FINDING ELODIE

SEAL Team Hawaii, Book 1

SUSAN STOKER

CHAPTER ONE

Attention. Attention. This is Captain Conger. The ship is under attack by pirates. This is not a drill. Repeat, not a drill. Do what you can to hide, but do nothing to put yourself or anyone else in danger. The authorities have been notified. If you have access to a radio, and it's safe to do so, use the emergency frequency to talk to anyone who might be listening and can help. We know this ship better than they do. Hunker down and if you're the praying sort...pray.

Elodie Winters, known to the crew on the *Asaka Express* as Rachel Walters—or simply Chef—was moving before the captain had finished his announcement over the loudspeaker. The entire crew had been briefed a few days ago that they were entering the dangerous waters of the Gulf of Aden, near Somalia and Yemen. She'd been scared enough to wear her clothes to bed. But deep down, Elodie hadn't thought it would truly be a concern.

The cargo ship she was working on had hoses on the deck that could spray an insane amount of water down on anyone dumb enough to try to approach, and it had been years since she'd heard of any large ship like theirs being taken hostage.

She had no idea if the hoses had malfunctioned or how the pirates had gotten onboard.

But here they were.

Her heart pounded a million miles an hour as she moved around her room in the bowels of the ship. The engineers and higher-ranking officers had rooms on the upper floors, but Elodie hadn't minded being lower down in the ship. She liked being near her kitchen.

When she'd come aboard, she'd been surprised to learn that everyone had their own room; she'd been expecting to share. But then again, there were only twenty-two workers on this ship, unlike cruise ships, which had hundreds of crew and thousands of guests.

In theory, Elodie knew why pirates attacked the large ships that went through the Gulf of Aden, but the reality seemed impossible. She'd seen the movie on the takeover of the cargo ship, the *Maersk Alabama*, and had been surprised at how easy it seemed to be for the pirates to get aboard. The *Asaka Express* was about the same size as the *Maersk Alabama*, but Captain Conger had reassured everyone that the safety measures put into place since that hijacking were much improved.

It seemed there was room for even *more* improvement.

Elodie took time to put on the boots she had by the side of her bed and grabbed her emergency radio. All the employees had been issued one. She could talk to the bridge with it, and access additional frequencies if needed.

Gripping the radio like a lifeline, she quickly opened her door—and let out a small shriek in fright when she almost ran into someone in the hallway.

"I was just coming to make sure you were awake," Manuel said, the terror easy to hear in his tone.

Elodie was the chief cook onboard. She had one assistant, the second cook. Manuel reported to her and was responsible for the pastries and serving the crew and officers. The rest of

2

the employees hired by the shipping company were engineers and officers. She was the only female onboard, and she'd thought that might be weird at first, but most of the men were respectful and didn't pay her much attention.

There was one officer, Valentino, who thought she'd jump at the chance to join him in his bed, and when she'd politely declined, he'd gotten offended. She'd learned to avoid him.

"Rachel?" Manuel asked, and Elodie shook her head, trying to concentrate on the disaster at hand. "What should we do?"

"What we've been trained to," she told him. She regretted not choosing a name closer to her own, but then again, she hadn't exactly had a choice. She'd had to settle for the identity on the fake documents she'd bought.

The reason why she was using a pseudonym was a concern for another day. Right now, she needed to get somewhere safe, and her room definitely wasn't. They'd been warned in safety-training sessions that pirates would most likely ransack the individual rooms looking for valuables and money. And the last thing she wanted was to be found. She felt relatively safe amongst the men on the ship, but she had no idea what pirates would do if they found a woman onboard.

"Go down to the engine room," Elodie told Manuel.

"What about you?" he asked.

"I'm headed to the galley. I can fit inside many of the cabinets if I need to. You can't. Besides, with the vegetable room, the freezers, and cold room, there are plenty of places for me to hole up. We also don't know how long this will last. You guys will need food if the pirates decide to stay. I can use the dumbwaiter to send food down to the engine room if necessary. It's safer if we aren't wandering all over the ship while the pirates are onboard."

"But if those pirates are here for very long, they're gonna come down here. They're gonna need food and water too," Manuel said reasonably.

Elodie knew he was right, but the place where she felt the safest was her kitchen. Besides, the captain said he'd gotten ahold of the authorities. She didn't know who he'd managed to contact, but she had confidence that the hijacking wouldn't last for weeks.

"They'll be busy elsewhere for a while," Elodie told her assistant.

Manuel looked like he wanted to protest. Wanted to insist she come with him, but the sound of a door closing from the stairwell nearby clanged loudly in the hallway, and Manuel looked over his shoulder, his eyes wide with terror.

"Go," Elodie ordered.

He moved without any more prodding, running in the opposite direction from where they'd heard the noise. Elodie had no idea if the pirates were already running around the ship or how many there might be, but she wasn't going to stand in the hallway and wait for them to find her.

She hadn't come all this way, escaped what she had in New York City, only to fall prey to a random pirate now. Still gripping the radio, she jogged for the stairwell. The engine room was four decks high, and there was an entrance on this level, but the galley was two floors above where her room was located. She needed to move.

"Manuel will be fine," she said softly. She'd always had a tendency to talk to herself, had tried to break it, to no avail. Because much of her life had been spent alone, she'd started talking to herself to break the monotony.

"Walter has this under control," she muttered as she cautiously opened the stairwell door. The captain had asked everyone to call him by his first name, and while it seemed weird at first, she'd gotten used to it. He was in his early fifties, had gray hair, and was always smiling. He was down-to-earth and treated everyone with the utmost respect. She respected him back and felt safe with him at the helm.

John and Troy appeared in the stairwell above her and

4

raced past with barely a glance. They were engineers and obviously headed down to the engine room.

She heard other footsteps heading toward the upper decks and assumed it was officers going to the bridge. Elodie ran as fast as she could to the floor where the galley was located.

She hadn't lied to Manuel, there were lots of places to hide in the kitchen complex. She'd already scoped them out, but not because she was afraid of pirates.

She was scared of Paul Columbus.

The man had said more than once that the only way out of his employ was in a pine box, and she believed him. She hadn't known he was the leader of one of the most dangerous mob families in New York when she'd accepted a job as his personal chef. She'd just been excited for the opportunity to get out of the restaurant business. The money had been hard to turn down too.

At first she'd been utterly clueless as to how the Columbus family made their millions. She was happy to stay in the kitchen, minding her own business, creating delicious food for Paul and his frequent guests. But eventually she was clued in that the man she worked for was beyond evil. He didn't care who he hurt, as long as he found a way to make money illegally.

Everything she was surrounded by in his home had been purchased with dirty money, even the food she used to find such satisfaction in preparing.

Knowing she didn't have time to reminiscence over all the mistakes she'd made in her life, Elodie entered the officers' mess room. All the rooms in this part of the ship were connected in one long horizontal line. First was the officers' mess, then the officers' pantry, the galley, the crew pantry, and then the crew mess. There was a door in the galley that led to a hallway containing the food storage rooms. There was a general freezer, a fish freezer, three refrigerators, and several pantries for dry food storage.

She'd scoped out all the cabinets she could fit in, and even how she might be able to get to the elevators and stairwells undetected if she had to. She wouldn't have the first clue where to hide down in the engine room, which was another reason she wanted to come here. This was where she was comfortable. She knew if the pirates decided to stay for any length of time, they'd make their way to the galley, as Manuel had said. While that made things more dangerous for her, she would also do what she could to make sure their trips to the galley were as short as possible.

Keeping the radio tucked into a large pocket of her cargo pants, Elodie worked as fast as possible. She moved three bundles of bottled water into the main kitchen area, where they'd easily be seen. Then she took out several boxes of crackers, a few loaves of bread, and bags of potato chips, and strategically placed them around the galley and both crew pantries. Generally, the food was stored in cupboards, secured so the boxes and cans wouldn't go flying in rough seas. She wanted the food to be readily accessible for the pirates but at the same time, she didn't want it to look like anything had been left out intentionally. She wanted the pirates to think they'd hit the mother lode with the food in plain sight, and not bother to dig much deeper.

Elodie ran her arm across her brow. She was sweating and hated not knowing what was happening high above her head in the bridge. Were the pirates onboard? Had they gotten into the bridge? Were they hurting the captain and the other officers?

And most importantly, what did they want?

The radio she'd stuffed in her pants squawked, scaring the shit out of Elodie.

"Holy crap!" she exclaimed, putting one hand over her racing heart and using the other to pull out the radio. The voices were muffled, but she could hear heavily accented males yelling, and Walter trying to placate them.

Confused about what she was hearing, Elodie stood in the middle of the galley trying to decipher what was going on. It took a minute, but she finally realized that someone had activated a radio up in the bridge, and it was broadcasting everything that was happening to the others onboard.

Chills raced up her spine as she listened to Walter doing his best to calm the pirates. It was hard to figure out how many there were, but it seemed as if it was more than a handful. Her stomach clenched in fear. The more pirates there were, the easier it would be to control the ship, to leave some up with the captain and the officers on the bridge and send others to prowl the decks, looking for crew and anything of value they could steal. The last thing Elodie needed was to be held for ransom. Her face would be plastered all over the news...which meant Paul Columbus could use his extensive mob network of soldiers and associates to find her.

"Where is the safe?" one of the pirates asked loudly.

"Not here. It's downstairs in one of the chart rooms," Walter told him.

"You go, get money."

"You can have all the cash we have, then you'll go," Walter said.

"No go," another man said sternly. "You take ship where we say. Our men come on. You open containers."

"That's...it's not safe," Walter stammered.

"No care. We open. You drive!" the man shouted.

Then Elodie heard scuffling and more shouting. A gunshot went off—and she held her breath, waiting to hear who, if anyone, had been hurt.

"Stop! Okay, okay! We'll open whatever containers you want, but don't shoot that thing again!" Walter yelled desperately.

The pirates merely laughed.

"We shoot when and where we want. We shoot *you* if you do not give us what we want. No hostages, too hard to get money. But if you don't do what we say, we kill," one of the pirates said.

"You can't shoot Walter," Elodie whispered. "We need him to drive this damn thing."

As if the captain could hear her, he said, "If you kill me and my officers, this ship will run aground. The Bab el-Mandeb Strait is tricky as hell to navigate."

"I am fisherman. I can drive boat," one of the pirates said, unconcerned.

Elodie snorted. Driving a super ship like this one was way different than the skiffs the pirates were probably used to.

"We know there are others onboard," someone else said. "We will find and start killing *them* if you don't do what we ask."

"Nobody needs to get hurt," Walter said quickly. "We'll do what you want. Just don't hurt my crew."

There were more scuffling noises and the pirates began to talk amongst themselves in a language Elodie couldn't understand.

Things were getting out of hand, and she was terrified. But Walter had said he'd called the authorities. Someone would come to help them, wouldn't they? Didn't the US Navy have ships in this part of the world? It was unfathomable that these pirates could just steal a huge cargo ship like this one.

Deciding her best bet for now was to lie low, Elodie exited the galley and went into a dry goods pantry. There was a cabinet at the back of the room she knew she could fit into. She squeezed herself into the cramped space, moving large bags of potatoes and other goods back in front of her. It wouldn't fool someone if they were really looking for people hiding, but she thought it should be good enough if someone merely opened the door to glance inside.

She held the radio in her lap and stared down at it. She

couldn't really see in the dark, but the lights on the device calmed her. Mentally, she began making notes on what she was hearing. She didn't know if they would be of any use, but maybe after they were rescued, she could help recount what had happened.

Elodie didn't do drama. She was a chef, for goodness sake. How could one person get into so much trouble in one lifetime? Paul Columbus had already vowed to kill her for refusing to do his bidding, and now she was hiding from pirates on the high seas.

All she'd ever wanted was to live a quiet life. Maybe find a man and get married, have a kid or two, and cook food for a living. Now she was thirty-five years old, and somewhere along the way, her simple life plan had been seriously derailed.

This cargo ship job had seemed like such a blessing. She could get out of the country and away from Columbus and his network, who were trying to eliminate her. What could be better than being isolated on a ship in the middle of the ocean? She'd be perfectly safe.

"Yeah, perfectly safe," she mumbled, closing her eyes and resting her temple on the back wall of the cabinet. She had to believe this would be over soon. Walter would do what the men wanted and they'd get whatever valuables they could find in the containers they could reach and open, then they'd go. Back to wherever they came from, letting her and the rest of the crew get on with their lives.

Right. That was how it would happen in a Hollywood movie, but this was real life. And with how things were going, she'd probably end up being taken hostage and forced to marry some African tribal chief.

* * *

Scott "Mustang" Webber glanced over at his SEAL team. Midas, Aleck, Pid, Jag, and Slate were completely focused on the paperwork in front of them. They'd been on a mission in Pakistan when they'd been notified of a change in plans. They were pulled from the desert and flown by helicopter to the *USS Paul Hamilton*, a guided-missile destroyer currently undergoing joint Naval operations in the Arabian Sea. There were several other vessels—the *USS Lewis B. Puller*, *USS Firebolt*, *USCGC Wrangell*, and the *USCGC Maui* —in the area as well. His team had arrived onboard and immediately been taken to a conference room, where the admiral onboard had brought them up to speed on their current mission.

Apparently, a medium-sized cargo ship had been boarded by pirates in the Gulf of Aden. The captain had put out a distress call saying he was currently being boarded by an unknown number of pirates and that he needed assistance ASAP. Since then, there had been no communication with the captain or the pirates.

The *USS Paul Hamilton*, along with the other ships, were headed that way, but as of right now, they had no information to work with.

Mustang remembered hearing about the *Maersk Alabama* incident, and how Navy SEAL snipers had taken out the pirates who'd hijacked the captain and forced him into one of the cargo ship's lifeboats. Mustang and his team weren't snipers, and frankly, he hated close-quarter rescues, such as on a lifeboat. He'd much prefer to have the run of the cargo ship itself. There were plenty of places to hide and take out the pirates one by one.

"What's their heading?" Midas asked.

"Right now, they look like they're on their scheduled course," the admiral said. "Due west toward Djibouti. They're supposed to turn northward and go through the Bab el-Mandeb Strait and dock in Port Sudan."

"That's a pretty tricky strait to navigate," Aleck observed.

"It is," the admiral agreed.

"Do we have any idea what nationality the pirates are? Or what their plan is?" Pid asked.

"Unfortunately, not as of yet. We've been trying to reach them, to get someone to talk to us, but either their comms are down or we're deliberately being ignored."

"Shit," Jag swore under his breath.

Mustang agreed. Without information, it was almost impossible to come up with a plan.

Almost.

"So, we're going in blind?" Slate asked.

Mustang couldn't help but smile. Slate was usually the first to volunteer for a dangerous mission. He always wanted to get the show on the road, so to speak.

"Unless we can get someone to talk to us...yes," Mustang answered before the admiral could.

It was just lucky they were already in the area and could be taken off their previous mission. The team had been on a few cargo ships in the past and knew they were full of corridors and nooks and crannies. As much as he hated that the crew members onboard the *Asaka Express* were probably scared out of their minds, he was looking forward to the challenge of finding, and taking out, each and every pirate.

"Sorry to interrupt, Sir," a lieutenant said as he stuck his head inside the door.

"What is it?" the admiral asked.

"We have communication from the *Asaka Express*."

"Thank fuck," Midas said.

"Can it be patched through?" the admiral asked.

"Yes, Sir. Just a moment." The lieutenant disappeared from the doorway once more.

Mustang and his team waited impatiently for the connection to be made to the cargo ship. When the sophisticated radio in the middle of the table finally squawked, Mustang blinked in surprise at the voice on the other end.

"Hello? Is anyone there?"

"Yes, ma'am, you've been connected. Please tell the admiral what you just told me."

"Um...okay. I'm on the *Asaka Express* and there are pirates onboard. We need help." The woman's voice was shaking, she was obviously scared, but she was keeping her composure.

"This is Admiral Light, I'm in charge of the *USS Paul Hamilton*. We're headed in your direction. What is your name?"

"El— Um...Rachel Walters."

Mustang looked over at Jag, who raised an eyebrow at hearing her response. Most people didn't stumble over their own name. Even in an extremely stressful situation like the one Ms. Walters had found herself in.

"And in what capacity do you work onboard?"

"My job? I'm the cook."

It wasn't unheard of to have females onboard the large cargo ships that constantly sailed through the waters in the Middle East, but it was still rare enough to be interesting.

"What can you tell us about the situation?" Admiral Light asked.

"Right, um, well, I can only tell you what I've heard. I—"

"What do you mean, you heard?" Mustang asked, interrupting her.

"Oh, uh...there're more than just the admiral there?" she asked.

"Yes," Mustang answered. "My SEAL team is here and we're going to come help you, but we need as much information as you can give us before we do. How many pirates are onboard?"

"Here's the thing," Rachel said. "I haven't actually *seen* any of them. They have pretty thick accents and it's hard for me to understand them. Walter...er...Captain Conger told everyone onboard to hide, so that's what I did. I'm in the galley...well, not the galley, but in one of the pantries nearby. I've got a radio, and one of the officers must've turned on a radio on the bridge, because it's been broadcasting. I can hear everything that's going on up there, but again, it's hard to understand. I can't see what's happening."

"How many crew are onboard?" Aleck asked.

"Twenty-two, including me," Rachel answered without hesitation.

"What channel were you listening to the bridge on?" Pid asked.

"Ten."

"And what channel are you on now?" Pid asked.

"Um...five, I think. I was just changing channels and seeing if anyone could hear me when you guys answered."

Pid reached into his pack on the floor and started rummaging around. He was the team's electronics expert, and Mustang knew he was going to try to tap into the radio frequency Rachel was using and listen to what was happening on the bridge of the *Asaka Express* himself.

"If you had to guess, how many men would you say boarded the ship?" the admiral asked.

Mustang heard Rachel sigh. "I don't know," she said. "We were all sleeping when it happened and woke when the captain made an announcement, telling us what was going on. But I think it's more than just a handful. There was talk of searching the ship earlier, and I'm not sure they'd do that if they only had three or four people, but I'm not an expert on forcefully taking over a ship, so I don't know for sure. They want money, and for the captain to open the containers. They said something about more men coming onboard when we got somewhere and that they didn't want hostages."

Not wanting hostages could be good or bad. It could mean the pirates really did just want money and valuables. After the *Maersk Alabama* incident, when the pirate in charge had been taken back to the States and thrown in prison and his comrades had been killed, hostage-taking by pirates had fallen out of favor. But not taking hostages could also mean the lives of every single one of the crew were in danger. It was easier to shoot to kill than to try to wrangle two dozen men.

And Mustang really didn't want to think about what they'd do to a woman if they found her onboard.

"Oh, crap...I hear something!" Rachel said.

"Stay quiet, turn down the volume on your radio, but don't disconnect," Mustang ordered.

"Okay...um...can I ask your name? I just...it feels more personal."

"I'm Mustang," he told her. "And my team is all here. Midas, Aleck, Pid, Jag, and Slate."

There was silence for a second, then a slight huff of breath. "I had to ask," she muttered.

Mustang hadn't thought twice about sharing his team's nicknames, but he'd forgotten how weird they'd sound to a civilian. "Scott," he said quietly. "My name is Scott."

"Scott. Okay," she whispered, then inhaled sharply as a loud bang sounded through the connection.

All six SEALs leaned forward, as if that could somehow help keep the woman on the other end of the line safe from whatever was happening. Admiral Light sat tense in his chair as he listened as well.

They could all hear raised voices in the background. Mustang closed his eyes and tried to distinguish what language was being spoken. He wasn't a language expert, but it sounded like a mix of Arabic and French to him.

"Stop pushing me!" a man's voice said in English.

Rachel's breathing was loud and fast. Mustang wanted to comfort her. Tell her to slow her breathing before she passed out, but he didn't dare say a word in case it would give away her hiding place.

"There's no one here," said the man speaking English.

"Men will regret not show themselves," a man said, obviously one of the pirates by the sound of his accent.

"Where more food?" another man asked.

"There are a few freezers in this hallway," the crew member said, "and more storage, but the best bet for stuff that can be eaten quickly, without having to cook it, is in the pantries on either side of the galley. That's where the snacks and things are kept. Back here is mostly flour, sugar, stuff like that. Things the cook uses to make the meals."

"Show us these pantries. And no try anything."

"I'm not," the officer said. "I'm doing exactly what you've told me."

"We come back for water and food," one of the pirates said. "We look more for money now."

Everyone in the conference room strained to listen for footsteps retreating, or for more conversation, but all they could hear were Rachel's terrified breaths.

"You're okay," Mustang said softly after a long moment, not able to keep quiet any longer. "They didn't find you."

"I know," she whispered back in a voice so low, everyone had to struggle to hear.

"Who was that?" Midas asked.

"I think it was Bryce...he's one of the officers who works with the captain on the bridge."

Mustang saw the admiral writing the name down, though he was sure someone was working on getting a list of every crew member onboard the *Asaka Express*.

"Had you heard either of those two pirates before?" Aleck asked.

"I don't know. I'm sorry. God, I wish I was better at this," she moaned.

"You're doing fine," Mustang reassured her.

"I'm not. So far I've told you nothing you probably didn't already know," she said.

"Other than the original distress call, you're the first communication we've had from your ship," Mustang countered.

"I am?" Rachel asked. "That's weird. I mean, we've all been trained to use the radios to call for help."

"Are the others in the engine room or in the bowels of the ship?" Pid asked.

"Probably both, but I'm guessing most are in the engine room. It's loud down there and easier to hide. A cough or movement can more easily be masked by the noise of the engines," Rachel said.

"And being lower in the ship, surrounded by all the steel, makes it more difficult for radio transmissions to get through on a handheld radio," Pid told her.

"I guess that makes sense," Rachel mused.

"Why aren't *you* in the engine room?" Mustang couldn't help but ask.

"I'm the cook," Rachel told him, as if that explained everything.

"And?" Slate asked.

"And depending on how long the pirates are here, the guys are gonna need food and water."

Mustang shook his head. He was impressed with Rachel's dedication to her job, but she was putting herself in danger. Someone should've realized that, besides the captain, Rachel was probably the most vulnerable on that ship. The pirates could use her to force the other crew members to do their bidding.

He didn't even want to think of all the other ways they could use and abuse her.

"I'm in," Pid said triumphantly as he nodded to the radio in front of him.

"Already?" the admiral asked.

"He means, what took you so long?" Aleck corrected with a chuckle.

"You're in?" Rachel asked.

"I've patched into your radio frequency. We're listening to channel ten now."

"You are? Okay, good," Rachel said. "So...does this mean you're still coming?"

"Yes," Mustang told her. He wanted to tell her that they'd be there soon, but unfortunately, nothing worked that fast in the Navy. They needed to make plans, prepare the Zodiac and, most importantly, wait for night to fall...which was still too many hours away.

"The crew channel is three," she told them. "When you get here and kill the pirates, you can let us all know it's safe to come out on that channel."

"Bloodthirsty thing, isn't she?" Jag said under his breath. "I like her."

"Thanks for telling us," Mustang said, ignoring his team-mate. He wasn't surprised, anyone who worked on a cargo ship had to be pretty rough around the edges. He pictured a stereotypical ship's cook...an older, tall, overweight woman wearing a stained apron and covered in tattoos, with short hair and a bad attitude.

Then he felt like a douche for even thinking about her looks. That didn't matter in the least. Besides, from the sound of her voice, he guessed she was probably around his age, mid-thirties or younger, and she didn't seem to have a bad attitude in the least. She was doing her best to stay calm and give them any information she could. "You just stay hunkered down, no matter what, okay?"

"Okay—but Scott?"

Hearing his given name felt a bit odd. It had been a long time since he'd heard anyone call him that, but Mustang said, "Yeah?"

"What if they threaten to kill some of the officers if we don't show ourselves? What should we do?"

"Fuck," Slate said softly.

"You stay where you are," the admiral said sternly. "Under no circumstances should you or anyone else put yourselves in danger."

17

"I'm not sure I can sit here and listen to them kill the men I've become friends with," Rachel answered.

"I wish I had a better answer for you," Mustang told her. "I wish I could tell you that the pirates would be bluffing and they won't actually kill anyone. I wish I could say that if you, or anyone else, went up to the bridge, they'd not follow through with their threats, but there's no telling *what* those men will do."

"And I'm a woman," Rachel whispered.

"And you're a woman," Mustang agreed. "We're coming," he assured her.

"I don't know how the pirates got onboard," Rachel said, "but there's a hole in the very front of the ship. Not a hole, but like...an access port. Shoot, I don't know the official word for it. Where chains and stuff can be used without putting them over the railing. But when we got a tour, Walter joked that it was big enough for someone to fit through. With the bridge being at the back of the ship, and the containers stacked high, no one would see you if you came aboard that way."

Mustang saw his teammates smiling. They weren't making fun of her, it was obvious the woman was scared yet still doing her best to try to help, which was appreciated. But it was also obvious Rachel hadn't thought through the logistics of what she was suggesting. Getting onboard a moving vessel through the very front of the ship was dangerous as hell, and there wouldn't be very much cover on the forward deck.

"Thanks for the suggestion," Midas told her diplomatically.

"You're welcome."

"Stay on this frequency," Pid told her, "so we can communicate with you."

"But, then I can't hear what's going on with Walter and the others on the bridge," she said.

Mustang nodded at his teammate. It was a good suggestion. If the shit did hit the fan, none of them wanted her to hear it. "We can," he told her.

"Oh, right. I'd forgotten. Okay. Will you— Never mind."

"What?" Mustang asked.

"It's stupid."

"What?" he asked more forcefully.

"I was just going to ask if you could come onto the radio now and then and let me know that you're still out there and still coming to help? I'm terrified, and knowing someone is coming makes me feel a lot better."

"Yes," Mustang told her. "We're going to be in constant contact because we need to know what's going on below decks where you are." That was only partly true. Since Pid had patched them into the channel one of the officers had opened on the bridge, they had a direct line to the most important room on that ship. But that wouldn't help them if the pirates split up.

"Okay. Thank you for coming. And be safe. These guys sound really...angry."

When was the last time someone had told them, a notoriously badass Navy SEAL team, to be safe? How about never? "We will," Mustang told her. "Try to relax, and *you* be safe too."

"I'll try." There was a slight pause, then she asked, "What now? Do we say over and out or something?"

Midas chuckled softly.

"No need. We'll be in touch," Mustang told her.

"Right. Okay. Um...bye for now then."

Mustang shook his head. Damn. She was adorable. And it was completely fucked up that he was thinking that about someone in the middle of a damn op.

Then he didn't have any more time to think about Rachel Walters as Pid turned up the sound on the radio channel he'd tapped into on the bridge. They had intel to gather, a plan to make, and a ship of almost two dozen crew members to save.

CHAPTER TWO

Elodie felt better after talking to Scott. She'd never met a real live Navy SEAL before. She didn't know what she'd expected, but he was so...normal sounding.

Listening hard, she didn't hear anything from outside her hiding place. Her legs were hurting from being scrunched up in the cabinet for so long. She wasn't super tall at five-six, but she also wasn't quite small enough to be able to fit in her hiding place for long without discomfort.

Her heart beat fast as she made the decision to venture out. Moving slowly, just in case one of the pirates had been left behind as a sentry, she peered out of the cabinet.

The lights in the pantry were still on, and she didn't see anyone in the storage room. She awkwardly climbed out and stood, stretching her muscles so they would hopefully work correctly if she needed to make a fast getaway.

Putting the radio in her cargo pants pocket once more, Elodie crept to the door. She listened and, after hearing nothing but her own heartbeat, slowly cracked the door open.

The hallway was empty. She couldn't hear anything but the hum of the freezers nearby and the rattling of dishes caused by the vibration of the ship. It had taken a bit of getting used to when she'd first come aboard, but now she barely even noticed it.

She wasn't sure where she was going or what she was doing, but just knowing that someone was going to be coming to help them made her feel a little braver. She crept into the galley and saw one of the packages of water bottles she'd put on the counter was now gone, as was some of the food. Good. Her plan had worked...for now.

For a second, Elodie thought about doing what Steven Seagal had done in the movie *Under Siege*, making a microwave bomb, but she immediately dismissed the idea. First of all, there was no way to time it correctly to go off just when one of the pirates was in the vicinity. She never understood how that had worked in the movie. But second of all, and more importantly...she had no idea how to make a microwave bomb.

She wondered if Scott would know.

"He might, but he's not here," Elodie said softly.

She was walking through the galley when something caught her eye. The block of knives she used while cooking.

No one onboard was allowed to have a gun. She'd been relieved when she'd read that in the rules and regulations she'd received from the shipping company. Now she realized that it put them at a decided disadvantage against the pirates. But just because they didn't have guns didn't mean they couldn't still arm themselves.

Her knives were sharp. Very sharp. She made sure to keep them in top condition. The thought of actually using one against someone made her physically ill. But if it was stab someone or be raped and tortured, she'd choose to protect herself every time.

Briefly, Paul Columbus flashed through her mind. The man was seriously unbalanced. It made no sense whatsoever that he'd decided she had to die simply because she'd refused to do as he asked. Who *does* that? But if it came down to staying alive, or being at the mercy of Paul, any of his henchmen, or the pirates, she'd choose life. And if that meant using one of her cooking knives to buy her some time, so be it.

Elodie didn't have a good way of transporting the knife, no holster of any kind, but she quickly realized if she chose one of the more slender blades, it would fit through the belt loop of her pants and the hilt would keep it from falling to the ground. It wasn't ideal; if she fell, she could seriously hurt herself. But she definitely didn't want to be unarmed.

Walking slowly, Elodie went to the crew pantry and saw that it had been ransacked. Food had been pulled out of the cabinets and was spilled all over the floor and counter. She had no idea if the pirates had been looking for valuables or for something to eat. It was ridiculous, the idea that there'd be anything worth a substantial amount of money in the pantries. This was a kitchen, not a secret hiding place for a safe or something.

Feeling disgusted at their stupidity, Elodie went through the crew mess to the door at the end of the room and opened it an inch. After hearing nothing out of the ordinary, she peered out into the hallway. She had no idea what she was looking for. Pirates? Some of the other guys who worked on the ship? The captain?

Suddenly, she felt completely alone. It was silly, as she knew there were many other people onboard. She'd never really liked the game hide-and-go-seek, always afraid the "seeker" would get bored with the game and quit. Leaving her in her hiding spot, waiting in vain to be found. For a moment, she thought about going down to the engine room and finding some of the other guys. Maybe Ari or Troy. They'd help keep her hidden. The thought was tempting.

Curiosity got the better of her, and Elodie pulled the radio out of her pocket. She hadn't heard from Scott or anyone else from the US ship since they'd answered her desperate distress call. Making sure the volume was turned down extremely low, she changed the channel to ten and put the radio up to her ear.

She needed to know what was happening on the bridge. Maybe Walter and the other officers had managed to subdue the pirates and she was slinking around for no reason.

But instead, what she heard made her blood run cold.

"You're going to run us aground," Walter said, the agitation easy to hear in his tone, even through the radio. "Do you even know what you're doing?"

"I a fisherman. I know boats," one of the pirates claimed.

"Yeah, but a ship this size is very different from the skiffs you've operated."

"I in charge!" the man yelled, scaring the shit out of Elodie.

There was the sound of scuffling—and then the unmistakable sound of a semi-automatic rifle being fired.

Men shouted, someone screamed, more gunfire.

Elodie stood stock still and prayed for the officers on the bridge.

Then the pirates began yelling in their own language. It sounded as if they were arguing with each other.

Suddenly, the lights blinked out without warning.

Elodie was plunged into pitch darkness. She couldn't see her hand in front of her face. The only light in the room was coming from the blinking red dot on the radio in her hand.

There was more swearing from the men on the bridge.

"What happen to lights?" one of the pirates asked.

"I'm not sure." Elodie heard Bo, one of the officers, say in a shaky voice.

"You fix!" he ordered.

"I can't!" Bo exclaimed. "First, you just killed Danny, he was the expert on the gauges and shit up here. He knew what every single one meant and when something was wrong with them. Second, everything is controlled from the engine room!"

Elodie inhaled sharply. Danny was dead? "No," she whispered. Danny had a wife and two kids back home in Wyoming. He couldn't be dead. Her entire body began to shake.

"You go down and make lights go back on!" one of the pirates ordered Bo.

"If we're going to make it through the Bab el-Mandeb Strait without ramming this thing into Perim Island or Djibouti on the other side, you need me up here. Without the captain's expertise, I'm still not sure I can do it, but I know this ship a hell of a lot better than you do," Bo said in a shaky voice.

A tear fell from Elodie's eye. She didn't like the sound of that at all. Had they also killed Walter? How many of the other officers had they killed?

The next thing she heard was another loud gunshot and a thud.

She gasped and pressed a hand over her mouth.

The pirates began speaking to each other in their own language once more.

How long Elodie stood in the darkness not moving, she wasn't sure. But eventually her sadness and shock turned to anger. How dare these men come aboard their ship and start killing her friends? And if Bo didn't think he could get the ship through the small passageway of water that led to the Red Sea, and their destination port in Sudan, how in the world did these pirates think they could?

Which led to another thought—the pirates obviously didn't care about the lives of the people on the ship. So if they steered into that island Bo was talking about, they wouldn't care one whit. All they wanted was money or things they could sell.

Suddenly, the ship intercom squawked and one of the

pirates began speaking, his voice echoing throughout the galley and mess rooms around her.

"This is Hamza. I in charge of boat. You do as I say or you die. Your captain no listen, he is dead. The others, they no listen. They dead! You be dead too if lights no come on. You have ten minutes to put lights on, or we come down and find you. All we want is money. We no care about you. Save yourselves."

Elodie narrowed her eyes. Bastards. She really wished she knew how to make that microwave bomb right about now. These guys thought they could kill all the officers and engineers and somehow still get this massive ship where they wanted it to go? They were delusional.

Turning, Elodie was glad for all the time she'd spent in the galley. She knew this place like the back of her hand. With her arms out in front of her, just in case a chair had been moved, she made her way back through the crew mess, gingerly shuffled through the crew pantry room, and headed straight for the back wall in the galley. It took her several seconds to find what she was looking for, but when her hand brushed against the flashlight on the wall, she grabbed it triumphantly.

There was emergency lighting she could activate, but she shook her head. "Why make it easier for them?" she muttered softly. Then she stood in the middle of her galley, with the flashlight beam pointed toward the floor, and debated with herself.

"I could sabotage the place," she reasoned. "Break some glasses and spread the pieces around, pour out a few gallons of oil...but that would alert the assholes that someone was definitely here. But can I really sit around here and do nothing? Like a sitting duck? El, you aren't Superwoman, what can you really do against armed assholes? Well, one thing you can do is try to make sure they don't get any other weapons."

Hearing the sound of her own voice, even if it was whispered, made her feel better. As did having a plan. Quickly, Elodie began to search the galley for any kind of sharp implements. She didn't want to make it obvious that all the knives had disappeared. She also didn't want to make it easy for the pirates to find them if they went looking. So she slid one big butcher knife under the chiller. Another went into one of the ovens. And so it went. She hid the cutlery all over the galley.

That done, she looked around, wondering what else she could do.

The ship lurched under her, almost sending Elodie crashing to the floor.

The vibrations she'd gotten so used to suddenly stopped, leaving behind an eerie silence. The unmistakable sound of the watertight doors cranking down filled the air. She knew there were ways of getting around with the doors shut, but it made things much more difficult. And she hated not knowing if the doors had been shut because of what the engineers were doing down in the bowels of the ship, or if they'd come down automatically because they'd run aground or hit something.

Pulling the radio out of her pocket once more, Elodie saw that she'd somehow bumped the dial off of channel ten. She turned it slightly and heard the pirates speaking in their own language. Knowing she wouldn't be able to understand anything they were saying, she turned it to the channel she'd used to reach the US Naval ship.

"...Mustang, come in. Damn it, Rachel, where are you?"

Elodie had never been so happy to hear anyone's voice in her life as she was Scott's. "I'm here," she said softly.

"Thank fuck," Scott breathed. "I've been trying to reach you for at least twenty minutes. There have been some updates to your situation."

"I know," she admitted. "I know you told me not to, but I had to find out what was going on. They shot Walter. And some of the others."

"I'm so sorry."

"They were good men," Elodie told Scott. "A little rough around the edges, and some of the officers were a little conceited, but they didn't deserve what happened to them."

"No, they didn't," Scott agreed. "But now we've got bigger problems."

"Yeah, they don't know how to drive this thing, and now they want to kill all of us on sight."

"Exactly. I need you to hunker down and stay put."

"The watertight doors just closed," Elodie told him.

"What?"

"The watertight doors. Are we sinking? Or was that the guys downstairs?" she asked.

"You aren't sinking," Scott told her.

Elodie let out a breath of relief. "Okay."

"But things are gonna get dicey when they attempt to navigate that strait."

"Are you still coming?" she couldn't help but ask.

"Yes. But it's too dangerous to do so in the daylight."

"Shit!" Elodie said.

"You're going to be all right," Scott told her.

She appreciated him trying to comfort her, but she didn't feel very reassured right about now. "The engineers cut off the lights too. So it's really dark in here."

"We'll handle it."

"Okay. Scott?"

"Yeah, Rachel?"

Damn. She'd forgotten *again* that everyone thought Rachel was her name. "If something happens to me...there's no one to contact. Just give me a burial at sea and be done with it. Okay?" She wasn't sure how well her fake identification would hold up...and she didn't have a family to contact anyway.

"You're going to be okay," Scott told her firmly.

"But still—" she started.

"I need you to think positive. The worst thing you can do in a situation like this is give up."

"I'm not giving up," she told him. "Right now, I'm mad. Pissed that Walter and the others were killed unnecessarily. Many of those guys had wives and kids. This *sucks*."

"It does," Scott agreed.

"Do you?"

"Do I what?" Scott asked.

Elodie knew she should get off the radio. She was risking her life by continuing to talk to him. Besides, he probably had other things he could be doing...like planning how he was going to get onto this ship and kill the bad guys. But she couldn't bring herself to break the connection. Scott was literally a voice in the darkness, and he made her feel not quite so alone. "Have a wife and kids," she said.

"No to either."

"That's good, I guess."

"Yeah. Hang in there, Rachel. You're doing a good job."

"I hid the knives," she blurted.

"What?"

"I thought about breaking a bunch of shit and creating obstacles here in the galley, but then I figured they'd know someone was here and would turn everything upside down looking for me. So I decided it was better to keep everything as it was the last time they were here. Maybe then they wouldn't stay very long and wouldn't try as hard to search for anyone. But I didn't want them to get any more weapons, so I hid all the knives."

"Smart."

Elodie wasn't sure about that. "I kept one though. It fits through the belt loop on my pants."

"Be careful. You can't win a gunfight with a knife," Scott told her.

Amazingly, Elodie chuckled. "Is that some ancient saying or something?"

"No, common sense," he answered.

Elodie could hear the humor in his tone. And for just a second, she felt...normal. As if she and Scott were two people who'd met online or something and were getting to know each other. But then his next words snapped her back to reality.

"Do what you need to do to stay hidden," Scott told her. "Do *not* let them find you, Rachel. Okay?"

"Okay," she whispered.

"This is gonna be over soon."

"I hope so."

"I know so."

"I'd always heard you guys were cocky, but I have to say, it's kind of refreshing right about now."

"It's not being cocky if it's true." Then his voice lowered. "I'm sorry about your friends."

"Thanks."

"I'll talk to you soon—and *see* you soon, as well. Just try not to shank me or anyone on my team, would ya?"

Amazingly, Elodie chuckled. "I'll try."

"Mustang out."

Elodie put the radio back in her pocket and listened for any sign of the pirates coming down into her area. When she heard only that same eerie nothingness of the engines silenced, she headed back into the hallway with the storage rooms. She had the perfect hiding place. She'd thought of it a few weeks ago but had forgotten it until now.

She went into the smallest of the pantries and took a deep breath before reaching a hand toward the shelving units. She carefully climbed up to the top shelf, a good eight feet off the floor and at least three feet deep. She moved boxes from the back to the front and shimmied herself behind them. It was a good defensive position if she was spotted, although the wooden shelves wouldn't stop a bullet. But hopefully the pirates would never know she was there, hiding in the dark, even if they searched the room.

Putting her head down on her hands, Elodie closed her eyes and prayed for the day to pass quickly. The sooner night fell, the better, because that meant help would arrive.

CHAPTER THREE

Mustang reviewed the list of employees on the *Asaka Express*. Slate had marked those men he believed had been on the bridge, and thus had likely been killed, leaving just two officers and all of the engineers unaccounted for. Along with Rachel Walters.

They'd received a list of relatives of everyone onboard, as well as copies of the rudimentary background checks that had been done on everyone. Everything looked copasetic... except for Rachel's.

"There's nothing in her background beyond three years ago," Pid said.

Mustang nodded.

Everything listed was pretty generic. Her college graduation year, the fact that her parents were both deceased and she had no siblings. She'd been working at a restaurant in Los Angeles before taking the job aboard the *Asaka Express*. There was a glowing letter of recommendation, supposedly from the owner of the restaurant where she'd worked, but when Pid had run that man's name, he'd not been able to find any record of him owning any kind of restaurant anywhere in the country.

"Remember when we asked her name and she stumbled over it?" Midas asked.

"She's not who she says she is." Aleck pointed out.

"But does that make her an accomplice to what's going on now?" Jag asked.

"Can we please stop talking about her as if she's in cahoots with the damn pirates?" Mustang asked in frustration.

"Look, none of us really think she helped set this up," Aleck said reasonably. "But everything we've found so far leads us to believe she's keeping some big secrets."

"It would make sense that she took a job on a cargo ship if she's trying to hide from someone," Slate said.

"Like an abusive ex," Midas threw out.

"She could've changed her name because she's deep in debt," Jag offered.

"Does any of this matter right now?" Mustang asked.

"No," Midas said immediately. "As far as we're concerned, at the moment, she's as much a victim as anyone else on the ship. But that could change once we take control of the situation."

Mustang sighed. He knew that. If she was on the run, or trying to hide from someone, this situation had made it very difficult for her to lie low. The authorities would want to interview her, the media might want her side of the story, not to mention the US Navy would need her statement as well.

"She seems to have taken a liking to you," Midas said. "I'm thinking when we get onboard, you should be the one to track her down. If she trusts you, she might open up to you. Tell you what's up."

"And if we can help, we will," Aleck added.

"I hate bullies," Pid muttered. "If she's hiding from one, I'm all for *keeping* her hidden."

"Seems the last thing she'd want is a spotlight on her if she survives this," Jag agreed.

"There's no if about it," Slate said. "If darkness would hurry the hell up already, we could end this shit."

This was why Mustang loved working with these men. They were true champions of those who needed help. It was why they were all SEALs in the first place, to try to right the wrongs of the world no matter where they might be.

Mustang had no problem being the one to search for Rachel, ensuring her safety. Hell, just the thought of her relying on any of his friends was…unsettling. There was something about her that intrigued him. Made him want to get to know her better. Shield her from any danger on that cargo ship.

He didn't know Rachel's story, or if Rachel was even her real name, but he was curious to find out. He hadn't known her very long, but he was a good judge of character, and how someone acted in the face of a true crisis said a lot about who they were as a person. And Rachel Walters seemed to have a spine of steel.

* * *

Mustang sat in the back of the Zodiac and held on as the pilot steered them closer and closer to the huge cargo ship.

Throughout the day, officials on the USS *Paul Hamilton* did their best to talk to the pirates, to no avail. They weren't answering the hails from the various US Naval ships around them. They had to know they were screwed. They had to have seen on radar the armada of ships surrounding the cargo ship they'd taken over. But so far, they hadn't communicated with anyone.

It looked like the *Asaka Express* was floating dead in the water. The current would eventually push the massive ship closer and closer to the shoreline of Djibouti. Government officials were contacted, but they refused to get involved, saying until the ship was officially in their jurisdiction, they weren't willing to act.

It was frustrating and infuriating, but there was nothing Mustang, his team, or the US officials could do. If the pirates didn't talk to them, give them some idea of what their plan was and what they wanted, there would be no way to negotiate for the lives of the employees onboard.

Now darkness had fallen, and the SEALs could finally make their move. There were indications that over a dozen small boats were making their way toward the stricken *Asaka Express* from the northern part of Djibouti. US intelligence experts assumed they were more pirates, coming to pilfer as many goods as they could from the cargo onboard the ship.

Mustang and his team were in a race to get there first. Once they had the cargo ship secured, the US Navy would bring their warships closer and protect the vessel until it could be made seaworthy once more. They were also going to intercept the smaller boats if possible. Prevent them from adding to the chaos onboard the *Asaka Express*.

The plan was simple. Get onboard, then play hide-and-go-seek with the pirates, taking them out one by one. They'd been given permission to shoot to kill anyone onboard the ship illegally. The Navy wasn't fucking around.

The pilot of the Zodiac slowed the boat as they neared the eerily dark cargo ship. There were lights flickering in the bridge, but the team had approached from the port side, the side closest to the shore, undetected. Amazingly, the ladder the pirates had used to originally go aboard was still hanging from a railing.

"I'm sure that's how they're planning on the others getting onboard," Midas said.

"Most likely," Slate agreed. "We'll ditch it once we're on. No sense making it easy for more pirates to join the party."

No one had even the slightest thought to use the ladder to get aboard themselves. It could be booby trapped or monitored. Mustang ordered the pilot to move fifty feet forward from where the ladder swung back and forth with the movement of the waves.

"You think they'll be dumb enough to try to join their friends onboard?" the pilot asked.

"They'll try," Aleck said with a nod.

"Their only motivation is the bottom line," Pid agreed. "But the Navy won't let that happen if they can help it."

"Less talk, more action," Mustang said, looking up. They were lucky this cargo ship wasn't any bigger. It wasn't going to be easy to make their way up the side of the ship as it was. Jag moved to the side of the Zodiac and took a deep breath, then he was moving.

Using top-secret, super-spy type gear, Jag made it up the side of the ship within minutes. As they'd planned, he threw down a rope after securing it on the deck, and one by one, the team shimmied up onto the cargo ship. The Zodiac pulled away as silently as it had arrived the second Slate's boots had left the bottom.

Mustang and his team plastered themselves to the side of the shipping containers, fading into the shadows. He gestured with his head to the aft of the ship, and Midas and Aleck quickly headed in that direction. Pid and Jag began the long walk toward the front of the ship. They'd gotten the specs and blueprints of the *Asaka Express* while on the USS *Paul Hamilton*. It was over three hundred feet long and would take three or so minutes walking at a normal speed to get from the back to the front.

There were also fifteen lashing bridges, five cargo holds, and the engine room was four decks deep. The captain had been right, there were innumerable places for the crew to hide, and Mustang prayed they'd all been able to do just that. They were obviously doing everything in their power to make things difficult for the pirates, dropping the watertight doors below decks, shutting off the engine, and cutting the lights.

Darkness might be a disadvantage for the pirates, but it wasn't for the SEAL team. With their night-vision goggles, they could see almost as well as if it was daylight. Mustang and his team were on a hunt. They'd take out the pirates and hopefully this hijacking would be ended swiftly and with only one outcome— dead pirates.

Mustang usually wasn't so bloodthirsty, but this was war. If the pirates hadn't killed anyone, their orders might've been different...capture and interrogate. But because they'd upped the stakes by killing the captain and the other officers, they'd sealed their own fate.

Each of the men were wearing radios in their ears. They were voice-activated so they could quickly and easily communicate with the rest of the team.

"Ladder's disabled," Midas informed everyone.

The plan was to secure the outer decks before heading straight to the bridge. By throwing the ladder the pirates had used overboard, they'd made it more difficult for additional pirates to climb aboard and taken away a method for the current pirates to flee.

They'd take out anyone who was on the bridge, then search the rest of the ship. They had no idea how many pirates were wandering around, but they'd eventually find everyone and exterminate the threat to the employees onboard.

Midas and Aleck would continue around the back of the ship, while Pid and Jag secured the front before heading aft. Mustang and Slate would clear the mid-deck, then make their way back to the bridge, as well.

Through the radio in his ear, Mustang heard his team reporting the all-clear as they moved about the ship. No one was on the outside decks, which made for a quick and silent trip to the bridge. As he and Slate approached the rear of the ship, he saw Midas and Aleck already hunkered down, waiting for their arrival. The four of them would storm onto the bridge from starboard. Pid and Jag would hang back on the port side, out of the line of fire, in case any of the pirates attempted to flee the bridge on their side.

Mustang moved around his teammates, not reluctant in the least to take point. He held up his hand and counted down from three. He heard Slate say "go" through the radio even as he swung the heavy metal battering ram they'd lugged onboard for the sole purpose of knocking down the door to the bridge.

It flew open with one hit, and the four men poured into the space, overwhelming the two pirates who were inside.

The first reached for the rifle hanging around his body, but never had a chance to get ahold of it. Mustang's bullet pierced his head and he fell to the floor without a sound.

The other man immediately turned and went for the door on the opposite side of the room, firing blindly behind him as he ran. Mustang and the rest of the team took cover behind whatever they could. The man ran out the door and two shots rang out, indicating that Pid and Jag had done their job.

The entire operation was over within seconds.

Standing, Mustang surveyed the bridge. There were six men, obviously dead, lying in a heap along the back wall. Even though they weren't wearing uniforms, Mustang knew they were the captain and his officers. That meant there were still sixteen *Asaka Express* employees onboard.

"Only two?" Midas asked as he entered the bridge with Aleck.

"Yes," Mustang agreed.

"Fuck. That means there's probably still a handful of them wandering around then," Midas said.

Mustang's belly rolled. Normally he wouldn't care so much, might have even looked forward to the cat-and-mouse game they were about to engage in. But he felt differently now, knowing Rachel was onboard. The thought of her being hurt, or killed, was unacceptable. He'd briefly checked in with her another time or two before sundown. Probably less than an hour's worth of conversation, all told, since her first hail. And she'd somehow made this mission personal for him, which wasn't something he'd ever experienced before. He wanted to know her better. Know what made her tick.

"Should we use the intercom to inform the employees we're here?" Jag asked.

Mustang pressed his lips together. On one hand, it would be a morale booster for everyone to know help was at hand, but on the other, he didn't want to inform the pirates they were aboard...and he didn't want anyone to let down their guard and possibly get shot before their team could hunt the pirates.

"I think no, not yet," Mustang said after a beat.

"We could use channel three, the one Rachel said the crew uses to communicate," Slate suggested.

Mustang nodded. It wasn't perfect, but it might prevent the employees from mistakenly thinking they were the bad guys. There was no way of knowing if anyone would be listening, but it was the only way they had to communicate with the crew without tipping off the pirates.

He pulled out his radio and turned to channel three. "*Asaka Express* crew, this is a representative of the US Navy. We have secured the bridge and will be sweeping the ship for tangos. For the moment, stay where you are. I repeat, stay where you are."

Mustang nodded at Slate, who he heard reporting back to the *USS Paul Hamilton*. He knew, after the bridge and outer decks had been cleared, the plan was for additional personnel to come aboard to help secure the ship. Not only that, but because the cargo ship was floating adrift, they were sending someone who could pilot the large ship so it hopefully wouldn't run aground. Slate and Jag would stay on the bridge to keep it secure. If any of the pirates returned, they would take them out.

Pid and Aleck would patrol the outer decks until backup could arrive and take over. For now, it would be only Midas and Mustang patrolling the lower decks. They'd work as a team, searching room by room for the missing pirates. It was disconcerting that they didn't know how many men they were looking for, but ultimately it didn't matter. They'd find them all and make sure they weren't a threat any longer.

"Stay in contact," Mustang told his team unnecessarily.

They all nodded. Their team leader wasn't telling them anything they didn't already know.

Mustang once again took point as he and Midas headed for the door that led to a set of stairs right outside the bridge. The second the door closed behind them, they were plunged into darkness. It was dark on the bridge and outer decks, but with the stars and moon overhead, they'd still had a bit of light. Being in the interior of the ship afforded absolutely no ambient light whatsoever.

Pulling the night-vision goggles over his eyes, Mustang gave himself a moment to adjust to the green world that suddenly appeared through his lenses. Then he slowly began to walk down the stairs toward the first floor they had to clear.

This was obviously where the officers' and the captain's rooms were. The doors were all open and the rooms had been ransacked. Drawers had been emptied and the men's belongings were strewn all over the floor of each room. The pirates had searched for anything worth stealing.

Anger welled up inside Mustang. He'd seen a lot of awful things in his time as a SEAL, but nothing got him more riled up than needless violence and death. The pirates didn't have to kill the men up on the bridge. They could've locked them inside one of these rooms if they wanted to make sure they didn't get in the way of their mission. But instead, they'd ruthlessly snuffed out innocent lives.

Midas and Mustang found no evidence of any pirates on

the first floor and made sure to lock and close each of the doors after they'd searched the rooms. The last thing they wanted was someone sneaking back up here and hiding out, forcing the SEALs to re-clear the area.

The next floor looked much the same as the previous, individual living quarters that had been ransacked. Mustang and Midas painstakingly made their way through each room, checking every nook and cranny for anyone who might be hiding out, then locking and closing the doors. They reported back to the others, informing them of their progress.

Mustang itched to reach out to Rachel, but he didn't dare. He concentrated on the job at hand, and could only hope she was lying low, safe, wherever she'd decided to hole up.

* * *

Elodie cursed herself. Why had she left her hiding space? Because she was stupid, that was why. She hadn't heard anything in so long and had needed to use the bathroom. She figured it was safe enough—but she'd been wrong. The second she'd come out of the small restroom next to the officers' mess, she'd heard someone in the galley.

For just a second, she'd had the hope that it was Scott and his team. That the Navy SEALs had finally arrived and everyone was safe. But then she'd heard the man muttering in a foreign language and knew she was in deep shit.

She froze, looking around for a place to hide. But the officers' mess had nothing in it but a long table and chairs. There weren't any cabinets or any other place to hide. She could go back into the bathroom, but she'd be a sitting duck in there. And she'd already been lucky whoever was in the kitchen didn't seem to have heard her exiting the small room.

If she could make it to the officers' pantry, she might be able to get into one of the lower cabinets, but the pirate would definitely hear her moving around.

Elodie panicked. Any second, she was going to be seen. The man would walk into this room and find her there. The only thing she had going for her was that it was dark. She wanted to kiss whichever engineer below deck who'd had the great idea to turn off the electricity.

An idea struck her then. It was risky as hell, and if she made any noise, she'd surely be caught, but at the moment, she literally had no other options.

Moving slowly, she felt her way around the large oval table in the middle of the room. Elodie moved the chairs on the far side so they were a little closer together, making sure not to scrape the legs against the tile floor. When she thought they were positioned where she wanted them, she got down on her hands and knees and crawled under the table. She'd never been so thankful that whoever had furnished the ship had been too cheap to get chairs with armrests.

When the man in the other room seemed to finish whatever he was doing in the galley, she heard him enter the officers' pantry. He was only one room away from her right now, and she knew if she'd gone into that room to try to hide, she would've been caught.

Barely breathing, Elodie eased herself up onto the row of chairs she'd pushed together, under the table. Her belly was resting on one chair, her upper chest on another, her legs on a third. Stretched out flat, she held her breath as the pirate ransacked the cabinets. She had no idea what he was looking for, all that was in there was food and supplies, but he seemed to be taking great pleasure in throwing stuff on the floor and breaking bottles.

Elodie hoped that when he came into this room, all he'd see was a table and chairs, and with nothing to look through, he'd continue on. He had a flashlight of some sort; through the small circular window in the door, she'd seen the light wildly flicking around the room and walls. She prayed he wouldn't decide to shine it under the table for any reason.

She held her breath as she slowly reached for the knife she'd put in her belt loop. She pulled it out and clutched it in her fist, then waited to see what the man in the pantry would do next.

Minutes passed slowly. Elodie had no idea how long she'd lain on the uncomfortable chairs so far, but if the man didn't do something soon, her heart wouldn't be able to take the stress. It was going a hundred miles a minute and she felt as if he'd be able to hear it pounding.

When a radio suddenly crackled and one of his fellow pirates began speaking, Elodie nearly leaped out of her skin. She jolted badly and almost dropped the knife she was holding, which would've been a disaster.

The man on the other end of the radio sounded agitated, and Elodie wished she knew what he was saying. The man next door swore...at least, that's what she thought he was doing.

Then he yelled, "If anyone is here, you come out now. I won't kill!"

Elodie didn't dare move a muscle.

"If you hide, you die!"

She still didn't move. Elodie wondered briefly who the man suspected was down here before he suddenly shot off a volley of rounds from his rifle. She jerked and gasped. Luckily, the sound of the shots was slightly muted, since the pirate was shooting in the pantry behind a closed door.

"That was warning!" the man yelled again.

Nothing about him shooting his weapon made her want to come out of hiding.

Then he muttered something under his breath before speaking on his radio once more.

He was still speaking when the door to the officers' mess opened.

If Elodie hadn't turned her head at the exact right moment, she wouldn't have seen the two sets of legs entering the room. A sliver of illumination from the pirate's flashlight, flickering through the pantry window, momentarily highlighted the figures. The door shut without a sound, and she almost threw up with fear when she lost sight of the men.

Were these more pirates? If so, why weren't they calling out to their friend? She was confused, but didn't dare make a move, much less breathe. She couldn't see what was happening, but she could faintly hear the fabric of their pants as the two figures walked past the table, and her hiding spot.

The pirate in the galley seemed to be arguing with someone on the radio now. He sounded upset and pissed off. Then he stopped talking—and the sound of something large being thrown against the wall made Elodie jump in surprise yet again.

Apparently, while the pirate was throwing his temper tantrum, whoever had entered the officers' mess had opened the door to the pantry. The sound of gunshots made a small whimper escape her lips. The shots were much louder, since the weapon was fired in the same room where she was hiding. Now she could hear little but the ringing in her ears. Elodie strained to hear what was going on, and for several seconds heard nothing but her own heart racing.

"Tango down in the galley."

With the ringing and her heartbeat, Elodie wasn't sure she was hearing correctly.

That sounded like *English*. Non-accented English. And she was pretty sure her fellow *Asaka Express* employees wouldn't use a word like "tango" to describe the pirates. She also didn't think they'd be slinking around like these two men were.

She'd waited what seemed like forever for Scott and his team to arrive—and it sounded like they finally had.

It had been a couple hours since she'd been in contact with Scott, which she understood. He was busy planning a way to get onboard, and he couldn't exactly take the time to reassure her every other minute. But each time he'd reached out, it had made her feel so much better. Less alone.

"We need to find Rachel," one of the men said. She knew it was Scott because she recognized his voice.

"Maybe we should leave her where she is," the other man said.

"No. She would've heard the shots and is probably freaking out," Scott argued.

The last thing she wanted to do was get shot, so Elodie knew better than to pop up out of her hiding spot and surprise the men, but she definitely didn't want to stay where she was either.

"I'm here," she said softly, hoping she didn't startle them badly enough that they'd turn around and start shooting.

But she should've known they were too professional to do something like that.

"Rachel?"

Elodie winced at hearing the name from his lips.

She wanted to tell him that wasn't her name...but she couldn't. She'd changed her name in the first place because Elodie was too unique. It wouldn't be hard for Paul to find her if she'd kept it. But the drawback was that she sometimes forgot to respond when someone called her Rachel.

"It's me," she said.

"Where are you?" Scott asked.

"Lying on the chairs, under the table."

She heard more than saw movement on the other side of the table.

"Damn, that's smart," the other man said. "You fit perfectly up there, and in this darkness, even if someone looked they probably wouldn't see you."

"How are *you* seeing me then?" Elodie blurted. She hadn't been blinded with a beam from a flashlight.

"Night-vision goggles," Scott said.

Elodie jerked because his voice sounded from right next to her.

"Easy. How can I help you get out from under there?" he asked.

"I got it," she told him, amazed that she hadn't heard him come over to the side of the table. She kept her voice down as she climbed off the chairs. "I had to improvise. I snuck out of the pantry in the other hall to use the bathroom and when I came out, that guy was in the galley. I literally had nowhere to hide other than under here."

She crawled out from under the table and stood, using the table as a crutch. Her legs felt shaky from the adrenaline dump.

"Careful with that knife," Scott told her.

Elodie hadn't even remembered she was holding the thing. Now, she realized her fingers hurt from grasping it so tightly. She looked up, toward where she'd heard Scott's voice, and was frustrated when she couldn't see him. The flashlight the pirate had been holding was lying on the floor in the room next door, but it didn't give her enough light to see either of the men.

"Are they all dead?" she asked, proud when her voice only shook a little. It was surreal that she was talking about killing people so nonchalantly, but she supposed she could be forgiven, given the circumstances.

"No," Scott said, dashing her hopes that they could get in touch with the others onboard and have the electricity turned back on.

"This is the first pirate we've run across," the other man said.

"Which one are you?" Elodie blurted.

He chuckled. "I'm Midas."

"Hi."

Just then, the radio the pirate had been using cackled to

life, and a man began speaking urgently in whatever language the pirates used.

"Shit," Scott muttered.

Elodie felt a rush of air as he moved away from her.

"I don't suppose you're a language savant and can understand what they're saying, are you?" Midas asked.

She'd already told him and the other guys on the team that she couldn't understand the pirates, but she appreciated that he was trying to lighten the mood. "Sorry, no," she told him. "But right before you got here, he was talking to his friends and none of them sounded happy. He threw something big and it broke."

"Yeah, I think it was a jar of spaghetti sauce," Midas said, seemingly unconcerned.

She heard more sounds in the other room, but didn't dare move from her spot next to the table. Then Scott was back. She wasn't sure how she knew he was there, but she did.

Then he spoke, confirming his location. "Okay, we have to continue clearing the ship. You need to go up to the bridge—"

Elodie didn't let him continue. "No!" she said frantically.

"Yes," he countered.

"I'm staying with you," she insisted.

"We've cleared the floors above this one. It's safe for you to go back up to the bridge. Two other members of my team are up there, they'll keep you safe."

Elodie was shaking her head. She knew she was being completely irrational, but the thought of being alone even for the short trip to the bridge was terrifying. "You don't know where the other pirates are. You said yourself that you're clearing the ship. And I think they somehow know, if that conversation I overheard was any indication."

The radio Scott had taken off the dead pirate came to life again. "Djama?"

A few more words were said after that. It was obvious his friends were trying to get in contact with him.

"They're going to come looking for him," Elodie said. "And if I go up to the bridge, I could run into them. And you don't have time to escort me up there. They could be hurting or killing my friends. And if they find me, they're not going to hesitate to kill me either. The safest place on this ship at the moment is with you guys, so that's where I want to stay."

She held her breath as she waited for them to comment. She was laying it on pretty thick, and she knew it. She also knew she was probably wrong about them being her safest bet. They were *looking* for the pirates. Would be shot at when they encountered them. But something inside her was telling Elodie to stick with Scott. He'd been her lifeline throughout the day when she was scared. He was calm and confident. Now that he'd found her, she didn't feel comfortable letting him out of her sight.

When they didn't immediately agree or disagree, she blurted, "I've seen *Under Siege*...bad things will happen if I'm not with you."

She heard Midas choke on a laugh, but Scott didn't even try to hold his back. He wasn't loud, but he was definitely laughing at her.

"Right. First, I'm not Steven Seagal, and you aren't...what was that character's name in the movie?"

"Jordan Tate," Elodie supplied helpfully. She loved that cheesy movie and wasn't ashamed to admit it.

"Right. Anyway, I don't want to hurt your feelings, Rachel, but you'll slow us down. We don't have an extra pair of night-vision goggles, and we aren't exactly going on a moonlight walk," Scott told her.

"I know. But I can hold on to your belt or something. I know I'm a liability, but I can also be an asset. I know this ship. I can help you get around the watertight doors and if the crew sees me with you, they'll know you're one of the good guys."

Scott and his teammate didn't say anything for a long moment, and Elodie panicked.

"I swear I won't scream if you kill someone. I'll carry all your extra stuff so you don't have to." Again, she knew she was being ridiculous. These men didn't need her to carry their shit, and without night-vision goggles of her own, she'd be hanging on to them like a helpless baby monkey. "I'll do whatever you say without hesitation," she said desperately.

"Like go up to the bridge?" Midas deadpanned.

Elodie nervously bit her lip and stared up at where she thought Scott's face might be. He had to let her go with them. He just *had* to. She didn't feel safe with anyone else.

She heard him sigh, then he said, "All right, but if anything happens, you hit the deck. I mean flat on your stomach on the floor. Understand?"

She nodded. "Absolutely. Yes. On the floor. Got it."

A hand brushed against her arm, and Elodie flinched before she could stop herself.

"Sorry. I should've warned you," Scott said.

"No, it's fine," she told him.

"Give me your hand," Scott told her.

Elodie blindly held it out, and she swallowed hard when Scott took it in his own. He wore gloves, but he was still so warm. She hadn't realized how chilly she was until right this moment.

Without a word, Scott tugged her behind him as he headed for the officers' pantry. "Stay here for a second," he ordered.

Elodie nodded and stood stock-still. She heard rustling, then he was back in front of her. "Have you ever shot a gun?"

"A few times. At the firing range. I got scope eye when I tried out a rifle for the first time."

She heard chuckling from behind her, and didn't blame

Midas for laughing. It *was* pretty funny. She hadn't realized she shouldn't shove her eye right up to the scope while she was firing the damn thing. The kickback had pushed the scope right into her eye socket. She'd had a black eye for a week.

"Right. There's no safety on this thing, so do *not* point it at anyone you don't want to die...especially me or my team, okay?"

"Okay," Elodie agreed, possibly a little more energetically than the situation warranted. She wasn't planning on shooting anyone, but she'd carry the weapon if that meant she could stay with the SEALs.

"Describe to me the layout of this floor," Scott demanded after she'd put the strap of the rifle around her chest. "We studied the schematic of the ship, but tell me whatever you can about the immediate layout. Where do these doors lead?"

Elodie had a feeling he didn't need her to tell him a damn thing, and was just trying to keep her mind occupied with something other than the fact they were sneaking around looking for people who would kill them without a second thought. Reminding herself that she'd asked to go with them, *begged*, she swore not to be a bigger pain in the ass than she already was.

It was a good thing she knew the galley and all the rooms on this floor like the back of her hand, because Midas had switched off the flashlight the pirate had dropped shortly after they'd killed him. It really *was* pitch black. No matter how many times she blinked, all Elodie saw was darkness.

"We'll walk while you're talking," Scott told her. She felt him pick up her hand and guide it to the back of his pants. He turned away from her and Elodie latched on tightly. She wasn't going to let go of him under any circumstances.

"Walk carefully," Midas warned.

Knowing she probably looked stupid, but not caring since there wasn't anyone other than the SEALS to see her, Elodie exaggerated her steps as she followed behind Scott and Midas, and they slowly and carefully made their way through the officers' pantry and into the galley. She told them everything she could think of about the layout and did her best to walk as quietly as possible. She might regret begging to stay with them later, but for now, she was relieved she didn't have to wander around the dark ship on her own.

CHAPTER FOUR

Mustang couldn't get the picture out of his mind of Rachel biting her lip and tipping her chin up bravely. When they'd arrived on the deck with the galley, he'd hoped they would be able to find the cook alive and well, and she'd shocked the shit out of him when she'd spoken up. Even with the night-vision goggles, both he and Midas had walked right past her. She'd come up with literally the only place to hide in that dining room, and it had been absolutely perfect.

And Rachel Walters looked nothing like he'd expected.

He admitted that what he'd pictured in his mind was unfairly stereotypical, but seeing her in person, even through the night-vision goggles, had given him a jolt.

Her hair was long, hanging messily around her shoulders. He guessed she probably had to wear it up when she was cooking, but since they'd been woken up in the middle of the night when the pirates attacked, she obviously hadn't had time to worry about it. He couldn't tell what color her hair was through the goggles, or her eyes. She was petite, at least half a foot shorter than his own six-foot frame.

But it was her face that drew his attention. Even in the dark room and with the goggles, he could read every thought that flitted across her expressive face. She'd been scared when she'd first stood up, but determined to try to be brave. She'd been relieved, happy to not be alone, then terrified when he'd told her to go up to the bridge. Her brows had furrowed in determination when she'd proposed staying with them, even as she'd bit her lip.

He was so used to being around his teammates and other soldiers and sailors who kept a straight face no matter what was happening. Being able to read her expressions so easily was refreshing...and appealing.

He could feel her fingers clutching the loop of his pants at the small of his back, and unexpected goose bumps broke out on his arms as she adjusted her hold, brushing against him in the process.

He couldn't believe how quickly she was getting under his skin. Had that ever happened to him before? No, he didn't think so.

Mustang had let Midas take point and he was currently scanning the hallway connected to the galley for movement. He gestured for them to follow when all seemed well.

"The door at the far end, to our left, goes to a set of stairs," Rachel whispered. "If you go up, you end up on a floor with living quarters, if you go down, there's a hallway with storage rooms. Toilet paper, that sort of thing, and the laundry facilities. Below that is another floor with bedrooms, it's where my room is, and then the engine room. At least the top deck of it. It's huge, and there are actually four levels in there. It's usually really loud, and hot, but with the electricity being off, I have no idea if it still will be."

Mustang nodded. He and the others had studied the blueprints of the engine room carefully. That was where they figured most of the pirates would be, hunting for the missing employees.

He was having second—and third—thoughts about Rachel being with them. When they got into that engine room, things were going to get exponentially more dangerous. He'd much rather stash Rachel somewhere safe, but he knew as well as they all did that, technically, nowhere was safe with the pirates running around. He had to assume they knew something was wrong because their friends weren't responding to their radio calls, so they'd be even more trigger happy as a result.

They quickly cleared the level under the kitchen and headed down one more to the floor where more crew quarters were located. So far, Rachel had done everything he'd asked. She'd been silent, and was doing a good job of moving quietly. She wasn't quite as light-footed as he and Midas, but for a civilian it was pretty impressive.

"There are five rooms on this floor. My assistant and I stay down here, and the head engineer and two other guys. They like being close to the engine room," she whispered.

The pirates hadn't spared this floor from their ransacking. Peering into the first room, Mustang saw clothing strewn around on the floor and the furniture had been upturned.

When they got to the last room in the hallway, Mustang was glad Rachel couldn't see what he was seeing through his night-vision lenses.

Her room had also been torn apart—but her underwear and bras were on her bed, as if whoever had discovered them had displayed them for his viewing pleasure. Now they knew there was a woman onboard. But what Mustang wasn't sure about was whether Rachel would be a larger target or not.

"This is my room," Rachel said softly. "Is it as bad as you said the others were?"

"They searched it too, if that's what you're asking," Mustang said.

"Right."

Her tone of voice was...off. She sounded upset, which wasn't unusual. Anytime someone was robbed it felt like a violation. When he turned to look at her, her eyes were wide in her face and she was biting her lip again.

He wanted to ask if there was something inside that she was particularly worried about being stolen, but now wasn't the time. They needed to keep moving.

Mustang heard Slate telling the team that the first round of reinforcements were roughly thirty minutes out from boarding the ship. He'd explained earlier that help was delayed when several boats full of Djibouti nationalists had been apprehended while heading for the *Asaka Express*. They claimed they were out fishing, but because of the amount of weapons onboard—and the large ladders with hooks on the ends, found on each boat—the US officials assumed they were the pirates' compatriots coming to help pilfer goods and valuables from the ship.

They were securing the last of those men now, and there was a veritable US Navy fleet surrounding the cargo ship, so they didn't have to worry about any more pirates joining the party onboard, but they still had to find and eliminate the rest of the men who were currently hiding in the nooks and crannies of the ship.

"The ship's getting dangerously close to shallow waters," Slate informed everyone. "We need to get the electricity back on, stat. We should be getting a pilot up here with the first wave of reinforcements, but we need to get communications with the engine room up and running to get the ship out of danger."

"Ten-four," Midas replied quietly. "We're two minutes away from heading down there. Stand by."

"Watch your six," Pid chimed in. "Found one man on the outer decks, he was more worried about what was in the container he'd managed to open than whoever might be sneaking up behind him, but the second he saw me, he fired. It was too late, of course, but these guys are shooting first and asking questions later."

"Got it," Mustang said. "Do we have any idea yet how many tangos we're looking for?"

"No," Jag said.

"Damn," Midas muttered.

Rachel could only hear their side of the conversation because she didn't have an earpiece, but she kept quiet and didn't ask for more information. Mustang's respect for her grew.

He turned his head and asked, "Ready, Rachel?"

When she didn't comment, almost as if she hadn't heard him, Mustang thought about the background her employer had run on her...and how fishy everything had seemed. It was becoming pretty obvious that Rachel wasn't her real name. Especially when she hadn't reacted to it just now.

He reached back and touched her arm. She jolted as if he'd stuck her with a stun gun.

"Sorry. I didn't mean to startle you. Are you ready to do this?" he asked. "It's not too late to head up to the bridge. The outer decks are clear and you should be good to go."

"I'm ready, and no, I'm staying with you," she said, softly but firmly.

It was a mistake, but Mustang wasn't ready to let her go. Something was telling him she was right, that the safest place for her was right there with him. Especially after seeing her room. He didn't want the pirates to get their hands on her.

"If you don't do exactly as we say, you could get us all killed," Midas told her.

"I know, and I'll do what you tell me," she promised.

"And if we say to go upstairs right now?" Midas asked.

Mustang looked back and saw Rachel wrinkle her nose before she sighed. "I'd go if you forced me to," she said after a moment.

Mustang looked over at Midas, and they stared at each other for a long moment. They'd worked together long enough to be able to read each other pretty well. Midas finally shrugged and lifted his hand in the air and made a circular motion with his finger...essentially saying, "let's get on with this."

Mustang nodded at his teammate then turned back to Rachel. She was staring up where she thought his head was with a worried look on her face. He wanted to soothe the wrinkles he saw in her forehead, to tell her everything would be all right, but he was aware that they really did need to get going. Things would get very tricky if this ship grounded itself on a reef or even the coastline of Djibouti.

The engine room needed to be secured so they could return to the USS *Paul Hamilton* and the employees of the *Asaka Express* could get on with their lives. There were dead bodies to secure, and the shipping company would have to deal with the transportation of their employees back to the States.

In other words...they had shit to get done, and standing in a dark hallway staring at a woman who intrigued the hell out of him was wasting time.

"Stay close," Mustang told Rachel. "And be as quiet as you can."

She nodded, obviously relieved they weren't making her leave.

Midas brushed past them and headed back down the hall the way they came. They needed to get to the engine room.

The next few minutes were tense as the trio made their way down the stairwell and entered the vast engine room. There were ducts and pipes everywhere. The lighting was eerie, as there were emergency lights scattered here and there that were on, illuminating some of the space while throwing other areas into shadow. The lights screwed with the night-vision goggles and both Mustang and Midas were forced to remove them.

They stood against the wall overlooking the engines for a

long moment as they waited for their eyes to adjust. Rachel didn't say a word the entire time.

Mustang studied the layout of the space. There was a catwalk running from the level they were currently standing on, across the vast decks below, obviously built so the workers could easily access the ductwork and pipes that ran across the space.

If they leaned over the railing, they'd be able to see all the way to the floor four decks below. According to what Rachel had said, there were offshoot hallways and work rooms on the lower three floors, all filled with machinery and containers built to hold trash, water, oil, fuel, and all other manner of necessary equipment needed to keep a ship this size seaworthy. It was going to be a bitch to clear this space, and the longer Mustang stood there, the more he realized they needed help. They could do a preliminary search, but anything extensive was going to take more bodies.

"Shit," he muttered.

"We're gonna need backup," Midas agreed. "And shooting off any kind of round in here is seriously fucking dangerous."

Mustang nodded. "Don't get too close to the railing. If someone's standing below, they could see us and pick us off."

Midas nodded in understanding. "We'll clear what we can, see if we can find some of the missing men. Then we'll wait for reinforcements."

Mustang knew he was talking to the rest of the team more than he was telling Mustang what to do. They were already on the same page. He'd had hopes that they'd be able to tackle this on their own, but seeing the blueprints didn't convey how big this room really was and how many places there were for someone to hide.

The trio hugged the wall and headed around the perimeter of the room, making sure to stay away from the railing. They made it around to the left side and found a room filled with pipes that snaked every which way. Also inside, a small control room sat off to the right, the door standing wide open. There was only one emergency light in the ceiling, concealing more than it was illuminating because of the shadows created by the light.

"Stay here," Mustang ordered Rachel.

He felt her fingers tighten on his belt loop for a second, then she nodded and let go of him. She brought the rifle that had been hanging on her back around to the front of her body and held it at the ready. She would've looked damn cute if there weren't real bullets in the weapon and they weren't in the middle of a deadly game of hide-and-seek.

He nodded at Midas, and they split up as they began to search the room. Their search didn't result in finding any of the pirates or ship employees. So they continued into the next room, away from the main part of the engine room and where they'd left Rachel.

Their search continued into yet another room, and then one last small room at the end of the deck. While there, they finally found one of the crew members. He'd folded himself behind one of the large ducts.

"US Navy," Midas said.

"Oh, thank God!" the man said.

"What's your name and what's your position on the ship?" Mustang asked.

"I'm Manuel. I'm the second cook."

Mustang was glad to see the man alive and well, but he'd been hoping to find one of the engineers.

"I was too scared to go any farther into the engine room when we were told the ship was overtaken," the man explained. "Is it safe to go back upstairs?"

"No, not yet. We advise that you get back in your hiding spot. Our team is making notes on where the crew is holing up. We'll make an announcement when it's all clear," Midas told him.

"Okay," Manuel agreed. "Oh, hey, did you find Rachel? She's the cook, she was hiding up on the galley level."

"We found her," Mustang told the man, not elaborating.

He sighed in relief. "Good."

"Stay put," Mustang told him once more and watched as Rachel's helper scooted back behind the duct where he'd been hiding.

Midas and Mustang made their way back through the side rooms to the large atrium space. Rachel was still standing right where they'd last seen her, rifle in hand, eyes wide, lips pressed together in determination.

"Did you find anyone?" she whispered in a tone so low, Mustang almost couldn't hear her.

"Yeah. Manuel."

"Was he all right?"

"Yeah. Scared but hiding."

"Thank God."

Mustang reached out for Rachel's hand and curled it back around his belt loop. Without a word, they continued around the huge open atrium to the next set of rooms.

They quickly cleared the first floor and all the rooms as best they could, then made their way down to the next level of the engine room. The noise steadily got louder as they headed down. The electricity and engine might be down, but the pumps and other machines were still running. The temperature also climbed the farther they went into the bowels of the space, as well.

When Midas and Mustang had swiftly and preliminarily cleared the three levels above the main engine room floor, they were faced with the decision of whether to continue or to stay put and wait for backup. They hadn't been able to search as thoroughly as they'd like, but a more intensive search would be done once backup arrived and the lights had been turned on.

They'd found four more employees, all hiding in various

rooms on one of the upper three floors. That still left a lot of the crew to be discovered. The last thing Mustang wanted was to be ambushed by a ship employee if they thought he and Midas were pirates. Not to mention, they hadn't found any of the remaining pirates themselves.

For a second, Mustang wondered if they were on a wild goose chase. Maybe there *weren't* any more pirates. But he immediately dismissed that thought. The authorities had listened to the recordings of what was happening on the bridge and estimated at least six men had taken over the ship. That meant there were at least three more to find.

He and Midas were standing at the base of the stairs leading to the upper levels. There was a half wall behind them, with three large storage tanks behind it. He motioned with his head to Midas and his teammate quickly cleared that area. When he returned, Mustang turned to Rachel. "Stay here. We'll be back."

She opened her mouth to protest, but then pressed her lips together and nodded.

He wanted to reassure her. Tell her that they'd be fine, that *she'd* be fine. But there wasn't time. He took hold of her arm and led her to the half wall then gently pushed her down behind it. She'd be safe there. He had to believe that, otherwise he'd never be able to leave her. But for the search he and Midas were going to need to do down here, he couldn't have her hanging on to him.

She looked up at him, and even though they were in the shadows, he could still see the fear in her eyes. A piece of her hair was sticking to her forehead, and before he'd thought about what he was doing, Mustang reached out and gently smoothed it back. Then, without a word, he straightened and returned to Midas's side.

"How long until backup arrives?" Mustang asked his other teammates.

"Less than five minutes," Aleck told him.

"We can come down and help now, before the others get here," Jag offered.

"No, we need you up there in case the rats try to flee the ship," Mustang said softly. "We'll take a quick look around then hold steady for the extra eyes."

"Watch your six," Slate said.

Mustang gave Midas a nod, and with one last thought for the courageous woman behind the wall, they headed out to see if they could find the pirates.

* * *

Elodie stayed crouched behind the half wall, gripping the rifle in her hands tightly. She didn't dare put her finger anywhere near the trigger. She was jumpy and scared to death and the last thing she wanted was to accidentally fire the dang thing.

She'd wanted to protest when Scott and his teammate told her to stay hidden here. But she'd told them she'd do whatever they said, and the thought of prowling around the engine room wasn't exactly high on her list of fun things to do.

So she stayed right where she was, praying the SEALs either found the pirates or that more help arrived so they could all get the hell out of there.

Elodie wondered what her next steps would be. She'd taken this job because it had seemed safer than being in the States, trying to stay two steps ahead of Paul Columbus. She'd read about pirates, but it had seemed like such a remote possibility that they'd actually get hijacked. She hadn't heard of any attacks recently.

She'd tried to stay under the radar and somehow had found herself in the spotlight anyway. This hijacking would be big news, she knew it. With the captain and his officers killed, everyone would be reporting on it. And the fact that she was a woman was unique enough for all the reporters to want her take on what had occurred.

She couldn't let that happen. If even one picture of her got out, she was as good as dead.

Could she get off the ship in Sudan and disappear again? Shit, she had no idea if the ship was even going to continue to Port Sudan anyway. She also hadn't been able to see anything when they'd stopped outside her room, but the way Scott tensed made her think that it was bad. She wondered if her real identification papers and documents she'd hidden in an air duct had been found by the pirates. It was stupid of her to bring them, she realized now. Had Scott seen them? Is that why he'd tensed?

She had a feeling the SEALs didn't miss much. She also knew she'd failed to respond to her name being called at least once. Did they suspect she wasn't who she said she was? Would they blow her cover?

Maybe she'd be taken into custody when the Navy came onboard. Maybe they'd take all the surviving crew members off the ship and interrogate them. Elodie had no idea what would happen once all the pirates had been captured or killed. But she had a feeling her life was going to be upended once more.

Sighing, she rested her head against the wall and closed her eyes. It was hard to believe that less than a day ago, her biggest worries were what to make for dinner and trying to convince Valentino that she didn't want to sleep with him.

She was so lost in her head that she wasn't paying attention to what was going on around her. The hum of the machinery, the heat of the room and the stress were actually making her sleepy. Considering they'd all been woken up in the middle of the night to news that their ship was being taken over, then she'd been awake all day trying to stay hidden, and now it was nighttime again, it wasn't any wonder she was exhausted and her eyes wouldn't stay open.

But a noise nearby jolted her back into awareness quickly.

She scooted farther back behind the wall, then went so far

as to back up slowly behind one of the large storage tanks. She peered out from behind it, holding the rifle at the ready. She tried to tell herself that it was probably Scott and Midas coming back from their patrol, but the hair on the back of her neck was standing up and she honestly didn't think they'd be back so soon.

Trying to slow her breathing, Elodie's eyes widened as she saw a dark figure creeping down the stairs she and Scott and Midas had come down not that long ago. He wasn't one of the crew, she knew that immediately. He was in a black T-shirt and torn dark shorts. He was also wearing a pair of flip-flops. No one on the ship was allowed to wear anything other than closed-toe shoes when they were outside of their rooms.

She'd never seen this man before, and her adrenaline immediately spiked.

He turned in the direction Scott and Midas had gone, but instead of following them, he slunk behind the very half wall she'd been crouched against thirty seconds ago. If she hadn't moved, he would've run right into her.

Elodie's heart was beating a mile a minute, and she didn't know what to do. Should she shoot him? The thought was repugnant. She'd never hurt anyone in her life before and didn't want to start now. But when Scott came back, he'd go right to the spot where the pirate was crouched, thinking he'd find her there. He'd be ambushed and killed before he'd had a chance to defend himself.

Sweat dripped down her temple, but she didn't dare move to wipe it away. The last thing she wanted was to bring any attention to herself. Elodie could smell the man's body odor where she was hidden and it physically made her ill.

Several minutes passed, and Elodie thought she was going to have a heart attack.

Then the man shifted, bringing his rifle up.

Elodie looked where he was aiming and saw movement.

Scott and Midas were returning—and they had no idea they were about to be gunned down.

Swallowing hard, Elodie moved without thinking. She went down onto her knees and raised her own rifle.

She must've made some noise that the man heard over the sound of the humming machinery, because his head turned... and they made eye contact.

His eyes widened, probably because he realized how close she'd been to him the whole time. He started to swing his rifle around to point it at her...

Elodie squeezed the trigger of her own weapon before he could complete the movement.

The sound of the rifle firing was surprisingly loud, and Elodie flinched, but she squeezed the trigger two more times almost without thinking.

The man who'd been waiting to ambush Scott and Midas looked down at his chest, then fell forward, flat on his face.

Elodie panted as if she'd just run the forty-meter dash and couldn't take her eyes off the man she'd just shot. A small pool of blood began to spread around his body, making her gag.

"Rachel!"

Looking up, Elodie saw Scott kneeling next to her. She had no idea how long he'd been there or how many times he'd said her name before she realized he was talking to her. Her ears were ringing slightly. Midas was standing near the stairs with his weapon at the ready.

"We need to get out of here," Scott told her urgently.

"He came from up there," Elodie told him woodenly, looking at the stairs and the level above them.

"Shit, all right. He must've looped around and we missed him in our search," Scott said.

"He was going to shoot you," Elodie said.

"I know."

"He was waiting for you."

"You saved our lives. Thank you," Scott said.

Elodie realized she was still gripping the rifle tightly. She wanted to be badass and indifferent about what she'd just done, but she couldn't find it in her.

"Come on, we need to get you out of here," Scott said, grabbing her elbow and pulling her to a standing position. "We found a group of the engineers. They're ready to turn the electricity back on when we give them the go-ahead. But we need to wait until we've got backup, so we can protect the crew when they go to their stations to get the ship functional again."

Elodie barely heard the words.

"Rachel? Are you listening?"

"Uh-huh."

"She's in shock," Midas said from nearby.

"I know," Scott told his friend. "I should've left her upstairs."

Elodie focused on him then. "But then you would've gotten shot."

"Maybe," Scott said. "Come on, the engineers pointed out an emergency stairwell in the back of the room that we can use to get up to the front of the ship and then to the bridge."

Something else occurred to Elodie. "If I wasn't here, you wouldn't have had to come back for me...and you wouldn't have been in danger."

Scott leaned down and framed her face with his gloved hands. He tilted her head up so she had no choice but to look at him. His face gleamed with sweat and she could more clearly see his beard and mustache. The beard touched his upper chest but wasn't scraggly or unkempt.

She had the sudden urge to run her fingers over the hair to see if it was fine or coarse. She'd never been this close to anyone with a beard like he had. There was a deep wrinkle between Scott's eyes as he frowned down at her.

Frankly, the man was gorgeous. It was a shock to realize

65

that now, after she'd been talking to him all day and then following him around in the dark.

"You were right. The safest place for you was with us. The fact that this guy got behind us somehow and was lying in wait proves it. You might've run into him at some point on your way up to the bridge. I know shooting him was hard, but you saved us, and we're forever in your debt. All right?"

She nodded. What else could she do?

"We gotta get going," Midas warned.

Without another word, Scott grabbed ahold of Elodie's hand and pulled her behind him as he stepped around the dead man on the floor and headed back into the bowels of the engine room.

Elodie held on to his hand tightly, conscious of the fact that he hadn't directed her to hold his belt loop. She was now between Scott and his teammate, and they moved quickly, weaving around the pumps and pipes. They arrived at a door, half the size of the normal doors around the ship. She'd have to get down on her knees to go through it. She saw not a stairwell on the other side, but metal rungs, like a ladder.

Movement to her right scared her so badly, she jumped and reached for the rifle she'd let fall against her back once more. But Midas grabbed hold of her arm, preventing her from arming herself.

"It's okay, they're the good guys."

Elodie focused on the dark shapes and realized they were Troy, Ari, and Pablo.

She couldn't stop her reaction; she lunged for them and gave each man a fierce hug. "Thank God you're okay!" she told them.

"We're glad to see you too," Troy said.

"What about everyone else?" she asked.

"They're around here somewhere," Ari said vaguely. "We managed to take out one of the pirates, but the others have been much more cautious since then," he told her.

"Rachel took care of another a few minutes ago," Midas said, and Elodie would swear she heard pride in his tone. But she didn't want to think about what she'd done.

"So there's what, two more left? Three?" Pablo asked.

"Something like that. Maybe only one," Scott said.

"Is it true that they killed the captain?" Troy asked.

Elodie nodded. "And the rest of the officers who were on the bridge with him."

"Damn."

"Yeah."

"I need to get Rachel upstairs," Scott said, interrupting them.

"Right. Sorry," Troy said.

"Don't get complacent," Midas ordered. "Even if there's only one guy left, he's going to be desperate. Stay tuned for the signal to turn the lights back on, then stay hidden. Soon, this place will be crawling with good guys and this'll all be over."

The three men nodded and disappeared into the shadows around them.

"I'll go first," Midas said.

"We'll be right behind you," Scott told his teammate.

Elodie watched as Midas got down on his knees and somehow squeezed himself through the hatch.

"Up you go," Scott said.

She looked at him in surprise. "Me? I thought I'd be last."

"Nope, I've got your six."

"But who has *yours*?"

He smiled at her then, and she could've swore he leaned toward her a bit before he said, "I think you've proven that *you* do. Now, up you go, Midas is waiting."

Not thinking too hard about his words, and how good they made her feel, Elodie shimmied into the small escape hatch and started upward. She smelled the fresh air before she got halfway up, and it made her climb faster. She heard

Midas open the latch at the top and before she knew it, he was helping her up and out to stand on the open deck.

It was still dark outside, but the wind was blowing and the smell of the salty sea air had never been as welcoming as it was right that second. She hadn't realized how stuffy it was down in the galley and engine room.

She heard something to her right and turned in alarm, only to relax when she saw four men coming toward them dressed the same as Midas and Scott.

"The bridge is secure."

"There're two dozen of our men onboard, with more coming."

"Good to see you two."

Elodie listened to the exchange with wide eyes. It seemed as if the Navy didn't mess around. When they said they were sending help, they were really sending help.

"There's at least one more tango below decks somewhere," Midas informed the rest of the team.

"Heard she took care of one of them," one of the newcomers said.

Feeling awkward and out of place, Elodie kept her mouth shut as she stared up at them.

"She did. Saved our asses. He was hunkered down where we'd left Rachel, and we would've walked right into him if she hadn't taken him out. Guys, this is Rachel. Rachel, this is the rest of my team. Aleck, Pid, Jag, and Slate."

Elodie nodded at the men. They were standing right under an emergency light at the front of the ship. There were large hydraulic mooring wenches around them, and the containers were stacked high above their heads. She'd been up here more times than she could count, but never at night, and never with only the emergency lights on. It seemed surreal, like a different planet.

Especially when she was standing with these six men, all looking at her as if she was something special.

It was hard to tell the guys apart, since they were all wearing black clothes and bulletproof vests. Scott was the only one with a full beard, and she liked how it made him stand out from the rest of the team.

Not really liking being the center of attention, Elodie said softly, "Hi."

All six men grinned at her, and she immediately had a feeling she was missing something.

"She doesn't look badass enough to have saved your worthless hides," Slate stated.

Elodie couldn't help but frown at him.

The others all chuckled.

"She ready?" a voice asked from behind her.

Again, Elodie startled badly. She had a feeling she'd never like being snuck up on again after this experience. She turned to see another group of men standing on the back deck.

"Yeah," Scott answered for her.

"Ready for what?" Elodie asked.

"Rocco and his SEAL team are going to escort you to the bridge, where we know you'll be safe while we head back below deck to secure the ship once and for all," Scott told her.

Elodie looked from Scott to the other men, then back at Scott. "You're going down there again?"

"Yeah. We need to finish this."

They stared at each other for a long moment. Elodie wanted to tell him not to go. To stay here and let the other SEAL team hunt the last terrorist, but that would be rude... and not very nice to admit she'd rather put the men she *didn't* know in danger, rather than Scott and his team.

Scott took a step closer, seeming to put them in a private bubble. "You'll be safe with them," he told her. "They're among the Navy's best, stationed in California. They won't let anything happen to you."

"Is that where you're from?" she asked, knowing she was deliberately trying to postpone the inevitable.

Scott smiled. "No. My team and I are stationed in Hawaii. Honolulu."

"I've always wanted to go there. I bet it's nice."

"It's Hawaii, Rachel, of course it's nice." He grinned wider.

Hearing the fake name on his lips brought Elodie back to the present. What was she doing? Flirting with the man? In the middle of a hijack situation? Nothing could happen between them. She was on the run and he was a respected Navy SEAL.

She took a step back. "Right, I'm ready. The sooner you guys can find the pirates, the sooner we can all get back to our lives."

She hated the look of disappointment on Scott's face, but she ignored it, giving him a small smile and waving to his teammates, who were standing behind him. Then she turned her back on them and headed toward the other SEAL team.

"Rachel..."

"Rachel!"

Once again, Elodie remembered too late that was the name she was going by, and she turned. Scott was frowning at her, but when he saw that he had her attention, he said, "I'll make sure you're all right before we leave."

She wanted to thank him, to smile in her obvious relief. But the sooner she got it through her thick skull that she was destined to be alone, the better. She wouldn't drag someone down into the goatscrew that was her life. She wouldn't put anyone in danger. Paul Columbus would find her one day and kill her. She knew that for certain.

So she simply nodded and turned her back on Scott once more as she joined the second SEAL team. They surrounded her and began the long walk down the deck toward the bridge.

CHAPTER FIVE

Mustang appreciated his team not giving him shit for his short conversation with Rachel. He knew they'd hear every word through the radios they were still wearing, but he hadn't cared. Of course, they hadn't said anything intimate, but he couldn't deny he liked that she seemed to want to know more about him. Telling her he was stationed in Hawaii wasn't exactly a state secret, but it made him feel good that she was interested.

But then she seemed to close down. He'd seen her wipe all emotion from her face as if he'd said something offensive. He wracked his brain trying to figure out what he'd said or done wrong, but came up blank.

What he *did* know for certain was that Rachel wasn't her name. And that bothered Mustang more than he cared to admit. He'd called her name twice before she'd turned around, and he didn't think it was because she hadn't heard him. Nor did he think she'd been using the pseudonym for long, otherwise she would've reacted to the name immediately.

One thing Mustang didn't like was a mystery. Especially when it was attached to someone he admired.

Rachel Walters, or whoever she was, had saved his and Midas's lives. They hadn't seen or heard that pirate come down the stairs, and they would've walked right up to him behind that wall before they realized it wasn't Rachel waiting for them.

She hadn't liked killing him, that was obvious, but she had. She was an enigma, and Mustang wanted to solve the mystery of who she really was and what she was doing on this ship in the middle of nowhere.

But first he and his team, with the help of Rocco and the other SEALs, had a pirate to track down and eliminate.

An hour and a half later, the *Asaka Express* was up and running once more. It had taken forty minutes for the SEALs to find the last pirate. He'd climbed inside one of the air ducts and had attempted to crawl his way to freedom. He'd been found when the duct collapsed under him and he practically fell into their laps. He'd also made the mistake of trying to shoot his way through them, which wasn't a good choice when surrounded by six armed Navy SEALs.

As the sun began to rise, an announcement had been made that the ship was clear and the engineers had immediately turned the electricity back on. The cargo ship had narrowly missed being grounded on a shallow reef off the coast of Djibouti, and after the SEALs had been extracted from the vessel, it would continue to Port Sudan with an armed escort of three US Navy ships.

Once there, Mustang had no idea what would happen to the crew. Most likely the company would give them the option of staying onboard or being flown home. He had no doubt a replacement crew would be available almost immediately, this time hopefully with a few more safety precautions being taken if the ship continued operating in this part of the world.

He and his team would be returning to the USS *Paul Hamilton* and, from there, sent back to Hawaii. All part of a day's work for them.

But he hoped to be able to catch Rachel before they left the ship. The decks were crawling with Navy personnel at the moment. There were probably more people onboard than had ever been on the ship's decks at any one point.

Mustang headed toward the bridge with the rest of the team. They all wanted to at least say hello to Rocco and his crew before heading home. Things on the bridge were chaotic when they arrived. The bodies of the captain and his officers had been removed; Mustang assumed they'd been brought down to one of the freezers...which Rachel probably wouldn't like.

He ran his eyes over the people in the room and saw the few officers from the *Asaka Express* who'd managed to escape the slaughter by hiding down in the engine room, now working with the sailors who'd been brought over from the other Naval ships in the area.

Rocco was standing with Gumby, Ace, Bubba, Rex, and Phantom on the opposite side of the long room, simply observing what was going on. The one person he didn't see that he most wanted to find was Rachel.

He saw Rocco making his way over to meet them. "Hey."

"Hey," Mustang returned, shaking the other man's hand. "Good to see you. Thanks for the assist."

"Of course. We just happened to be in the area," Rocco said with a smirk. "You all headed home?"

"As far as I know, yes. I'm sure there will be a ton of paperwork that needs to be done, and two after-action reviews, since we were pulled off another job to come here."

Rocco nodded. "Yeah, same here. We'd finished our original mission, but still, two AARs suck."

As his friends and Rocco's teammates greeted each other and shot the shit, Mustang argued with himself, wondering whether he should ask about Rachel.

"She's good," Rocco said as if he could read his mind.

Not pretending he didn't know what he was talking about, Mustang asked, "You sure? She was pretty tapped out there at the end."

"I'm sure," Rocco said. "She's a trooper. We were gonna take that rifle away from her, but she seemed to really want to keep it. It wasn't until we arrived at the bridge, and she saw for herself that things seemed to be safe, that she allowed Phantom to take it from her."

"Where is she now?" Mustang asked.

"Not sure. One of the officers seemed very glad to see her, and after the all-clear, he escorted her below decks. They left a few minutes ago."

Mustang clenched his teeth together upon hearing that. Which was ridiculous. Rachel had a life, and she was probably very glad to see someone familiar. He'd kinda had hopes that she'd want to see him off, but she'd probably be relieved never to see his face again. Especially after everything that had happened.

"Want some advice?" Rocco asked.

Mustang shook his head, realizing he'd zoned out for a second. "From the one and only Rocco? Of course," Mustang quipped.

But Rocco didn't rise to the bait. "Women can be confusing as hell. They say one thing and do another. They can be shy on the outside, but badass warriors on the inside. And if I've learned *anything* by being married to Caite, I've learned to never assume I know what she's thinking."

Mustang nodded in appreciation. He knew all about how Rocco had met his wife on a mission, and how she'd saved his life.

Mustang tried to be open-minded, to not assume

someone was weaker than he was simply because of their gender. Hell, he'd seen some amazingly strong women in the Navy, so it wasn't that he thought women should be barefoot and pregnant or anything. Still, Rachel had shocked the shit out of him by not hesitating to kill the pirate. She'd even said she didn't really like guns, despite shooting them before.

"She intrigues me. I know nothing about her, and yet I can't stop thinking about her. I know it's ridiculous. She could be dating that officer she's with, or married, or a lesbian...it's making me crazy."

Rocco grinned. "For the record, if the long look back at you as we were walking away was any indication, I don't think she's into women or married. Of course, I could be wrong. But here's the thing, Mustang, there aren't a lot of women who can handle what we do. Kissing her goodbye and not being able to tell her where you're going or when you'll be back sucks. You need to find someone who's strong enough to handle the stress that comes along with being a SEAL's partner.

"She saved your life, man. I never thought I'd ever be in a situation where I needed a civilian to save *my* hide, but I did, and Caite is literally the best thing to ever happen to me. My advice is to go find Rachel. Tell her you'd like to see her again. I don't know where she's from or how that'll work, but if you're that interested, I advise you to do everything in your power to make it happen. At least make it clear to her that you want to see her again. You'll regret it if you don't."

It was a long speech, which surprised him, but it was what Mustang needed to hear. He felt a bond growing with Rachel he hadn't felt with many people in his life. She'd been scared to death, and yet she hadn't hesitated to do what needed to be done.

"She's the cook," Mustang told his friend. "I bet she went down to check out her kitchen. Or at the very least, make sure the bodies of her crew mates were properly stored."

"If anyone asks where you are, I'll make sure they know you're doing official SEAL shit so you'll have time to talk to her."

"Thanks, Rocco. I owe ya."

"Nah, it's what friends do."

They shook hands once more and Mustang turned to head for the exit.

"You goin' to find her?" Midas asked as he passed him.

"Yeah. I just want to make sure she's okay after everything that happened," Mustang said.

"Tell her thanks from the rest of us," Aleck told him. "It would have sucked to have to get used to a new guy on the team if you'd gotten killed."

Mustang rolled his eyes. Aleck had gotten his nickname partly because his last name was Smart, and partly because he *was* a smart aleck.

"Might do you all good to get someone new as team leader. They wouldn't put up with your shit," Mustang fired back.

"You know you love us!" Pid chimed in.

"Yeah, you'd be super sad if we weren't around to give you that shit," Jag added.

Slate just crossed his arms and smirked.

"I'll be back soon. Don't leave without me," Mustang told his team.

"Never. Who'd do the paperwork if we left you?" Midas asked.

Mustang chuckled as he left the bridge. He passed a few Navy sailors who were standing guard and headed for the stairs leading down to the lower decks. He wasn't sure what he was going to say to Rachel, but hopefully he'd figure it out by the time he found her.

* * *

Elodie felt horrible. She was exhausted and every muscle in her body hurt. Probably from all the exertion she wasn't used to. Not to mention the stress and bouts of extreme terror she'd yo-yoed through for over twenty-four hours.

When she'd been escorted up to the bridge by the other SEALs, she'd been both relieved she was out of the engine room and terrified for Scott and his team. She knew they were going to go right back down into the bowels of the ship to try to find the missing pirate, or pirates, if there was more than one left lurking about.

She couldn't believe she'd actually killed someone. Even though she'd lived through it, it felt as if the last few hours had happened to someone else. She wasn't GI Jane, not even close, and yet she hadn't really even hesitated to take that man's life. What if he had a wife and children? Would they ever know what happened to him? No, he wasn't exactly doing nice things, but did that make it okay for her to take his life?

She'd known deep down in her bones that he was going to kill Scott and Midas. He wouldn't have hesitated, which is why she'd pulled the trigger. It was him or the men who'd risked their lives to save her, and everyone else left onboard.

When she'd gotten up to the bridge, there had been a bunch of people she'd never seen before doing what they could to try to keep the cargo ship from running aground. A female sailor was trying to manually steer the ship without the use of electricity or the engines. There had been lots of swearing, but amazingly she'd been able to straighten out the ship so it wasn't sitting sideways in the middle of the strait.

Elodie had stayed as far away from the dead bodies of the captain and the others as she could. The men on the other SEAL team had moved to stand between her and the bodies, which she appreciated more than she could say.

She'd been relieved when word came up to the bridge that Scott and his team had found the last pirate. Not long after that, a few officers who'd taken refuge in the engine room appeared on the bridge...including Valentino. Elodie was glad to see he was alive, but she wasn't prepared for him to throw his arms around her and hug her as if they were an item or something. She'd had to pry herself out of his arms and reassure him that she was fine.

The other officers told her they were glad to see her and had gotten to work helping the sailors get all the systems up and running again, now that the electricity was back on and they could communicate with the engineers below decks once again.

The SEAL team helped the sailors remove the bodies. She'd known they were taking them downstairs to the freezers. The thought of ever again going into whichever freezer they planned to use was revolting. Now that the danger was over, the only thing Elodie wanted to do was get off the ship altogether, which wasn't possible at the moment.

She'd stayed on the bridge for a while watching the activity around her in a semi-trance. She wasn't sure what she was supposed to do. Valentino offered to escort her down to the galley to check it out, and Elodie supposed she needed to clean things up down there. Remembering the way the pirates had rifled through the pantries and had broken glasses and stuff made her wince. The jar of spaghetti sauce Scott said the pirate had thrown against a wall would definitely need to be dealt with.

Yeah, even though she wanted off the ship, she still had a job to do. The crew still needed to eat, and they were probably all very hungry after not eating for so long.

So she'd agreed to Valentino's escort. He wasn't exactly a big strong Navy SEAL, but his company was better than the alternative...going below decks by herself. It would be a long time before she felt comfortable walking around the ship alone again, if ever. She knew she'd imagine pirates jumping out from behind every corner from now on.

When they got downstairs, the galley was a mess. Broken glass and food everywhere. Elodie was trying to decide where to start cleaning when Valentino took hold of her arm and pulled her into his embrace.

He held her with a grip that was too tight to be comfortable.

"I'm so glad you're all right," he murmured into her ear as he held her.

Elodie held herself stiff in his arms. "Thanks. You too."

"I was so scared for you," he went on. "I wanted to come up here and find you, to protect you, but we had no idea where the pirates were. And after hearing they'd shot the other officers, I knew they'd kill me on sight."

Elodie wanted to roll her eyes. It wasn't just *him* they would've killed. He'd always thought himself above the other employees on the ship. He rarely spoke to the engineers during meal times, and he'd been the one to suggest different workout times for the officers and the rest of the crew. It was ridiculous, but he seemed to think being an officer made him better than anyone else.

Elodie tried to step away from him, but Valentino tightened his hold.

"I know you need comforting. Just let it happen."

That was it. Elodie was done.

She pushed as hard as she could and Valentino finally let go of her. "I'm good, thanks," she told him. She didn't want to tell him off, as she'd always hated confrontation, but she couldn't stand in his embrace a second longer.

"I'm here for you," Valentino told her. "Anything you need, I'm here. Don't be ashamed to need someone," he said. "You know what they say, extreme situations often bring people closer, and I feel very close to you right now. I could've died along with the others if I'd been up on the bridge."

Elodie frowned. "Why *weren't* you up there?"

"I...well...I wasn't on duty," Valentino stammered.

"I don't think Danny was either, but when the captain came on the loudspeaker, he went straight up to the bridge," Elodie said. She knew the schedules of most of the men onboard because she needed to know how much food to cook and who would be eating in the dining rooms at various times.

"I was going to go up there," Valentino said defensively. "But I decided to check on the engineers first instead."

That was such bullshit. Valentino had never felt the need to make sure *anyone* was all right. He'd totally gone down to the engine room to hide. Her disgust for the man increased tenfold.

Obviously not sensing her disdain, Valentino stepped into her personal space once again. He lifted a hand and brushed a piece of hair back from her face.

When Scott had done that, Elodie liked it. When Valentino touched her? Not so much.

"I can make you feel alive," he said suavely. "Give you a way to prove to the universe that you're still here."

He couldn't be saying what she thought he was saying —*could* he?

"Sex is a great stress reliever," he went on. "A good orgasm gets the endorphins going, and I guarantee I can make you forget what happened, at least for a little while."

Elodie took a step backward. Ew. "I can't believe you're still hitting on me! Especially *now*, when your friends are dead and stacked up in a freezer on the other side of this wall! You seriously think I'm gonna jump at the chance to get into bed with you? Not happening, Valentino," she said firmly.

For just a moment, she saw anger flit across his face. He took a step toward her, and Elodie had no idea what he'd planned on doing—and would *never* know, as a deep voice sounded from the doorway behind Valentino.

"I wouldn't get any closer to her. I hear she's pretty damn good with knives."

Elodie looked over Valentino's shoulder and saw Scott standing in the galley doorway. He'd come in through the crew mess and pantry. Now that the lights were on, he seemed even taller and stronger than she'd thought when she'd seen him in the dark.

She drank in his features. He was still dressed all in black, but now she could see his hair was short on the sides and longer on top. She still had an urge to feel his beard, to see if it was soft or scratchy. He was taller than her by at least half a foot, and the sight of him had her wanting to throw herself into his arms. If it had been him who'd embraced her, instead of Valentino, she would've gladly snuggled in and let him comfort her. His brown eyes were glaring at the officer, and she could see the muscles in Scott's arms flexing, even under the black long-sleeve shirt he had on.

This was a man on the verge of pouncing. Like a sleek panther.

Elodie held her breath, waiting to see what would happen next.

Valentino kept his eyes on Scott, which was the smartest thing he'd done since they'd come downstairs. He obviously knew where the threat was...all six feet of him standing in the doorway.

Scott didn't wait for Valentino to speak, he strode into the room and not so casually put himself between the officer and Elodie. "I'm thinking you're needed on the bridge," Scott told him. "They could use all the help they can get up there, and that's where your duties lie. Not here."

"I was offering to help," Valentino muttered.

"Help, yeah, that's what it sounded like to me," Scott said sarcastically. "I think Rachel's got things under control here. It's her kitchen, after all."

Valentino opened his mouth to say something. Probably

something unwise, but Scott didn't give him the chance. He leaned into the other man and said in a low, threatening tone, "Leave her alone, Valentino. She said she wasn't interested. Very clearly, I might add. I heard her as I came through the door all the way back there," Scott said, indicating the crew mess with his head. "Stop thinking with your dick and start using your brain. You're an officer. Act like it," Scott said.

Valentino glared at Scott, then turned and headed for the door that led to the hallway alongside the galley. The one with the freezers and storage rooms. He slammed his hand on the door and left without another word.

Elodie let out a sigh of relief.

"If that asshat pulls that shit again, you need to report him," Scott told her.

"I will."

"I mean it. Guys like him have a hard time believing that any woman wouldn't want to sleep with them. And since it's obvious he's got his sights on you, and you're the only woman onboard, you need to be careful."

"I will. I think he's simply feeling off-kilter after everything that's happened," Elodie hedged.

"Right. The man who deserted his fellow officers and hid like a coward in the engine room until it was safe to come out," Scott drawled.

"But didn't I do the same thing?" Elodie asked. "I hid here in the galley."

"Not the same thing," Scott told her, stepping closer.

Interesting that when Valentino crowded her, it made her skin crawl, but when this man did it, Elodie wanted to step closer.

"Let me guess, because I'm a woman?" she asked, doing her best to not embarrass herself by throwing herself at him. She had no idea what it was about this man that did it for her. She'd just met him, for goodness sake. But he'd done what no other man had been able to do for a very long time...make her want to lean on him. To confide in him.

But she couldn't do that. It wouldn't be fair.

"No. Your gender has nothing to do with this. He's an officer. He's supposed to be a leader on this ship. To lead by example. And being a coward isn't being a leader. I'm not saying he should've been happy to get shot, but he should've done what *you* did...attempted to get help for his crew and fellow officers."

Elodie stared up at Scott. "What are you still doing here? I thought you'd leave right after you found all the bad guys."

"Yeah, well, I wanted to talk to you before we left," Scott said.

Elodie's eyes widened. "You stayed because of me?"

"Yeah, Rach, I did."

She couldn't help but wince at hearing a shortened version of a name that wasn't hers.

Scott reached out and took her hand in his and walked her back toward the crew dining area.

He'd taken off his gloves, and his hand was warm and comforting around her smaller one. He pulled out one of the chairs around the table and urged her to sit. She did, keeping her eyes on his as he crouched down in front of her, still holding her hand.

"I know we don't really know each other, but you can trust me," Scott said.

Elodie nodded. But he didn't say anything else, as if waiting for her to respond.

"Um...okay."

Scott sighed. Then he reached into a pocket of his pants and pulled out a small notepad. He dropped her hand and got out a pen and scribbled something on the paper. He ripped it from the notebook and held it out to her.

Elodie looked down at the paper and took it without thinking. He'd written his name and a phone number on it.

"That's my personal cell number," he told her. "You need help with anything—anything at all—you give me a call or text."

Elodie was dumbfounded. And confused. She looked at the man still crouched in front of her. "Why?"

"Because I admire you. Because you saved my life, and I owe you. Because I know something's up with you, and you're too scared to admit it. I know your name isn't Rachel, and the only reason someone uses a fake name is because something's wrong. I don't know what it is, and I don't really care."

"What if I'm wanted? Like, I killed someone?" Elodie whispered.

Scott laughed. He flat-out threw his head back and laughed as if she'd told him something extremely funny. When he had himself under control, he took her free hand in his once more. "You haven't killed anyone," he said firmly. "You were shaking so hard after you killed that pirate hell bent on shooting me and Midas, you couldn't even walk very well. No, whatever it is you're running from, it isn't the law."

Elodie swallowed hard. She couldn't remember the last time someone had done something so...generous?

"Whatever it is you're hiding from, I can help you," Scott said softly. "I'm guessing you thought taking this job would keep you far from your demons and allow you to disappear. I have no idea how widespread the press is going to be on this incident, but considering the *Maersk Alabama* had a movie made about what happened, I'd say the reporters are probably going to meet the ship at Port Sudan in droves."

Elodie bit her lip.

"Yeah. And being the only woman onboard...it's going to be tough to keep your name and face out of the spotlight. Your name might not be an issue, since it's obviously not your real one, but..."

His voice trailed off. He was right. If even one picture got out of her, Paul would definitely be able to track her down.

She'd kept her job as a chef because she enjoyed it, but when he discovered that was what she'd been doing on the *Asaka Express*, it would give him another avenue to try to find her.

"My team and I are in Honolulu," he reminded her. "If you need a place to go, you can come to us. We'll keep you safe."

Elodie couldn't believe what she was hearing. It had been so long since anyone had gone out on a limb for her, and this man didn't know her at all. He was offering his support without even knowing what she was running from.

It was unbelievable, and she wanted to latch onto his offer with both hands. But would that be fair to him? The Columbus family was one of the largest and most powerful mob families in New York, and she'd learned the hard way that their reach was mighty and vast. Could Paul do something to get Scott in trouble with the Navy? Make him lose his job? She wasn't naïve enough to think that Paul would let anyone who helped her get off scot-free.

No, she'd defied him—and no one went against Paul Columbus.

"Thank you," she said quietly after a long moment.

"I mean it," Scott said. "We can help you. We've got connections, lots of them. When you get off the ship and are trying to decide what to do next and where to go…Hawaii is open to you as a place to regroup. I…I'd like to get to know you better. I already know you're brave and resilient, and I'm guessing you have to be halfway decent as a chef, since you were hired to make all the meals onboard." He smiled, letting her know he was teasing.

"I know you're determined and smart enough to understand instinctively where you're safest, if the grip you had on my belt loop was any indication." Scott brought a hand up and cupped her cheek. "You intrigue me, Rachel, or whatever your name is. And that hasn't happened to me…ever."

Elodie desperately wanted to tell him her real name and

her situation, but she pressed her lips together until the urge passed.

"Will you at least think about it? About coming to Hawaii?" he asked.

Elodie was nodding before she even realized what she was doing.

"Good. I'm gonna worry about you," he told her. "So even if you don't want anything more to do with me or my team, and if you don't end up coming to Honolulu, will you consider still dropping me a line to let me know you're out there somewhere, alive and well?"

Gah. He was killing her. "Yeah. I can do that."

"Thank you." He hadn't moved his hand from her face, and now his thumb was gently caressing her cheek, as if he wasn't conscious of doing it. "You know, there have only ever been five people who I'd consider giving my life for. My team. They've saved my sorry hide, and I've saved theirs. Now there's six."

Elodie couldn't have spoken if her life depended on it.

"Use that," he ordered, using his head to nod to the paper she was still clutching in her hand.

"I will," she told him shakily.

She could've swore Scott leaned closer, and Elodie held her breath, wondering if he was actually going to kiss her—until the door behind them slammed open.

Scott moved immediately, standing and blocking her from whoever had entered.

"Oh, sorry, didn't mean to startle you!" Manuel said. "I'm here to help Rachel clean up. Everyone's starving, and I figured if I cleaned, she could get something started so people didn't start gnawing on their arms."

Elodie quickly put the paper with Scott's number in her back pocket as she stood. She put one hand on Scott's back and felt nothing but hard muscles shifting under her touch. "I was just about to get started," she said softly, bending the truth a bit.

"I think we're going to have extra company onboard until we get into port," Manuel said. "The Navy guys and gals are staying for our protection, and to make sure there are enough people to steer this thing."

"Thanks for letting me know," she told her second cook. Mentally, she began to calculate how much food she needed to make. Definitely a larger portion than normal, simply because people were hungry. They'd need protein and carbs, and it would need to be something fast and easy. Maybe chicken parmesan with plenty of noodles.

She'd been so lost in her head, she'd almost forgotten Scott was standing there. Manuel headed for the pantry and the galley, and she looked up at the SEAL in front of her. He had a small smile on his face.

"What?" she asked a little self-consciously.

"You like what you do."

"I do," she agreed. "Are you and your team staying, or the other SEAL team?"

"Unfortunately, no," Scott told her, and Elodie couldn't help but feel disappointed. "But you've got my number. You can talk to me anytime you want," he reminded her.

Elodie wanted to be able to give him her number in return, but she didn't have a cell phone. Didn't even have an email address. She'd found out the hard way how easy that stuff was to track. Besides, she didn't have anyone she wanted to stay in contact with. No family. No friends. She was truly alone in the world.

"Thank you again for saving my life," Scott said.

"Thank you for saving *mine*," Elodie retorted.

"Be happy," he told her as he took a step toward the exit.

"You stay safe out there," Elodie returned.

"Always."

Then he nodded at her and disappeared through the door.

Elodie stood in the middle of the crew dining area staring at the door for several moments. Her life had been so crazy in the last twenty-four hours, she wouldn't have believed it was possible if she hadn't lived through it.

"Rachel! Get a move on!" Manuel called out teasingly.

Closing her eyes for a second, Elodie patted her back pocket, making sure the paper was still there before turning and heading for the galley. She had no idea what her next steps would be, but it was nice to have at least one option, even if that option would put Scott and his team in danger. She didn't think she'd accept his offer, but it was comforting to have all the same.

Putting thoughts of what she was going to do once the ship arrived at port out of her head, Elodie concentrated on doing what she did best...cooking.

Days later, Paul Columbus sat in his office in New York City and stewed. He owned the entire fiftieth floor of the apartment complex he lived in. The penthouse. He had more money than he could spend in two lifetimes. People both feared and respected him.

And yet he was deeply unsettled.

Being the head of one of the most powerful mob families in New York meant he had to constantly be on his toes. It wasn't as easy to escape the scrutiny of the law as it had been in the old days. His grandfather used to pay off the cops, and that left him free to do pretty much whatever he wanted.

Paul's father had to be more careful, but he'd still had some of the older detectives on his payroll. After he'd died, Paul had done what he could to cultivate friends on the police force—even through coercion and blackmail—but he hadn't been very successful. That meant he had to run his empire with extreme caution.

He relied heavily on his people. And months ago, after a thorough search, he'd found who he'd thought was the perfect addition to his staff. The damn woman had almost no one. No family. Few friends. She also had no street smarts. She was incredibly naïve...the perfect choice to groom for his organization.

He'd treated her kindly, done his best to make her feel at home, to build her loyalty to the family, and he'd thought he'd succeeded. She'd seemed happy and content. Grateful.

Which was what he needed.

Without cops on his payroll, it was damn difficult to kill his enemies. His grandfather had had it easy compared to him. Paul had no idea how many men his grandfather had gotten rid of in his lifetime, but he hadn't spent a single day behind bars for his actions, thanks to an army of law enforcement at his back.

Paul, conversely, had surrounded himself with loyal employees. People who did anything and everything he requested, including lying their asses off to the authorities when necessary. In return, they received generous salaries, nice places to live in the city, and became a part of his influential family.

But his private chef...

Paul had a lot of enemies. Shooting them was messy and noisy. And with all the cameras in the damn city, hit-and-runs would inevitably be captured on film.

But killing someone in the privacy of his home? Without them fighting back? Without the mark even knowing what was happening until it was too late? That was ideal. He could dump the bodies in the river and make it look like a drowning. Stick a syringe in their arm and leave the stiff in a back alley somewhere.

There were countless creative ways he could get rid of bodies once they were poisoned.

And Paul thought he'd found the perfect person to assist in his plan.

He'd been wrong.

Dead wrong.

When he'd approached his chef, explained what he wanted her to do...she'd had the gall to say no! To *him*.

She was in *his* house, and under *his* protection. She should've said "yes, sir," and done what he'd asked. That was the only acceptable response.

All she had to do was put some of the arsenic he'd secured into one of the bowls of soup she'd been planning on serving for dinner. That was it. His mark had already been arrested a few times for selling drugs, so when his body was found, the cops would just assume he'd overdosed. It was the perfect plan—except for the bitch shaking her head and gaping at him in shock when he'd told her what to do.

Paul hadn't been able to make her pay for such disloyalty right then and there; he'd had dinner guests waiting. But he'd definitely gotten his point across that she was in deep shit.

After his guests left, he'd planned on making doubly sure his chef understood she wasn't allowed to say no to him. Ever. That she'd do *anything* he told her to do from now on.

But she'd bolted. Hadn't even taken most of her belongings with her. No, the only thing she'd taken was a small bag... and she'd dumped the damn bottle of arsenic he'd left in the kitchen, in the hopes she'd come to her senses.

Stupid bitch. She was too stupid to even take the bottle with her...the only evidence.

But she still had something on him. Still knew his plan. And there was no way Paul Columbus was going to chance being taken down by a thirty-something mousy fucking cook. A dumb one at that.

Paul stood and paced his office, mumbling under his breath. Occasionally he gripped his hair tightly, his gait twitching as he walked back and forth. Small tells his son would have noticed in a heartbeat.

Paul knew his eldest son, Jerry, thought his old man was crazy—but he wasn't. He'd do anything to safeguard his family and his name. And the fact that there was a woman out there who knew what he'd planned for his dinner guest, and who could go to the cops with her suspicions, was eating at him.

No, Paul didn't think he was crazy, but he *was* paranoid. If his employees weren't with him, they were against him.

Twitching nervously, Paul growled in frustration. He'd been searching for the damn chef for months. He'd thought he'd located her a couple times, only to be disappointed.

He hadn't said anything to his son, or his head capo...his uncle, who was in charge of some of their soldiers. No, this was *his* fuckup, and he needed to make it right.

And as long as Elodie Winters was out there breathing, there was a chance she'd talk. Blab her mouth about what he'd asked her to do. She had information that could potentially bring him down. And for that—and for having the *nerve* to tell him no—she had to fucking die.

But first, he had to find her.

They'd located her in Pennsylvania and Los Angeles, but hadn't been able to kill her before she'd disappeared both times. She had no family he could threaten her with. No real friends whose fingers he could chop off and mail to Elodie... not that he'd know where to mail them anyway.

The woman was a ghost. A ghost with no friends and no connections. He'd thought that would made her the perfect employee, but he'd been wrong. And Paul Columbus hated being wrong.

A knock on his door brought Paul out of his head. "Enter!" he called out.

Andrew stepped inside the office and closed the door behind him. Andrew was one of his capos, but he wasn't related by blood. He was lower in rank than Paul's uncle, loyal as hell, and Paul trusted him implicitly. He was the *only* one he'd trusted with his current problem, and Andrew had been working for months to find Elodie.

Andrew had a shit-eating grin on his face and looked way too fucking cheerful for Paul's current mood.

"You better have something for me. If you don't, you can turn right around and leave. I'm not in the mood today."

"I've got something," Andrew said immediately, striding over to the desk.

Paul rounded the desk and sat. Andrew placed a thumb drive on the desktop, then stood back, still smiling.

"Well? What the fuck is that?" Paul asked.

"It's a video I think you're gonna wanna see."

"I only want to see it if it's got that bitch on it," Paul muttered. But he leaned forward and grabbed the drive as he spoke.

Andrew didn't respond, and Paul's heart began to beat faster.

Was this their first real lead since the bitch had disappeared into thin air? It was improbable that someone so stupid had been able to cover her tracks as well as she had.

He plugged in the thumb drive and waited impatiently for a window to open. He clicked on the video file and watched as a newscast began to play. It was in German, with subtitles. Playing behind the newscaster was a clip featuring a huge cargo ship with the name *Asaka Express* on the side. Paul remembered hearing about how the dumbass captain had gotten himself and some of his crew killed. He had no idea how in the world backwater pirates could ever take over such a large ship like the *Asaka Express*, but he hadn't really cared enough to find out more about the incident.

"Look closely, boss," Andrew said. "At the crew members getting off the ship."

Paul leaned in and watched as men in overalls came off

the ship one by one. Then there were a few officers wearing white uniforms. US Naval personnel were escorting them, and Paul knew they'd been called in to help pilot the ship into port safely.

The crew all assembled at the bottom of the gangplank and paused for a group picture. Paul was about to ask what the fuck Andrew had brought him, and why, when one of the crew members caught his eye. He was shorter than the others and standing slightly behind one of the officers.

Squinting, Paul leaned closer. That wasn't a guy. It was a female.

As he watched, one of the officers turned and put his arm around her shoulders, hauling her to his side before the video cut out and the German newscaster was on screen again.

Rewinding the video, Paul paused it right at the end.

He looked up at Andrew. "It's her."

"I believe so, yes."

"Where is she?"

Andrew's smile dimmed. "I don't know. But if she was on the *Asaka Express*, there should be records of where she went from there. I did find out the chef onboard was going by the name Rachel Walters."

"That last name can't be a coincidence," Paul said.

"I agree," Andrew told his boss.

"Good. And find out who that asshole is with his arm around her shoulders. If we can find him, we might be able get more info, maybe even finally have some leverage to use against her."

"Already on it, boss," Andrew said. Then he nodded and turned and headed for the door.

Paul had already refocused on the video. He played it again. And again. Then he leaned back and sighed in relief as he stared at the slightly blurry screen shot he'd taken. He couldn't tell at first glance if it was the woman he was looking for, but the height was about right, and the hair color. And the fact that she'd been working as a cook onboard the vessel.

He needed Elodie Winters dead. And no matter how long it took, it was gonna happen. No one in his family could know why she'd left. His eldest son wouldn't be happy if he knew what he'd done, that he'd risked their entire organization by trying to involve the cook in family business.

Eventually, Jerry would take over the family, but not as long as Paul was alive and well. He'd not take his place until Paul *said* he could. And if his eager son found out about the loose end who could possibly put a large chink in the Columbus family armor, he'd use that to his advantage, try to kick Paul out.

He wasn't having that. He was in charge, dammit, and as soon as he found and killed the bitch chef, he could relax and enjoy being the head honcho once more.

"You can run, but you can't hide forever, Elodie," Paul said. He leaned back in his chair and smiled for the first time in a very long while. "I'm gonna find you...and you'll regret saying no to me," he muttered.

CHAPTER SIX

"It's been two months, man, you've got to stop moping around and checking your phone every two seconds," Slate told Mustang after their morning PT run. The first thing he'd done after they'd arrived back at their cars was check his phone.

Mustang sighed. "I know." And he did. He'd hoped that Rachel would get in touch with him by now, but it was becoming obvious she had no plans to call or text.

"Sorry, man. I know you thought you two had connected," Jag said.

"We did," Mustang insisted. "Look, I know it sounds weird, but there was just something about her that intrigued me. We definitely connected."

"It's true," Midas confirmed. "I mean, I liked Rachel, but those two were in tune with each other. It's as if once she'd latched onto his belt loop, they became...one...or something. Sounds completely fucked up and corny, but it's true."

Mustang didn't know if he should thank his friend or tell him to fuck off.

"You really think she's in trouble?" Pid asked.

"I don't know *what* to think," Mustang admitted.

"You want to see if we can get Tex involved?" Slate asked. "You know he'd probably love to see if he could track her down. It'd be a challenge or something for him."

Mustang was shaking his head before his friend had finished speaking. "No. I have no idea why she took the job on that cargo ship or why she's using a fake name, but I don't want to dig into her history, only to have that somehow ping whoever's looking for her and end up leading someone right to her."

"First, you know Tex is better than that," Aleck said with a shake of his head. "Second, we don't know for sure Rachel's not her name."

"It's not," Mustang said. He was one hundred percent certain of that. He'd had a hard time getting her attention by calling her name more than once. And he couldn't get the sad look in her eyes out of his mind, when he recalled calling her Rach that last time they'd talked. He'd bet his entire SEAL career Rachel wasn't her name.

"So what now? You just hope and pray she gets in touch with you for the next year or so?" Slate asked.

Mustang wasn't shocked by his friend's attitude. Slate was always the impatient one of the team. When they got information about a mission, he was the one who wanted to move immediately. He valued the intel from research, but he was more of a doer rather than a sit-around-and-discuss-shit kind of guy.

"Pretty much," Mustang said. "I'm not sure what else I can do. She didn't have a phone or email, so I couldn't get her info."

"Who doesn't have an email in today's day and age?" Midas mused.

"Exactly," Aleck said. "Which means Mustang is probably right, and she's hiding from something or someone."

"I still say Tex could help," Slate uttered.

Mustang knew Slate was right, and he'd considered calling

the former Navy SEAL more than once. Tex was a genius with electronic shit. Pid was good, but Tex was unmatched. Not only that, but the man had some pretty powerful friends. Men who ran teams outside the government's watchful eye. Men who could get shit done without worrying about pesky things like laws.

It used to bother him that there were former military men out there who'd banded together to essentially go out and kill people. But then he'd read about a case where a known sex trafficker in Peru had been ambushed and assassinated, and he'd understood. The man had been taken out by one of the teams Mustang had previously disapproved of. After learning about the horrors his victims went through, including a woman who'd been kidnapped from Las Vegas and held captive for a decade, he got it.

Rumor had it that there was also a team out of Indiana that was doing the same thing, taking care of the worst of humanity. While Mustang knew he wasn't cut out for that kind of work—he'd much rather save someone than kill—he'd realized the value of having people out there willing to put their lives on the line to rid the world of evil.

But he wasn't ready to call Tex and interfere with Rachel's life. He had no idea what she was hiding from, but the bottom line was that if she didn't want him involved—and obviously she didn't, considering he hadn't heard from her—then he wasn't going to get involved. He'd never forced himself on a woman before and he wasn't going to start now.

But it still sucked, because he *knew* they'd clicked. And he liked Rachel.

"What are you thinking about so hard over there?" Pid asked. They were all standing around their vehicles in the parking lot next to the beach, winding down after their morning workout.

Mustang realized that he'd been staring out at the waves while lost in thought. He sighed. "Nothing much."

"You know what I think?" Midas asked.

Mustang braced himself to hear one of his teammate's crazy ideas. Midas was the one who always seemed to come up with the most outlandish activities for them to do. He liked to push the envelope, loved any kind of adrenaline rush. He was a great SEAL because of it, but when they weren't on a mission, he still needed that kind of excitement in his life. Mustang used to worry about him, but had learned it was easier, and better for Midas's mental health, to let him go a little crazy.

"Oh, Lord, here we go," Aleck said on a sigh.

"Please don't let it be swimming with sharks again," Pid muttered.

"Or volunteering to hike around an active volcano to get lava samples," Jag added.

"No, nothing like that," Midas said. "I was thinking deep-sea fishing. I think we all need the break. We can charter a boat and spend the day on the water."

"Because we don't get enough time at sea," Jag quipped.

Mustang hid a smile. His teammates cracked him up.

"Oh, come on. It'll be nice not to have to be on the water because we're on a mission. We can have some beers, relax, and maybe snag a marlin or ahi while we're at it," Midas cajoled.

"I'm in," Mustang said. It actually did sound fun. He hadn't been deep-sea fishing in a long time, and he truly enjoyed hanging out with the guys on the team.

"I know a guy," Aleck said. "I'm sure he'd take us out. I don't want to go with any of those cheesy tourist companies with guides who don't know their asses from their heads."

"They aren't all that bad," Midas said.

"I know, but still. This guy has his own boat, it's got enough room for all of us so we won't be sitting on top of each other the entire trip, and more than that, I trust him. His boat'll be up to code and we won't have to worry about being stranded out at sea or some such bullshit," Aleck told them.

"Great. So...this weekend?" Midas pressed. "What do you all have planned?"

"Well, there were these twin sisters..." Pid started, letting his voice trail off.

Jag smacked him on the back of the head. "Maybe in your dreams," he joked.

Pid chuckled. "Right, of course I'm free. Since when have any of us had a life lately?"

"We've been too busy to have any kind of social life," Aleck said.

"Which suits me just fine," Slate added.

"Great. So, Mustang, you're in?" Midas asked.

"Sounds good," Mustang agreed. He might as well go. It wasn't as if he needed to sit around his apartment waiting for Rachel to call.

The team all said their goodbyes then and got into their cars. They had an hour and a half before they were expected to be on the Naval base, which was plenty of time for them to go home, shower, change, and fight the traffic to get there.

On the drive home, and as Mustang got ready for work, he thought of nothing but Rachel...including their last conversation on the ship. Maybe he hadn't been clear enough that she could trust him?

Maybe he'd freaked her out when he'd leaned forward to kiss her...

It had been instinctive. Impulsive. And if her second cook hadn't come into the room at just the right—wrong?—moment, he would've done something he hadn't ever done before.

Kissed a woman within hours of meeting her.

He wasn't a prude, but meaningless sex had never been Mustang's thing. And at thirty-six, it still wasn't. He liked to know a woman before he initiated any kind of intimacy.

But he supposed what they'd been through was enough to bring them close in a short period of time. Rachel had literally saved his life, and she'd held up so well throughout the entire ordeal. Mustang couldn't help but admire her. Want to get to know her. Find out what made her tick.

Sighing, he stood in the small but functional kitchen in his apartment and stared out the window at the ocean. He'd taken the apartment because he could see the waves from the kitchen and the master bedroom. There were only two bedrooms, the master and a tiny room he currently used as a workout space. But he could lie in bed and see the ocean in the distance, and that made it well worth the exorbitant price.

Then again, nothing in Hawaii was cheap. Food, lodging, clothing...it all cost a pretty penny.

Knowing he needed to get a move on if he was going to get to base on time, Mustang swallowed back the rest of his coffee and put his mug in the sink. He hoped wherever Rachel was, she was safe and happy. He might be bummed that she hadn't reached out to him, but he never wanted to be with someone who wasn't one hundred percent into him. He'd seen too many relationships in the Navy that didn't work. He wanted to find a woman who would support and love him, and in return, he'd be one hundred percent devoted to her, as well.

* * *

Elodie rolled over in bed and groaned. The last couple of months had been extremely stressful, and when push came to shove and she had to make a decision about where to go after getting off the *Asaka Express*, she'd made a split-second choice she hoped she wouldn't regret.

She'd been in Hawaii for a month and a half now...and

wasn't any closer to finding Scott as she'd been the first day she'd arrived.

It was stupid to come to Honolulu, really. But she hadn't had anywhere else to go...so here she was. Now the odds of her being able to find the handsome Navy SEAL who'd come to her rescue were slim to none.

She'd been a dumbass and had lost the piece of paper with his number on it.

The days after the SEALs had left the *Asaka Express* were crazy. They'd had several meetings with Naval and government officials. They'd had to tell their stories over and over to several different groups of people. The company that owned the ship had given everyone a hefty bonus...Elodie had kind of felt as if they were trying to pay them off, so they wouldn't say anything bad about the security or what had happened. But since she needed the money, she'd had no problem taking it, feeling only a little guilty afterward.

Elodie and Manuel had been extremely busy with cleaning up the galley and the other rooms under their control, not to mention cooking meals for the crew and the extra men and women who were onboard.

After one very long day, when the company had told everyone they had twenty-four hours to decide what they wanted to do next—stay on the *Asaka Express*, move to a different ship, or quit with a healthy severance package—Elodie had seriously considered Scott's offer to go to Hawaii.

She knew going back to the East Coast wasn't an option. Paul Columbus had too much power there. He might be a New York mob boss, extremely ruthless and powerful, but he knew people. Lots of people. And they'd all do whatever he told them to do without hesitation—including killing a former employee who knew too much and refused to get onboard with his nefarious plans.

She'd left the United States because she hadn't felt safe anywhere. But the more she thought about it, the more

Hawaii appealed. Honolulu had millions of tourists. They constantly came and went, and it should be easy enough for her to blend in there. Since the tourist industry was so robust, she could work for a while, and no one would blink if she decided to up and move a few months down the line.

Elodie had hopes that one day she might be able to let down her guard a bit. Maybe even get married and start a family. But she wouldn't risk doing that until she was sure Paul had given up on finding her. Maybe if he realized that she hadn't snitched, hadn't gone to the cops to turn him in, he'd decide she was going to keep her mouth shut and forget about her.

Sighing, Elodie stared at the popcorn ceiling of her studio apartment. It wasn't really an apartment, merely a room off an elderly woman's house that she'd rented. There were marks on the ceiling from water leaking in from somewhere and no air conditioning. Most of the time that didn't bother her, as the ocean breeze blew through the room in the afternoons. But the humidity was harder to get used to. Everything felt damp. And when she licked her lips, she always tasted salt.

Closing her eyes, Elodie remembered the day on the *Asaka Express* when she realized she'd somehow lost the piece of paper with Scott's number. She'd needed to do laundry, and could've sworn the slip of paper was in another pair of jeans. She'd loaded up her duffle bag to drag down to the laundry facilities, where she normally double-checked her pockets before tossing stuff in the machine, but she'd been in a hurry. While in the laundry room, she'd run into Valentino, who'd tried to hit on her...*again.*

It wasn't until a short while later, when she couldn't find the paper with Scott's number, that Elodie realized she must've washed it. By that time, it would've been mush inside the washer. And of course, she hadn't memorized the number either. She knew the area code for Honolulu was 808, and that there was a zero, a few threes, and a one in his number, but that was it.

Despite knowing it was stupid, she'd still decided to come to Hawaii, even without a way to contact Scott. She'd hoped that she'd be able to find him somehow. Maybe even just run into him randomly. But that was a joke. There were too many people on the island, and way more service men and women than she'd thought. And it wasn't as if she could just saunter onto the Naval base and start asking questions.

So, she'd taken the severance and hush money she'd received and found the cheapest place to rent that she could. But even that had been more expensive than she'd expected. She'd had to find work, otherwise she'd have ended up homeless on the streets with the countless other men and women she saw on a daily basis.

Despite knowing she could probably find a job in a restaurant somewhere, Elodie had resisted. For one, she was scared that it would give Paul a way to find her. If he did somehow find out she'd been working as a chef onboard the *Asaka Express*, it would be natural to assume she'd found another job as a chef elsewhere. And she was afraid he had the resources to somehow find her if she continued working in her field.

But second...Elodie was tired of the kitchen.

Once, she'd loved it. Loved coming up with new and exciting dishes. But being on the run and always looking behind her had dimmed her joy of cooking.

It had taken two weeks, but eventually she'd found a job working for a charter fishing business. The work wasn't hard or very cerebral, which was actually nice. The two men who owned the boat were married and in their early forties. Both were friendly, but not overly so. After fending off Valentino's advances and doing everything in her power to not get into a situation where she was alone with him, it was a refreshing change.

On days when tourists chartered the boat, they left early

in the morning, around six. Her job was to be friendly with the guests, help entertain any children that accompanied their parents, keep the boat clean, make sure everyone signed the appropriate paperwork, serve a light lunch and snacks, and to take pictures. She was paid just enough to buy groceries and cover rent.

The boat usually came back to the dock in the early afternoon, and after she cleaned up, putting everything back in its place for the next day, she had the rest of each day to herself. Since Elodie didn't have a car, she couldn't exactly explore the island, but she'd quickly learned how the public transportation system worked and did her best to get out and about.

She wasn't going to accidentally run into Scott if she spent all her time in her room, though she'd quickly realized that despite visiting all the touristy places associated with the Naval base, like Pearl Harbor and the Battleship Missouri Memorial, Scott wasn't going to appear out of nowhere, take her in his arms, and be overjoyed to see her.

Elodie wasn't sure what her long-term plans were. She liked her job well enough, but she couldn't work on a charter fishing boat forever. She was thirty-five years old, a renowned chef, a half-decent person, and unfortunately, on the run from a crazy mob boss she'd had the misfortune to accept a job from.

When the alarm on the bedside table went off again, Elodie reluctantly clicked it off and headed for the bathroom. Today, she didn't have to make any decisions about the rest of her life. All she had to do was smile, be friendly to whatever tourists had decided to charter the boat, and make it through another day. Maybe when she got off work she'd go down to Ewa Beach. She'd heard good things about it, and it definitely wouldn't be as crowded as Waikiki. She'd gone there just once, and that had been enough. Too many people, too many stores, and not enough space.

She knew she shouldn't complain. After cheating death

not once, but twice—first when she'd managed to escape New York and the Columbus family's reach, and second when the *Asaka Express* had been hijacked—Elodie was trying to learn to be all right with her boring life. Boring was better than dead.

But she couldn't help but wonder frequently what Scott was doing. If he thought about her at all.

She'd thought about him almost every day since he'd walked off that cargo ship. He'd sounded so sincere when he'd offered his help. She didn't know how he'd realized Rachel wasn't her real name, and she'd been so tempted to confide in him. But they hadn't had time.

She hadn't wanted to put him in danger by coming to Hawaii, but she was. She knew that. But she was scared. She had no idea what to do next. So she'd come, despite the fact that she might be putting Scott at risk.

Elodie felt weak for being afraid of Paul, for being so lonely. Scott made her feel safe. She just hoped, if she ever found him, that he was still willing to help, and that he'd forgive her for dragging him into her shit.

Late at night, when she was in bed with the ocean breeze drifting over her, Elodie fantasized about what might have been. If she wasn't on the run. If she could be with him. Would they click in the normal world like they had on the ship? Or was the danger the only thing that made it seem as if they'd had a connection?

Elodie had dated in the past. Nice, safe men. Businessmen who'd thought since she was a chef, she'd like nothing more than to spend her days and nights off cooking for them. Instead, Elodie had always wanted adventure—and she'd gotten way more than she'd bargained for, that was for sure.

Sighing, she pulled on her bathing suit and forced herself to get a move on. Things with Scott probably never would've worked out anyway. He was...larger than life. A hero. She was a stupid chick on the run. She wished she was brave enough to fight back against Paul. Go to the cops, something. But she hadn't and she wasn't.

She also wasn't an idiot. He'd win. He didn't fight fair, as evidenced by the many people who'd ended up dead before they could testify against the family. She'd been ordered to participate in the killing of a man, and her refusal to put poison in his meal had led to her life on the run.

And now she was in paradise, where she was surrounded by people every day. She smiled and laughed, but still felt so very alone.

Doing her best to shrug off her melancholy, Elodie tried to look on the bright side of things. She was alive. Living in Hawaii. Had a roof over her head and food to eat. So what if she didn't have friends? If she didn't have a boyfriend? She was fine...just fine.

A tear rolled down her cheek as she headed out to the bus stop. She wasn't fooling anyone, least of all herself. Coming to Hawaii was a bad idea. It just made her think about Scott even more and regret being stupid enough to lose his number. She had no idea if things with him would've gone anywhere, but at least she would've had a friend. Wouldn't have felt so alone in the world.

"Maybe I'll move to Australia," Elodie said as she took a deep breath and wiped her face clear of her tears. It wouldn't be good for the tourists to see one of the employees red-eyed and weepy.

She knew she'd been hired not only because she'd been available to start immediately and hadn't flinched at the low pay, but also because she looked halfway decent in a bathing suit, and most of the charters were men. Sure, it was discriminatory and disgusting, but beggars couldn't be choosers. And she did actually like Perry and Kahoni, the owners of the boat. They didn't allow their guests to make her uncomfortable in any way. One of them went on every trip, along with the only other employee, a local guy in his early twenties, Kai.

As she sat on the bus headed for the harbor, Elodie thought about where in Australia she might want to go. Maybe Adelaide. It wasn't as big as Sydney or Perth, and she'd worked with a guy once who'd been from there. He'd always talked about the city in glowing terms, including how amazing the restaurants were. It would be too dangerous to try to find anyone she'd worked with previously, because she knew Paul would already consider any of her past contacts. He wouldn't hesitate to hurt or kill someone if he thought they had information on her whereabouts. But she could go to Adelaide and find a small, out-of-the-way restaurant and make apple crumble cake and meat pies all day.

The harbor came into view, and Elodie gathered up her stuff. She'd learned the hard way that sunscreen wasn't enough to protect her skin when it came to the Hawaiian sun. She'd splurged and bought a long-sleeve shirt that had built-in UV protection. It was made of a material that would dry quickly if it got wet and didn't leave her looking like a lobster at the end of the day.

After climbing off the bus, she walked past the row of boats parked in the harbor until she got to the *Fish Tales*, the boat Perry and Kahoni owned.

Perry waved at her as she climbed aboard and Kai gave her a slight chin lift. Both were busy getting the boat ready to go for the day. Kahoni would be meeting their clients back at the small shack on the pier.

"Aloha, Melody, how's it shakin'?" Kai asked as he worked.

Elodie had learned her lesson, and she'd used a good chunk of the money she'd gotten after leaving the *Asaka Express* to get some custom paperwork for a new identify. She'd needed a name that was closer to her own so she'd remember to answer to it. Melody was close enough to Elodie that she didn't think twice when she heard it.

"I'm great, but gettin' better. You?" she asked. This was

their tradition. She had the same answer every morning when he asked.

"Good. Ready to find some marlin today!" Kai told her. He said that every day, as well.

It was good to have a routine. Safe. It was what Elodie needed.

Twenty minutes later, two couples headed to the boat with Kahoni. They were smiling and looked as if they couldn't wait to go fishing.

Saying a prayer—like she did at the start of every trip— that the clients wouldn't be susceptible to seasickness, as it was her job to deal with the barf bags, Elodie smiled in welcome as they climbed aboard. Eight hours and counting until she was free to roam Oahu in the hopes that by some miracle, she'd run into the man she couldn't get off her mind.

CHAPTER SEVEN

Saturday morning, Mustang wondered what the hell he was doing. On one of the very few days of the week he had to sleep in, he was up at the ass-crack of dawn meeting his friends, people he saw every damn day, to spend an entire day in a boat on the ocean, something else he spent quite a bit of his life doing. He'd been looking forward to this fishing trip at first, but now he was having second thoughts.

But Midas seemed super excited about the prospect of catching a huge marlin, and Mustang couldn't deny that sitting around shooting the shit about things that didn't involve national security or some evil terrorist was appealing. So he hauled himself out of bed and got ready to meet Aleck when he arrived to pick him up.

Aleck was there right at seven o'clock, and they headed down to the harbor, where they'd meet the guy Aleck knew. The man's boat was large and comfortable. After the rest of the team showed up, they headed out.

It was a beautiful day, sunny with a nice breeze. The guys laughed, drank a few beers, and generally had a good time.

Pid caught a huge marlin, which had taken all of them to help reel in. Aleck's friend, the guy who owned the boat, was going to filet it when they got back to shore so each of them could have some. They all agreed to donate the rest of the fish to the man, in thanks for taking them out for the day.

It was still early afternoon when they arrived back at the harbor. Mustang was sitting near the front, enjoying the sun and wind on his face. There were a good number of tourist boats entering and exiting the mooring area. Mustang smiled at the little kids who enthusiastically waved at him from boats as they headed out for an afternoon of whale watching, snorkeling, or parasailing.

Despite his reluctance that morning, he'd needed this. A day to completely relax. To not worry about what was going on in the world...or whether or not his phone rang. Today, he was simply Scott Webber, average Joe, not Mustang the Navy SEAL.

His teammates were shooting the shit behind him, and Mustang wasn't really paying attention when something onshore caught his eye. A boat was tied up to the dock not far from where they were headed to tie up themselves, and two couples, obviously tourists, had just exited the craft. They were shaking hands and thanking the guides when something about the smallest one made him look twice.

Her dark hair was up in a ponytail, and she had on a long-sleeve white shirt and a pair of black board shorts. It wasn't until she smiled at the couples that Mustang realized who he was seeing.

Standing up abruptly, he yelled, "Rachel!"

But the woman didn't turn her head or otherwise act as if she'd heard him.

"Rachel!" Mustang called out again.

"What the fuck, Mustang?" Aleck asked, coming up beside him.

"It's her!" Mustang said impatiently.

"Who?"

"Rachel! The girl from the *Asaka Express*."

"You know that's pretty unlikely, right?" Pid asked, coming up to the front of the boat to see what the commotion was about.

"It's not. I'm almost positive it's her!" Mustang insisted. He turned to stare back at the pilot. "Pull this boat over!" he exclaimed.

"Our berth is just up there," the pilot said, indicating a spot in front of them with his chin.

"Shit!" Mustang swore, turning back around and craning his neck to keep his eyes on the woman he was almost positive was the one he'd met a couple months ago on that hijacked cargo ship.

"Where is she?" Midas asked, also crowding into the front of the boat.

"There," Mustang said, pointing to the boat that was behind them now. "On the *Fish Tales*."

Midas squinted his eyes and watched as the woman climbed back onboard the smaller fishing boat with two other men. "I don't know, man," he said after a moment.

"I'm telling you, it's her," Mustang insisted.

"How could she be here?" Jag asked.

"And if it *is* her, how come she hasn't called you?" Slate added.

"I told her if she ever needed anything that I was stationed here, and I'd help her," Mustang explained to his friends. The only person who knew he'd offered his assistance had been Midas. The others knew he'd given her his phone number, but not that he'd given her a direct invitation to come to Honolulu. "And I don't know why she hasn't called me," Mustang admitted.

"Dude, she's hanging out on a charter fishing boat. I can't imagine she'd come all this way and take a job like that. Isn't she a chef?" Aleck asked.

"Yeah," Mustang said. He craned his neck again as the other boat fell out of view. His heart pounded in his chest. If that was his Rachel, he needed to talk to her, make sure she was all right. Find out why she was here and why she hadn't contacted him.

"Jeez, I'm usually the impatient one," Slate joked as Mustang anxiously waited for the boat to get close to the dock.

Usually Mustang would help to get the boat tied down and clean up their trash, but all he wanted to do was get onshore and find out if the woman he'd seen was Rachel. It took several minutes, but finally the pilot had gotten the boat close enough to the dock that Mustang could jump onshore. He took off at a run, knowing his friends would gather his shit.

He could see the boat named the *Fish Tales* ahead of him, but he panicked for a moment when he saw no movement onboard.

Looking behind him, toward the parking lot, Mustang spotted the woman he'd seen earlier walking with a taller man. He sprinted toward them and couldn't stop himself from calling out once more.

"Rachel!"

The couple didn't slow down or look around.

"Fuck," he muttered. Mustang knew he probably looked like a crazy man, running and yelling like he was, but he was desperate to get to the woman before she disappeared. If it wasn't Rachel, it was her doppelgänger.

"Rachel!" he tried again.

This time, the man turned around and looked at him, then glanced down at the woman next to him and said something. When she turned around to see who was yelling, and why, she looked shocked as he ran toward them.

"Rachel?" he said in a more normal tone as he got closer.

The woman's face had paled, and she stared at him with wide eyes...but she still wasn't saying anything.

He stopped a few feet away and drank her in. He had no idea why she wasn't saying anything.

"Why is he calling you Rachel?" the man next to her asked.

Mustang ignored him. All in all, she looked good. She had a pair of flip-flops on her feet and the shorts she wore showed off toned legs. The white top clung to her curves, and Mustang couldn't deny that he liked what he saw. Back on the *Asaka Express*, he hadn't been able to get a good gauge of her size, not only because they'd been in the middle of a dangerous op, but also because she'd worn an oversized shirt and baggy cargo pants that hid every inch of her body.

Her black hair was pulled back in a ponytail and the tip of her nose was pink, but it was obvious she'd gotten some sun since she'd been in Hawaii, as her skin was a shade darker than he remembered it being out in the Middle East. Her brown eyes were staring at him in disbelief, and he could see various emotions churning in their depths.

But no matter the differences between two months ago and now, this *was* Rachel. The woman who'd saved his life on that cargo ship.

"Melody? Why is he calling you Rachel?" the man asked again, moving so he was standing slightly in front of her, as if protecting her from Mustang.

Mustang wanted to snort. Like this surfer dude could get the drop on him. Wasn't happening. But he wasn't there to scare Rachel...or whatever her name was.

"Scott?" Rachel whispered.

"Yeah. It's me," he told her.

Then she was moving toward him, pushing past the man next to her. Practically throwing herself into his arms.

Mustang let out a small *oof* as she hit his chest, taking a step back to keep them both upright. Putting his arms around her and holding her tight had never felt so right.

"All-righty then, guess you *do* know him," said the man she'd been walking with.

"I do," Rachel mumbled, nodding.

"You good then? You still want me to give you a ride home?" he asked.

"I can take the bus," Rachel answered, not picking her head up from Mustang's chest.

"I'll take her home," Mustang told the other man.

"I'm Kaikilaonāoneko'olau," the man said, holding out his hand. Then grinned at the look of consternation on Mustang's face. "But I go by Kai."

Mustang chuckled and lifted a hand from Rachel's back to take Kai's outstretched palm into his own. "Mustang. Also known as Scott."

"It's good to meet you. Melody hasn't talked about much since she started working with us. Nice to know she's got some friends." He nodded his head, indicating something behind Mustang.

He glanced back and saw Midas and Aleck walking down the dock toward them.

"She does," Mustang agreed.

"Aloha, Melody. See you tomorrow."

"Thanks, Kai," she said, finally pulling away from Mustang.

He tightened his hold on her, not ready to let her go yet.

The second Kai was out of hearing range, Mustang asked, "Melody?"

He felt more than heard the woman in his arms sigh. "My name isn't Rachel."

"Is it Melody?"

She shook her head slightly but wouldn't look up at him.

Mustang moved slowly, putting a finger under her chin and lifting her head so she had to look him in the eye. "What's your name?"

"Elodie Winters."

Mustang had no idea if she was telling the truth, but figured she was. A name like Elodie wasn't exactly common, and if she was going to make up a fake name, he figured she'd use something more commonplace.

"It's smart to use something close to your own name. Melody, Elodie...they're very similar."

"I learned my lesson. As you saw before, and now, I forgot to respond to Rachel more often than not."

"Yeah, I noticed," Mustang told her with a smile.

"But you can't call me Elodie in public," she said softly.

"I have a million questions for you, but they'll have to wait," he told her.

"I can't believe you're here," Elodie told him.

"I think that's my line," Mustang said with a smile.

"Hey, Rachel, it's good to see you again!" Midas said as he approached.

"Damn, Mustang was right. It *is* you!" Aleck said in amazement.

"Guys, I'd like you to meet Elodie Winters," Mustang said quietly. "Elodie, you remember Midas and Aleck, right?"

"Scott...I thought we just agreed—"

He interrupted her. "We did. But these are my teammates. They're going to help me...you, *us*...figure out what's going on and fix it."

"I'm not sure it can be fixed," Elodie said softly.

"Elodie. That's unusual," Midas said.

"It's French. Over there, it's pronounced with the emphasis on the O, but my parents said it like Melody without the M," Elodie said, as if she'd explained her name many times in the past.

"We all thought Mustang was losing his mind when he said he saw you," Aleck told her. "But we should've known. There's a reason he's our team leader. He's pretty damn sharp."

"We're glad you showed up. He's been checking his phone

like a squirrel waiting for a bird feeder to be re-filled," Midas said.

"What?" Aleck said, staring at his friend as if he had horns growing out of his head. "What kind of an analogy was that?"

"You know, the little buggers get used to stealing food from a bird feeder, then get impatient when it's empty," Midas said.

"Good Lord, you're a dork," Aleck said, shaking his head.

Elodie giggled, and Mustang's heart felt as if it grew two sizes. It was a sound he hadn't heard from her before, and he wanted to hear more of it. She sounded happy. Carefree. Whatever trouble she was running from hadn't completely diminished her ability to laugh. "What's your schedule for the rest of the day?" Mustang asked her.

She looked up at him, and even though she was smiling, he could still see the shadows in her eyes. He'd noticed them back on the cargo ship and had hoped maybe her troubles were behind her, but with her still using a fake name, it was likely they weren't.

"I'm off for the rest of the day," she told him.

"I came with Aleck. How about he takes us back to my place, where I can change, then I'll take you back to *your* place so you can do the same, and maybe we can have dinner somewhere together and talk?"

She stared up at him for a long moment, and Mustang felt as if he were seventeen again and waiting on his crush's response to his invitation to prom.

"Okay," she finally said.

"Okay," he agreed. He didn't like that she sounded a bit reluctant, but she'd said yes.

When the rest of the team caught up to them on the dock, he reintroduced everyone once more.

"This is Elodie...previously known as Rachel and, for now, Melody, when we're around others."

"Hey," Jag said.

"Good to see you again," Pid added.

Slate merely gave her a chin lift in greeting.

"I...were you guys really fishing today?" she asked a little hesitatingly.

"Yup," Pid told her. "Things have been fairly intense at work and we needed a little downtime."

"Did you catch anything?" she asked.

"Yeah. A big-ass marlin. Aleck's friend was the pilot, and he sliced us each a big filet and he's keeping the rest," Pid said.

"Cool," Elodie said.

"You like fish?" Mustang asked her.

"Hate it," she answered immediately.

Everyone was taken aback for a moment, then Slate said, "But you work on a charter fishing boat."

"I do," Elodie agreed with a small smile. "I couldn't afford to be picky when I was looking for a job. And there's no requirement I have to eat what the clients catch. I have no problem being around the fish, helping to bring them onboard and things like that, but I don't think I'll ever grow into liking to eat anything that comes from the ocean."

"You're a chef?" Pid asked with a frown.

"I am," Elodie agreed. "But where in the chef handbook does it say you have to like everything you cook?"

"She's got you there," Mustang said with a smile. She'd stepped away from him as they'd talked to his teammates, but he kept his hand on the small of her back. A part of him felt as if she'd disappear once more if he didn't keep her within reach. It was ridiculous, but he was so relieved to see her again, to have her there, that he wasn't going to fight his instincts.

She was still dealing with something, and until he knew what it was, and what demons he needed to slay, he'd stick as close to her as he could. There was always the possibility she'd up and leave again if she got too scared, so he wanted to do what he could to mitigate that possibility.

Despite no contact whatsoever, the two months since he'd seen her had somehow made him feel even closer to Elodie. It made no sense whatsoever. But he'd played back their entire encounter on the *Asaka Express* over and over in his mind. And he'd become even more impressed with what she'd done. How she'd acted. It was crazy, but he'd always been a man to act on his instincts, and right now they were telling him Rachel Walters—or Elodie Winters—was a woman who would be worth getting to know.

"Are we gonna stand out here baking in the sun all day or what?" Slate grumbled.

Mustang couldn't help but snort out a laugh. Leave it to Slate to get them all moving. Whoever he ended up with would have to have the patience of a saint.

As natural as breathing, Mustang took Elodie's hand in his and started walking toward Aleck's car. He said goodbye to the rest of his teammates and opened the back door to Aleck's yellow Jeep. They'd given him shit about it, but Aleck always said that he liked the color, that it kept others from hitting him because there was no way they could miss him driving alongside or in front of them. He probably had a point, but they still liked to rag on him about the bright color.

Once he had Elodie settled, Mustang walked around to the other side of the Jeep and climbed into the back seat next to her.

After Aleck put their bags in the back storage area, he got behind the wheel and grumped, "Great, now I look like a chauffeur or something."

"Home, James," Elodie quipped, then blushed as if she'd forgotten where she was and who she was with.

Mustang loved that she felt comfortable enough around him and his friends to tease. Her personality seemed different here. Bigger. More relaxed. He'd always thought Hawaii was good for the soul, and that was obviously the case for Elodie. She was still stressed and still had some pretty deep secrets, but he liked this side of her. The sun and sand fit her much better than the dark and dank lower decks of the cargo ship she'd been hiding out on.

Mustang couldn't keep his gaze from flicking repeatedly to Elodie as Aleck drove toward his apartment. He was grateful his friend kept the conversation flowing, as he couldn't do much beyond staring at the woman next to him.

By the time they pulled up to his place, Mustang had no idea what they'd talked about, but since Elodie seemed relaxed and happy, he didn't really care.

"Mustang? Can I have a minute?" Aleck asked.

He really didn't want to leave Elodie alone for even a second, but he nodded anyway.

"I'll just wait over there," Elodie told him, indicating a patch of shade under a tree near the entrance to the apartment complex.

"Okay. Elodie?"

"Yeah?"

"Don't worry."

She snorted. "Scott, I've been one big ball of worry for months now. I'm not scared of what you and your friend are going to talk about. I'm more worried about you—*any* of you—getting involved in my issues and having it come back to bite you in the ass."

Her words just made him like her all the more. A lot of people would jump at the chance to let a team of Navy SEALs take on their problems, but not Elodie. He had a feeling she'd do what she could to downplay whatever was going on just to try to keep them safe.

Fuck that.

She didn't give him a chance to respond, but turned to

Aleck, thanked him for the ride, then strode over to the tree to wait for him.

The second she was out of earshot, Aleck turned to him and the easygoing smile he'd had on his face disappeared. "You gonna find out what the fuck is going on?" he asked.

"Yes." Mustang's answer was immediate and determined.

"Good. Because I like her."

When Mustang scowled, Aleck chuckled.

"Not like that. It's obvious to anyone with eyes that you guys are into each other. I just like her gumption. I don't know why she didn't contact you, but I'm willing to bet she's got a good reason. Find out what you can, and Pid can use his skills to find out what we're really dealing with. If he needs to, he'll contact Tex."

Mustang held up his hands. "Easy there. I'm thinking we don't want to invade Elodie's privacy the day after we meet up with her again."

"We won't be. Pid will," Aleck said, completely serious.

"Just give me some time to talk to her," Mustang said sternly.

Aleck sighed. "Fine. But you know Slate is gonna want information like, yesterday."

"I know. But I have a feeling I need to tread carefully. She's afraid."

"She is," Aleck agreed. "She does a good job trying to hide it though. Okay, fine. Find out where she's been the last two months, why she didn't call you, where she's been living, and if she's been in contact with the other employees from the ship or anyone else. We'll need to know how well she's hidden her tracks. If she *is* on the run, we'll also need to know when we might expect company."

Mustang freaking loved that his teammates had no problem wading into whatever was going on with Elodie. It was obvious that he'd been preoccupied the last couple months worrying about her, and now that she was here, they were one hundred percent devoted to solving whatever problem she had.

"I'll see what I can find out," he told Aleck.

"Good."

"But you need to give me today and tomorrow. I'll talk to everyone at PT on Monday."

"Well, shit," Aleck pouted. "We have to wait that long?"

"You do know that you sound like Slate, right?" Mustang said with a grin.

"Damn, I do. Okay, she's been all right this long, another day and a half probably won't make a difference," Aleck said on a sigh.

"Let the others know, would ya?" Mustang asked.

"I will. Mustang?"

"Yeah?"

"I think she's good for you."

Mustang blinked in surprise. "You've known her for what, twenty minutes?"

"Maybe, but we all know what she did back on that cargo ship. How she didn't hesitate to save your and Midas's lives. Not everyone would've done that. And she's funny. And it was obvious she was just as glad to see *you* as you were her. That kind of connection doesn't come along every day. My suggestion is that you just go with it. See where it leads you."

"And if it turns out she's broken the law and is a black widow or something?" Mustang asked.

Aleck rolled his eyes. "That woman is no criminal. No fucking way."

Mustang believed that too. If he didn't, she wouldn't be standing patiently waiting for him to bring her up to his apartment. He was a pretty good judge of character, and Elodie Winters needed a champion more than anyone he'd ever met. She wouldn't ask him to be one for her; he instinctively knew that too. But she'd sealed her fate when she'd pulled the trigger on that rifle back on the *Asaka Express*.

When she'd saved his life, she'd earned the thanks and respect of his team. And if they could help her in return, they would.

"I agree," Mustang said.

"But seriously, if anything is majorly wrong, call before Monday. Okay?"

"I will," Mustang promised. "Thanks for hooking us up with your guy today. I had a good time. I'd forgotten how much I enjoy fishing...and just being out on the open water with no agenda."

"Same. I'll see you Monday."

"Later."

Mustang headed for Elodie. She was standing with her back to the car, gazing out at the sliver of ocean that was just visible off to the side of the complex.

"Ready?" he asked as he approached.

She turned, and he could see the apprehension was back in her gaze. Instinctively, Mustang took a step backward, giving her some space.

"This isn't a good idea, Scott," she said softly.

Damn, talking with Aleck had given her time to second-guess his intentions or fret about whatever was going on with her. Mustang slowly took a step toward her, and relaxed when she didn't tense up or move away from him. "Why did you come to Hawaii, El?"

She stared up at him but didn't speak.

"Personally, I think this is the best idea you've had in a long time. I don't know why you didn't get in touch with me right when you got here, but I'm fucking thrilled that I happened to see you today. Maybe you're trying to let me down easy. Maybe it's just coincidence that you're here. Maybe you have a husband and eight kids you're needing a break from, I don't know...but I *do* know that I haven't been able to get you off my mind for two months. And when I saw you on that boat, it took everything I had not to leap into the water and swim over to you to make sure you didn't disappear into thin air before I had a chance to talk to you."

He saw her swallow hard. "I'm not married and I don't have children," she said quietly.

That didn't tell him much...but Elodie walking toward him and resting her forehead against his chest told him everything he needed to know.

Wrapping an arm around her shoulders, Mustang cradled her close. "Come on. I smell like fish and need to change. We'll get you sorted, get something to eat, then we'll talk. Okay?"

"I shouldn't be here," she said, but she didn't fight him as he began to walk them toward the entrance to the building.

"But you are," Mustang said.

She nodded and said nothing more.

They headed to the elevator, and even though no words were spoken between them, Mustang still felt as though they were communicating. He could feel her muscles begin to relax and she leaned against him ever so slightly.

It would take time and patience for her to trust him, but he had a feeling earning that trust would be one of the most satisfying and rewarding things he'd ever do.

CHAPTER EIGHT

Elodie stood in Scott's kitchen and stared out the window above the sink. She could see the ocean from where she was standing, which she loved. All she saw from her windows was the concrete driveway and sometimes her neighbor's naked butt as he walked around his house. But beggars couldn't be choosers, and she was grateful she'd been able to find a place she could afford.

She could hear the shower in Scott's bedroom, and surprisingly it comforted her. For the first time in a very long time, she didn't feel quite so alone. Though, Elodie knew she should probably leave. Shouldn't involve Scott or the rest of his team in her problems.

Was Paul still looking for her? Was she running and using a fake name for nothing? She hadn't seen anyone who looked suspicious in months. She'd done everything she could think of to not bring attention to herself.

She'd never forget how angry Paul was when she'd told him she wouldn't put the poison into her soup. He could've killed her right then, and she figured he might've, if there wasn't a roomful of people waiting to eat the four-course dinner she'd made. If Paul killed her right then, it would've brought a lot of attention onto him. So he'd had to go back out and pretend all was well.

The second she'd plated the desserts, Elodie had left. She knew if she'd stayed, she probably wouldn't have lived to see another sunrise.

But now, after all this time, she was doubting herself. What if she'd acted too impulsively? Yes, Paul had been upset, but did that really mean he was going to *kill* her?

Sighing, Elodie took another sip of the water Scott had given her when they'd entered his apartment. Honestly, she felt pretty safe here in Hawaii. She had absolutely no connections to the state. There was no way for Paul to know where she was. Even if he saw the news clip of the day the *Asaka Express* came into Port Sudan, and recognized her, she'd done her very best to leave no clues where she was headed. She'd even lied to Human Resources and told them she'd be headed to Paris to stay with a friend.

So why was she still feeling so unsettled?

"You look like you have the weight of the world on your shoulders."

Elodie jerked in fright and spun around to see Scott standing in the entryway of the kitchen. He was leaning against the wall, and his gaze seemed too intent. Too knowing.

"Sorry. I didn't mean to scare you. I thought I made plenty of noise when I came in."

"No, it's fine. I was just thinking," Elodie told him.

He studied her for a long moment. "How about this...how about we spend the rest of the day talking about nothing important? We can get to know each other without worrying about when and how to bring up the elephant in the room."

Elodie stared at Scott. He was wearing a pair of board shorts that went down to his knees. His legs were tan and there was something especially intimate about seeing his bare feet. He had on a navy-blue T-shirt with the words Leonard's

Bakery on the front. His arms were muscular, and she could see the hint of a tattoo peeking out from the left sleeve of his shirt. It intrigued her and made her wonder what else she didn't know about him.

At first glance, he looked somewhat gruff, his beard and mustache and muscles making him seem kind of scary, but Elodie had gotten to know him well enough onboard the cargo ship, and she wasn't scared of him.

Not having the pressure of when, how, or if she was going to tell him about Paul Columbus appealed. For once, just for a little while, she wanted to pretend she was a normal woman.

"What do you think?" he asked when she didn't answer him.

"I'd like that," Elodie told him.

"Me too," Scott admitted. "I mean, I want to help you, if you'll let me, but I also want to get to know you without you thinking I'm trying to pump you for information. Have no doubt, I *do* want to know what's going on with you. Why you're using fake names. But I can put off my curiosity for a while. I'm just so damn happy you're here."

"I lost your number," Elodie blurted.

Scott blinked. "What?"

"I lost the piece of paper you wrote your number on. All I remembered was the area code and a few numbers. I was going to get in touch with you but couldn't. Then I decided to come here and see if I could find you. Which was incredibly stupid, I realized pretty much as soon as I stepped out of the airport. But I decided to stay anyway, hoping against hope that maybe I'd find someone who worked on the Naval base who might know you."

Scott pushed off the wall and walked toward her. Elodie kept her gaze on his and tilted her head back as he got closer. He stopped right in front of her and took the bottle of water out of her hand and put it on the counter next to her. Then he opened his arms.

Elodie didn't hesitate. She felt comfortable with this man. She never would've come to Hawaii if she didn't. She rested her head on his shoulder and felt his arms close around her. She slowly wrapped her own around him, and they stood like that for quite a while.

Scott smelled like soap and...man. She couldn't say exactly why, but was comforted whenever she was around him. She'd never felt like this before in her life. Safe. As if she could be whoever she wanted to be and do whatever she wanted to do and no one would dare stand in her way.

It was an uncomfortable thought, simply because she knew she ought to feel that way on her own, not because she had a man at her side. She'd worked her ass off to be an independent and strong woman. But right now? She was nearly at the end of her rope. On the outside, she looked put together and confident, but deep down she was terrified.

She wanted to hope that Paul had given up and was satisfied she wasn't living in New York City anymore, but she had a feeling the ruthless head of the Columbus family would never give up until she'd paid for saying no to him...as crazy as that might seem to any rational person.

"You're thinking too hard," Scott said, his chest rumbling under her ear with his words.

She looked up at him.

"You hungry?"

Elodie shrugged. "I could eat."

"Good. You been to Helena's yet?"

"Who?"

Scott chuckled. "Helena's Hawaiian Food. It's a restaurant. A damn good one. There's a dine-in option, but it's always completely packed. It specializes in homestyle Hawaiian cooking. I thought maybe we could pick up some food then come back to this side of the island, to Barbers Point Beach Park. By the time we get there, most of the tourists—the ones who bother coming to this side—should be heading back to where they came from. It's a public park, but it won't be overrun by people."

"Sounds great. I haven't seen much of the island," Elodie told him.

"You haven't had time to get out and about?"

"It's not that. I don't have a car and have been using public transportation. And I don't really know the cool places to go. I went down to Waikiki and there were just too many people around for my liking."

"Yeah, Waikiki isn't bad, but if you're looking for pristine beaches and privacy, that isn't the place to go. I'd be happy to show you some of my favorite spots and hikes if you want. We can go up to the North Shore sometime as well if you're interested."

Elodie wanted to immediately agree. But she needed to rein in her enthusiasm. Once he learned who she'd worked for, and heard the entire story about why she'd been using different names, he might feel differently about hanging out with her.

Taking a deep breath, Elodie stepped back and Scott immediately dropped his arms, giving her space. Her stomach chose that moment to rumble.

He chuckled. "Right, and that's my cue to get my butt in gear and get us moving. Let me grab some shoes and we can go. We'll make a stop at your place, then we'll go downtown, grab the grub, then head to the beach. Sound okay?"

"Sure. Scott?"

"Yeah, El?"

Hearing even the shortened version of her real name felt good. It had been so long since she'd been Elodie, she hadn't realized how much she'd missed it. "Thanks." She didn't know what she was thanking him for. For being trustworthy. For seeming to be excited to see her. For offering to give her a day of normal instead of immediately asking her to spill all her secrets. For making things so easy.

He reached up as if he was going to touch her, then stopped himself mid-reach and dropped his hand back to his side. "You're welcome." Then he turned and headed into the small living area of his apartment.

Elodie waited by the entrance of the kitchen and had to smile when he came back to her. He hadn't put on a pair of sneakers, but instead he wore flip-flops. She tried to hide her smile, but obviously wasn't successful because he asked, "What?"

"I just...I wasn't picturing you as a flip-flop kind of guy."

Scott laughed along with her. "I wasn't before I moved here. I was a boots guy all the time. I wanted to be ready for anything. But it's hot here. And I have to wear my combat boots at work and my sneakers when I work out. It feels good to let my toes breathe. And I'll have you know these are super-authentic Hawaiian flip-flops, and they're comfortable as hell."

Elodie looked at her own feet. She held one up. "These are super-authentic ABC Store flip-flops and they suck, but I still love them."

Scott laughed. "Right, the ABC Stores are handy on the island, carrying anything and everything a tourist could want, but I'll have to bring you to the store where I got my kicks so you can see the difference between those cheap plastic things you're wearing and the good-quality ones."

Elodie would have agreed, but she had to be very careful with her money. She couldn't exactly spend like she had an unending supply of cash. Unfortunately, she never knew when she might have to pack up and flee. At the first sign that Paul had tracked her down, she'd need to leave.

"There she went," Scott muttered. He reached for her hand and held on tightly as he pulled her toward his door. "No thinking," he ordered. "Today's for good food and getting to know an old friend."

He was exaggerating their connection, but Elodie still

appreciated the sentiment. Scott *did* feel like an old friend. Even though they'd only met a short time ago, they'd been through something intense, and that made her feel more connected to him than if they'd just met in passing.

She was somewhat embarrassed to let Scott see where she was staying, but Elodie straightened her shoulders. There wasn't anything wrong with it. No, it didn't have an ocean view, and it was only a room in a nice old lady's house, but it had been exactly what she'd needed when she'd arrived.

Scott held the door as she climbed into the passenger side of an old beat-up pickup truck, then he walked around and got behind the wheel. Trying to make conversation, Elodie said, "So...your truck is...nice."

He snorted. "She's a piece of shit, but the engine is perfect and I have no worries that she'll break down. I bought it from this guy that a former SEAL who lives up at the North Shore hooked me up with. The guy built the engine from scratch and she runs perfectly. And a bonus is that I don't have to worry about anyone trying to steal her... no one in their right mind would take a second glance at this thing."

When he started the engine, Elodie had to agree that it sounded pretty smooth. Not that she knew anything about cars or engines. She could make a mean parmesan risotto with roasted shrimp, but didn't have the first clue about how to even change a tire. It was probably a good thing she didn't have a vehicle right now.

"Why do guys always say their car is female?" she asked as Scott pulled out of the parking lot and headed toward her place.

"I suppose because a car is pretty important to men. They usually have their own personalities and we spend a lot of time with them. I like to pamper my car and make her run as well as she can, and thus I treat her as if she's my wife...and now that I'm trying to explain it, it sounds ridiculous."

Elodie lifted a brow at him. "I'd argue that referring to cars as female promotes the ideology that women are objects, things seen as property owned by men. It's subconscious, and maybe not even something men think about, but it still perpetuates the notion and it's detrimental in the long run."

Scott was silent for a long moment after she'd spoken.

Elodie wrinkled her nose and mentally smacked herself in the forehead. Jeez, giving Scott a lecture wasn't how she wanted to start out getting reacquainted with him.

"You're right," he said. "I definitely don't see women as property, and I can understand how it would be harmful."

Elodie stared at him, not sure how to respond.

"What?" he asked.

"I just...I'm not a diehard feminist, but I've been through my share of discrimination in my field. Many times people expect women to be sous chefs instead of in charge of a kitchen. I've had to fight hard to get my opinion across with male-dominated staff, and it's annoying as hell. I didn't mean to start a philosophical debate or anything. You can call your car whatever you want."

"What would you name this beast?" Scott asked, not seeming put out in the least.

Elodie thought about the question for a bit, liking that he didn't rush her or try to fill the silence with meaningless conversation.

"Ben," she said after a couple miles had passed.

Scott burst out laughing. "Ben?"

"Yeah. Ben is the name of a guy who on the outside is nothing special. Maybe he blends into a crowd and isn't noticed a lot. But underneath he could be a rocket scientist. There's Benjamin Franklin, Benny Hill, Benjamin Harrison... and I had a neighbor growing up whose name was Ben. To look at him, you would think he was the biggest nerd, and maybe he was, since he was on the chess team, which is shitty of me to say because it's a huge stereotype. Especially after I just lectured you about objectifying.

"Anyway, he was also one of the most generous guys I've ever met. He was always organizing fundraisers for people and paying for students' lunches and stuff like that. Everyone liked him too. The jocks, the band geeks, the theater people. So I think Ben is the perfect name for your truck. On the outside, he looks a little rough, but under the hood he's a perfect gentleman and will get you where you need to go."

When Scott didn't immediately say anything, Elodie started to feel awkward. Shit, there she went, being weird again.

But then Scott turned to her with a huge smile on his face. "Ben. I like it."

She sighed in relief. "Oh! Sorry, the turn is right up here," she said, pointing to a street ahead on the left. She gave him directions through the narrow streets past some of the newer homes to the older section in the back. There, the homes were closer together and much smaller, but almost all of the families had been welcoming. They teasingly called her Haole. She'd learned that a haole was a person who wasn't a native Hawaiian. It was often used as a derogatory term, but since everyone who'd called her that in the neighborhood did so with a huge smile—and when they brought her native Hawaiian dishes—she didn't take offense. She was the only white person in the neighborhood, after all, and she stood out.

In some ways, that made her feel safer. If Paul or his henchman ever found her and staked out the place, her neighbors would definitely notice.

Scott parked in front of the house she lived in and she said, "I won't take that long. I'll tell Kalani that you're with me so she doesn't worry."

"Take your time, El. I'm good out here."

"Okay. I'd invite you in, but—"

"It's fine," Scott said, interrupting her.

But Elodie still wanted to explain. "I just have one room. There's a bathroom, of course, but the room itself is crowded. Heck, I think there's probably more space in this truck than in my room."

"I said it's fine," Scott repeated quietly. "You don't have to defend where you live to me."

She kind of felt like she did, but she let it drop. "All right. I'll be back soon."

"No rush. Do you trust me to order for you? I can call in our order to Helena's so it'll be ready when we get there."

"Yes. Although remember, I don't eat seafood."

"I remember. I'll get a variety of things so if there's something you don't like, you won't starve."

"Thanks." Elodie could have told him that, other than the seafood thing, she wasn't all that picky. She'd eaten her share of odd things in her lifetime, and it was hard to be a chef if you were a picky eater. But she was interested in seeing what he thought she might like.

She climbed out of the truck and hurried around to the side entrance, to her room. She paused to knock on the door that led into the main living area of the home. She told Kalani about Scott and explained that he was a soldier on the nearby base, and that he was with her. Then she hurried into her room to shower and change.

Fifteen minutes later, Elodie was ready. Her hair was still wet, but it would dry soon enough in the warm afternoon air. She felt energized and excited. Scott's suggestion that they not talk about any deep subjects today made all the difference. She looked forward to getting to know him as a man, not as someone who wanted to "save" her.

She'd put on a flowered sundress she'd bought at one of the ABC Stores. It was made of cheap cotton and only cost fifteen bucks, but it made her feel pretty.

She had no illusions about why she wanted to look nice either.

Scott Webber was one hell of a good-looking man. And she couldn't deny that she was attracted to him. Had been from the first time she'd met him...and that was before she'd even gotten a good look at him. He hadn't treated her as if she was helpless. He'd trusted her to tail him and Midas. And he hadn't hesitated to offer his gratitude after she'd saved his life.

Yeah, it was safe to say she was attracted to the Navy SEAL and had been more than glad to see him chasing after her earlier that afternoon. The look of relief and excitement in his eyes when he realized it was her still made Elodie's skin tingle. Had any man ever been that happy to see her? She didn't think so.

For the millionth time, Elodie kicked herself for losing his number. She should've memorized it the second she'd looked at that piece of paper.

She walked out to the truck and saw he was scrolling on his phone. Elodie knew she should've picked up a cell, but she hadn't really needed one. Her room had a land line, and Kalani even supplied her with a phone. If she needed to get in touch with Perry or Kahoni, she could, and they knew she didn't have a cell, so they called her in the mornings or evenings if they wanted to get ahold of her.

Scott looked up right before she reached for the door handle. She opened the door and climbed in, and by the time she was settled, Scott still hadn't said anything. Wondering what was wrong, Elodie looked over at him. "What?"

"I just...you look nice. Pretty. I like that color on you."

Elodie knew she was blushing. The color of the dress was bold, dark purple with large white flowers all over it, interspersed with hot pink smaller petals. "Thanks."

They stared at each other for a long moment...then Scott shocked the shit out of her by slowly leaning closer.

Elodie's belly flipped, but she couldn't deny she wanted this. Wanted him.

Scott's hand touched her first, lifting her chin, putting her in direct alignment with his mouth. She wondered if she was being crazy, letting him kiss her this soon.

But then his lips were on hers, and she couldn't think about anything but him.

His beard was soft instead of scratchy, and the feel of it against her skin was something she'd never experienced before. He was tentative at first, lightly brushing his lips against hers, as if testing, making sure she was truly okay with what they were doing.

Elodie's hand moved to the back of his neck and squeezed.

As if all he'd been waiting on was a sign from her that she wanted more, Scott moved. His head tilted to get a better angle, then his tongue was running along her lips, seeking entry. She opened for him, closing her eyes and inhaling his unique scent into her lungs.

She could feel her nipples hardening under her flimsy bra and her heart raced as she finally got a taste of the man she hadn't been able to get out of her mind for months. The slight taste of peppermint lingered from when he'd brushed his teeth earlier. His tongue playfully dueled with her own as they kissed. He retreated, and she followed, loving their give and take.

He was the one to finally pull back. His hand was still on her chin, and his thumb caressed her cheek lightly. "Should I apologize for that?" he asked huskily.

"Only if you're sorry," she told him.

"Hell no, I'm not sorry," he said. "I've wanted to do that for months. Regretted not being able to do it back on the ship."

Something inside Elodie settled. She'd felt the same way, but understood he'd been there on official business and it wouldn't have been right to ask for a kiss when he was in SEAL mode.

"You're under my skin," he admitted. "I've been watching my phone for months waiting to hear from you."

"I'm so sorry," she told him. "I wanted to get in touch. Then I thought maybe I'd get lucky and run into you if I was here. I even went to Pearl Harbor one day because I knew that was near the Naval base, but when I got there it was obvious it wasn't a place you'd be."

"Yeah, it's a bit touristy. Our offices aren't anywhere near there. I couldn't believe it when I saw you on that boat today. What are the odds?"

"Slim to none," Elodie said softly.

"Exactly. I want to know everything about you, Elodie. Your likes and dislikes. Where you came from, your family, how you got into your profession...being a chef, not a charter fishing boat employee...where you grew up, how you got that job on the *Asaka Express*, what happened after I was gone...everything."

"Same," she said as she stared into Scott's eyes. This was too fast, but it felt right. She felt a connection to Scott like she'd never known before. As if they were truly meant to be together.

Elodie knew she was opening herself up for heartbreak. Something this intense couldn't last...but she couldn't make herself slow down. Didn't *want* to slow down. She wanted to experience passion like she'd only read about in books and saw in movies. Maybe they'd fizzle out after finding out how different they were, but oh, how she wanted to feel something other than fear and suspicion for a while. Friendship and lust would do.

And maybe, if she was really lucky, love.

"There's so much going on behind those eyes of yours," Scott said softly. "I can't wait to find out what makes you tick. And for the record, this isn't normal for me. I'm usually the guy who wants to go slow. Wants to take a woman out on several dates before moving in for that first kiss. Who thinks sleeping together before six months is too fast. But right now, all I can think about is what you're wearing—or not wearing—under that dress. It's crude, and rude, and I feel like a dick even admitting it. But there's just something about you that makes me act in ways I normally wouldn't."

Elodie felt her face flush and she squeezed her thighs together tightly. Good Lord, this man was lethal. But she had to admit that she liked knowing he was as discomfited as she was.

Her eyes dropped down to Scott's lap, and she quickly brought them back up to his face.

He smiled. "Yeah, the second I saw you in that dress, I got hard. It seems to have a mind of its own, but don't worry, you're safe with me. I swear."

"I know," Elodie said. And she did. This man wouldn't hurt her, wouldn't try to take anything she wasn't willing to give. And it was taking everything she had not to invite him to go back into her room right that second.

But her stomach had other ideas. It growled again. Loudly and insistently.

Scott chuckled. "Yeah, okay, I need to get you fed." His thumb caressed her cheek one last time before he leaned forward, gave her a quick peck on the lips and sat back. "Buckle up, El. I'll give you the two-cent tour as we head into town. I'm not an expert on the history of this area, but I'll share what I know."

Elodie put on her seat belt and sat happily in the seat next to Scott as he drove them toward Helena's. At some point, he reached over and took her hand in his. Their clasped hands rested on his thigh as he drove. He pointed out landmarks and explained that the traffic wasn't all that bad right now, but in an hour and a half it'd be at a standstill.

It was hard to believe she was actually here with Scott,

and he was holding her hand. Or was she holding his? It didn't matter. She was so thankful to be here, she didn't even care what they were doing. She'd come to Oahu in the hopes of running into the man she couldn't get off her mind, and it was a miracle she'd done just that.

Elodie was happier than she could remember being in a very long time. She clung to that feeling and prayed with all her might that Paul Columbus had given up on finding her, and she could live her life free and without worry.

CHAPTER NINE

Mustang looked over at Elodie and smiled. He'd ordered them kalua pig and pipikaula short ribs with rice instead of poi, then couldn't resist stopping to get some malasadas for dessert on the way to Barbers Point. It had taken longer than he'd wanted, and he hated that Elodie was obviously hungry and had to wait to eat.

They'd found a spot near the beach, away from the tourists who hadn't left yet, and he'd loved how she hadn't hesitated to dive right into the food. They sat next to each other on a volcanic rock wall and watched the waves crash against the beach as they concentrated on their meals.

As Mustang ate, he couldn't stop replaying the kiss they'd shared. He hadn't meant to do it, but the second he saw her walking toward his truck in that cute-as-hell Hawaiian-print dress, he was a goner. He'd been attracted to her when she'd been wearing boots and cargo pants on the ship, and he'd definitely taken more interest on the boat dock. But with her damp hair making it all too clear she'd just gotten out of the shower, and in that pretty dress, he'd lost his mind.

He was glad he'd suggested they put off all serious talk and simply get to know each other. Mustang wanted to remember this moment forever. Elodie looked relaxed, as if she didn't have a care in the world. He would always want that for her. Hated to see her stressed, and it seemed as if he'd seen her that way just about every minute they'd known each other...until now. And maybe back in his truck outside her place.

Mustang remembered how her fingers had dug into the skin on the back of his neck when they were kissing. It was burned into his memory.

He wanted her. Didn't want to go slow. Felt almost desperate to have her under him, over him, any way he could get her.

And that wasn't like him. He was usually very cautious, as he'd told her. Liked to move slowly with women. Wanted to get to know them. But that was the thing...he felt as if he knew Elodie. Oh, he didn't know the details. But he knew *her*. Who she was deep down. He'd seen that loud and clear on the *Asaka Express*.

"Beach or mountains?" she asked.

They'd been doing this for the last twenty minutes. Asking either/or questions as to which the other liked better, and then discussing when either wanted clarification.

"Seriously?" he joked.

"Yeah."

"Beach. I'm a SEAL. I need the water."

"Fair enough," Elodie said with a shrug. She had some sugar from the malasadas on her cheek, and he leaned over and wiped it off with his thumb and showed her.

She wrinkled her nose adorably. "Your turn," she told him.

For a second, Mustang thought she meant he had something on his face too, which would be hard to see with his beard, but then he realized she meant for him to ask a question. "Let's see...parasailing or paragliding?"

"Gliding," Elodie said without hesitation.

"Wow. You answered that really fast. You ever done it?"

"Nope. But...and I suppose this is a point that might make or break our friendship...I don't like the ocean all that much," Elodie said.

Mustang stared at her in confusion. "What? I don't understand."

"What's not to understand? Sand, salt, sharks, jellyfish, rip currents, killer fish, manta rays...need I go on?"

"But wait—you took a job on a cargo ship. Which is on the *ocean*, I might remind you. And now you work for a charter fishing company...which again, the fish are in the ocean, and thus you have to spend your time on the boat looking for them...on the ocean."

Elodie giggled, and Mustang couldn't help but let his gaze drift toward her chest. She wasn't hugely endowed, but her tits jiggled a bit when she moved and laughed, and it didn't help that one of the straps on her dress kept falling off her shoulder.

"I know, but I grew up in Indiana. There weren't any oceans as far as the eye could see. I like water, in a pool or hot tub. I don't mind looking at the ocean, but being in it freaks me out. And when I was on the *Asaka Express*, I wasn't *in* the ocean, I was *on* it. There's a big difference. Same with my job now. So while parasailing isn't exactly in the ocean, there's a chance the rope could break and I'd end up in the water. At least with paragliding, that isn't the case."

Mustang could go into all the reasons paragliding was more dangerous than being tied to a boat by a rope and being towed behind it with a parachute, but he kept his mouth shut. If there was a malfunction while paragliding, she'd end up in a crumpled heap on the ground. But she was being adorably cute and he wanted to know more.

"Do you have any brothers or sisters?"

Elodie shook her head. "No, I was an only child. My parents were professors at a community college."

"They still around?" Mustang asked.

141

"Unfortunately, no. Mom had a heart attack about six years ago. She didn't make it. And I think my dad was so sad about her passing that he couldn't go on. He developed a blood clot and died about a year after she did."

"I'm sorry," Mustang told her.

"Thanks. I miss them a lot, but know neither of them would've wanted to live without the other. They were so much in love. They did everything together. Drove to work, ate lunch, went to shows, cooked. It drove me crazy when I was younger. I couldn't understand why they didn't want to have their own friends and their own hobbies. But they were content with each other's company. Today I look back and I get it. They were lucky."

They were quiet for a moment before she asked, "What about you? Are your folks around? Do you have siblings?"

"No brothers or sisters, I was an only child like you. My parents are still alive, they live in West Virginia, where I grew up. They're hard working, but not all that interested in higher education. They're happy living in our small town, playing bingo on the weekends, and making moonshine in their not-so-secret still in the woods behind our house."

"You're kidding, right?" Elodie asked with a laugh.

"Nope. Sailor's honor. The local sheriff knows they make the stuff, but since they give him a bottle every month, he doesn't give them grief about it."

Elodie snorted. "Wow, okay."

"They're good people," Mustang said. "But they never had the kind of wanderlust I did growing up. They were content to live in the same place, see the same people, and not go anywhere. I wanted to see the world. They also never understood how I could actually *like* school. Let's just say they aren't exactly the scholarly type. But they're generous, and they love me to pieces. I just have to go to West Virginia if I want to see them."

"How'd you get your nickname?" Elodie asked.

"I'd tell you, but then I'd have to kill you," Mustang joked. He never told the story behind his nickname to people unless he knew them really well. He wasn't sure why, he just didn't feel comfortable sharing something so personal.

But the fact that he had no reservations telling Elodie was just another way he knew she was different. Special.

"Kidding," he said before she could respond. "It's kind of embarrassing, but at the time, I thought I was doing my buddy a favor."

"Oh, this I gotta hear," Elodie said.

Mustang was distracted by her licking sugar off her fingers after eating the malasada, but he did his best to stay on track. "I had just graduated from boot camp and was feeling like I was all that and a bag of chips. My nickname at that point was Webb, based on my last name. I was headed toward the barracks at the end of the day, and one of the guys in my unit, a guy who'd been in for a while, asked for my help. I'd bragged earlier that week that I knew how to hot-wire just about any kind of car, and he said he'd lost his keys and wanted my help in hot-wiring his car so he could get home.

"I was feeling pretty good that the guy had asked me for help, considering how low my rank was, so I gladly helped get his Mustang started. But right after, while I was feeling all proud of myself, the military police came racing up and threw me in handcuffs. The guy who'd asked for my help had fled, and it turns out the Mustang belonged to the commander, not the guy in my unit."

"Oh my God!" Elodie said, her eyes wide. "Did you get in trouble?"

"I thought I was going to end up in the brig for sure, but luckily, after hearing the story, the commander thought it was kind of funny. He declined to press charges and I was let go. But word got out about what happened, and people started calling me Mustang."

"And did the other guy get in trouble?"

Mustang smirked. "Oh, yeah. The commander made him do extra duty for six months. He was cool with it though; he knew he'd gone too far with the prank, and we actually ended up becoming pretty good friends. When I tried out for the SEALs, we lost touch."

"That's hilarious," Elodie said. "I guessed there had to be some sort of story behind your name, but I figured maybe you raised horses growing up or something."

"Ha. Nope. So...how'd you become a chef?" Mustang asked.

Her smile slowly dimmed as she stared out at the waves. Mustang instantly regretted his question. He hadn't wanted to talk about anything that would make her sad or depressed. "You don't have to answer that if you don't want to."

"No, it's fine," Elodie said immediately, looking up at him. "My parents always cooked together, and when I got old enough, I joined them. At first I was just doing measuring and chopping, easy stuff like that, but after a time, I got more into it and was trying complicated recipes on my own. I started watching as many cooking shows as I could, and before I knew it, I was obsessed.

"I went to the community college where my parents worked, after high school, and got my business associates degree, but I wasn't all that interested in going on to get my bachelor's degree, much to my parents' chagrin. I headed up to Chicago and went to culinary school. I loved it. I worked in a *lot* of restaurants after I graduated, and was even a sous chef for a pretty famous chef for a while. But eventually the hours got to me and I wanted a change of pace."

Mustang could see Elodie's shoulders slump as she spoke, and he knew whatever change she'd made had somehow led to the problems she was having today. He reached out and slid his hand to the back of her neck.

She looked up at him in surprise.

"Not now," he said softly. "I want to hear every detail

about what happened when you left Chicago, but for now, I want to enjoy the evening on the beach with you. Please don't think I don't want to know what's going on, I do, but I want to get to know you first."

He saw her swallow hard before she licked her lips and spoke. "Okay."

"Good." Mustang couldn't take his gaze from her lips. He wanted to taste them again. Wanted to nibble on that plump upper lip, and the vision of her taking his cock between those luscious lips sprang into his mind suddenly. He immediately got hard.

Shit, this wasn't like him. He never thought about sex so soon after meeting a woman. But then again, he'd been thinking about Elodie for months now. Wondering where she was and if she was all right.

"How about a walk?" he blurted, needing to move. If he didn't, he might pull her onto his lap and do some very indecent things on a public beach.

"I'd like that," she told him.

Mustang didn't let go of her for a long moment. He was warring with himself. Part of him wanted to slip his hand under her dress, and another part knew he needed to let go of her to get some of his control back.

"Scott?" she whispered.

"Yeah?" he replied just as quietly.

Her breasts rose and fell with her inhalations, letting him know he wasn't the only one feeling out of control.

"This is crazy, isn't it?" she asked.

"Yeah," he said. "But damned if I care."

"Me either," she said with a small smile. "But...I don't do this. I mean, I have in the past. When I was in my early twenties. I was killing myself to make it as a chef and was stressed way the hell out, so occasionally I'd go to bars and find a guy and go home with him. But I'd always feel guilty afterward, and it didn't make me any less stressed. Shit...now I'm babbling and you probably think I'm a whore."

"I don't think that," Mustang said immediately. "I've done the same thing a time or two, and you're right, sleeping with a stranger never really seems to be all that satisfying."

"Exactly."

"But you don't feel like a stranger to me," Mustang told her.

She nodded. "I know. Why is that? We've really only known each other for less than a day if you count the hours and minutes."

Mustang tightened his grip and ran his thumb over the skin behind her ear. She visibly shivered under his touch, and it made him feel so damn powerful. She was responsive as hell; he couldn't wait to see her reactions in bed. "I think it's because we formed a bond on that cargo ship. I helped you, and you helped me. It was pretty intense and our guards were down. I've thought about you every day since then. Wondered where you were, if you were all right, what you were doing."

"Same," Elodie said as she blushed. "I was devastated when I realized I'd lost your number. It felt as if I'd lost something precious. It was silly to come here to Hawaii in the hopes I'd somehow be able to find you, but I didn't know where else to go."

"I feel as if a higher power had a hand in us not only meeting, but in me seeing you today. Midas suggested we go deep-sea fishing out of the blue. It's amazing that we happened to be at the same harbor that you work out of."

"I know," she said.

Mustang watched as she licked her lips...then she leaned toward him slightly. He took the hint and met her more than halfway. He kept hold of her nape as he devoured her.

She melted in his arms, tilting her head back and letting him take what he wanted. How long they made out, he had no idea, but when he felt her hand slip under his shirt...then into the back waistband of his shorts...Mustang knew he needed to slow things down.

He wanted this woman with a longing that scared him. He needed to be naked with her, inside her, more than he'd ever needed anything in his life. But he wasn't going to do something that might embarrass her, or get either of them arrested on this public beach.

After pulling back, Mustang realized that his own hand had made its way under the hem of her dress...and he was kneading her thigh inappropriately, considering where they were. She'd spread her legs just a bit, giving him access, and his fingers were dangerously close to feeling exactly how ready her body was for him. He could smell the slight scent of her musk, and he had to close his eyes to get control of himself.

"That escalated quickly," Elodie said with a small laugh.

Opening his eyes, Mustang looked down at the woman in his arms. Her lips were even plumper now than they were before, flushed from his kisses. Her cheeks were pink and she seemed to be having a hard time catching her breath.

Both their hands were frozen, her fingers brushing the top of his ass cheeks under his shorts and his own on her inner thigh. Slowly and regretfully, Mustang removed his hand from under her dress. His cock jerked when she slipped her hand out of the back of his shorts.

"Still want to take that walk?" he asked.

Elodie nodded immediately. "Yeah, actually, I do. I've lived here for a month and a half and have yet to see a sunset from a beach. And it'll keep me from pushing you down onto the sand and jumping you right here." She grinned as she said it.

Relieved that she didn't seem ashamed or overly embarrassed about their very hot make-out session, Mustang smiled. He was glad he'd found a relatively secluded piece of the rock wall around the beach to eat. He stood and gathered their trash and then reached for her hand. "One romantic sunset on the beach, coming up," he said with a smile.

Elodie took his hand in her own and stood. The beach wasn't very long or wide, and wouldn't take terribly long to walk, so they took their time ambling down the sand, laughing and enjoying each other's company.

As they walked, they got to know each other more, talking about anything and everything they could think of. He told her stories about SEAL training and his teammates; she told him stories from her time as a chef in various restaurants. How awful customers could be when something wasn't exactly how they wanted it. He learned that she hated being cold, loved cats and guinea pigs, that she wished her feet were smaller so she could wear cuter shoes, that ever since the incident on the cargo ship, she had to sleep with a light on. She was a neat freak, loved to read romance novels, had a bad habit of picking at her fingernails, and was a secret ice cream junkie.

In return, Mustang told her that he wasn't really much of a pet person; while growing up, all animals had been kept outside. He hated having rugs in his house because he felt all they did was collect dirt and germs. Declared forest green was his favorite color, and he told her how he'd gotten the small scar under his chin.

By the time the sun finally began to set, Mustang felt even more as if he'd known Elodie forever. They had the same feelings about growing up as only children...they'd liked it, but had been lonely at times. They both thought three children was the perfect number for a family, and they loved living in Hawaii.

He stood behind her and put his arms around her shoulders, holding her against his chest as the sun ever so slowly fell below the horizon. "Don't blink," he warned Elodie as it began to disappear.

Neither said a word as they watched the sky turn from blue, to orange, to pink, then finally a light gray as the sun fell from view.

Elodie turned suddenly in his arms and rested her cheek against his chest. She looked up after a long moment. "Thanks," she whispered. "That was perfect."

"I should've taken a picture for you," Mustang said regretfully.

"No need. It'll be burned in my memory forever," Elodie told him.

They stared at each other for a beat, then Mustang lowered his head. He couldn't help it. Couldn't have stopped himself from kissing her right that moment if his life depended on it. A whole host of terrorists could've stormed down the beach right then and he wouldn't have done a damn thing about it. All his attention was centered on the woman in his arms.

The kiss was short, because Mustang knew if he lingered, he really *would* take Elodie to the sand and have his wicked way with her.

Elodie put a hand on his chest and looked up at him with big eyes. "Your place or mine?"

Mustang let out a huge sigh of relief.

He wanted this woman. Badly. But he hadn't wanted to overstep his bounds by suggesting she come home with him.

"Mine," he said firmly, then grabbed her hand and turned and headed for the parking lot.

He heard Elodie giggle behind him and couldn't help but smile. It seemed as if they were on the same page as far as intimacy went, and he couldn't wait another second to make Elodie his.

And she was.

His.

She might not fully understand what going home with him meant, but he did.

This was meant to be. *They* were meant to be. He'd hated having to leave her on the *Asaka Express* but now that he'd found her, he was keeping her.

"In a hurry?" she quipped as she stumbled after him.

Deciding walking was taking too long, and not wanting her to trip and hurt herself, Mustang turned and practically shoved their shoes at her chest. He'd been carrying both pairs of flip-flops as they walked in the sand. Surprised, Elodie grabbed hold of the shoes and let out a small shriek when he bent down and picked her up with one arm behind her back and the other under her knees.

She immediately wound an arm around his neck. "At least you didn't throw me over your shoulder," she said with a laugh.

"I thought about it," Mustang admitted.

She laughed harder. "Well, for the record, this is much more comfortable."

"Noted," Mustang told her.

He loved the feel of her in his arms. She wasn't light, but she wasn't too heavy for him to carry. He'd trained to haul his teammates around fully loaded down with gear. So she was light compared to Midas, who was four inches taller than Mustang.

When they arrived at his truck, Mustang lowered her legs and, after they'd put their shoes back on, he framed her face with his hands. "Be sure," he told her.

"I've never been more sure of anything in my life," Elodie told him. "I've second-guessed every decision I've ever made. Should I go to a four-year university, should I go to culinary school, should I work with this chef or that one, should I take that damn job in New York or the one on the *Asaka Express*? Should I go to Hawaii or somewhere else? But this is one decision I don't have to think twice about. I want you, Scott."

Mustang was a SEAL, he couldn't turn that off...and he

made a mental note about New York, but he pushed it to the back of his mind. First things first. Making Elodie his once and for all.

He kissed her hard on the lips, then opened the truck door for her.

She smiled as she got settled. When he went around and climbed behind the wheel and started the engine, she said quietly, "I kinda expected more than just a quick kiss."

"I'm on the edge here," Mustang told her as he headed out of the parking lot. "If I'd done more, we might be lying in the bed of my pickup right this second, your dress shoved over your hips and my head between your legs."

"Damn," Elodie whispered.

For a moment, Mustang thought he'd gone too far. That he'd been too blunt. But when he glanced over at Elodie, he saw she was fanning herself with her hand and smiling at him. She wasn't upset with what he'd said; if he wasn't mistaken, she was turned way the hell on.

"How do you want this to go?" he asked.

"Want what to go?"

"When we get to my place, I can pour you a glass of wine and we could sit on the couch and make small talk and maybe watch a movie. I can seduce you with long, slow kisses while we pretend to be interested in the television," he told her.

"Or?" Elodie asked.

"I can do my best to wait to take your clothes off until we get to my bedroom. No promises though. I'll make sure you're ready for me, then I'll fuck you hard and fast, getting our first orgasms out of the way. Then I'll eat you out, maybe convince you to suck on my cock, then we'll make love again. I'd like to say it'll be slow and sweet, but I have a feeling it'll be a long time before I can ever go slow once I get inside your hot, wet body."

"Holy shit," Elodie breathed. "That. I want that. The

second one. I feel as if I'm gonna go crazy if you don't get inside me."

Mustang shifted in his seat and brought a hand down to his crotch to adjust his cock. He saw Elodie's eyes fasten on his movements and smirked. "Sorry, I'm so fucking hard it's almost impossible to drive."

"Better you than me," she quipped.

"I've got condoms," Mustang told her. "Not because I've had anyone back to my place in months, but because they're a part of our regular kit when we get deployed. They're handy to make sure the muzzles of our weapons don't get wet, and a hundred other uses. I bought a new box the other week."

Elodie laughed. "You're a regular Boy Scout," she told him.

"Not even close," Mustang replied. "But I'll never do anything that would put you in danger. I'm clean, but as close as I feel to you, we don't really know each other well enough to have unprotected sex."

"I'm not on birth control," Elodie said. "I thought about it, but my body doesn't react well to the hormones. So I appreciate you not being a dick about wearing a condom."

"As I said, I'd never do anything to hurt you, El."

"I haven't had sex in a while."

"How long's a while?" Mustang asked.

"Over a year."

Mustang couldn't help but inhale deeply. He couldn't deny that he liked that. Liked that she hadn't been with anyone in so long. "I'll make sure you're ready for me," he told her.

"That's not gonna be an issue, Scott," she said. "I'm practically dripping right now."

"Fuck," he swore. "You can't say shit like that to me while I'm driving." He shifted again, trying to relieve the pressure on his dick. Luckily he was wearing shorts and not more restrictive pants, like jeans or his cargo pants, but his cock still wanted out of the confines of his boxers and shorts.

When Elodie reached over and put her hand on his thigh as he drove, it didn't help matters any. But Mustang covered her hand with his own, refusing to let her pull back. He wanted her hands on him any way he could get them, even if it meant he had to experience a little sensual pain.

As he pulled into his parking lot, he said, "Last chance to change your mind. That offer of wine and relaxation is still open."

Elodie squeezed his thigh and said, "No. I want you. I have for months. I've fantasized about this moment for too long to want to waste time with seduction and foreplay. I need you, Scott. All of you."

Slamming the truck into gear, Mustang hopped out the second he cut the engine. He went around the pickup and shut Elodie's door for her after she slid out. He didn't pick her up again, but wrapped his arm around her waist and pulled her into his side as he headed for the lobby of his apartment complex.

No one was around when they got into the elevator, and as much as Mustang wanted to pull the straps of her dress down her shoulders and feast on her tits, he refrained. He knew once he started undressing her, he wouldn't be able to stop. He could wait another thirty seconds. Maybe.

They walked down his hallway without a word, and Mustang unlocked his door. He put a hand on the small of Elodie's back and urged her inside.

The second the door shut and he'd locked it, Mustang was on her.

CHAPTER TEN

Elodie's back hit the wall next to Scott's front door and before she could take a full breath, his mouth was on hers. He was devouring her; there was no other word for it. And Elodie gave as good as she got.

This wasn't a gentle seduction. Their teeth gnashed together and their hands frantically tried to touch everything at once. Elodie felt the straps of her dress being pushed off her shoulders and down. Then she lost Scott's mouth as he bent toward her chest. She'd worn a strapless bra, and it didn't take much effort at all for Scott to wrench it down so it was around her belly. Her nipples peaked in the chilly air, and before she could think too much about what was happening, Scott had taken her into his mouth.

Groaning, Elodie did her best to undo the snap of Scott's shorts and shove them down. Then her hands pulled his shirt up, and for a second she didn't think he was going to remove his mouth from her breast to let her pull the shirt over his head. But he pulled away, tore his own shirt off, then bent to her breast again.

Elodie had a split second to see the tattoo on his left arm before she had to shut her eyes once more. The way Scott's beard was brushing over her chest was erotic as hell; she'd never felt anything like it before. He wasn't teasing either, was sucking at her nipple hard as his hand kneaded the sensitive flesh of her other breast.

"Scott," she moaned as she undid the clasp of her bra and let it fall to the floor.

He grunted and tried to push her dress over her hips, but it wouldn't go. She'd always been a little hippy, and the dress was made to slip over the top of her head. Not to mention, he hadn't bothered to undo the small zipper on the side.

Before she could help him, he'd simply torn the material, the ripping sound loud in the otherwise quiet entranceway.

"Sorry," he mumbled. "I'll get you another."

Elodie's stomach clenched at the carnal move. But he wasn't done.

Without lifting his head, Scott reached for her underwear and pushed them down as well. Elodie was butt-ass naked in his foyer, just as he warned her she might be.

He pulled his mouth off her nipple with a pop and went to his knees in front of her.

He shoved one of her legs out to the side, opening herself up to him. Elodie grabbed ahold of his head and held on as he leaned in. His eyes glanced upward and caught her gaze. She hadn't ever been this turned on before, and seeing him on his knees in front of her, feeling one hand gripping her hip and the other kneading her ass, made her feel sexy as hell—and powerful.

"Lick me," she ordered.

She saw him grin before he lowered his head once more. But he didn't take his eyes from her, and Elodie found she couldn't look away. She felt his tongue trace the seam of her pussy before he groaned low in his throat. She knew she was wet, she hadn't lied about that in the truck. She should've been embarrassed. This wasn't like her. Oh, she liked sex, but this was different. More intense. More passionate. Just...more.

Scott shifted and circled her clit with his mouth. She couldn't see where his beard ended and her pubic hair started. All she could see was his intense brown gaze boring into her own.

His chin moved as he began to suck on her.

"Good Lord!" she exclaimed as she bucked against his face. She'd never gone from zero to one hundred as fast as he was taking her. "Shit, Scott, yeah...just like that."

She couldn't help but close her eyes and lean against the wall behind her. She held on to his head for dear life as he ate her out more roughly than anyone ever had before. He wasn't gentle in the least as he sucked on her clit, pushing her toward a climax.

"Too much," she complained, even as she tightened her fingers on his head. Scott didn't listen to her anyway, flicking her clit fast, as if his tongue was a vibrator. She began to shake, and his hands gripped her hips tighter.

Elodie wanted to thrust but didn't have the leverage. She lifted one of her legs and threw it over his shoulder, and heard and felt him grunt in approval. He palmed her thigh and held on as she now teetered on one leg in front of him.

"I'm gonna come," she warned Scott, probably unnecessarily. He was most likely very aware that she was on the verge of a monster orgasm. Her belly clenched and her thighs shook. She whimpered as the feeling grew and grew inside her. It was almost scary how out of control she felt, but then she realized that there was no need to be frightened. Scott had her. He'd make sure she didn't fall.

Elodie held her breath as she went over the edge, overwhelmed by how good Scott was making her feel. Maybe it was the new position—she'd never come while standing up before—or maybe because she was teetering on one leg, but whatever the reason, this orgasm felt as if it was her very first. Overwhelming and all-consuming.

Before she could process what was happening, Scott was moving. He leaned down and picked her up, carrying her into the living room and lying her on her back on the couch. He crouched over her, rolling a condom over his large cock.

Elodie had been with her fair share of men. Small dicks, crooked dicks, fat dicks, thin dicks. But she'd never taken someone as thick as Scott. Excitement welled up within her. She spread her legs as wide as she could on the leather couch and arched her back sensuously.

His eyes took in her every movement, and she saw his cock jump in his hand. She loved knowing she could affect him. She wasn't afraid to take him inside her body. He'd more than made sure she was ready. She could feel her wetness dripping down her thighs and had the crazy thought that she was glad his couch was leather and would clean easily, before Scott leaned forward and notched the giant mushroom head of his cock between her folds.

They hadn't said much up till now, and Elodie could see a vein in the side of Scott's forehead pulsing.

He held himself over her and ever so slowly fed his dick into her welcoming body.

Elodie felt a pinch of pain, and she spread her thighs even wider as she reached down and grabbed hold of his rock-hard ass. Scott was one big muscle. He could easily hurt her, but he was going slow, giving her a chance to adjust to his size.

He groaned as if in agony when he got halfway in.

"More," she urged.

"I don't want to hurt you," he got out between clenched teeth.

"Scott, you just made me orgasm harder than I've ever come before. I'm so wet, I'm dripping all over your fucking couch. Just take me already!"

"Bossy," Scott said with a chuckle.

"Less talk, more action," Elodie complained.

He moved before she was even finished speaking. Slamming the rest of the way inside, making nerves she'd never felt come to life.

"Holy shit," she whispered, as she felt his pubic hair mesh with hers. Lifting her head and looking down their bodies, she saw they were as close as a man and woman could be. His cock was buried so far inside her, she couldn't see any part of it.

Then, as she watched, he pulled out, his cock shiny with her juices.

"So fucking beautiful," Scott muttered, and Elodie lost sight of his cock as he pushed inside her once more.

Her head fell back, bouncing on the cushion under her.

"I can't be gentle. You feel too good," he warned.

"Fuck me like you said you were going to," Elodie begged.

Scott shifted over her, moving his hands up so they rested almost in her armpits. "Hang on," he told her.

Just as Elodie grabbed hold of his biceps, he began to thrust. Her boobs bounced up and down as he slammed into her over and over. Every inch of her pussy lit up. She lifted her legs and urged him on by digging her heels into his ass.

Other than their harsh breathing and small grunts, neither said a word; they simply lost themselves in the pleasure.

Elodie had no idea how long they fucked, but it seemed way too soon when he said, "I'm coming." He planted himself as deep inside her as he could and grunted sexily. Elodie watched as Scott threw his head back and came.

She squirmed under him, wanting more but too embarrassed to ask for it or get herself off. But Scott seemed to know. Without pulling out of her, he sat up and reached between their legs. She could feel him softening inside her. When he began to pluck at her clit and one of her nipples at the same time, she jerked.

"Sorry, I couldn't hold off any longer. Next time, I'll wait for you. Come for me again. Come around my cock, babe."

Elodie obeyed. She was so primed, the feel of him stuffed inside her—and how sensitive she was from his earlier attention—made her come almost immediately. She let out a long moan and squeezed him with her inner muscles so hard, he slipped out of her body as she was coming.

They both groaned, and Elodie saw Scott's gaze was fixed between her legs. "Damn, woman, that is so fucking sexy."

Then he was moving again. She had no idea how he could do anything right now; she felt like a wet noodle. But he leaned over and picked her up as easily as he had on the beach and headed down the hall.

"We should clean the couch," she muttered.

"I'll take care of it. Right now, I need to hold you."

Elodie wasn't about to protest. He lay her down on his bed and helped her climb under the covers. He went into the bathroom briefly, she assumed to take care of the condom. And before he came back to bed, he turned on lights in the closet and the hall, leaving the door halfway open.

Her heart melted. He remembered that she'd said she couldn't sleep in the dark anymore. Damn, could he get any better?

The answer was yes, he could. Instead of getting under the covers with her, holding her close, he threw the covers back, exposing her to his gaze.

"Scott?"

"I want to see," he muttered. Then he began to kiss every inch of her body. He started at her head and worked his way down. Kissing, nuzzling, licking. Elodie reveled in his attention—and knew in that moment she was already irrevocably, dangerously in love with this man.

It made no sense. This was more like a one-night stand, but her heart had made its choice. Scott Webber was hers. Period. Full stop. There would be no one else like him, ever.

Damn.

* * *

Mustang's heart was beating as fast as if he'd just outrun twenty tangos while being shot at the whole way. He'd tried to hold back, to make their first time as good for Elodie as it was for him, but the second he'd pushed inside her tight sheath, he couldn't think about anything other than thrusting and getting off.

Thank God he'd made her come before he'd lost control. Thank God he hadn't completely blown it and had been able to give her that second orgasm after he'd selfishly taken her so roughly. But he'd warned her. And she didn't seem to be too concerned about his lack of restraint.

He'd make it up to her. Make it so she'd never want to leave him.

Mustang had no idea how he'd fallen so hard and fast. He was the cautious one. Always wanting all the information before he made any kind of move on the job. And here he was, jumping in with both feet and damn the consequences.

He'd just have to make Elodie love him. There was no other alternative. He'd keep her so happy that she'd have no choice but to fall hard. Starting with making up for ripping her clothes off, taking her on his fucking couch, and coming with a few strokes like he was a damn virgin.

But with her, he felt like one. He'd never been with anyone as hot, wet, and tight as Elodie. Her body had almost strangled his cock, and for a second he'd thought he wouldn't fit. But he had. They were a *perfect* damn fit.

He knew he should let her get some sleep. She'd worked all day in the sun, after all, but he couldn't bring himself to cover up her gorgeous body. She wasn't a hardbody, but he didn't mind, not in the least. Every wrinkle, every stretch mark, every blemish just made him love her even more. She was real. A grown-ass woman who'd chosen to be with *him*.

He kissed her forehead. Then her cheeks. Then one shoulder before moving to the next. He traced her collarbone with a finger before following it with his tongue. Her nipples were tight and hard, and he couldn't resist squeezing her tits. They weren't huge, but they weren't small either. They were fucking perfect.

Mustang envisioned his cock fucking her tits, and he writhed a bit. No, this was for her. There would be time for that later. He hoped.

He kissed her belly and found she was ticklish. He could smell her musk as he nuzzled her mound and barely resisted the urge to lick her folds. He wasn't done cherishing her. He kissed her inner thigh, then her knee, then her ankle. Her toenails weren't painted, and she had long, slender toes. Her feet were bigger than most women's, and he even thought *that* was cute.

He slowly began to work his way back up her body, his arousal climbing as he neared her pussy. He pushed one leg, and she opened to him. He loved how she willingly did exactly what he wanted.

He hadn't had time to really admire her earlier. He'd been too worried about making sure she really wanted him. He'd been terrified he'd look into her eyes and see reluctance, or some indication that she was using him because he was a SEAL. But all he'd seen was lust and want.

He played with her folds with his finger for a moment before sinking his index finger slowly inside her body. She groaned and lifted her hips a fraction of an inch.

"You like that?" he asked.

"Duh," she fired back.

He smiled. Fuck, this was fun. When was the last time he'd had fun while making love to a woman? Never, that's when. He'd always been too worried about making sure he wasn't hurting her, that she was consenting.

He slipped another finger inside Elodie's body and gently fucked her.

"More," she begged.

He could feel fresh wetness coat his fingers and fucking loved that he could turn her on like this. He wanted to see her come again. On his hand. He felt ten feet tall that he could push her over the edge. It was amazing to be able to control her pleasure. If that made him an asshole, so be it.

He brought his other hand up between her legs and began to play with her clit with his thumb, even as he continued to gently thrust in and out of her body.

When she began to thrust against him, he stilled his fingers, letting her fuck them.

Her nipples were tight, her tits jiggling as she squirmed on his sheets. And he was a fucking caveman, because he loved seeing her like this. At his mercy, straining for what only he could give her.

"Harder," she moaned.

"Your wish is my command." At that moment, Mustang realized he was kidding himself. He wasn't in charge here. She was. She had him wrapped around her little finger, and if she let him, he'd spend the rest of his life bending over backward to give her everything she wanted.

He stopped teasing and went to work making his woman come.

She flew apart quickly, and he'd never seen anything more beautiful. Then she surprised him by sitting up and pushing him backward on the mattress. Before he knew what she was doing, she had his cock in her hand and was lowering her head.

"El," he moaned.

She ignored him, tightening her hand around the base of his dick and taking the head between her lips. It was as carnal as he imagined it would be. Her mouth stretching to take him as she slurped and sucked.

She wasn't going easy on him either, she was sucking hard, as if she were trying to pull his come out of his body by force. When she lowered her hand between her legs and scooped up some of her own juices to lubricate him, Mustang almost came right then and there.

"Condom?" she asked, lifting her head. Her hand continued to pump him up and down, and Mustang knew in seconds, this would be over before it even started.

He turned, dislodging her hand, giving him a moment's reprieve before he lay back again and rolled a condom down his length.

"I don't know how you fit," Elodie said as she eyed him, but she gamely straddled his waist and reached for him. "But you did once, so I'm sure you will again."

"Damn straight I will," Mustang told her. "You were made to take my cock."

She grabbed his dick once more, and they both groaned as she fit him to her and slowly began to ease down.

Once he was all the way in, Mustang concentrated on her face. He knew if he looked down and saw how they were connected, he'd lose it way too quickly once again. He kneaded her tits as she slowly began to undulate on him. She didn't bounce up and down at first; she flexed her hips and rubbed her clit against him.

"Damn, I'm so full," she breathed.

He twitched inside her. Let her set the pace for a while. She rotated her hips in circles, then back and forth, holding herself up with her hands braced on his chest. She was sexy as fuck, her hair brushing against her tits and nipples as she moved. Mustang memorized the moment and knew he'd fantasize about this for many, many nights to come.

"Touch yourself," he ordered. "Make yourself come on my cock."

He loved that she didn't hesitate. One hand moved between them and she began to roughly massage her clit. He felt her inner muscles squeeze his dick, and he groaned. Fuck, she was perfect.

Her juices were rolling down his balls now, soaking him as she got herself off.

"You've ruined me for my vibrator," she said, looking down into his face as she got closer and closer to the edge.

"Good. You need to get off, you let me know and I'll let you use me just like this, anytime you want. I'll fill you so full, you won't feel anything but me." He continued to talk dirty, seeing that she loved it. "You're clenching me so tight, you're gonna leave bruises. I fucking love this. You on top, your tits begging for my touch. Come, Elodie. Fucking come already."

That did it. She arched her back and pressed down as hard as she could on his cock and exploded. Mustang grabbed her hips even as she was coming and lifted her, slamming her back down as hard as he could on his dick.

She screamed, and he did it again. And again. Prolonging her orgasm and setting off his own in the process. He came so hard and long, he saw stars. His heart almost beat out of his chest, and he knew he'd probably be sore in the morning from using muscles he wasn't used to using.

When they'd both stopped shaking, Mustang eased Elodie down onto his chest. She lay against him like a wet noodle. They were both sweaty and breathing hard, but Mustang couldn't keep the smile off his face.

"Holy shit," Elodie muttered. "Thank God I didn't go for the wine and slow seduction. I've never been so satisfied."

"I promise to do the slow seduction some other time," Mustang told her.

"Nope. I liked this. I choose a hard fucking every time."

His smile grew, and he ran a hand gently up and down her back.

They both groaned when his cock eventually slipped out of her body.

"Damn."

"Yeah. I need to take care of the condom."

"Okay," she said, rolling over.

He headed for the bathroom and was back in seconds. He straightened the blankets and covered Elodie before getting under them with her. He took her into his arms and they both sighed in contentment.

After a moment, she asked, "Are you sure this isn't weird?"

"This isn't weird," Mustang told her immediately. "It's so right, it's not even funny."

"I just...I didn't come to Hawaii for this. I mean, I wanted to find you, but I didn't come for sex."

Mustang laughed. He couldn't help it.

Elodie raised her head. "What's so funny?"

"I know you didn't come to Hawaii for sex. You're so amazing, I have no doubt you could get sex any day of the week and twice on Sunday. I'm glad you came here. I prayed I'd see you again. I wasn't lying, I regretted having to leave you before figuring out how I could help you. And I *still* want to help...but I also want more."

"More?"

"Yeah. I want *you*, Elodie. I want to take more walks with you, I want to cook with you, and have you show me up every way a chef can show up a shitty cook like me. I want you to get to know my team and hang out with us. I want to wake up with you by my side, and I want you to be waiting when I get home from a mission. I want it all...and if admitting all that makes this weird, so be it."

Mustang held his breath as he waited for her response. Had he gone too far? Yeah, the sex between them was great, but maybe that's all she wanted. Sex. To make the reason why she had to use a fake name go away.

But he still wouldn't doubt the feeling deep down that said she was the one for him.

Elodie went boneless against him. He hadn't realized how tense she was until that moment. "I want that too," she said quietly.

"Good. Then no more talk about this being weird. Yeah, we had sex right after we connected again. Big deal. All it did was knock through all the bullshit dating stuff. We're together now, we'll get to know each other even better as time goes on, and we'll have this," he squeezed her shoulder, "each night. Okay?"

"Yeah. More than okay. We're exclusive though, right?"

"Fuck yeah, we are." The thought of her dating anyone else made him a little crazy. It was just one more way Mustang knew he was a goner.

"Scott?"

"Yeah, babe?"

"I'm scared."

Everything in him wanted to leap out of bed and slay dragons for her, but Mustang forced himself to stay calm. "About what?"

"That my issues will get you hurt. Or one of your friends. Of screwing this up. Of you figuring out that I'm not worth the trouble, or getting sick of me. I'm scared of just about everything these days, if I'm being honest."

"Your issues will not get me or my friends hurt. You aren't going to screw *this* up. It's obvious you have no clue as to your appeal, and I should probably work on trying to change that, but I have no desire for you to figure out that *I'm* nothing but a Navy bum and have you look elsewhere for better."

She sighed and snuggled into him more. "Navy bum, my ass," she snorted.

Mustang smiled. "Sleep. We'll talk tomorrow. Do you have to work?"

"No, it's Sunday, I have the day off."

"Good. I do too. We'll spend the day together, talk, and figure out what happens next," Mustang told her.

"Okay."

"Just like that? Okay?" he asked skeptically.

"Yeah. I'm tired of running. So damn tired of looking over my shoulder. I want to believe that I'm good, that I can stop running scared. Nothing's happened in months. I have no reason to think I'm in danger...but what if I'm wrong? I'm okay with you helping me because I want this. *You*. And I can't have you if I have to relocate every few months."

Mustang's heart hurt for her, but her words also made him feel really good. She wanted him, and she had him. Lock, stock, and barrel. He was hers, just as she was his. She might not believe it yet, but he'd do whatever it took to make sure she could be Elodie Winters again.

Just so he could ask her to marry him and become Elodie Webber.

He couldn't help but grin.

"Thanks for leaving the light on for me," she said into his shoulder.

"I'll always leave the light on for you," he told her, then turned and kissed her forehead.

"Sleep, babe."

"Night."

"Good night."

Mustang drifted off with a huge smile on his face and slept harder than he had in a very long while, all because of the woman at his side.

* * *

"What did you find out?" Paul Columbus asked Andrew as he entered his office. It had been too damn long since they'd seen the news clip of the employees of the *Asaka Express* getting off the cargo ship in Sudan. He wanted to know where Elodie was. Now.

"It took a while, but I've got the name of the guy with his arm around her shoulders. Valentino Russo. He's Italian."

"Where is he?" Paul asked.

"I've got good and bad news about that," Andrew began.

"Just spit it out," Paul barked.

"Right. The bad news is that he's currently at sea. He was transferred to the *Asaka Freedom*."

"Fuck. How long?"

"His contract is for six months. But I've got their port schedule, and there's a good chance he'll take shore leave when they get to their next port. From what I've been able to find out about our guy, he considers himself a ladies' man and has a habit of visiting bars and whorehouses when he lands."

"I want intel," Paul said.

"And you'll get it."

"You go," Paul said. "I need you on this, Andrew. You're the only person who knows about this bitch. If my son finds out what happened, and that I let her get away, he'll push to take over the family—and I'm not ready for that to happen. I need her *dead*."

Even Paul realized he was becoming slightly irrational, maybe even obsessed with killing Elodie Winters...but he couldn't stop now. It was a matter of pride. It didn't seem as if Elodie had gone to the cops yet, at least no one had confronted him about anything, but if there was a chance she could, he needed to make sure it didn't happen.

She couldn't win. And right now, it felt as if she was winning. She was continually a few steps ahead of him, and Paul fucking *hated* it.

"I need you to take care of this personally. Go get this asshole. Find out what he knows about Elodie."

"I can do that."

"I don't care what it takes. *Any* information is better than what we have now, which is nothing. Use another identity so no one can trace you back to the family. This is all under the radar, got it?"

"I'll take care of it. And him," Andrew said with a hungry gleam in his eye.

Paul knew his friend was bloodthirsty and enjoyed seeing others suffer; it was what had made him such a good soldier, and now capo. He controlled his soldiers with an iron fist and no one dared cross him. He'd find this Italian Don Juan and get any information he had about Elodie Winters out of him. If the man tried to keep quiet to protect the bitch, he'd be singing like a canary when Andrew got done with him.

One of the things that Paul liked most about Andrew was that he wasn't afraid to torture their enemies for information. It showed his loyalty to the organization. To Paul.

Paul didn't feel bad in the least that this Russo had narrowly escaped being killed by pirates, only to die by torture at Andrew's hands. His only concern was finding the rock Elodie had crawled under. He wouldn't let her get away. He was Paul fucking Columbus. She should've been more grateful to him for giving her a job. Shouldn't have said no. Shouldn't have run. But now that she had, she'd signed her own death warrant. He'd look weak if he didn't take care of her.

Andrew nodded and left the room as silently as he'd entered, but Paul didn't even notice. He was too lost in the visions of payback running through his head.

More and more often Paul found himself obsessing over things that hadn't gone as he'd wanted. Replaying different outcomes in his mind. His sons had subtly indicated they were worried about his mental health, but Paul brushed away their concerns. His kids just wanted to be in charge. Especially Jerry. Paul knew they were calling him paranoid behind his back...but he'd show them. Once he took down Elodie, things would settle again. He didn't like loose ends, and the chef was a huge one.

Paul's impatience was reaching its peak, but knew he could count on his capo. Andrew would find Valentino and get the information they needed to find the bitch.

She might think she was safe. But no matter how much time passed, Elodie Winters would *never* be safe from him.

CHAPTER ELEVEN

"I'm going for a run."

The words barely registered in Elodie's brain. She squinted her eyes open and saw Scott hovering over her. He had on a tank top and a pair of running shorts. She frowned. "What time is it?" she asked sleepily.

He smiled and leaned down and kissed her forehead. "Early. Go back to sleep. I'll be gone about an hour and a half or so."

"You're going to *run* for an hour and a half? Are you nuts?"

He chuckled. "I'm a SEAL," he said as if that explained it. Then he turned and headed for the door. Before he got there, he turned again and came back to the side of the bed. He leaned over once more and put his hand on her cheek. "For the record...I like having you here in my bed. Thank you for last night." Then he kissed her on the lips and was up and moving before she could respond.

Shifting on the mattress, Elodie smiled. She was delightfully sore in all the right places. But glancing at the old-fashioned clock radio on the table next to the bed turned her smile to a grimace. Four-thirty. It was way too early to get up, especially considering it was her day off. She'd sleep for a bit, then get up, shower, and make breakfast for Scott.

She actually looked forward to cooking for the first time in a long while. Breakfast wasn't exactly haute cuisine, but she made a mean eggs benedict if she did say so herself.

Turning over, Elodie inhaled the scent of Scott, lingering on his pillow, and closed her eyes.

She woke up later groggy and disoriented. When looked at the clock again, she saw it was nearly nine in the morning.

Shit! She'd totally overslept. Sitting up, she also realized she was still completely naked. Bringing the sheet up to cover her chest, she inhaled deeply. It smelled like she was way too late to impress Scott with her prowess in the kitchen this morning. The scent of coffee, bacon, and bread filled the room.

Elodie climbed out of bed and went into the attached bathroom. She took a quick shower, making sure not to get her hair wet since it took forever to dry, and contemplated what she could wear after to greet Scott.

He had literally ripped her dress practically in half in his hurry to get her naked last night. Not to mention her underwear was probably still in the foyer of his apartment. She debated rummaging through his drawers, and decided she was going to have to. There was no way she was going to parade out into his living room without a stitch of clothing on.

Since it was a bit chilly in the mornings, she grabbed a long-sleeve gray dress shirt from his closet. She also found a pair of sweatpants that would work for now. They were huge on her, and she had to roll the bottoms so she didn't trip over them, but at least she was warm.

Elodie knew she looked ridiculous, but she didn't care. Wearing Scott's clothing was intimate, and after last night, when they'd both gone at each other like sex-starved jackals, she figured he wouldn't mind.

She took a long look out at the ocean from the window in his room and sighed. She didn't think she'd ever get tired of that view. She hadn't had time to appreciate it last night. And besides, it had been dark. But if she lived here, she'd buy one of those overstuffed comfortable easy chairs and plant it right in front of the window so every time she looked up, she'd see the serene Hawaiian surf. Looking at the waves was soothing; being in them, not so much.

In the past, when she'd woken up in a man's apartment or house after sleeping with him, and not really knowing him, she'd felt awkward, making up whatever excuse she could think of to slink out as fast as possible. But surprisingly, she wasn't embarrassed at all by her behavior from the night before. Being with Scott felt right. And easy. She couldn't wait to spend the day with him, despite knowing she needed to spill the beans about her complicated life.

Eager to see him again, Elodie wandered out of his room and into the living area of his apartment. He was sitting at the end of a small table next to the kitchen, drinking what she assumed was coffee.

The second he saw her, his eyes lit up and he smiled and stood. "Come 'ere, sleepy head," he said, holding out a hand.

Elodie padded over to him without hesitation. He pulled her into him, then sat, shifting her so she sat across his thighs.

"Morning," she said softly.

"Morning. You sleep okay?"

"Like a rock. You?" she asked.

"Better than I have in months," he returned.

"How was your run?"

"Good."

"I can't believe you ran for an hour and a half," she muttered.

"I actually felt so good, I went for two hours," he informed her.

Elodie shook her head. "Right, so we should talk about this now. I'm not a fan of exercise. I mean, I like to walk and hike, and go see beautiful wildlife and nature stuff, but I've never been the kind of person to like to exercise because it's a healthy, responsible thing to do. We'll never be the kind of couple to participate in partner marathons or stuff like that. I'll go and watch and cheer you on, but I'm not going to strap a number on my chest and run for fun."

Scott threw his head back and laughed so hard, Elodie thought he was going to fall out of the chair. When he got himself under control, he looked at her and said, "Noted. What about bike rides?"

"Only if there aren't any hills and you get me an electric bike," she quipped.

"Swimming?"

"In a pool or hot tub, where I can bob up and down and have a drink in my hand, yes. You already know how I feel about the ocean."

He chuckled. "Can you swim?"

"Of course I can swim," Elodie told him. "I'll never make the Olympics. And swimming back and forth, watching that black line on the bottom of the pool? That's boring as hell."

"On that, we agree," Scott said. "I don't expect you to do anything with me that you don't want to do or enjoy. We don't have to like all the same things, and we don't have to always be joined at the hip."

"Good," she said.

"Good," he echoed. "Now that *that's* out of the way... there's something else we need to do."

"What's that?" she asked, raising an eyebrow at him.

"Say good morning properly," he said, then leaned closer.

Elodie eagerly met him halfway, bringing a hand up and resting it on the back of his head as he kissed her. The kiss was long and slow, with none of the frenetic urgency of the night before. He tasted like coffee, and for some reason that seemed extremely intimate.

He leaned back, but Elodie didn't remove her hand from his nape.

"Good morning," Scott said huskily.

"Morning."

"And...in case you don't remember me saying it when I got up this morning...last night was one of the best nights of my life. I think most of the reason I felt so good on my run was because of you. Because you simply make me happy. I know that's sappy as hell, but so be it."

Elodie still had some reservations about what they were doing, how fast they were moving, but she was going to hold on to this happiness with both hands for as long as she could.

"I wouldn't have stayed if I didn't feel connected to you, Scott. I admit that I don't really understand it, but at the moment, I don't care. It was as if the second I saw you on that dock, something clicked inside me. Something I'd been missing since you left the *Asaka Express*."

"I feel the same way. It's as if I've known you forever... here." He put a hand over his heart.

Elodie nodded in agreement.

"Right, so no more talking about moving too fast or whether or not things are weird. We aren't, and they aren't. Okay?"

"Okay," she happily agreed.

Scott leaned back and pretended to inspect her from head to toe. "Love the outfit, babe."

She laughed. "Well, my pretty dress seemed to have gotten torn last night."

"It did, huh? That's too bad." Scott reached for the top button of the shirt she had on and deftly undid it. Then he popped open the next one, revealing quite a bit of skin. "But I have to say, I like what you've got on right now. I like seeing you in my clothes."

"They're huge on me. You're like a Bigfoot or something."

"I am not, I'm only six feet tall. Midas is the Sasquatch at six-four."

"Well, since I'm only five-six, you're all huge to me."

Scott leaned down and nuzzled the skin of her chest that he'd uncovered. "You showered," he complained.

"I did. After last night...well...let's just say I needed to clean up." It should've felt weird talking about something so intimate, but with Scott, it felt natural.

"I wanted to shower with you," he told her.

Elodie realized for the first time that he must've showered as well, because he certainly didn't smell like he'd been on a two-hour run. "But you already took one," she said.

"And?" he retorted.

"Right. Forgot, you're a SEAL. You're practically a water baby."

"That, and I'll pretty much never pass up a chance to see boobs."

Elodie burst out laughing. Had she ever laughed this much with a man before? She didn't think so. "Ah, the truth comes out," she said.

Scott took her face in his hands and kissed her hard and fast. "As long as they're your boobs, that is. Scoot off, I made you breakfast."

Elodie continued to sit in his lap, reluctant to move and trying to catch up to the topic change, so he shifted her off his thighs and then seated her in the chair. "Stay there. No moving. How do you like your coffee?"

"Black and strong," she said.

"Hmmm, I would've pegged you for extra-sweet with cream," he said.

"Nope. Long days and nights in kitchens have taught me to take my caffeine as undiluted as possible," she told him.

"I love getting to know little things about you," Scott said as he headed into the kitchen. The apartment wasn't all that big, and the kitchen wasn't too fancy, but the stove was gas burning and the refrigerator was stainless steel. It looked like the owners of the apartment complex had done their best to upgrade where possible. She watched Scott as he flitted around the kitchen, pulling out plates and opening the oven to retrieve whatever he'd stashed there.

"I'm sorry I slept so long," she told him.

"It's not an issue at all. There was no way I was gonna wake you, not when you looked so damn adorable all snuggled up in my bed," Scott said.

"You watched me sleep?"

"Oh, yeah. After I showered in the guest bathroom after my run, I stood in the doorway, drank a cup of coffee and tried to figure out how I'd gotten so damn lucky to have you here with me." He looked over at her. "And I know me running into you was pure luck, so I'm more grateful than I can say that someone was watching over us."

Elodie could tell he really meant that. She swallowed hard, feeling emotional all of a sudden. She'd felt so alone for months, and simply being with him now made her feel as if a ray of sunshine had suddenly sprung out from behind the cloud that had been hanging over her head for so long.

"Here you go," Scott said, not giving her a chance to respond. He placed a plate in front of her, and Elodie could only stare down at it in surprise.

"It's not homemade," Scott went on, "I'm not that talented. But I stopped on the way home from my run and grabbed some meat pies from a place not too far from here. I got you a chicken vegetable one. It might be a little spicy, but I've found that just brings out the flavor of the chicken more. I also grabbed a fresh mango and pineapple and cut them up as well. And because I'm a guy, I grilled some bacon to go with everything else. I pretty much limit myself to bacon on the weekends as a treat."

Elodie stared at her plate, struggling to gain her composure.

"El? What's wrong? If you don't like it, we can find you something else," Scott said, leaning toward her in concern.

Elodie shook her head. "It's not that. It looks delicious."

"Then what's wrong?" Scott asked quietly.

"I just...I can't remember the last time someone made me breakfast. Or dinner, for that matter. When you're a chef, it's just assumed that you'll be the one cooking. And when I was in New York, I didn't have time to date or for anyone to worry about what I was eating. On the cargo ship, it was much of the same. My job was to feed everyone else."

She saw Scott sigh in relief. "Well, I can't pretend that I won't enjoy anything you make for me, but I don't expect you to always cook for us. I enjoy grilling and experimenting now and then. I haven't starved after thirty-six years of life. And I have to admit, I like looking after you, taking care of you. That sounds patronizing, and I'm sorry. I know you can take care of yourself. Maybe pampering is the better word. I like pampering you, even if it's something small like picking up breakfast on my way home."

"Thank you," Elodie said softly.

"You're welcome," Scott returned. Then he leaned over and took her chin in his hand and kissed her before shifting back to his own seat.

They ate breakfast slowly, enjoying the morning and continuing to get to know each other. Elodie insisted on taking care of the dishes, since he cooked. There wasn't much to do, as he'd already cleaned up after making the bacon.

She put their plates in the dishwasher and turned, letting out an *oof* as she ran smack dab into Scott.

"Jeez, you walk quietly. I had no idea you were behind me."

He rolled his eyes. "SEAL, babe, remember?"

"I know, but still, it's uncanny. I'm gonna have to put a

bell around your neck so you don't scare the crap out of me when you're sneaking around."

He wrapped his arms around her waist, and she noticed how his gaze fell to her chest. She hadn't closed the buttons he'd opened earlier, and without a bra, she knew he was getting quite the eyeful from his vantage point.

His hands shifted under the waistband of the sweats she was wearing. His fingers caressed her hips—and his eyebrows went up. "You aren't wearing underwear under here?" he asked.

"Scott, the last time I saw my bra and underwear was in the foyer. I have no idea where they are now, and I wasn't going to put them back on anyway. They're dirty."

"They're in my washing machine," Scott admitted. "I was gonna wash your dress too, but unfortunately, I need to take it to a seamstress to get it fixed before you can wear it again."

He was damn cute. "It's fine. The dress cost like fifteen bucks at an ABC Store. It'll be cheaper to just go buy a new one."

Scott shook his head. "Nope. You're keeping that dress, and every year on our anniversary—the anniversary of when we found each other again—you're gonna wear it when we go out and I'm gonna strip it off you when we get home, just like I did last night."

God, she loved the thought of that. Not only the sex, but that he was thinking long term. It solidified her feeling that this wasn't a casual fling for either of them. "I might gain weight and not be able to fit into it in the future," she teased.

He shrugged, seemingly unconcerned. "Then I'll scour the Internet and find fabric just like it and have a new one made for you."

Gah, he definitely knew all the right things to say. Elodie smiled up at him.

"But now I can't ever wear those sweats again," he said conversationally.

"What? Why not?"

"Because I know your pussy has been bare under there, and there's no way my cock will be able to behave."

It was Elodie's turn to roll her eyes. "You're being ridiculous."

"Am I?" he asked, nodding down to his crotch. "Look, I'm hard and ready to go just thinking about you being bare under there."

"I think you need to have that looked at," Elodie said seriously. "That can't be normal. Not after last night and you running two damn hours this morning. You should be exhausted."

"You mean you *aren't* thinking about all the things I can do to you with my cock?" he asked.

"Nope," Elodie said, lying through her teeth.

Scott stared at her for a moment, then moved his hands up and began to tickle her.

Elodie screeched and squirmed, trying to get away from his fingers, without success. She broke away from him and ran toward the living room. Scott easily caught up to her and tackled her onto the couch, straddling her hips and continuing the tickle torture.

"No, no! Stop! I give up!"

"Tell the truth, or I won't stop!" he threatened.

"Okay, okay!" she said between giggles. "I may or may not have masturbated in the shower this morning as I thought about how hot you are, and how much I loved what we did last night."

His fingers immediately stilled, and he groaned. "Damn, woman," he complained. "Seriously?"

Elodie nodded shyly.

"It's a good thing we both have the day off," he said as he reached for the buttons of the shirt she was wearing once more.

Elodie grinned and didn't protest as he peeled his shirt

away from her chest and stared down at her. Feeling powerful and sexy, she arched her back slightly. Scott immediately moved, leaning down to take one of her nipples into his mouth, just as he'd done the night before. Elodie moaned and fisted his hair as he feasted on her.

An hour later, they were both lying back in his bed, sweaty and satisfied after another bout of intense lovemaking. The connection between them was powerful, and it wasn't just sexual either.

As if he could read her mind, Scott said, "Talk to me, El. It's time."

Elodie had known this was coming. And if she was being honest with herself, as much as she'd liked having the pressure taken off by not talking about her past before now, she was relieved to finally get it off her chest. To confide in someone.

She was still nervous about Scott's safety, but after months of not seeing anyone suspicious or feeling danger lurking nearby, she was beginning to think maybe she'd overreacted. That maybe Paul was happy she was gone and would leave it at that.

Turning her head so she could look out the window on the other side of the room, see the calming sight of the ocean, Elodie took a deep breath and began to spill her secrets.

CHAPTER TWELVE

Mustang did his best to stay calm as Elodie began to speak. He'd worried about her for months. Wondering if she was safe, and what could possibly be so bad that she'd taken a job on a cargo ship in the Middle East to get away from it. He'd come up with all sorts of scenarios in his mind...but not one of them was close to the truth.

"I was working in Chicago for a very well known Michelin star restaurant. But I hated it. I was tired all the time and the head chef was an ass. He stood around yelling at all of the sous chefs, station and line cooks, and specialty chefs. I understand how things work, but it still grated on my nerves when he took all the credit for everything, even though he didn't cook a damn thing.

"A friend I knew from culinary school emailed me and told me about an amazing opportunity in New York City. The job was somewhat mysterious, but involved being the personal chef to a very wealthy family in the heart of the city. Room and board was included, which is huge since everyone knows how expensive apartments are in New York. I'd had an especially bad day at work and applied on a whim, never thinking I'd get a second look. But I did.

"I flew out for an interview, and I liked the people I met while I was there. I prepared a dinner for a small gathering as a part of the interview, and I guess they were impressed, because I got the job. I quit my job in Chicago and immediately moved out to New York. And things were great for a while. I was in charge of my own kitchen and mostly left alone. The salary was generous, and I met the head of the family several times, and he seemed very nice..." Her voice trailed off.

"But he wasn't?"

Elodie shivered. "No."

"Who was he?" Mustang asked, not liking where this was going.

"I had no idea who he was when I took the job," Elodie insisted.

"Shhhh, it's okay." Mustang hated the defensive tone in her voice. He wasn't judging her, but he needed to know who the hell she'd worked for if he was going to help her.

"Paul Columbus." She tensed as if waiting for his censure.

"Is that name supposed to mean something to me?" Mustang asked, wracking his brain to try to think of who the man was and why Elodie was so terrified of him.

She sighed, as if relieved. "You really don't know him?"

"No. Never heard the name before," Mustang said.

She relaxed against him, and for the first time, Mustang realized just how much she'd tensed up while telling her story. "He's apparently the head of a mob family in New York."

"The mob?" Mustang asked in surprise. "Seriously?"

"Yeah. I had no idea, obviously. I suppose I should've known something was up, considering how high the salary was."

"No," Mustang said immediately. "There are lots and lots of millionaires in this country who aren't famous and whose names aren't plastered all over the media. Especially in New York."

"Yeah, I guess."

"So what happened?"

"I was working in the kitchen as usual, and Paul came in. He didn't enter the kitchen often, and I had my own apartment and entrance to the kitchen, so I rarely saw the rest of the Columbus family or anyone who worked for him, outside those who ran errands for me and helped serve the food. He... he put a small bottle down on the counter and told me to add the contents to one of the bowls of soup that would be served to his guests. He was staring at me with eyes so hard and cold, I seriously felt the temperature in the room go down twenty degrees. I asked him what it was, and without hesitation, he said it was arsenic.

"I was shocked. I told him I wouldn't do that, that it would be murder. He lunged toward me so fast, I didn't even have a chance to evade him. He backed me against the counter, leaned in—I can still remember how bad his breath was—and told me that I worked for him. That he *owned* me.

"Somehow, I found the courage to speak. I told him the soup for the night was a beef bouillon, and that his guest would surely taste it. I suggested that maybe it would be better to disguise it in a bisque, because it was thicker and chunkier, and I'd be happy to make that another night if I had some advance notice."

"Shit! How'd he take that?" Mustang asked, realizing she'd gone tense again.

"He wasn't happy," Elodie said. "I swear I thought he was going to kill me right then and there for defying him. I realized later, after doing some research, that arsenic is odorless, colorless, and tasteless. It's really a perfect poison. He *had* to know I was talking out of my ass...but for some reason, he didn't call me on it. Maybe he really knew nothing about the poison either.

"Anyway, I was already trying to think of what the hell I was going to do the next time he demanded I put poison in someone's food when he turned and grabbed one of my knives. He shoved my head against the counter and held the knife to the back of my neck as he said, 'If you say no to me again, it'll be the last thing you ever say.' Then he slammed the knife down hard, chopping off a hunk of my hair, before standing up and leaving as if he hadn't a care in the world."

"Holy fuck," Mustang swore.

"Yeah. Scared the shit out of me. My hands shook throughout the rest of dinner prep. None of the other assistants in the kitchen said anything, and I think it was because they didn't want to seem to be siding with me over Paul. I also think they'd all probably been threatened in the past too, or at least had firsthand knowledge of how dangerous Paul was."

"What'd you do?"

"I finished dinner. Poured the arsenic he hadn't taken with him down the drain, went back to my apartment, packed a small bag, and left. I couldn't stay, not after being asked to participate in the first-degree murder of someone, and not after he'd told me I had to do everything he demanded or he'd kill me."

"Damn, I knew you were strong, but I had no idea," Mustang said.

Elodie ignored his statement. "He wasn't happy. I didn't know where to go, so I stayed in New York for a while, trying to figure out what to do next. But one day when I was on the subway, I thought I was being followed. I immediately got off at the next stop, but so did the guy following me. It took me twenty minutes to lose him, and I thought I'd end up with a bullet in my head every one of those twenty minutes. I was scared to go to the bank and pull out more money, because I didn't know if he was watching my account. I had some money with me. I always keep an emergency stash of cash just in case, thank God.

"I immediately left New York and went to Pittsburgh. But

when I went in for an interview at a restaurant, I was told there'd been a mistake and I was no longer being considered. When I pressed for a reason, the owner told me she had no desire to make an enemy of the Columbus family. He'd spread the word that if anyone hired me, he'd make sure their restaurant failed every inspection and would have to shut down."

Mustang had been so relaxed after their morning romp, but now he felt as if he needed to take another two-hour run to excise the pissed-off energy he had inside him. "What did you do?"

"I panicked," Elodie admitted. "I used most of my money to take a bus all the way to Los Angeles. I figured that was as far from New York as I could get, but my name was too unique and Paul's reach was too long. I noticed a guy following me again while I was trying to find another job. I also got an email from someone I knew back in Chicago, breaking the news that our friend—the one who'd recommended me for the job with the Columbus family—had been murdered. Drive-by shooting. I just *knew* it was a message for me. So I cut all ties to anyone I'd known before. Terminated my email and social media accounts. Smashed my cell phone, and lucked out and found a guy who could get me some fake IDs."

"Thus, Rachel was born," Mustang said.

"Yeah. And the job on the *Asaka Express* seemed to fall into my lap. It was perfect. I'd be out of the country, with a new name, doing what I loved. But yeah, I guess karma has it out for me because then the ship got hijacked."

"And you met me," Mustang said.

She nodded. "True."

"So karma can't hate you too much."

"Well, unfortunately there were tons of reporters waiting for the ship when we docked in Port Sudan. I tried to keep my head down, but we had to pose for a group picture after we filed off the ship. I declined all interviews and had to decide what to do next. I was offered a job on the *Asaka Freedom*, but being trapped on a ship in the middle of the ocean didn't seem like the haven it had before. I had lost your number by then, but decided I might as well go to Hawaii, as I literally didn't have anywhere else to go. I used the second fake identification I'd bought...this time with a name closer to my own, so at least I didn't forget to answer to it." Elodie tipped her head up to look at him. "And here I am."

"And you've been here a month and a half?" Mustang asked.

She nodded.

"Have you noticed anything out of the ordinary? Anyone following you or making you nervous like you did in LA or New York?"

"No. I don't have a bank account, Perry and Kahoni pay me in cash. I know that's illegal, but I was lucky they bought my story about someone hacking into my last account and stealing all my money."

"Doesn't hurt that you're pretty," Mustang said with a smile.

Elodie blushed. "I hate lying to them, but I was desperate."

"I'm not judging you, or them," Mustang told her.

"And I appreciate it. They're good men, with families. I feel like I'm putting them in danger. I could've taken another chef position, there are lots of restaurants around here that are hiring, but I figured that would always be the first place Paul looked. I hoped maybe he wouldn't be able to find me if I'm a lowly deckhand on a private fishing charter. But what if Paul finds me and sinks Perry and Kahoni's boat or something? Or hurts their families?"

"Look at me," Mustang ordered. He felt sick inside that Elodie was obviously so scared. But he couldn't help being impressed that her first thoughts were for those around her. She had a tender heart, and it enraged him that this

Columbus guy had asked her to fucking poison someone in the first place.

The mob. Jesus, what were the odds? He had no idea the mob was still a thing in this country. But then again, people making money illegally would never truly disappear.

When Elodie tipped her chin up once more, he could see the fear in her eyes. Fear that he wouldn't believe her? That he'd tell her to get out? That he'd want nothing to do with her now that he knew her secret? Not fucking happening. If anything, he was even more impressed with her. She'd immediately left after finding out who she was working for and had managed to stay a step ahead of this Paul asshole and his cronies. "He's not going to get his hands on you."

She smiled weakly. "I appreciate you saying that, but you can't guarantee it."

He couldn't; that was the shitty thing. "I know, but I can do what I can to check into this Columbus asshole and mitigate the danger you're in."

"I actually feel pretty safe here. I haven't seen anyone suspicious and because I have no way of being tracked electronically, I'm hoping that he's finally given up."

"Maybe, maybe not," Mustang said. "But it's only been two months since you were photographed by those reporters. It could just be taking him this long to even see that footage. Did you tell anyone where you were going?"

Elodie shook her head. "No. When Human Resources insisted on a forwarding address, I made up a post office box number in Pittsburgh for my address and said I was going to go live with a friend in Paris."

"Good. I know this might be hard to believe, but I'm more than hired muscle. My team and I can look into this and see if anyone's on your trail."

Elodie reached out and gripped his arm tightly. "I don't want anyone else to get involved. The more people who know, the more leverage Paul will have against me."

"I can understand that," Mustang told her. And he could. But she didn't understand the kind of connections he had. She'd learn. "You're going to have to trust me to do what I think is best. And, El, I've been doing this secret SEAL shit for quite a while. I'm good at it."

She smiled slightly at that. "Okay."

"Okay? Okay...what?"

"Okay, you can do your super-secret SEAL spy shit. You can tell your team. I want to live my life without having to always look over my shoulder, and if the only way to do that is to let you do your thing, then okay. But...Scott?"

"Yeah?"

"I don't want to quit my job and hide out in your apartment all day. I need to *live*. If Paul is gonna find me and kill me, he's gonna find me and kill me. I don't want to regret not experiencing all there is to life in my last moments."

Listening to her talk about dying made Mustang even more determined to make sure that didn't happen. She wasn't dying, not on his watch. "All right, but at the same time, you can't just traipse all over the island as if you don't have a care in the world."

"I know."

Mustang's head spun with all the things he needed to do; talking to his team was on the top of that list. "How about this...I can take you to work and pick you up. I'm not sure it's the best idea to be using public transportation when you have no idea if anyone has figured out where you are. I can bring you back here, or to your place, but if you want to sightsee, I'm happy to take you. If you need to grocery shop, consider me your assistant. I just need you to be cautious until we figure this out."

"Deal," Elodie said quickly and without any reservation in her tone.

"Just like that?" Mustang asked suspiciously.

"Yeah, just like that," she agreed. "Scott, you basically just said that you'll take me where I want to go, when I want to go. You'll spend all your free time with me. Why would I argue against that?"

"Because you might feel stifled? Because you like your independence? Because I'm taking over?"

She chuckled wryly. "I've been alone for so long, I've almost forgotten what it feels like to have someone in my corner. I'm not saying I'm going to let you make all the decisions in my life for me, but I like being with you. I want to get to know everything about you. I'm more afraid of you getting tired of hauling my ass around than me getting tired of *you*. Oh! I hadn't thought about this...what about your job? You can't exactly be leaving in the middle of the day to pick me up all the time from the dock."

"If I can't, I'll have one of my teammates do it. If we're busy, or on a mission, there are a few other men on other SEAL teams here who I trust to do it. We'll figure it out. As long as I know you aren't opposed to a few restrictions and being cautious, I can relax a bit."

"You know what I want to do today?" she asked.

"What?"

"I want to go to the Dole Pineapple Plantation."

Mustang grimaced. "Really?"

"Yeah. I've heard their Dole Whips are amazing."

"I'm not doing that damn maze. Especially when someone might be after you. It seems as if it'd be the perfect place to take us *both* down," Mustang grumbled. He thought he might've gone too far, making light of the fact that the mob was after her, but she actually laughed.

"Right, I'm not a fan of mazes either. Thank you for believing me. And not locking me in your bathroom like a caveman."

"Don't think that didn't occur to me," Mustang warned. "Until we find out what the threat level is, I'm willing to be flexible, but if we find out that Columbus knows where you are, or that someone is here, I'll lock your ass down so fast your head will spin."

She continued to smile. "Okay."

"I mean it, Elodie. I'm not going to let you be TSTL."

She cocked her head. "What's that?"

"Too stupid to live. You know in the movies when the main character does something incredibly stupid to put him or her in the line of fire, to move the story along? That's not happening."

"Oh, like that insurance commercial where the teenagers are running from a serial killer and they're talking about where to hide and they're discussing their options. Like, hiding in the basement or something, and one of the girls says, 'Why don't we just get in the running car and leave?' and the guy asks if she's crazy and they decide to hide behind a wall of chainsaws instead."

Mustang just looked at her with a blank expression.

"Ha. Right, okay, you haven't seen that one, but believe me, it's making fun of those TSTL people you're talking about."

"I'll take your word for it. Now, were you serious about going to the pineapple plantation?"

"Yes."

"Then we need to get out of bed and get moving. Traffic's gonna be a bitch."

"You really don't mind taking me?" Elodie asked him.

"Nope. I'll do my best to show you whatever you want to see, and I've got some other out-of-the-way places I think you'll like as well. But I remember what you said earlier this morning, so I'll try to keep the hikes to the prettier waterfalls and views under ten miles."

Her eyes got huge, and Mustang struggled to keep a straight face.

"You're kidding, right?"

He lost it then, and burst out laughing.

She joined him and smacked his arm. "You're mean."

"Come on, lazy bones, I'll let you have the shower first."

"Lazy? Who was doing all the work not too long ago?" she asked suggestively.

And just like that, Mustang was hard again as he remembered how he'd taken her from behind, letting her fuck him... the way she'd rocked back and forth, taking him in and out of her body. "Elodie," he warned.

"I'm going," she said with a smirk. "I guess our showering together will have to wait too, huh?"

"If I get in that shower with you, we won't be going to the Dole Pineapple Plantation. Or anywhere else, for that matter," he threatened.

"Fine. I'm going," she said with a pout.

Mustang could tell she was teasing, and he loved it. He really *did* want to take her in his shower, but what she'd said earlier struck a chord in him. He wanted her to live her life. Not have any regrets when the end came. He was in a profession where that end could come sooner rather than later. Every mission he went on could be his last, and he wanted to experience as much as possible with this woman. Wanted to see her eyes light up as she tasted her first pineapple whip. To cook side by side with her, and experience a lot more sunsets on the beach.

She disappeared into the bathroom, then immediately stuck her head back out. "But we need to stop by my place so I can get some clothes."

"Of course," Mustang told her. "Might be a good idea for you to bring extras over here, just in case I get too excited and rip them off again later." He'd tried to be nonchalant, but obviously failed.

She stared at him for a long moment before she smiled. "I'll do that," she said softly, then disappeared again, still smiling.

Mustang flopped back on his sheets. He could smell their

combined scent on his bedding and knew he'd never take that for granted.

Elodie was here. With him. In his bed. In his heart. He was a lucky man, and he was going to do everything in his power to make sure no one took her from him. He wasn't perfect, was too intense, a bit too addicted to working out, and stubborn to boot, but he'd do whatever was necessary to make Elodie love him.

It might not be today. Or tomorrow. But hopefully someday, she'd realize he'd never let her down, that he'd always be there for her...and that he was head over heels in love with her.

CHAPTER THIRTEEN

"Did you find out what her deal is?" Slate asked Monday morning, when they'd all gathered around their usual conference table in the building where they worked on the Naval base.

Mustang had dropped Elodie at the dock and had re-met Kai, the young guy she worked with, and was also introduced to Perry, one of the owners of the boat. It had been weird to hear them calling her Melody, but he did his best to go with it. She'd never be Melody to him, now that he knew her real name. She'd always be his El.

After seeing her off, he'd gone to the base and had a long talk with his commander. He hadn't wanted to tell the older man everything, knowing he'd be told to let the police handle it, so he was vague about Elodie's issues, hinting that she had an ex who wasn't happy she was dating again, and was given permission to take his lunches a bit later in the afternoon so he could pick her up after she was done working for the day.

Now he was sitting with his team, ready to tell them Elodie's story. Mustang wasn't surprised Slate had been the first to bring it up. He would've laughed at the predictability of his team, but he didn't have it in him at the moment.

He'd been thinking about Elodie's situation, and the more he ruminated over what she'd said, the more it rankled. She'd done nothing wrong, just had the misfortune to accept a job with an unscrupulous man. She'd left at the first hint of trouble, and yet she wasn't out of the woods.

Did anyone escape the mob's wrath? Mustang knew next to nothing about the criminal underworld, but he had connections who would know plenty. Who'd be able to find out everything there was to know about this Paul Columbus guy—including his weaknesses.

Mustang was a SEAL. The trident he'd earned was a symbol of honor and heritage. He'd sworn to defend those who couldn't defend themselves, and his loyalty to his country and team would always be beyond reproach. He couldn't exactly go around killing people who did things he didn't approve of. He'd never stoop to that level. But if protecting and defending Elodie and his team meant someone died, so be it.

He had a feeling Paul Columbus would never get his own hands dirty. He'd send someone else to do his dirty work for him. So even if he dispatched someone who came after Elodie, there would always be someone else waiting in the wings to try to accomplish what the one before him had failed to do. Cutting off the head of the snake was the only true way to kill the enemy. That's how it was in war, and how it would be with the Columbus family.

Mustang had thought about the situation almost nonstop since Elodie had told him what happened. He'd smiled and laughed and enjoyed spending time with her at the pineapple plantation, but his mind never stopped mulling over her problem. Talking with his team would help make things clearer in his mind, Mustang knew that. But he also was aware that he'd be opening them up to whatever danger might lurk in the darkness, gunning for his woman.

And yes, Elodie was his. He wasn't going to fight it.

"Mustang?" Slate asked, interrupting his musings. "Are you gonna tell us or what?"

"Keep your pants on, Slate," Midas complained. "Give him a second to think."

Mustang smiled. He loved these guys. They were as close to brothers as he was going to get. He'd actually thought about keeping Elodie's story to himself, if only to protect these men. But if they knew he'd done that, they'd kick his ass for sure. They could take care of themselves without him playing protector. Besides, he needed their input. They always brainstormed before a mission and played devil's advocate with each other. They looked at all sides of an issue before deciding on a plan, and that's what he needed right now.

So he took a deep breath—and disclosed everything Elodie had told him the day before. About the Columbus family, about the poison, how Paul Columbus had threatened to kill her, how she'd been followed and about the restaurant in Pittsburgh being threatened, how her friend had been killed in a drive-by shooting, and finally, how she'd ended up on the *Asaka Express*.

He didn't leave anything out, and when he was done, the five men around him were silent for a long moment.

"The mob?" Pid finally said, breaking the silence. "The motherfucking *mob*? Jesus, Mustang."

"She's alive...that must mean she's doing something right," Slate deadpanned.

Mustang wanted to be pissed at his friend for being so blunt, but he was also correct. "That's kinda what I thought. It's been months since she left New York, and other than the people following her in Pittsburgh and Los Angeles, she hasn't seen anything out of the ordinary."

"You think the guy's given up?" Aleck asked.

Mustang sighed. "I'd like to, but no. And while she might not have any proof, the cops in New York would probably jump at the chance to have her testify against the man, if only to bolster some other shit they have on him."

"Yeah, the cops could use this as an excuse to look into him and his organization for *other* shit," Midas said. "But without evidence, there's nothing they can really do about Elodie's situation. It would be her word against his. And I'm sure Columbus would buy off his other employees to disparage Elodie, maybe say she's trying to blackmail him or something."

Mustang nodded. "And honestly? It seems as if this Paul guy might be a little insane. I mean, seriously...he wants to kill her because she told him no?"

"He could very well be mentally unstable," Pid agreed. "Could've taken her refusal personally. What do you want me to look up?" he asked.

Mustang knew he was talking about electronic searches. Pid might not be as good as the legendary Tex, but he was irreplaceable on their team. "I don't want to do anything that will ping on some mobster's radar," Mustang said.

Pid rolled his eyes. "As if I'd be that stupid."

"Right. Then I'm thinking we need intel on the Columbus family as a whole. Elodie said Paul's in charge, but who are his underbosses and does he have a consigliere?"

"What the hell's a consigliere?" Jag asked.

"Basically an advisor. Usually a trusted friend and confidant. He's the number three man in the hierarchy after the boss and underboss," Midas said.

Everyone turned to stare at him.

"What? I watch a lot of movies," Midas said in his defense.

"See if you can figure out who the capos are, the guys in charge of the soldiers. We need to know the family's usual MO. Are they into shit like sex trafficking and murder, or things like money laundering and blackmail? Basically, anything that will tell us what we can expect when it comes to them trying to find Elodie," Mustang said.

Slate leaned forward and rested his elbows on the table and pinned Mustang with a hard look. "What is it about this chick that has you so...invested? You spent a few hours with her two months ago, pined for her ever since, and it seems pretty obvious by the shit-eating grin on your face and your desperation to slay all her dragons that you slept with her this weekend. Does she have a magic pussy or something?"

Mustang clenched his teeth and wanted to punch his friend, but he didn't blame him—or any of the guys—for being skeptical. He opened his mouth to try to explain, but Midas jumped to Elodie's defense.

"That was unnecessarily crude, and you know it, Slate. But as someone who was there when we met Elodie, I'll tell you this...she's special. And I saw for myself the connection she and Mustang had."

"So since she saved your life, you decided she's 'the one'?" Slate asked. "I'm honestly not trying to be a dick here, I'm genuinely curious. She seemed nice enough when we met her, but we don't know her well enough to have much more of an opinion."

"No, that's not why. Although I can't deny I'm pretty damn grateful. She makes me feel...calm. Content. But excited at the same time. She has a positive attitude when life hasn't given her any reason for one. She's brave. And hard working. And she's blunt, like you, which I appreciate. She says what she's thinking and doesn't play games. She's got a big heart and worries about other people probably more than she should, and she's funny..."

Mustang trailed off when he saw all five of his friends smirking. "What?"

"We get it, she's the most amazing woman on the planet," Aleck said.

"So...she's it for you? After such a short time, you're sure?" Jag asked.

"I can't see into the future, but I sure as hell hope so," Mustang said without hesitation. "Here's the thing, I'm thirty-six. I've dated my share of women. And in my entire life, I've never felt the pull toward someone that I do with Elodie. I'm not saying we're running off to Vegas tomorrow, but yeah, I'm pretty sure she's it for me. It's a feeling deep down inside me that I can't explain. A...*rightness* that has no words."

The room was silent for a moment, as if everyone was digesting his words.

"I want you guys to get to know her. To decide for yourself. I want you to like her, of course, but I want you to like her for who she is, not because she's with me...if that makes sense," Mustang said quietly.

"You know it'll be hard for us to think anyone is good enough for you," Jag said seriously.

"We'd follow you into the depths of hell if you asked. Hell, even if you didn't ask," Pid added. "And any woman who's gonna be with you has to be pretty damn impressive."

"All I ask is that you give her a chance. Don't be a dick to her, she's been under a lot of stress," Mustang said, his voice a little harder.

"You should know us better than that," Aleck said. "We'd never be assholes to someone you're seriously dating. We might tell you later what we think, if we don't believe she's good enough for you or whatever, but we'd never make her feel like shit."

"I appreciate that. You're gonna like her. I have no doubt," Mustang said confidently. "She's damn likable. But just remember that I found her first."

Everyone laughed.

"So...look into the Columbus family, see if I can find

anything we can use against them if they do decide to show their faces here in paradise. Check. I can do that," Pid said.

"You gonna lock her down?" Midas asked.

Mustang shook his head. "No. I trust her instincts. They've kept her safe this far. She's agreed to let me take her to work and pick her up and not to use public transportation. She doesn't have email, a phone, a bank account or a car, so there's no worry they'll run her off the road or anything."

"But will they run *you* off the road if she's with you?" Slate asked.

"I guess maybe we'll find out," Mustang said, almost wishing they'd try. If he had the chance to have a one-on-one encounter with someone from the Columbus family who might be sent to kill Elodie, he'd make sure they knew she wasn't alone anymore and was well protected. He'd make it clear she was off limits, and it would be in their best interest to forget they knew her.

"So she's staying with you, then?" Aleck asked.

Mustang didn't hear any censure in his tone, and he answered honestly. "That's unclear as of yet. But hopefully, yes."

"The great and mighty Mustang hasn't gotten her to agree to move in with him after," Jag exaggeratingly checked his watch, "forty-eight hours of meeting up with her again?"

"Shut up," Mustang said, throwing his pen across the table at his friend.

"It would make things easier," Slate said—and everyone turned to stare at him incredulously.

"Weren't you the one who was questioning his immediate attraction to the woman?" Pid asked.

"Yeah. And he explained it. So now I'm onboard," Slate said matter-of-factly.

Mustang couldn't help but grin. These guys could be a pain in the ass, but they were loyal as hell, just as he was to them. They'd been through too much to be petty or assholes toward each other. They might disagree or play devil's advocate, as they were trained to do, but when push came to shove, they'd always have each other's backs.

"So we're playing this low-key and waiting to see if anything comes up?" Midas asked. "Should we be more proactive?"

"If we clue in the family that we're looking into them, it might tip them off about where she is," Pid said.

"But if we don't find enough information, they could sneak up on our six and ambush her," Slate said.

"So the question is, do we dig far enough that it might tip them off, or lay low, stay on our guard, and react if and when we need to?" Aleck added.

The room was silent for a moment as the men mulled over the decisions that had to be made.

"I think we see what Pid can come up with discreetly, and go from there. The last thing we want is to bring the wrath of the mob down on our heads," Mustang said. "Besides, our hands are somewhat tied in this anyway. Paul Columbus isn't going to be dumb enough to come here himself, and even if he did, we can't get away with murder."

"Exactly," Midas said, then lowered his voice. "But we know people who know people. We might not be able to act, but we know others who can. Including someone who lives here on the island."

Mustang nodded. He didn't want to call in favors, but he would for Elodie. She deserved to live a life free of fear. To be who she wanted to be and do what she wanted to do. If that was being a deckhand, fine, but if that meant opening up her own restaurant, with her name splashed across the front and all over the Internet, he'd do whatever it took to give that to her.

"I'll start seeing what I can find tonight," Pid said. "In the meantime...when do we get to hang out with you guys?"

Mustang smiled, grateful that the team wanted to get to

know Elodie. But at the same time, he was feeling a little self-ish. He wanted her to himself for a while.

"Maybe she can come work out with us one morning," Aleck suggested.

Mustang burst out laughing and shook his head. "Nope, she already informed me that she wasn't the working-out kind of woman."

"She could watch us?" Aleck tried again.

"She already gets up early for her job, and when she has the chance to sleep in, she takes it," Mustang told him.

"She's a cook, right? Maybe we can have a cookout and she could make the food," Pid suggested.

Slate reached out and smacked him on the back of the head. "We aren't going to make her cook for all of us the first time we meet her. Jeez, you're an idiot."

"It was just a suggestion!" Pid said. "No need to get violent."

"I'll figure something out," Mustang told his friends.

The door to the conference room opened and their commander stuck his head in. "You guys ready for a debrief on the situation in Benin?"

The men all got serious and nodded. Benin was a country in Africa, near the equator, that shared a border with Nigeria. They'd been watching internal factions fighting for a while now and it looked like the country was on the verge of a coup. If they were sent in, their job would be to rescue US and other foreign nationals who were caught in the fray. Everyone had been advised to vacate the country, but there were always a few people who denied what was happening right in front of them or who thought they'd be safe if they stayed.

The topic of Elodie was dropped, but Mustang felt better knowing his team was now aware of her situation. He was satisfied, for the moment, that she wasn't in imminent danger, but he was grateful that Pid would be looking into the

Columbus family. He'd be thrilled to find out Elodie had misread the situation and the family wasn't actually part of the mob. But he didn't doubt her fear was real. No one gave up their life like she had if there wasn't some truth to what was happening.

No, he was sure Elodie felt as if her life was in danger. The question was...how deep was the threat? He'd find out, and then he and his team would take care of it so Elodie could live the life she wanted...hopefully with Mustang by her side.

* * *

Scott was waiting for Elodie when the *Fish Tales* pulled into dock that afternoon. She'd been distracted most of the day, fluctuating between insanely happy and wondering what the hell she was doing. She wasn't the kind of person to dwell on the negative, but it seemed so much shit had piled on top of her over the last year, it was hard to see anything positive. Meeting Scott had been a light in her otherwise dark life.

The weekend had been amazing. She'd been afraid to tell Scott about Paul and what had happened in New York, but he hadn't freaked out. Hadn't told her to get the hell out or yelled at her for possibly bringing the mob straight to his doorstep. Not that she'd thought he'd do either of those things, but there was always the possibility.

Even better, he hadn't immediately tried to take over her life. He hadn't ordered her to quit her job and go into hiding. He hadn't insisted she go to the cops and tell them what happened. He'd listened and made suggestions—things she'd readily agreed to. She didn't think she'd ever met someone so tuned in to what she was feeling and thinking as Scott.

And then there was the sex. She couldn't deny she'd thought about how things would be between them, but the reality had been so much better than her fantasies. Scott was rough and a little aggressive, and she loved it. She felt like a completely different person when she was with him. Oh, there was more to a relationship than sex, but they were definitely starting out on the right foot as far as she was concerned.

"See you tomorrow, Melody!" Kai called out as she stepped off the boat and headed for Scott, who was standing at the end of the dock waiting for her. It was crazy how even a few days of her real name coming from Scott's lips made hearing Kai call her by a different name feel so wrong.

She waved at him and called out, "Aloha!" and continued toward Scott.

He was smiling by the time she got to him. "Hey, babe."

"Hey," she said, stepping into his personal space and tipping her head back. He obliged by bending and kissing her hard and deep, right there in front of all the tourists and locals milling about.

When he lifted his head after several moments, Elodie knew she had a ridiculous smile on her face.

"How was your day?" he asked, putting his arm around her shoulders and steering her toward his truck.

"Good. The clients each caught a marlin. They were thrilled."

"Glad to hear it."

"How's your day been?" she asked.

"About like normal," he said.

"Did you...did you talk to your team?"

He knew what she was referring to. "I did. And it's all good. I'll tell you about it tonight. You want me to take you to my place or yours?"

Elodie thought about it for a second, then said, "Mine, please."

She liked that he didn't complain or try to talk her into going to his place. He merely stood by as she climbed into his truck and shut the door behind her when she was settled.

The drive to the house where she was renting a room was done in silence, but Elodie felt a little better when Scott reached over and took her hand in his as he drove.

When he pulled up in front of the house, he cut off the engine and turned to her. She held her breath, because the serious look on his face made her extremely nervous.

"The guys wanted to know when they were going to get a chance to meet you. They had all sorts of ideas...like working out with us, or having a cookout—for which they volunteered you to cook all the food." He rolled his eyes and smirked. "I said no to both, by the way. I have no problem with them meeting you, but I'm not ready to share you yet. I hope that's okay. It's not that I'm trying to hide you or anything, I just...I'm feeling selfish and want to spend every second of my time off getting to know you, not playing host with my team."

Elodie's nervousness evaporated. "Okay."

"I know that's crazy, and I *do* want you to meet them. I think you'll get along great. It's *not* that I'm afraid you won't like them or vice versa."

She smiled. "I feel kinda selfish of your time myself, and I wouldn't mind learning more about you before I'm thrown to the wolves, so to speak."

Scott smiled. "Good. And I told them about your situation...and they're looking into it."

Elodie felt the blood drain from her face at the latter news.

"Don't panic," he ordered. "Pid's good at what he does. He's not going to do anything that will alert them to your whereabouts. He's discreet. We just need to know what we're dealing with here. How serious they are about finding you and how dangerous they really are. Trust us. Trust *me*," he said urgently.

Elodie reminded herself that she knew this would happen when she opened up to Scott. It wasn't even a question that he'd talk to his team about her, but she wasn't as sure about them poking into the situation. Eventually, she nodded.

"We got this," he said softly. "We'll figure this out and then put it behind us and live happily ever after. Okay?"

Elodie took a deep breath. "Okay."

"Unfortunately, I need to get back to base, we've got more meetings this afternoon."

"Is everything all right?" she asked. She had no idea what Scott normally did during the day, but important meetings couldn't be a good thing for a SEAL, could they?

"Everything's fine," he said without seeming stressed. "We've always got our eyes on what's going on in the world, and trying to keep up to date on the latest developments means we're always in meetings. You want me to pick you up when I'm done?"

Yes! Of course she wanted that. But she didn't want to seem too eager either. "If you're going to be tired at the end of the day, it's okay if you just want to go home."

Without warning, Scott leaned over and palmed the back of her head and pulled her into him. He kissed her hard, then, staying nose to nose, said, "I'll never be too tired to see you."

Butterflies took off in her belly. "Okay, then I'd love for you to pick me up. I'd offer to let you stay here, but the view from your apartment is much better. As is your kitchen. Can I cook for you tonight?"

"Yes, but only if you don't go out of your way."

"I won't," she promised, her mind already racing to think of what she might make for him.

"Do you need to go to the grocery store? We can stop by after I pick you up."

"No, I think I'm good," Elodie told him as she mentally reviewed what she had in her landlord's pantry.

"Okay. We need to talk about getting you a phone, but I'll call your land line when I'm on my way."

Elodie didn't want to argue over the cell. She didn't want

Scott to pay for a phone for her, as she knew they weren't cheap, and she still wasn't comfortable carrying anything on her person that could be traced. She had no idea if Paul or his family had the connections to digitally trace someone, but she had to assume so, and didn't want to take any chances.

"Right. I'm going to have a hard time winning that argument, aren't I?" Scott asked with a smile. "It's cool. I'll see you in a few hours. El?"

"Yeah?"

"This is gonna be fine. We're gonna work out, and Columbus isn't going to win, *we* are. All right?"

She nodded. What else could she do? She wanted to believe him, with all her heart she wanted him to be right.

He leaned in, kissed her forehead gently, then sat back. Elodie climbed out of the truck and waved as she headed down the gravel driveway toward the side entrance to her room. She needed to shower, change, then decide what she wanted to make for dinner.

It had been a long time since she'd been excited to cook. She had no idea if this was a one-time thing, and once she actually got back into the kitchen the spark would die, as it had so many other times recently. But it was one more thing she could be grateful to Scott for. He was already changing her life in so many ways, she was losing track. And she couldn't help but smile about that as she entered her apartment.

CHAPTER FOURTEEN

The last three weeks had been amazing. Stupendous. Better than Elodie could've ever imagined.

She'd kinda thought things between her and Scott would've gotten less intense as the weeks passed, as the newness of their relationship faded, but that hadn't been the case. She still got butterflies when she saw him after work, and they hadn't run out of things to talk about to each other.

Every day, she learned something new about Scott. How he absolutely hated spiders, but had no problem with picking up snakes. How he had a soft spot for the turtles on the island and even volunteered once a month to stand on Lani-akea Beach on the North Shore to protect the giant green turtles that frequently crawled up on the sand to sun themselves there. Without volunteers like himself, the tourists would get way too close to the turtles and most likely act stupid—like put their children on their backs for pictures and other nonsense. She'd gone with him one Sunday, and she'd happily spent three hours sitting in the shade, watching her man educate the tourists and protect the turtles.

He'd come on two charter fishing trips with her, as well. Both on the weekends. He'd been funny and charming, and both sets of tourists had left feeling as if they'd gotten their money's worth and happy with how attentive everyone had been. Kai loved Scott, and he'd asked a million questions about the Navy, including whether he ever regretted joining.

Kahoni had been on the boat both times when Scott had joined them, and he'd pulled her aside after the second trip and told her that she'd caught herself a good one, and advised her to not throw him back. The corny fishing analogy aside, she was relieved to know her boss approved of Scott.

She was even more relieved to find she loved cooking with him. He took directions well, and was so pleased when something he'd made turned out perfectly. Despite knowing she was a chef, he never insisted she cook for them. Many nights, he'd planted her on his couch and told her to relax as he took care of fixing them something to eat.

He was thoughtful and caring, and he had a very definite sense of right and wrong. They were watching the news one night—something Elodie hated doing, but tolerated because Scott needed to keep abreast of what was happening in the world—and a clip came on about a five-year-old kid who'd stolen his parents' car. He'd been stopped on the interstate going twenty miles an hour below the speed limit. Instead of getting in trouble, the kid was a momentary celebrity, everyone laughing and thinking his stunt was hilarious, even if incredulous.

When the newscaster said a big-time football star heard about what happened, that the kid was trying to drive to California to meet him, he'd flown to his house with a car full of free shirts and goodies. Scott had lost his shit, insisting it was ridiculous that the kid was being rewarded for doing something so wrong. He ranted and raved about how lucky he'd been that he hadn't killed anyone, that the parents should've grounded him for three years instead of allowing all the publicity and positive attention.

Elodie had agreed, but it illustrated how passionate Scott could be about what he believed to be right and wrong.

As the weeks passed, Elodie had also opened up to Scott. He knew she could get up early if she had to for her job, but she really wasn't a morning person. He'd learned the hard way that she cried at those sappy Hallmark Channel movies. He'd come home from work one day and found her bawling on his couch, and she'd had to work really hard to convince him that nothing was wrong, that she was safe, just crying because of a show on the TV.

She loved to people watch, and he'd spent a hilarious afternoon at the beach with her while she came up with elaborate stories about the tourists who walked by. He'd learned that she'd much rather save money and stay home than spend twenty bucks to see a movie in the theater (and forget about buying snacks; they were overpriced and such a rip-off).

And their physical connection was just as combustible as it had been that first explosive night together. They didn't have sex every day; sometimes neither of them felt like doing anything other than cuddling. There were nights when Scott was so worked up from his meetings about what was happening in the world that he needed to stay up late watching mindless movies or working out, while she fell asleep alone in his bed. But she always woke up in his arms, which made her feel cherished and blessed.

While they might've only been together for a few weeks, it felt more like months. They were completely in tune, aware of each other's feelings.

So when Scott came home from work on Friday night, she could tell immediately that something was going on.

"What's wrong?" she asked when he approached.

"How do you know something's wrong?" he asked, avoiding the question.

"Because I know you. You have this little line between

your eyes that gets deeper when you're stressing about something."

Amazingly, he chuckled. "If someone would've told me two months ago that I'd be here today, I wouldn't have believed them."

"If you were where?" Elodie asked, confused.

"Here. Standing in my apartment with my very serious girlfriend telling me she knew me well enough to know when I was thinking too hard about something, simply by taking one look at my face." He stepped toward her and almost yanked her into his arms.

Elodie bounced off his chest and looked up at him just as he took her face between his palms and kissed her. As usual, she gave herself to him. Letting her body relax as his tongue entered her mouth and explored. He wasn't aggressive, he took his time, and when he finally lifted his head, Elodie was turned way the hell on...and even more worried.

"Talk to me," she implored. "Did Pid find something new? Has Paul found me?"

"No," Scott said, immediately shaking his head. "Nothing like that."

"Then *what*?" she asked as she gripped his biceps hard. "You're freaking me out."

"We're being sent out on a mission next week," Scott said, then paused as if waiting for her reaction.

"And?" Elodie asked.

He blinked. "And what?"

"That's what you're stressed about? Why? Is it going to be dangerous?" She shook her head. "No, don't answer that, of course it is. You're a SEAL. But is it gonna be more dangerous than usual? Is that why you're all worked up?"

"I'm all worked up, as you call it, because this will be the first time I've been deployed since we've been together."

Elodie still didn't understand. "I'm sorry, I don't get it. I mean, I've known you were a SEAL since we first met. You've been working very hard over the last few weeks, and I know it's because you've been getting a lot of intel about something happening somewhere. It's not a surprise to me that you're going to be sent off to save the world...so what aren't you telling me?"

Scott seemed to relax right in front of her eyes. He sighed and his shoulders fell. She could feel the muscles in his arms get less tense as well. The little line between his eyes—a dead giveaway that he was anxious—got less prominent. "I was worried how you'd take me leaving," he admitted.

"Scott," Elodie said, completely exasperated now. "If you think I'm going to fall apart when you leave, I'm not. I mean, I'm gonna miss you terribly, and worry about you incessantly, but you're an adult, and you've been a SEAL for a long time. I'm in my mid-thirties, I think I can survive without you for a while. Wait...do you know how long you'll be gone? Are we talking days, weeks, months?"

He was grinning now, and Elodie found herself getting annoyed with him. It didn't happen a lot, and the feeling usually faded quickly, but he seemed to love to egg her on in situations like this.

"I don't know, but it won't be months," he said, still grinning. "You gonna stay here while I'm gone?"

Elodie blinked in surprise. "Um...no? This is *your* apartment."

"Yeah, and you've spent every night but three here since we got together," he retorted.

"You counted?"

"Hell yeah, I've counted," Scott told her. "The first time you said you wanted to go back to your place for the night, I slept like shit. I tossed and turned and wondered what I did or said to piss you off."

"You know it wasn't anything like that. I had cramps and didn't want to bother you with them," Elodie reminded him.

"I know. And I told you not to do that shit again. That I

don't give a crap about your period. I mean, I hate that you have bad cramps, but I'm not going to wig out about the fact that you have a period every month. It's kind of a part of life. And the second time was when Kalani fell and hurt herself. You didn't want to leave her, so you spent the night on her couch until her kids could get there from Maui. I completely understood, but I still missed holding you as I fell asleep."

Elodie stared at him in surprise. She couldn't believe he remembered every minute detail of the times she hadn't slept over at his apartment.

"And the third time was when you saw that news story about a fire at that restaurant in New York. I knew it made you start thinking about your own situation, and that you were running scared. I hated that you were running *from* me instead of *to* me when shit got real, but I let you do it because you're a grown-ass adult."

"And I called an Uber at one in the morning to bring me back to your place because I couldn't sleep and knew I'd been a dumbass," Elodie said softly.

"You *were* a dumbass," Scott agreed, but he smiled when he said it so she knew he was teasing. "I'd never been so mad at someone and so glad to see them at the same time."

"The woman driving the Uber was nice," Elodie defended.

"Not the point. You could've been taken advantage of, taken somewhere to be robbed and raped. And, might I remind you, you promised never to do that again."

"I know. And I won't," she told him.

"So back to my point, you are more than welcome to stay here. You're practically living here anyway, other than the few hours you spend at your place in the afternoons when I drop you off after your shift. Kai said it would be no problem to pick you up and drop you off here before and after your trips, and if he can't, I can arrange for a friend from the base to come get you."

"I could drive Ben. I mean, if you trusted me with your truck," Elodie suggested.

"I trust you with everything I have, but it's simply safer if you aren't alone. We talked about this."

They had. But Elodie hated to be a burden on anyone. Having Scott chauffeur her around wasn't weird anymore, but having someone else go out of their way seemed like such an imposition. "I haven't felt anyone following me since I've been here," she argued. "And you said yourself that your team hasn't found out anything that would make you think Paul knew where I was."

"I did, but that doesn't mean he won't suddenly find something while we're gone," Scott countered. He leaned down and rested his forehead on hers. "I just need you to be safe while I'm not here," he said quietly. "But if you really want to drive my truck, I won't say no."

And this right here was one of the many reasons why she'd fallen for this man. He wasn't overbearing and demanding. He had his say and ultimately left the decision about what to do up to her.

"Kai can pick me up and drop me off," she told him.

Scott straightened. "Thank you. And now, there's something else."

"Something else? What?" she asked.

"Sunday, you, me, and the guys are going to hike the Maunawili Falls Trail. I know what you said about hiking, but I think you'll have fun. It's not too strenuous, less than three miles round trip, and I've done this one several times. We'll leave early in the morning, before all the tourists get there. We'll get wet though. And muddy, so be prepared. Afterward, we'll head to Aleck's place. He lives in a condo with a huge pool and gazebos with grills."

Elodie waited until he was done, as it was obvious he was nervous and talking fast so she wouldn't interrupt him. "Sounds fun."

Scott stared at her for a second, as if trying to read her mind. "Are you just saying that, or do you mean it?"

"I mean it," Elodie told him.

He sighed in relief. "Good. The guys have run out of patience with me keeping you to myself. They said if I didn't plan something, they were going to hogtie me and kidnap you just so they could get to know you."

Elodie laughed, but then realized Scott wasn't joining in. "Wait, you're kidding, right?"

"Nope. Not at all."

She shook her head. "Well then, it's a good thing I said yes, huh?"

"Yup. I appreciate that, for my sake as well as yours. Because if they'd kidnapped you and scared you, I would've had to beat the shit out of them."

Elodie had a feeling he wasn't kidding about that either. "So you came up with the hiking plan?"

"Yeah. And figured Aleck could buy all the burgers and shit. His place really is amazing. We gave him crap about renting such an expensive place, until he told us he wasn't renting, that his family owned the condo. Apparently they're loaded, and when they found out he was going to be stationed here, they gave it to him and bought another for themselves, for when they visit the island."

"Wow," Elodie said.

"Yeah. You wouldn't know it by looking at him that his family's rich. I think he was on the team about six months before we even found out. I figured we might as well take advantage of the perks of the complex."

Elodie was looking forward to seeing Scott's friends and teammates again. There was no chance to get to know them aboard the *Asaka Express*. She couldn't help but hope they liked her.

"You have nothing to worry about," Scott said, as he took her hand in his and pulled her toward the kitchen. "With how much I've talked about you, they already like you. Come on, I'm hungry. I didn't eat lunch today because I was worried about telling you I was leaving. Now it feels as if my stomach is eating itself."

"Scott," she scolded. "You can't skip meals. It's not good for you."

"I know. What'd you want tonight?"

They went back and forth about their options and finally decided on sriracha shredded chicken tacos. They were quick and relatively healthy.

Since Elodie had to work in the morning, they headed to bed early, and after Scott had gotten her off twice, and had orgasmed once himself, they lay together, their arms and legs intertwined, replete and relaxed.

"Be safe next week," Elodie whispered into his shoulder.

"You know I will be. I've got an amazing woman to come home to now. There's no way I've found you, only to get taken out by some asshole now."

She smiled against him. "I'm gonna worry about you every second," she told him.

"Only appropriate, because I have a feeling I'm gonna be worried about how you're doing as well," he said.

Elodie lifted her head and frowned. "No, that's not allowed. You need to concentrate on what you're doing. I'm gonna be fine. You're the one who'll be in danger."

"Until we know exactly what's going on with Columbus, you don't know that."

"I'm going to go to work, be on the ocean all day, then come back here. I'm not going to be gallivanting all over the island. I'll be holed up in your apartment."

"Our."

"What?"

"*Our* apartment," Scott said easily.

Elodie smiled. She liked that. No, she freaking loved it.

"So if it's our apartment, you'll let me pay half the rent?"

"Not a chance," Scott told her.

Elodie hadn't really expected him to agree. That was just the kind of man he was. But she could easily find ways to contribute. The man ate a lot. She could order groceries to be delivered, just as she'd been doing at Kalani's. He didn't pay attention to what was in his fridge or pantry very much. And if he thought a grocery fairy was visiting and restocking, she didn't mind.

"You need to talk to Kalani about your lease," he told her. "There's no reason to pay rent when you're here all the time."

He was right, but Elodie wasn't quite ready to give up her room. She knew she'd be hard pressed to find anything as cheap and nice as what she had right now. It was only one room, but still. For just her, it was perfect. And she liked Kalani, and knew she could use the extra money as well. Besides, as much as she thought things between her and Scott were going well, if his friends decided she wasn't a good match for him, or if he changed his mind, she'd need somewhere to go. She made a noncommittal sound in the back of her throat.

He sighed under her. "I know, it's not fair of me to ask you to give up your place. But you and me are going to work out, El. It's okay if you keep it until you're sure."

That was the thing, she *was* sure, but it seemed like a huge step to give up her place. She was practically living with him already, as he'd pointed out, but still. "Thanks," she said after a beat.

Scott hugged her, and she traced his tattoos on his opposite shoulder and upper chest. They looked kind of like the designs on the Indian pottery she'd seen from the American southwest. He'd admitted that he'd gotten them right after he'd joined the Navy, when everyone else was getting inked. He didn't regret the design, but they also didn't have any deeper meaning.

"I think I've been more content this last month than I've

ever been," Scott said quietly. "I know things won't always be so hunky-dory between us, but now that I've seen how well we mesh, I'm gonna try even harder to not be a dick and ruin what we've got."

Elodie felt like a pile of mush. "I don't think you could be a dick if you tried."

"Oh, yeah, I can, but I'll do my best to control it around you."

She chuckled. "I feel the same. I never really cared much about having a boyfriend. I was happy with my own company and always so busy. But I feel as if you're my best friend, as well as my boyfriend. It's nice to have someone to talk to, who you know won't judge you or think badly about you."

"Well, there was that time when you said you actually like pineapple on pizza," Scott quipped.

She smacked his stomach, and he let out an exaggerated *oof*. He caught her hand in his and brought it up to his mouth and kissed her palm, before wrapping his fingers around hers and resting their joined hands on his belly. "We're gonna live happily ever after. I know it," he declared.

Elodie was too satisfied, too happy, to even try to be rational about their relationship. Nothing about it had been normal, but she was all right with that.

"Go to sleep, babe. I'll make sure you're up in time to eat a good breakfast before we have to leave for the harbor."

That wasn't anything new, he'd been fixing her healthy breakfasts since the first time she'd spent the night at his apartment. "Are you running in the morning?"

"Not tomorrow. We're taking it easy on PT since we're heading out on a mission next week."

Elodie hated being reminded that he was leaving, but she tried not to let it get her down. It was a part of who he was, as she'd known all along. "'Kay," she said sleepily.

Scott tightened his arm around her, and she felt him kiss the top of her head.

The light from the bathroom shone into the room, and it reminded her of one more reason why she'd fallen so hard for this man. He knew about her demons and did whatever he could to help banish them, even if that meant sleeping with the light on.

The words "I love you" were on the tip of her tongue, but she held them back. Now didn't seem the time to share those feelings. Instead, she turned her head, kissed the warm skin of his chest, and settled her cheek against him contentedly.

Her life may not have gone the way she'd thought it would, but she didn't regret one damn thing, since everything had led her to this moment right here and now.

CHAPTER FIFTEEN

Elodie eyed the beginning of the trail with surprise. She and Scott had left his place early, and there hadn't been any traffic as they'd cut up the middle of Oahu to get to the neighborhood where the trailhead for Maunawili Falls was located.

"This is really different than back in the States, huh?" Elodie said as she took in the nearby homes. She wondered if the residents got annoyed with all the people parking on their street to go hiking.

"Yeah, and it's a shame that some people have no respect," Scott said as he bent to pick up a plastic bag full of trash someone had dumped on the street. She helped him pick up a few more pieces of trash and they put them in the back of his truck.

They heard a vehicle approaching and turned to see Aleck's bright yellow Jeep pull up. He and Midas and Jag all hopped out after he'd parked behind Scott's truck.

"Hey." Scott greeted his friends with a manly chin lift.

"So she's *not* a figment of your imagination," Jag told Scott.

"Ha. Very funny. Elodie, in case you don't remember

everyone's names, this is Jag. The big yellow monstrosity belongs to Aleck, and of course you remember Midas."

Elodie had remembered who everyone was because Scott talked about them constantly. She smiled shyly and gave them a lame wave. She didn't want to shake their hands, that would just be weird, and hugging was out since she'd barely met them.

She was spared any awkwardness as another car drove up then, and Slate and Pid got out. More introductions were given, and soon they were ready to head out. Elodie had worn a pair of board shorts and a cheap pair of sneakers she'd picked up at another ABC Store. Scott had warned her that this trail got very muddy, so she hadn't wanted to ruin her only other pair of nice shoes. She had on a swimsuit under her T-shirt and shorts because, again, Scott had told her about the swimming hole at the end of the hike below the waterfalls. He'd also told her how fun it was to jump from the waterfall into the water, but she wasn't so sure about doing that.

They'd packed some snacks, drinks, as well as towels and a change of clothes. Scott insisted on bringing a first-aid kit as well. She supposed she'd have to get used to the man always being prepared for anything.

"Ready?" Midas asked the group.

Everyone agreed, and Elodie hung back to take up the rear—but none of the guys moved. They just stared at her. "What?" she asked without thinking.

"Go ahead, you can fall in behind Midas," Aleck told her.

"I'll just go last. I don't want to hold you guys up," she said.

Every single one of the men smiled at that. Elodie had no idea what was so funny, but Scott quickly explained.

"You aren't going to hold us up. We're going to take this at your pace, babe. And for the record, this isn't a workout. We aren't planning on force marching you to and from the waterfalls. If you see something along the way that you want to stop and look at, we'll stop. If you need to rest, we'll stop. And no way in *hell* would we ever expose your six by having you go last. You'll stay between us so if anything happens, you slip or a large grizzly bear appears out of nowhere, we can fight it off like the big bad Navy SEALs we are."

Elodie rolled her eyes. "There aren't any bears in Hawaii," she said with a laugh.

"That you know of," Pid retorted. "Maybe one escaped the zoo."

"Fine," she said with a shake of her head. "I'll walk between you guys, but if I go too slow, just tell me."

"Yeah, sure, we'll do that," Scott told her.

Elodie felt a little bad at first that she was the only one without a pack on her shoulders, but quickly decided she was glad after they'd started. The trail wasn't difficult. It seemed to be following a river, but like Scott said, it was very muddy. It was hard to keep her footing and after slipping a few times, she had mud caked all the way up to her thighs.

She would've been embarrassed about the fact she kept losing her balance, but the other guys were stumbling just as much. When Midas, who was walking in front of her, went to step over a rock and his feet went flying out from under him, she couldn't help but laugh. He'd looked hilarious sitting in the mud in the middle of the trail. Luckily, he wasn't hurt and laughed right along with her.

After that, they began to talk as they walked, and she was enjoying getting to know him a little better.

"You're doing okay after what happened on the cargo ship?" he asked.

"Surprisingly, yeah. I still think about Captain Conger sometimes and feel bad though," Elodie said.

"If it makes you feel any better, after reading the report, it was obvious he did everything right. He hadn't made any stupid decisions that made the *Asaka Express* vulnerable to attack. It seemed as if you guys were just in the wrong place at the wrong time."

"You read the report?" Elodie asked in surprise.

"Yeah, we all did. Why?"

"I just..." She shrugged. "I guess I thought doing that sort of mission was kinda routine for you guys. And reading the official reports of what happened on every mission you go on would get old." She didn't really know anything about how SEAL teams operated or what their standard procedures were, but it seemed odd to her that they'd go out of their way to revisit a mission once it was over.

"Well, it's always good to evaluate what we did while on a mission so if we made mistakes, we don't repeat them next time. Besides...you made quite the impression on us, which made us all even more curious as to the circumstances of how the cargo ship got hijacked in the first place. We were kinda looking for someone to blame, and realized there wasn't anyone, really. It was just shitty timing."

Elodie's respect for Scott's team went up a notch. She knew they were well trained and elite special forces soldiers, but she honestly hadn't realized how much they did both before and after their missions. "What's your story?" she asked. "I mean, shouldn't you be a professional basketball player or something?"

Midas laughed. "Because I'm tall? I had no interest in playing ball. I was a swimmer. I spent every summer in our neighborhood pool, from the time it opened until dinnertime. I think my dad would've liked me to be interested in a more manly sport than swimming, but there was this girl..." His voice trailed off, and he turned and winked at Elodie. "She was two years older than me, and when I realized she was on the swim team, and I could hang out with her at meets and practice—and see her in a swimsuit while I was at it—I was all in."

"Were you any good?" Elodie asked.

"I was okay," Midas said.

"He's full of shit," Aleck said from behind her. "He got his nickname because his senior year, he won all three of his individual events at State and was on three winning relays. He had so many gold medals, everyone started calling him Midas."

"Wow, that's kinda impressive," Elodie told him. "Did you end up dating that girl?"

Midas grinned. "Nope. Turns out she was into women, but I did find several other girls who thought it was cool to date a swimming stud."

Elodie laughed. "Right. And I'm sure checking you out in your Speedo had nothing to do with that." For a second, she was aghast at what she'd just blurted, but when all of the guys burst out laughing, she relaxed.

"I plead the Fifth on that one," Midas said.

"Ask him what his specialty stroke was," Pid called from behind them.

Amazingly, Elodie saw a flush of pink steal over Midas's cheeks. "Oh my God, you were a breaststroker, weren't you?"

The guys behind her were laughing so hard now, she wasn't sure how they were all staying upright on the muddy trail.

Midas shrugged. "I was a sprinter too," he said, as if that would make her forget his teammates' ribbing.

Having pity on him and deciding not to tease him, she asked, "Does it come in handy to be a state champion when you're a SEAL?" she asked.

"Yes and no. When we have water ops, we aren't exactly sprinting through the water. We're trying to be stealthy or we're swimming underwater."

That made sense. The group came up to a place in the trail where they had to cross the river. There were rocks strategically placed in the rushing water, but Midas didn't bother attempting to use them. He waded through the water without hesitation.

"Here, grab my arm," Aleck said as he came up next to her. Looking back, Elodie saw Scott was bringing up the rear of their little group. She didn't mind that he wasn't right at her side, she knew without having to think about it if things got awkward or it looked like she was uncomfortable, he'd come up to hike with her, but she appreciated him giving her space to get to know his team.

Grabbing Aleck's arm, she did what Midas had done and tromped through the chilly water without trying to keep her feet dry. They were already soaked, and it actually felt good to wash off some of the sticky mud that was stubbornly clinging to her sneakers.

They continued on the trail, and now Elodie found herself walking behind Aleck. "So, you have a fancy condo, huh?" she asked.

Without seeming to be embarrassed about it, Aleck nodded. "Yeah, it's sweet. It's got three bedrooms, a huge kitchen, and the balcony is to die for. It overlooks the court-yard, not the pool—which, trust me, is a big deal. The last thing you want to hear is screeching kids day and night when you're trying to relax after a long day or mission."

"What do your parents do? Am I allowed to ask that?"

"You can ask whatever you want. They're in real estate. They started out renting their own house a long time ago, when they moved after they got married and couldn't sell it. Things kind of went from there, and now they own way too many properties for me to even remember."

"I don't think I'd want to rent out anything I owned," Elodie said. "I mean, I've seen and read too many horror stories about renters to want to risk it."

"Right? I feel the same way, much to my parents' chagrin. I know they were hoping I'd follow in their footsteps, but when I joined the Navy, I think they realized I was a lost cause. But I have to say, I'm thankful every time I fall asleep with my patio door open at night, listening to the sound of the ocean waves, that they're as successful as they are."

"You aren't afraid to sleep with your door open? I mean, aren't you worried someone will come in?"

Aleck chuckled. "If someone manages to climb up to the fortieth floor of the complex to rob or kill me while I'm asleep, more power to them."

"Wow, the fortieth floor?"

"He lives on the penthouse floor," Pid said from behind her.

Elodie's eyes got wide. "Seriously?"

"Yup. When he says his parents have been successful, he's not kidding," Midas said from in front of them.

"Successful?" Aleck said with a snort. "They're fucking loaded. Oh, sorry for swearing."

Elodie waved off his apology. "I never would've guessed. I mean, you're..." Her voice trailed off before she said something to offend Scott's teammate.

Aleck chuckled. "I don't seem spoiled? I'm not. My parents made sure I knew how lucky I was when I was growing up. We volunteered a lot at our church, helping others less fortunate than us. My parents worked their asses off to get where they are. I'm glad they don't have to worry about retirement or anything like that. They've earned everything they have."

"And he's working on paying them for his condo," Pid threw in. "Just in case you were thinking he's a rich kid living off his parents' money."

"They're being stubborn about it," Aleck added. "Every time I transfer money to them, they put the exact amount in the retirement account they started for me when I was a kid. It's annoying."

"Oh, yeah, poor baby. So annoying," Elodie teased.

"Hey, watch it," Aleck retorted.

Elodie thought he was teasing her right back, so she rolled her eyes. But a second later, she tripped over a tree root growing across the trail and went flying forward. She careened into Aleck's back, knocking him over. Just before she fell in a heap on top of him, Pid grabbed her waist from behind.

For a second, Elodie had no idea what happened—then she struggled hard not to laugh at poor Aleck. He'd landed face first in a thick patch of mud in the trail, and when he stood, he was literally covered from head to toe in the thick dark brown muck.

"I-I'm sorry," she stuttered. "I thought you were responding to my snarky comment. I didn't know you were actually trying to warn me about the trail! But...oh my God... you look hilarious."

Everyone was laughing now, so Elodie didn't feel too bad about laughing with them.

Then, before she could even react, Aleck lunged forward and wrapped his arms around her, pulling her into a bear hug.

"Ack! Gross! No!" she screeched as she squirmed and tried to get out of his hold. When he finally let her go, Elodie looked down and saw that he'd managed to transfer quite a bit of the mud to *her*.

"There. Now we're even," Aleck said with a grin. His teeth looked very white in his mud-smeared face and he seemed awful proud of himself.

Elodie turned to look at the rest of the guys, and saw that Scott was laughing just as hard as the others. She tried to keep a straight face, to feign upset, but she couldn't do it. She started giggling, and soon she couldn't stop. The seven of them probably looked like lunatics, standing in the middle of the trail, laughing their heads off, but she didn't care.

She'd needed this.

These men were so down-to-earth. She should've known

they'd be amazing people with the way Scott talked about them.

"Come on," Aleck said, holding out his hand. "Truce?"

She immediately took it. She liked Scott's friends. They treated her as if she were their little sister, even though she knew she was older than most of them.

Aleck held her hand and helped her through the thick mud he'd fallen into, releasing it when they were on the other side, then they continued with the hike. She laughed and joked with Midas, Aleck, and Pid as they continued toward the waterfall. She was having a great time getting to know the three men. Jag, Slate, and Scott brought up the rear, talking quietly amongst themselves.

It didn't take as long as she'd thought it might to get to the end of the trail and to Maunawili Falls. There had been some beautiful views of the surrounding mountains as they'd walked, and Aleck had pointed out Kailua in the distance, but Elodie hadn't seen anything as beautiful as this waterfall in a long time.

She felt an arm go around her waist as she stood at the edge of the swimming hole at the base of the falls, simply staring.

"Pretty, huh," Scott asked.

"It's beautiful," she breathed.

"Come on, around that way is a good place to set our stuff down so we can go for a swim."

She followed the rest of his friends, who'd obviously done this many times before. They set their packs down and Aleck was the first one to climb the path leading up to the top of the waterfall.

"Is he really going to jump?" she asked.

"Oh, yeah," Scott said. "We all are."

Elodie shook her head. "*You* all are, maybe."

"It's fun," Scott insisted.

"It's initiation," Pid told her. "You have to do it."

"We aren't in high school, and peer pressure doesn't work on me," she told Pid.

"Come on, you're missing out," Midas cajoled.

"Nope, not happening. It might not be the ocean, but there are still critters in there. Probably," Elodie told them.

To his credit, Scott stayed with her as they watched the other guys climb to the top of the water—the very top—and leap off with loud banshee yells.

Elodie smiled as she watched their antics. They were like little kids, having the time of their lives.

"Having fun?" Scott asked. He was standing behind her now, with his arms around her waist and his chin resting on her shoulder.

Elodie nodded.

"The guys aren't being annoying, are they?"

"Not at all."

"Good, I warned them to all be on their best behavior."

Elodie shook her head. "You didn't have to do that," she said.

"Uh, yeah I did. Otherwise they'd have been telling you embarrassing stories about me."

Elodie turned in his arms. "Yeah?" she asked, raising one eyebrow. "Maybe I want to hear these stories."

"No, you don't," Scott told her. "Are you sure you don't want to jump?"

"Very sure. But you go on. I know you want to."

She realized exactly how much he'd been dying to do just that when he absently kissed her, then raced up the trail toward the top of the waterfall.

Elodie sat down on a rock and watched as her boyfriend and his team reverted to being teenagers once again, having the time of their lives as they climbed up to the top tier of the waterfall and jumped into the cold water over and over again.

At one point, Pid came up and sat next to her. He pulled

his pack over and produced two bottles of water, handing one to her. They drank in silence for a while until Pid said, "You did the right thing."

Confused, Elodie looked over at him. "Pardon?"

"You did the right thing," he repeated. "I'm sure Mustang has told you, but I'm the electronics expert on the team, and I've been looking into the Columbus family. You were smart to get out when you did."

Elodie wasn't sure she wanted to think about her past right now, not when she was so relaxed and having fun, but she was also curious as to what Pid might have learned. "Thanks," she said.

"There's been a lot of internal unrest in the Columbus family over the last few decades. Lots of people wanting power and killing their own family members to get it. Drug trafficking, extortion, and loansharking are their main methods of making money. Not to mention murder. That seems to be their go-to way of dealing with people they don't like, or who don't do what they want. If you'd have used that poison to take out whoever Paul Columbus was mad at that night, you'd have ended up right where they wanted you. They would've blackmailed you to continue doing what you were doing, and if you refused, I'm sure you would've ended up just like all the other people who they couldn't control."

Elodie shivered and brought her knees up to her chest and wrapped her arms around them. "I might've done the right thing, but why does the right thing have to be so hard...and scary?"

Pid leaned over and nudged her with his shoulder affectionately. "The only easy day was yesterday."

She looked at him in confusion. "What?"

"It's a SEAL motto. It means that every day you'll need to work harder than the last. But when you work hard every day, and see what you've accomplished and what you're now capable of, yesterday seems easy."

"I'm not sure that's all that comforting," she told him with a small snort.

Pid wrinkled his nose. "Okay, yeah, when I think about it from your point of view and situation, maybe it wasn't the best motivational quote to use."

It wasn't, but Elodie felt better anyway. This man was trying to help her. He didn't know her, didn't have any loyalty to her, and yet, he was helping anyway. She put her hand on his arm. "Thanks, Pid."

"For what?"

"For trying to help me."

"Here's the thing," Pid said. "You're with Mustang, and he's one of the best men I've ever met in my life. He's saved my life too many times to count. I'd do anything for him. Being with you makes him happier than I've ever seen him, and I want that to continue. We were already impressed with your actions back on that cargo ship, so helping you isn't a hardship. Threaten one of us, you threaten all of us. That's the way it's always been and how it will always be."

Elodie loved that Scott had the kind of bond and friend-ship as he did with these men. She didn't care if they were helping her only because she was with Scott.

"Aren't you uncomfortable with all that mud on you?" Aleck asked from behind them.

Elodie startled so badly, she would've fallen off the rock she was sitting on if Pid hadn't grabbed her arm. She looked behind her and saw water dripping off Aleck's hair. He'd taken off his shirt, and she couldn't help but admire his physique. She wasn't attracted to him sexually, but she could appreciate a well-built man when she saw one.

"I'm okay."

"You don't have to jump, but I'm gonna feel guilty if you walk all the way back to the cars all muddy like that. The water's chilly but it's refreshing. Please?"

Elodie sighed. How could she refuse? And Aleck was

right, she was sticky and the mud was starting to itch on her legs. "Okay, but if an anaconda drags me under, I expect all of you to come and save me."

"Deal!" Aleck exclaimed happily. "Come on."

She once again took his hand and let him lead her to the edge of the swimming hole. He immediately plunged into the water, while Elodie bent down to take off her shoes.

"Leave 'em on," Jag told her.

Elodie looked up. Jag hadn't said much thus far, and not just to her, but anyone. She didn't think he was being rude, so much as it was just his personality. He was the silent but deadly type. At least that was the impression she got. He was also the shortest of the men on the team, but still taller than her by a few inches.

"There are some sharp rocks at the bottom, and it'll be easier to walk with them on. Not to mention it'll clean them off," Jag said.

Elodie nodded and decided to wade in with her shorts and shirt on. Yeah, she wore her suit underneath, but she'd wash off the mud first, then take off her clothes. She was very thankful at that moment that Scott had insisted on throwing in an extra set of clothes for them both in his pack. She'd thought he was being overly prepared at the time, but he'd obviously known what he was doing.

She waded in cautiously—then shrieked with laughter when Scott came up behind her and hauled her up into his arms. He strode into the water, holding her above it.

"Don't drop me!" she yelled, latching her arms around his neck.

He smirked at her.

"I mean it," she threatened, but she didn't think she sounded very adamant.

He walked out into the water until she could feel it lapping against her ass. She tried to arch her back to get away from the cold, with no luck.

"Hang on," Scott told her.

She wasn't about to let go of him, and Elodie closed her eyes in anticipation of him dropping her—but instead, he kept hold of her and plunged them both down into the water.

It was freezing. The guys kept saying it was "chilly" but they'd totally lied.

After dunking them both, Scott immediately stood back up, and Elodie gasped in air. "Holy crap, it's like ice!" she told him.

He laughed. "It's not so bad."

"Right, I forgot, you're a big bad Navy SEAL and impervious to cold."

He backed up closer to the shore, then lowered himself again, sitting on a big rock in the water. When he settled, the water came up to around the middle of his chest. "You'll get used to it in a second." Then he propped her ass on his knees under the water...and used a hand to inch his way up her body. He caressed her thigh, then her stomach, then her chest.

Elodie's eyes widened as his touch turned intimate.

"Scott?"

"Just cleaning the mud off," he said with a gleam in his eye.

Elodie looked around nervously.

"No one's watching," he said. "And I'd never do anything inappropriate in front of my friends, or anyone else, that would embarrass you."

She had to admit that, thanks to his touch and being immersed in the water, she was warming up. Elodie relaxed, trusting Scott to hold her up in the water. "Thanks suggesting this today. I'm having a good time, and it's nice to get to know your friends."

"They like you," Scott said.

Elodie shrugged. "I mean, it'll take longer for us to really get to know each other, but it's obvious you're all close. I feel honored to have been invited into the inner circle, at least a little bit, if that makes sense."

"It does. You feeling more comfortable now?"

"With them?"

"With them, and in the water now."

"Yes to both."

"Good." He stood up, letting her legs fall, and Elodie realized the water wasn't actually all that deep. She stood, and the water came to just below her breasts. Scott pulled her close and she snuggled against him. He'd taken his shirt off too, and she loved how the sun glinted off his tan skin and his tattoo. His beard dripped, and once more, she realized exactly how good-looking her man was. She went up on her tiptoes, and he immediately lowered his head. The kiss was intimate and deep, but they kept it short.

Voices sounded in the direction of the trail and when Elodie turned to look, she saw they were no longer alone.

"And here they come," Scott murmured.

She was disappointed, but understood that this was public property. Tourists were just as welcome to use the area as they were.

"Come on, man! Come take a few more jumps before this place gets overrun!" Midas called out.

"Go," Elodie told him when he hesitated.

"You sure?"

"Of course. I'm good."

Scott gave her a boyish grin, then kissed her once more, hard and fast, before turning and heading for shore.

Elodie dunked herself, slicking back her hair, before doing her best to get the rest of the mud washed out of her shirt and shorts. Then she headed back up to where they'd left their stuff and stripped out of her clothes. She felt a little shy, and was relieved Scott and his team were otherwise occupied. She noticed they had no problem stripping down to their shorts to play in the water, but even with Scott's praise and worship of her body when they were in bed each night, she wasn't exactly comfortable flaunting herself around the very obviously in-shape SEAL team.

She sat on the rock near their packs once more and basked in the sun as the men played. They began a splashing war with a few teenagers who'd arrived, then showed them how to get to the two different jumping platforms above the waterfall. By the time the area around the waterfall and swimming hole got too crowded, they were all ready to head back.

Elodie put on the extra set of clothes Scott had packed and they all started down the trail. This time, Slate was leading the group. Everyone made fun of him for being impatient. Now that their fun time was up, all he wanted to do was get back to the vehicles. Elodie couldn't really blame him though. Walking in wet shoes and socks, as well as a damp bathing suit, wasn't exactly comfortable.

She stared at Slate's wide shoulders as they walked, dividing her attention between them and the trail at her feet. The large man surprised her when he turned and said, "Let me know if I go too fast for you to keep up."

"I will. Thanks."

"You hanging in there?" he asked.

Elodie was even more surprised he was initiating conversation. He and Jag had been fairly quiet all day. "Yeah, I am. I wasn't sure about this hike at first, but it's been great."

"I meant with everything else."

"Oh, I guess so. I don't really have a choice."

"You always have a choice," Slate said. "No matter what happens in life, you always have a choice. You might make the wrong one, but the choice is there."

Elodie wondered what kind of wrong choices he, or maybe someone he was close to, had made in the past. Because it certainly sounded as if he was talking from experience and not in general.

"You're right. I chose to take that job in New York

without looking too hard into it. I should've known it was too good to be true, but I was blinded by the need to get out of the restaurant business and by the salary."

Slate grunted. It wasn't exactly encouragement to keep talking, but she did so anyway. She kept her voice low so only Slate, and probably Jag, who was walking behind her, could hear. "And I chose to take the job on that cargo ship, thinking it would get me as far away from New York as possible, and bad things still happened. And now I'm here. I don't know if my choice to come to Hawaii will end up backfiring, and if I'll bring danger straight to Scott's door, but you have to believe me when I tell you that I'll do *everything* in my power to prevent that."

"Even leave?" Jag asked.

Yup, she was right. He could hear her. She turned to look at him, nodding. "Yes."

Jag nodded back, as if she'd said what he wanted to hear.

"That's not gonna be necessary," Slate said, and Elodie turned to face forward again. "If anyone from that family manages to track you down and threatens you, we'll take care of it."

"Why?" Elodie asked. "I'm a stranger to you. I'm possibly putting your friend in danger."

"Because we don't like bullies," Jag said. "We've spent our entire military careers fighting against assholes who prey on others."

"And," Slate added, "we like you."

Elodie blinked. He liked her? He hadn't said more than a few words to her all day, except for the last few minutes. But his assurance meant the world to her. She could understand them helping her because of Scott, had even expected that. Pid had said as much earlier. But to hear Slate say that he liked her? She felt as if she'd somehow managed to win the lottery. She didn't think Slate openly admitted to liking many people.

"And for the record, I'll gut anyone who lays a hand on you," Jag added.

Elodie shivered. Yeah, he was definitely the silent but deadly type. She made a mental note to never get on his bad side.

"Thanks, you guys," she said. "I appreciate that more than I can say. But honestly, I'm more worried about Scott than me at this point. He doesn't deserve for any of my shit to come down on him. Don't let him do anything that might get him in trouble with the Navy, all right? He lives and breathes serving his country, and if something happened because of me, and he couldn't be a SEAL anymore, it would destroy us both."

"We've got his back. And yours," Slate told her.

"Jeez, you guys in a hurry for some reason?" Aleck called out from behind them.

Elodie realized for the first time that they'd begun to walk much faster as they were talking. Maybe it was a subconscious attempt to make sure Scott didn't overhear.

Without thought, she turned and yelled, "What? Can't keep up, Aleck? Wuss!"

Everyone laughed, and it felt good to be joking around with these guys. Aleck and the others jogged to catch up with them and a good-natured shoving match occurred between the guys, who were all trying to take over the lead. Elodie stepped out of the way and watched with a huge smile on her face. She turned to Scott, who'd come up next to her. "You aren't joining in?"

"Hell no," he said. "I only brought one change of clothes, and the last thing I want to do is drive to Aleck's condo covered in mud."

The guys quickly got themselves sorted out and they were once more walking toward their vehicles. They passed groups of hikers every couple minutes, and Elodie was glad they'd gotten up early to beat the crowds. Her stomach growled, and she realized it was close to noon.

Without her having to ask, Scott dug out a granola bar and handed it to her.

Smiling, Elodie sighed in contentment. She was truly happy. Her life wasn't perfect, she still had a pretty damn big cloud hanging over her head, but right now? Walking in the mud with these six men and being treated as one of the team? She was content.

CHAPTER SIXTEEN

Mustang stood under the gazebo and watched as Elodie stood with Jag at the grill and helped cook their burgers. She'd done exceptionally well that morning, and he'd been relieved she seemed to have a good time. He'd taken a risk with the hike, but had chosen a relatively short and non-strenuous one, and he'd loved seeing the way she laughed and talked with the guys.

"She's good people," Midas said as he stood next to Mustang, drinking a bottle of water.

She was. Definitely. "You think she'll be all right when we head out next week?" Mustang asked.

"Yes," Midas said without hesitation.

His immediate response made Mustang relax a fraction.

"Pid's been monitoring Paul Columbus and all his capos and everyone is where they should be. In New York."

"That doesn't mean they can't call in a hit man or send a soldier to do their dirty work," Mustang said. It was something they'd talked about in the past, and it had bothered him ever since.

"True. But at the moment, Paul is floundering as the head of the family. Sounds like he's got his hands full with Jerry

Columbus trying to take over. I'm not saying he's given up, because a man like that never forgets someone who betrays him. He's also not going to want to admit that he let Elodie escape his grasp; it'll make him look weak. But I'm thinking at the moment, her whereabouts are still a mystery to him."

"Elodie didn't betray him," Mustang said harshly.

"I didn't mean it that way. I know she didn't, but that's not how he'll look at it. She was an employee of the Columbus family, and they're expected to always obey whatever the boss says. And she directly defied him by refusing to poison that food. He's not going to want to let that go."

Mustang nodded and took a deep breath. "Right. I know."

"Good. Do we have any estimation on how long we'll be gone for this mission?"

"A week. Maybe ten to twelve days."

"She's gonna be okay, Mustang," Midas said. "She's smart, doesn't take chances, and was able to get away from him on her own for months."

Mustang nodded again. His friend was right. Elodie wasn't stupid. She was extremely cautious, and she was doing everything possible to stay under the radar. He hated having to call her "Melody" when they were in public, but he understood why it was necessary. They spent a lot of time together in his apartment. Watching movies, cooking, making love, and simply enjoying each other's company. She didn't seem to need a lot of social interaction and he knew that was helping to keep her safe.

"Burgers are ready!" Jag called out from near the grill.

Mustang moved closer, as did his teammates, and they all filled their plates with food. He took a bite of his hamburger —and his eyes nearly rolled back in his head.

"Holy shit, Jag, this is fucking amazing!" Aleck said with his mouth full.

"Yeah, what'd you put in this?" Midas asked.

Jag shrugged and gestured to Elodie with his head.

"Wasn't me. When I went upstairs to the condo to grab the meat, Elodie was tinkering in the kitchen. That's the result."

Mustang beamed as his team praised Elodie and begged to know what she'd done to make the hamburgers taste so good. He'd been giving her space all day, wanting her to get to know his friends, and for them to know her. He'd been ready to step in if someone overstepped their bounds or made her uncomfortable, of course, but he'd been thrilled to see that Elodie could hold her own when the teasing got a bit intense.

"You guys are acting like you've never had a good hamburger before, jeez," she said with a shake of her head.

"I thought I was a pretty good griller," Pid said between bites, "but seriously, this tastes like we're at a five-star restaurant."

Elodie laughed. "Well, I *was* a chef at a five-star restaurant once upon a time," she told them.

"Damn, Mustang, you better watch out or I'm gonna steal your girl," Aleck told him.

"Not a chance, Aleck," Mustang retorted, deciding it was time to reclaim his woman.

He wandered over to where Elodie was standing near a table filled with condiments and snacks. The second he got close, she put her arm around his waist and leaned into him, making him feel damn good.

"If you guys really want to know the secrets to a good burger, it's pretty simple. A thumbprint in the center of the formed patty, use salt and pepper *only* to season, use high heat, and *definitely* don't squish them down while they're cooking. You should only flip them once; just let the heat do its thing and stop messing with the burger once it's on the grill. And when it's done, you have to let it rest, let the juices redistribute throughout the meat. If you cut into it right away, or bite into it, the juices will go everywhere and make everything soggy. Oh...and mix the cheeses you use. American and cheddar are fine, but I used Monterey jack to give it a bit of a bite, and muenster."

"Aleck had muenster cheese in his fridge?" Midas asked in mock astonishment.

"Yes, I did, asshole," Aleck said. "I might like peanut butter sandwiches and tuna, but I grew up eating at country clubs, so I developed a taste for good food. Not the slop you guys eat all the time."

Mustang smiled as the banter flew back and forth between his friends. He leaned down and kissed the top of Elodie's head. "Having a good time?" he asked quietly.

"The best," she told him. "I really like your friends."

"Good. Because I have a feeling after these burgers, your presence is going to be requested at any get-together that has food. Not that they only want you around because you can cook or...I mean, because you're a chef, but...oh shit. I'm gonna stop talking now before I put my foot any farther in my mouth."

She chuckled. "It's okay. I know what you mean. And honestly, it's fun to cook for friends or with you. I'd lost my love of cooking for a while. Making meals for a crew of twenty or for patrons in a restaurant isn't the same. It gets monotonous quick."

"I can imagine. You thought about what you want to do when this Columbus business is over and behind you?" he asked.

"No."

Her answer was short...and almost bitter sounding.

"El?"

She sighed and looked up at him.

"What's wrong?"

"It's just...I can't think past today. I have no idea what my future holds, and the last thing I want to do is plan for something and then be disappointed when I have to give it all up and run and hide again."

Mustang put his plate down on the table and turned to Elodie. He took her plate out of her hand as well, then tilted her face up to his. "Listen to me, babe, you want to know what your future holds?" He didn't give her a chance to answer, but went on. "Me. This, relaxing with friends on the weekend, not looking over your shoulder, and definitely planning for what we're going to do a week from now, a month, a year."

She gripped his wrists and looked at him with eyes so filled with pain, worry, and hope, it nearly killed him. "You can't know that."

"I can and do," he argued.

"Elodie, this Paul guy isn't going to win," Pid added quietly.

Mustang had almost forgotten where they were, and that his team could hear every word of their conversation. Almost. He'd known they would back him up...he needed Elodie to believe that they were doing everything in their power to make sure she would be safe to live her life.

"No fucking way," Jag agreed.

"He might be head of that family for now, but he's a fucking idiot, and his second in command is gonna take over soon. Mark my words," Slate added.

"You ever talk to Jerry Columbus?" Midas asked.

Mustang took a breath and released Elodie's face, but grabbed her hands and squeezed them as she turned her head to look at his team.

"Paul's son? No. I mean, I knew he was around, but he never came into the kitchen and wasn't involved in hiring me," Elodie said.

"Right. Well, he seems a lot more savvy than his dad. Less hotheaded. But of all the members of the Columbus family, he's the most dangerous," Midas told her.

"And this is supposed to make me feel better?" Elodie asked under her breath.

"Yeah, it is," Aleck joined in. "Because from what it looks like, he doesn't know anything about you. Doesn't care. He's more concerned about Paul and his fuckups. He's been pretty vocal about his dad's...outbursts. We get the feeling it's not exactly a secret in the family that dear ol' Dad is a bit unstable. The team and I have talked about this, and we have a feeling Jerry is gonna make a move to take over the family sooner rather than later, and when that happens, it's likely you'll be in the clear."

She sighed. "It's all just so *stupid*," she said. "I mean, I left. I'm obviously not going to go to the cops or I would have by now, and even if I did, I don't have any proof of what I was asked to do."

"Men like Paul Columbus don't care about any of that. They just want to win," Slate said quietly. "Especially if he's not in his right mind."

"Well, he's not going to win," Mustang said firmly. "We're on this, El. Pid's keeping track of his capos, basically his military captains who are in command of the soldiers in the mob. The guys who do the actual work. As far as we can tell, they're all in New York doing their dirty deeds. They aren't out looking for you."

Mustang felt her let out a relieved sigh.

"If you think we're gonna let some asshole get his hands on you, you're crazy," Aleck told her. "Mustang has been a hell of a lot nicer and easygoing this last month. The last thing we want is him going back to being the hard-ass, ball-busting team leader he was in the months between when he met you on the *Asaka Express* and when he ran into you again."

"Fuck off," Mustang told his friend. "Just for that, I think we'll do our run with our packs on for PT on Monday."

Everyone groaned.

Elodie giggled. It was the most beautiful sound Mustang had ever heard. Aleck wasn't exactly wrong with his assessment of his temperament. Being around Elodie had softened him in a lot of ways. Regular sex probably had something to do with that as well, but he'd never admit to something so crass...especially not in front of Elodie.

"If we're gonna get our asses kicked on Monday, I want to stuff my face now to prepare. Are there any more burgers?" Pid asked.

"You guys want more?" Elodie asked in surprise. "We already made like a dozen of them."

"They're always hungry," Mustang informed her as he squeezed her hands once more then reached for the plate he'd abandoned.

"I could eat another, but I'm more interested in watching how Elodie cooks these things," Jag said.

"Same," Midas agreed.

"All right, I'll show you on one condition," Elodie said with a completely straight face.

"Anything."

"Of course."

"Depends on what it is," Slate said suspiciously.

She smiled at him. "Ah, there's one smart guy in the bunch," she quipped. "Wanting to know what he's agreeing to before he says yes. All I was gonna ask is that you promise to come back safe and sound from your mission next week."

Everyone went silent at her request.

After a pregnant pause, Mustang knew he had to step in and explain why they hadn't all immediately agreed.

"Babe...here's the thing. As good as we are, as much as we plan and prepare, shit can always go sideways. We're trained to deal with that...but from the first day we started working together, we made a pledge that when we had girlfriends or got married, we'd never promise to stay alive. We do everything in our power to make sure that happens, but we can't promise."

He saw Elodie swallow hard, then nod. "I understand, and I shouldn't have said anything. It's just...you guys are my only friends. And now that I know all of you, *really* know you, not just what Scott has told me about you, I can't imagine any of you not being here. You're a unit, a team, and it's obvious how close you are."

Surprisingly, it was Slate who approached. He tugged Elodie into his arms and gave her a long and heartfelt hug. "We can't promise not to die, but we *can* promise to not do anything stupid or to put ourselves in situations that would be less than ideal."

Elodie chuckled against Slate's chest. "Less than ideal, yeah, that's totally SEAL speak for 'fucked up beyond all recognition' for sure."

Slate loosened his hold and glanced down at her. "How'd you know what FUBAR stands for?"

"Because I'm not an idiot?" she quipped. "I know how to use the Internet. And I may or may not have used Scott's phone to research military acronyms. Since I'm dating a military guy now, I need to know that stuff so I can understand Scott when he talks. And along with the normal things, like the ranks and ridiculous stuff like COMNAVSEASYSCOM —who actually uses that one?—I looked up some of the more fun ones. Like FUBAR, FARP, BLT, BOHICA, DILLIGAFF, and SWAG."

Mustang couldn't help but laugh along with the rest of his friends. Then Slate passed Elodie to Pid, who gave her a long hug of his own, then Aleck, Midas, and lastly, Jag. Mustang had no problem whatsoever with his friends comforting Elodie. He trusted them with his life, and Elodie's, and if they could make her feel better with a hug, he was thrilled.

His heart kind of hurt thinking about her saying they were her only friends. He wanted to fix that, but wasn't sure how without putting her in danger.

For what seemed like the hundredth time, he mentally cussed out Paul Columbus. It was true that he wouldn't have met Elodie if the man hadn't caused her to flee for her life, but he hated that she was so alone right now. Afraid to make any deep connections in case she had to bolt once more.

He stood back and watched as Elodie charmed his team. She showed them how to put the thumbprint in the middle of the patties and smacked Jag's hand when he reached for the burgers with the spatula.

"I said no touching," she scolded. "Let the heat do its thing."

Mustang thought it was hilarious that his slip of a woman actually had the audacity to smack Jag. He wasn't exactly Mr. Jovial, but she knew he wouldn't do anything to hurt her.

By the time the afternoon was winding down, Mustang could tell Elodie was exhausted. It was no wonder; they'd hiked, swam, hiked some more, then she'd cooked and kept up a constant conversation with everyone. He knew she had to be good at small talk for her job on the fishing boat, but it could be stressful to hang out with people you didn't know and constantly be "on."

After they'd cleaned up the gazebo area they'd used and had helped bring utensils and leftover food back up to Aleck's condo, they'd all headed back down to the parking lot. Elodie had given each of the men a long hug and told them all to be safe. Mustang enjoyed spending time with his team, but he was more than glad to have Elodie to himself once again.

He drove back to his own apartment, which seemed tiny compared to Aleck's. For just a moment, Mustang worried that what he could give Elodie paled in comparison, but as if she could sense his concern, she turned to him the second they were inside. She hugged him hard. "I loved Aleck's place —who wouldn't?—but yours is so much cozier."

God, she was fucking perfect.

"You look tired," he said.

"That's because I am," she replied with a smile.

"How about a bath?"

"I'd love one."

"Go on, then. You want me to bring you a glass of wine?"

She smirked. "That will always remind me of the first time we came here, and you asked if I wanted a slow seduction with a glass of wine or if I wanted you to take me hard and fast just inside the door."

Mustang's cock twitched. He'd never, ever forget that either. "I knew you were perfect for me by your reply."

Elodie sighed happily. "You want help with our stuff, getting it in the wash?"

"Nope. I got it. Go on and get settled. I'll be in there in a bit with your wine."

"Thanks, Scott. And for the record...you have amazing friends."

"Yeah, they're pretty awesome."

With that, she went up on her tiptoes, kissed him briefly on the lips, and headed for the master bedroom.

Mustang watched her go and knew if something ever happened to her, he'd be completely lost.

For the first time in his Naval career, he didn't want to go on a mission. He wanted to stay here, with her, making sure she was safe. He knew Elodie would tell him he was being ridiculous, but the thought of her possibly needing him when he wasn't there was abhorrent.

Taking a deep breath, he reached for the pack he'd brought inside. Their clothes were wet and had to be washed, then he needed to get a glass of wine for his woman and make sure she was as comfortable and relaxed as possible. After she was mellow and warm from her bath and the alcohol, he'd take her to their bed and show her exactly how much she meant to him.

Smiling at the thought of making love to her later, Mustang headed for the small laundry room off the kitchen. He had a few days before they left for Africa, and he was going to take advantage of every minute he had to spend with Elodie.

* * *

On Wednesday, Elodie did her best to keep herself together as Scott drove her toward the harbor. He was taking her to work and then he'd be headed out on his mission. She was scared for him, but determined to put on a brave face. This was what women who were married to or dating military guys did. They made sure their men could go off and serve their country without having to worry about the people they were leaving behind. She could do this. She'd been on her own for quite a while now.

Scott pulled up and hopped out of the truck without a word, as she did the same. They met at the front of his truck and he immediately reached for her hand. Her backpack with a change of clothes was over one of his shoulders, and she couldn't help but be proud of how handsome he looked in his blue camouflage Navy uniform.

"You okay?" he asked quietly as they walked toward the *Fish Tales*.

"Yeah. You?"

"I'm just thinking about how much I'm gonna miss you," he admitted.

"Same. But you'll be busy and time'll go by fast." She had no idea if that was true or not, the time-going-by-fast thing, but she hoped so for his sake.

"Kai said he could pick you up and take you home, but if he gets sick or can't take you, call either of the two guys we talked about. I work with them on the base, and they said they'd have no problem driving you back to my apartment."

"I'll be fine, Scott."

"And if you need or want to go back to your place, make sure you lock the doors and don't leave your windows open at night. I know you like the breeze, but it's not safe since you're on the ground level."

"Scott—"

"And don't forget to take the disposable phone I bought for you wherever you go. Even if it's just to the store, although we did set up the grocery delivery straight to my apartment, so you shouldn't have to go out."

"Scott—" Elodie tried again, but he kept talking over her.

"I wish I knew how long I'll be gone, but I don't. Ballpark is two weeks, but we could be back before that or, if things don't go as planned, we could be gone for up to a month. Be smart, and if you sense anything is wrong or off, call my commander. I updated him on what was going on—about Columbus and everything. I know you weren't happy with me, but he needed to know so he could step in if the shit hits the fan while I'm deployed."

"Scott!" Elodie said for the third time, moving so she was right in front of him and he had to stop walking or run right into her. "It's going to be fine. *I'm* going to be fine."

She saw him take a deep breath. "I know," he said softly.

"Thank you for being worried about me. It's been a long time since anyone has cared about what I'm doing."

"I care," he said in a tone she couldn't read.

"You are not allowed to dwell on what I'm doing when you're gone. You *know* what I'll be doing—working, sleeping, and eating. That's it. I'm not going to decide to take a stroll down Waikiki Beach, or hang out at the Ala Moana Mall or something. You need to concentrate on your mission and the guys. They aren't going to be happy if they get a bullet in the butt because you're distracted and wondering if I'm okay."

Elodie was relieved when Scott smiled. "I know."

"Good. Now, kiss me like you mean it and go kick bad guy butt."

"This morning wasn't enough kissing for you?" he asked with a smirk.

Elodie couldn't help but blush. Scott had woken her up an hour before her alarm was set to go off and shown her without words how much he was going to miss her. That was on top of the amazing sex they'd had the night before. He'd taken her so hard and fast, she'd been nothing but a pile of goo afterward, then he'd changed things up and tortured her by bringing her to the edge of orgasm so many times, she'd begged him to please let her come already. They'd laughed, then she'd cried a bit, thinking about how much she would miss him, and she felt as if they were even closer emotionally as a result of their intense lovemaking sessions.

"I'll never get enough kissing from you," she admitted truthfully.

His smile disappeared as he leaned toward her. They made out in the middle of the dock for who knows how long, and probably would've continued and embarrassed themselves if Kai hadn't walked by and wolf whistled at them.

"The boat won't ready itself," he joked to Elodie as he continued toward the *Fish Tales* to prepare it for the day's charter.

Scott stared down at her for a long moment. Neither spoke, but they didn't need to. "Be safe while I'm gone," he finally said.

"I will. You too."

He nodded, then grabbed her hand and they headed for the boat once more. Elodie wanted to cry, but forced the tears back. Scott needed her strength right now, not her breaking down. This was the first time he'd left for a mission since they'd been together, but it wouldn't be the last. She could handle this. She *could*.

"Tell Midas I'll kick his ass if he lets you get hurt," she joked.

Scott didn't smile. "I will."

Realizing she was going to have to be the one to leave first, Elodie reached for the back of Scott's neck and pulled him down to her one more time. She kissed him briefly on the lips. "See you when you get back."

Scott licked his lips and nodded.

Elodie took a deep breath and let go of his hand, then turned and headed for the gangplank that led onto the *Fish Tales*.

"Hey, Melody, you ready for today? Four kids and two adults, here's to hoping they aren't obnoxious," Kai said with a smile.

Hearing the fake name was extra jarring now, especially when she heard her given name from Scott and his friends all the time. "Now you've jinxed us, way to go," she joked. Her heart wasn't in it, but she was doing her best.

She turned to look at Scott one more time and saw he was already halfway down the dock, headed for the parking lot.

"He's gonna be fine," Kai said softly.

"What?" Elodie asked, looking over at Kai.

"Your boyfriend. He's gonna be fine. He's badass, and he'll be back before you know it."

She smiled at him. Kai was a good guy. Young, in his early twenties, and still figuring out what he wanted to do with his life, but he was polite and respectful and a hard worker. She enjoyed working with him on the boat and knew she could've gotten stuck with someone a lot worse as a coworker. "Thanks."

"You already know he asked if I wouldn't mind picking you up in the mornings and bringing you home...but did you know he called me again and practically lectured me on making sure I drove the speed limit, always wore my seat belt and, if I had even a drop of alcohol on the boat, not to get behind the wheel when you were with me?"

"He did?" Elodie asked.

"Yup. That man is head over heels for you, Mel. It's weird, because he's this muscular, bearded tough guy, but with you, he's a giant marshmallow. I can only hope to be in a relationship like you guys have one day."

Elodie smiled. Yeah, Kai's description of Scott was really accurate. "He's pretty awesome."

"Good morning!" a deep voice called out.

Elodie turned to see Perry headed their way.

"Ready for today?"

She wasn't, but Elodie smiled and nodded anyway. She had a feeling Scott would be on her mind every second of every day until he returned to her safely. She hadn't asked for his promise, not after the talk with his team, but oh how she'd wanted to. She just had to hope and pray that everything went as planned on their mission and he'd be back sooner rather than later.

It was kind of nice to worry about someone else for a change, instead of about Paul Columbus and what he was doing.

CHAPTER SEVENTEEN

Paul sat at his desk, drumming his fingers on the top. Andrew had left weeks ago to try to track down this Valentino guy who'd worked on the *Asaka Express* with his former chef. His friend and capo was using fake identification and had all the money he needed at his disposal to bribe and extort people for information about the man's whereabouts.

So far, he'd chased the ship the man was supposed to be on, the *Asaka Freedom*, from port to port without any luck.

Paul was running out of patience. Every day that bitch was free to run around was another day she could totally ruin his life. Jerry was chomping at the bit more and more, trying to take over the family, and if he heard about what had happened—and that Paul hadn't been able to find Elodie yet, and shut her up—he'd use that opportunity to undermine him.

Andrew had checked in a few days ago, and had said the *Asaka Freedom* would be docking in Tunis, Tunisia, today. They were five hours ahead of New York time, and so Andrew should've gotten back to him by now.

Just when Paul was working himself up into a nice rage,

his phone rang. The throwaway one he used only to talk to Andrew, that couldn't be traced to either of them.

"Talk to me," he growled as he answered it.

"Got 'im!" Andrew crowed.

"Thank fuck. What'd he say?" Paul asked.

"Well, nothing yet. I paid a prostitute to slip a mickey into his drink at the pub. Dumb bitch didn't ask any questions, all she wanted was the money so she could go shoot up. I'm gonna keep him out of it until I can get him stashed someplace where it's safe to interrogate him."

"Don't take fucking forever," Paul grumbled. "I want to know where Elodie Winters is, and I want to know yesterday."

"He'll tell me everything he knows," Andrew said, the glee easy to hear in his voice. "When I'm done with him, he'll be admitting to every fucking thing he's ever done wrong."

"Make sure there are no loose ends," Paul warned.

"I'm not an idiot," Andrew complained. "This isn't my first interrogation."

"I just don't want to have to find *this* guy after everything is said and done, to make sure he doesn't snitch."

"Oh, don't worry, he won't be snitching about anything when I'm done with him."

"Good," Paul said. "I need you back here as soon as possible. People are starting to question where you are, and our cover about your sister being sick isn't going to hold up much longer."

"A day or two at most, boss," Andrew said. "Then I'll be back and we can plan our next steps. This asshole is going to tell us what we need to know, I feel it."

"Keep in touch," Paul ordered, then hung up without another word. He hated this entire situation. Couldn't believe a wisp of a woman like Elodie had managed to stay one step ahead of him. She was a fucking *cook*, and he was the head of a feared and respected mob family.

If Jerry ever found out how long she'd been able to elude him, Paul was a dead man. Jerry, and everyone else, would lose all respect for him and most certainly take him out.

For a moment, he considered going to wherever the bitch was hiding and taking her out himself, but he dismissed that idea immediately. He needed to be here in New York, keeping tabs on his family and holding tight to his position. If he left, he was screwed. He had to rely on Andrew to do what needed to be done, both with this Valentino guy and Elodie.

And he was so close to finding the information he needed to end this once and for all.

As he thought about how scared the bitch would be when she realized she was going to die, Paul closed his eyes in satisfaction. Maybe he'd ask Andrew to film her death. It was risky, but he could delete the video right after he watched it. He wanted to see her suffer. *Needed* to see that.

He smiled in anticipation.

* * *

"You gonna talk now?"

Valentino squinted at the man in front of him out of the one eye that wasn't swollen shut. He had no idea where he was, or who the man beating the shit out of him was. The last thing he remembered was being at the bar in Tunis with a smokin'-hot chick. He'd been onboard the ship so long, if he didn't get some pussy, his dick was going to fall off.

He'd been denied shore leave at the last two ports since he was the newest officer on the ship, and he'd been so fucking happy to get approval to go ashore when they'd arrived in Tunisia, he'd pretty much ignored the safety warnings and gone straight to the part of the city where whores frequented.

He'd almost immediately started talking to a woman who was all over him. She'd gone to the bathroom, and he'd decided to stop dicking around when she got back. He wanted to fuck, and he didn't need all this seduction bullshit that went along with it. He wasn't going to date this woman, he was going to slake his need then send her on her way. Maybe he'd find someone else to suck him off later.

He needed to get off as many times as he could before he had to be back onboard the next afternoon. Stuck on a ship filled with men for who knows how long until he could get off at the next port.

But somewhere between the woman agreeing to bring him to her place to fuck and now, something had gone extremely awry.

He was in a room he didn't recognize with a man he'd never seen before in his life. The guy hadn't told him why he was beating the shit out of him; he just was.

Valentino was sitting on a chair with his hands cuffed behind him and his legs tied apart. His shirt and pants were nowhere to be seen, and he didn't have his boots and socks on anymore either. He was sitting there in nothing but his underwear.

But the most alarming thing about the situation was that there was a huge piece of plastic under the chair—and the man in front of him wasn't wearing a disguise at all.

Valentino could describe him to the police in detail. He had longish black, greasy hair, which was tied back from his face with a rubber band. He couldn't see any visible tattoos, but he wore a black shirt and a black pair of pants. His teeth were yellow and his nose was crooked from being broken at some point in his life. At the moment, the man's knuckles were bloody and scraped from beating on his face, and Valentino couldn't help but eye the knife in a sheath on the man's belt with terror.

"I think you're ready," the man said, answering his own question.

"Who are you and what do you want?" Valentino asked, hating how weak and slurred his own voice was.

"Who I am doesn't matter, but what I want...yes, that's the right question."

The man stalked toward him, and Valentino wanted to spit on him, wanted to kick him between the legs and get the fuck out of this room. But as if the man could read his mind, his fist struck out, hitting him so hard in the face he couldn't breathe for a second.

"I want to know where Elodie Winters is."

"Who?" The question popped out without thought.

The man beating him didn't even hesitate, he turned and headed for the other side of the empty room and grabbed something that had been propped up against the wall. Valentino hadn't noticed it earlier.

It was a long piece of wood. Without a word, the man brought it up high, then swung it low and hard against one of Valentino's shins. Then he did the same to the other one.

He howled as pain radiated up his legs, making him retch all over his own lap.

The man beating him simply chuckled and hit him again.

"Where is she? All you're doing is making this harder on yourself," the man said.

"I don't know anyone with that name!" Valentino protested.

"Protecting her is valiant, but stupid," the man told him, and brought the board down on his thighs.

"I don't know who you're talking about!" Valentino yelled, desperate for the man to believe him.

Thankfully, the guy paused in his beating. "Hmmmm. I think I might believe you. She may have been using another name. She was on the *Asaka Express* with you. You had your arm around her fucking shoulders when you docked in Sudan after the ship was hijacked. Am I ringing any bells?"

Valentino blinked. "You mean *Rachel Walters*?"

The man beamed as if Valentino had just told him he'd won a million bucks. "Ah, Rachel Walters. Yes, that's her. I remember now, that's what the newscast said her name was. Where is she?"

Valentino's heart dropped. The guy had been fucking with him all along. If he knew Rachel's name the entire time, why was he beating him to try to get it out of him? Nothing made sense, and Valentino was in so much pain he couldn't think straight. He opened his mouth to tell this asshole that he had no idea where the damn cook was, but before he could say anything, a piercing agony went through his thigh.

Screaming, Valentino jerked his hands, forgetting they were restrained behind him. Looking down, he saw the hilt of the knife that had been at his tormentor's waist, now sticking out of his thigh.

"Oh, I missed," the man said, then reached for the knife.

"No! Don't!" Valentino yelled, but he was too late. The man yanked the blade out of his leg, and Valentino threw up once more.

"This will all stop if you just tell me what you know about Rachel and where she is. You looked awfully buddy-buddy with her when you got off the ship. Don't lie and tell me you don't know where she went. Is she on another ship?"

Valentino's mind spun. He'd do anything to make the pain stop, even give up Rachel. He had no loyalty to her. No way. But the problem was, he honestly didn't know where she was. He'd done everything he could think of to get the frigid bitch into his bed, but she'd resisted. He'd assumed she was gay... until he saw her with that fucking Navy SEAL. It pissed him off enough to try one more time to fuck her, but she'd lit into him after he'd put his arm around her at that news conference. Bitch.

Apparently, he'd been quiet too long, because the knife came down once more, this time dangerously close to his dick. Valentino screamed, then shivered. He was cold, so damn cold. And tired.

He closed his eyes, only to open them when he felt the knife being pulled out of his leg once more. It almost didn't hurt anymore. Blood pooled under his ass on the chair, and Valentino knew he was in deep shit.

"Tell me and this stops," the man said almost gently.

"I don't know," Valentino whispered.

"Wrong answer," the insane asshole said.

Then the pain came from Valentino's shoulder. His head lolling to the side, he saw the hilt of the knife inches from his face, sticking out of his upper arm.

"Where is she?" the man asked as he ever so slowly pulled the knife out of his flesh once more.

"I don't know!" Valentino said more forcefully. "After the news conference, I never saw her again!"

"You have to know *something*," the man insisted. "Did you overhear her talking to anyone from the corporate office? Did she call anyone? She couldn't have just disappeared. Tell me what you fucking know."

Valentino wracked his brain. He needed to come up with something to give this guy, otherwise he was going to continue to be tortured. The pain wouldn't stop.

Then something he'd all but forgotten flashed to his mind.

"The number!" he shouted.

"What number? You better start talking, or the next thing I'm gonna cut is your dick."

"I tried to catch her alone in the laundry room." Valentino almost tripped over his words, trying to get them out before this lunatic chopped off his cock. "She ran off, but there was a piece of paper. She dropped it! Must've come out of her pants pocket or something. It was a number."

"What kind of fucking number?" his torturer said, then punched him in the face for good measure.

Valentino could feel blood dripping off his chin but had no idea where it was coming from. His nose? Cuts on his face? His mouth? He felt around his mouth with his tongue and realized he was missing a couple of teeth. Shit, he'd always had perfectly straight teeth, and he hadn't even needed braces to get them.

"Damn, you're either stupid or *fucking* stupid," the man muttered, then leaned down in front of him.

Valentino had no idea what he was doing—until the most excruciating pain yet radiated up from his foot.

The man stood and triumphantly held up one of Valentino's toes.

"This little piggy went to market..." he singsonged, then threw the toe to the ground as if it had offended him in some way. "*Talk*," he ordered.

Valentino's gaze locked on that digit as it finally sank in that he wasn't going to live through this. This guy was certifiably crazy, and it was obvious the longer it took for him to get the information, the more he'd enjoy torturing him.

"A phone number. I don't remember all of it, but the area code was eight zero eight. That damn Navy SEAL gave it to her. There were some threes in the number, and a one, I think. I was gonna give it back to her but decided not to because she was being a fucking bitch."

Valentino spoke quickly, not caring that he was throwing Rachel under the bus. She'd rejected him. He had no idea who this guy was, or why he wanted the dumb bitch, but he could have her. It was *her* fault he was in so much pain. He'd tell this guy everything he wanted to know if it would just end the torture.

"She was upset about it. When someone asked why she was all mopey, she said she'd washed an important piece of paper that must've been in the pocket of her jeans. But she didn't wash it; I burned the fucking thing to a crisp," Valentino said, his voice slurring even more now.

"Eight oh eight, huh?" the man asked.

Valentino nodded.

"And it belonged to a Navy SEAL?"

"Uh-huh. One of the guys who came onboard to take out the pirates. She had the hots for him, wanted in his pants, and I guess the feeling was mutual. If she had more time, I bet she would've fucked him right then and there, but he had to go back to his ship, and we had to go into port."

Valentino sagged in relief when the man stood up and took a step away from him.

"You aren't lying to me, are you?" he asked.

Valentino shook his head as vigorously as he could. "No!"

"You know what? I believe you."

"Thank God."

"Since you were finally smart and told me what I wanted to know, I'm gonna kill you quickly."

Valentino opened his mouth to beg for his life, but didn't get the chance to say anything before the man lunged at him and sank the blade into his upper left chest.

Looking down, he saw the hilt vibrating back and forth, and he coughed.

"Right in the heart. You'll bleed out in a few seconds. Don't fight it," the man told him as he removed the blade from his flesh.

Valentino wanted to cry. Wanted to scream at the injustice of what was happening to him. But he didn't have the energy. His head slowly sank forward and his eyes closed as his heart stopped beating in his chest.

* * *

Andrew grimaced as he did his best to clean up the room. He hated this part. He much preferred torturing people then leaving the mopping to his soldiers. But he had to dispose of this asshole's body where the Tunisian police wouldn't find it. He'd arranged for a father and son to take the body out into the sea and mix it in with the chum they used to bait sharks.

Valentino Russo would disappear off the face of the earth as so many others before him had done. The ocean, thanks to the creatures that dwelled within it, was an amazing way to make shit disappear.

Making sure the man's toe was included in the plastic wrapping, Andrew mulled over what Valentino had told him. Elodie had taken a fancy to a Navy SEAL, and it sounded like the attraction had been mutual. She didn't have the paper with his number, since Valentino had destroyed it, but she could've memorized it. It sucked that Andrew didn't have it either, but there were only so many places Navy SEALs were stationed, at least that was what he thought. He didn't know shit about the military. Hadn't ever been interested in the government having that much control over what he could say and do, or how he could live. But knowing the area code would give him a huge leg up on locating the guy. And if he knew what city he lived in, he'd go and see what he could find.

Andrew had no proof Elodie was with one of the SEALs, but there had literally been no other sign of her anywhere. She was probably using another fake name, but narrowing down where she might've gone was a huge step.

He couldn't wait to get back to New York and do some research. Paul was gonna be fucking thrilled. And Andrew was sick of being a mere capo. He wanted to move up in the organization, maybe become Paul's consigliere. If he could be his advisor, he'd have a lot more power and respect amongst the other capos and fucking Jerry. The underboss was itching to move into Paul's spot—and if that happened, Andrew knew he'd have no chance of being anything other than what he was...a glorified gopher for the family.

Smiling as he recalled Valentino's cries of pain, he sealed

the ends of the plastic he'd wrapped around the man's body. Andrew loved seeing others suffer. It fed his soul.

If he hadn't found the Columbus family, he'd most likely be a serial killer. But now he could kill in the name of family and duty. He'd never felt better about what he did than right this moment.

He knew what Elodie had done, and why Paul wanted her found and silenced. Even Andrew could admit all this trouble was probably for nothing; if she'd planned to go to the cops, she'd have done so by now. But he didn't give a shit either way. All he cared about was seeing the terror on her face when she realized she'd been found and was going to die. His plan was to surprise her, appear out of the blue, not give her any warning before he killed her.

"I'm gonna find you, Elodie. Your worst nightmare is comin' for you," he said as he left the dead man in the corner of the rundown motel room for the father and son to pick up later that night. He knew they would too...because he'd kidnapped the man's wife. He told them he'd send word on where they could pick her up when they proved they'd disposed of Valentino's body.

God, he loved his job. He regretted not getting to kill the old woman, but sometimes leaving his victims alive was just as satisfying as killing them. Knowing others would suffer because of his actions was what got him off. And he knew without a doubt the man and his son would do whatever he told them to do, in order to get their loved one back. She was only a little worse for wear; he'd practiced a bit with his knife before he'd taken Valentino. She'd be fine...eventually.

Smirking, Andrew washed his hands in the sink one last time, then left the motel room without looking back. He had a plane to catch and research to compile.

CHAPTER EIGHTEEN

Mustang was tired, but he wasn't thinking about sleep. All he could think about was getting to the harbor and seeing Elodie.

Their mission to Africa had been relatively smooth. Surprisingly, while he'd missed her something terrible, it didn't seem to detract from the mission. If anything, he was even more focused, hyperaware of everything that could possibly go wrong. He knew it was because he wanted to make sure he got home to Elodie.

His internal clock was all messed up, but that wasn't anything new when they came home from a mission. And despite his exhaustion, he was far too excited to sleep. He had to see Elodie. To make sure she was all right and nothing had happened while they'd been gone. He thought about calling to let her know he was home, but after seeing it was close to the time when she usually returned from a charter, he'd decided to head down to the harbor instead.

He parked his truck and saw that the *Fish Tales* was already docked. He could see people moving around on deck and couldn't help but smile as he made his way toward it.

Kai saw him first, and he nudged Elodie.

Mustang saw the moment she realized who was walking toward the boat. She let out a little cry, then was running down the dock toward him.

"Scott!" she cried just before she got to him.

Mustang opened his arms and then she was there. He went back on a foot to keep them both upright and laughed as she latched onto him.

God, this felt good. He'd seen thousands of reunions between soldiers and their girlfriends, boyfriends, spouses, and children, and had been pleased for them each time. But nothing had prepared him for the feeling of...relief, contentment, when he got to hold Elodie once more.

She pulled back a fraction and looked up at him. "You're back!"

He chuckled. "I am."

"Are you all right?" She began to pat him on his chest and arms, as if seeing for herself that he was in one piece.

"I'm perfect, now that I've seen you."

She stopped her frantic inspection of his body and looked up at him. One second she was smiling, and the next her lip began to wobble.

"Babe," he crooned when tears began falling from her eyes. She pressed her face to his chest once again.

Mustang wanted to laugh, but he didn't. It wasn't funny that she was upset, but he figured these were tears of gratitude that he was back unhurt more than anything else. If he was being honest, he felt a little teary himself.

He gave her a moment to get control over her emotions, then kissed her temple. "You done here?"

She nodded and looked at him. Her face was blotchy from crying and her eyes were a bit bloodshot, but he'd never seen anything more beautiful. She reached up and wiped her face and said, "Almost. Kai and I were just finishing straightening up the boat while Kahoni did the paperwork."

Mustang grabbed her hand, brought it up to his mouth

and kissed the back, then started down the dock toward the boat. "Come on, let's see what else needs to be done so I can take you home."

"Aloha! Good to see you," Kai called out as they got close.

"Thanks. It's good to be home," Mustang said. Both he and Elodie walked up the short gangplank back onto the deck of the *Fish Tales*.

She was right; the cleanup looked mostly done. Mustang took in the small back deck with seats, where the guests could sit while fishing. Right behind it was a door that led into a covered seating area with two tables and more padded benches. A small kitchen was toward the front of the covered area, with a sink, refrigerator, and serving space. Mustang knew the charter included a lunch service. A tiny bathroom was located down three steps at the back of the covered space.

There were also stairs that led up to the wheelhouse, where all the electronics for operating the boat and for steering were located.

There was a spot for everything. Fishing poles were lined up against one of the walls just inside the covered area. Life jackets went under the bench seats. Several first-aid kits were screwed into the walls for easy access. It was a clean and well-maintained boat, and Mustang couldn't help but be impressed every time he was on it.

"Thanks for giving...Melody rides to and from work." It was very hard for Mustang to think of her as anything but Elodie, and he still stumbled over her name now and then when talking to others, but he'd rather die than do anything that would put her in danger or embarrass her. And having to explain why he wasn't calling her by her name would definitely be awkward.

"No problem at all. Assuming I don't need to pick her up tomorrow?" Kai asked with a grin.

"Nope. I do appreciate your assistance though," Mustang said.

"Anytime."

"We've got a regular schedule in the next few days," Kahoni said to Elodie and Kai after he'd welcomed Mustang back. He was looking down at his phone as he scrolled through his calendar. "Tomorrow we have a packed boat, with six guests—four adults and two kids—then Friday and Saturday, we've got four guests each day. And I got a call from a man who sounded desperate to get some pole time in. He's here on holiday with his wife and two daughters, but they aren't the fishing kind. I told him we didn't operate on Sunday, but he said he'd pay double. What d'ya think? Can you two handle it? I know Perry or I always accompany the charters, but with only one guest, I think it'll be easy enough. I'll pay you overtime."

"I'm in," Kai said immediately.

Mustang smiled. The prospect of earning extra money was never something he'd turned down when he was in his late teens and early twenties either.

Kahoni turned to Elodie. "I know your man just got home, but do you think you could do it?"

Elodie nodded. "Of course. I know it's your daughter's birthday on Sunday, and you've been looking forward to it for a while now."

"Thanks, Melody, you're the best. I swear I won't make a habit of this. I want to make sure you and Kai don't resent working for Perry and me, but it was hard to turn down the double pay," Kahoni said.

"It's fine."

"It's only a four-hour charter, and I'm thinking, based on the last few days of fishing, you could head toward the Pinnacle and see if you have any luck. If not, you could head to the Penguin Bank."

Elodie and Kai both nodded in agreement.

"The Pinnacle?" Mustang asked.

Kahoni explained. "Yeah, it's a section of ocean that's fairly shallow compared to fishing toward Kaena Point. Those areas also aren't too far from some of the FADs; fish aggression devices placed by the state of Hawaii."

Mustang shook his head. "Do I want to know what those are?" he asked. It was obvious he knew next to nothing about deep-sea fishing. Yeah, he enjoyed going out now and then, especially with his team, but he didn't pay attention to the details.

"They're buoys the state puts out to attract schools of tuna and other fish. I personally think it's kind of cheating, but hey, it certainly helps us find fish for the guests to catch, so I'm not complaining. It's not good business for someone to pay a premium to rent a boat and come up empty-handed," Elodie explained.

"I guess it wouldn't be," Mustang agreed.

"Right, so it's settled. I appreciate your willingness to work on your day off. I swear I'll make it up to you," Kahoni said. "But the good news is that you should be done by noon rather than two or three."

"Mahalo," Kai told his boss. "I'm all done cleaning up out here."

"And I was just about finished inside," Elodie added.

"You two go," Kahoni said with a grin. "Melody, I know you're probably anxious to spend time with your man, and the waves are calling you, Kai. I'll finish up here."

"Hang loose!" Kai said, flashing the shaka hand gesture at Kahoni. Then he grabbed his bag and was headed down the dock.

"See you later!" Elodie told her boss and grabbed her own backpack. Mustang took it from her and put his hand on the small of her back as they walked off the boat.

It was so good to be back, and to be with Elodie, it was hard for Mustang to keep his hand from straying into dangerous territory. She looked so good after he'd spent two weeks in Africa. She was wearing another pair of cheap flip-flops she'd bought at an ABC Store—one of her favorite places to shop—a pink tank top with a giant white hibiscus flower on the front, and board shorts that went to her knees. Her black hair was up in a messy bun, and his fingers itched to take it down.

She lifted her chin to look up at him, and Mustang couldn't help but notice the spatter of freckles across her nose, and that she looked tanner. Of course, being out in the sun every day would bring out the pigment in her skin. He probably wouldn't have noticed if he'd been gone for a short while. It was only by being apart that he noticed the small changes since they'd last been together.

"You look good," he blurted.

She smiled up at him. "Oh, yeah, after being in the wind and salt all day, I'm sure I'm ready for my walk down the runway."

Mustang caught her arm and stopped her. They were standing in the middle of the dock, but he couldn't wait a second longer. He lowered his head and kissed her as if his life depended on it.

She immediately gave control over to him, which just spurred him on more. He'd missed her terribly, and having her in his arms again was almost overwhelming. How had he lived without her in his life for so long? He didn't really understand how just being around her made all his troubles and worries seem so minuscule, but it did.

When they both had to take a breath, Mustang stared down at her, trying to memorize everything about her. The flecks of green in her brown eyes. The small wrinkle lines at the edges of her eyes. The way she licked her lips sensuously when she was turned on or wanted him to kiss her. "I missed you," he said quietly.

"I think I missed you more. Your apartment is very quiet without you there."

"I'm here now."

"Yeah, you are. And speaking of your apartment, I should probably tell you that when I'm stressed, I cook. And before you ask, no, nothing weird happened here. I didn't sense anyone following me or anything like that. I had no bad vibes, but I was worried about you and the guys. I couldn't help but stress about something going wrong on your mission. So there's enough food in your freezer to feed us for weeks. Oh! I know, we could bring some to the others! I'm sure Slate wouldn't mind getting a casserole. And Midas might like the meatloaf I made."

Mustang leaned down and kissed her again. She was smiling at first, and he loved feeling her happiness on his lips. He pulled back and took her hand and continued toward his truck. "No one's getting my food," he told her. "I'm not ready to share all that deliciousness with my team yet."

Elodie giggled. "It's only food, Scott, we can make more."

"Nope. You made it, it's mine."

"You're selfish, you know that?" she asked with a grin.

"When it comes to you and your food? Absolutely," he said without remorse. "What else did you do while I was gone?"

Mustang made sure to check out the area as he approached his truck. Nothing stood out as being suspicious. There were groups of people walking around the docks, to and from the boats, a couple of men with fishing poles set up at the end of one of the docks and, as always, a few homeless men and women hanging around in the grassy areas under the trees nearby.

He held open Elodie's door for her and waited until she got settled, then walked quickly around the truck to the driver's side.

When he put on his seat belt, he glanced over at Elodie

and saw she was staring at him with a huge grin on her face. "What?"

"Nothing. It's just...you look good. Healthy. I was worried about that."

"About what?" Mustang asked as he started the truck.

"About you not eating right. Sleeping in the dirt. Pushing yourself too hard." She shrugged. "I know it's stupid. You're a SEAL. You've trained to do all that stuff. But that doesn't mean I don't worry about it."

Before he pulled out, Mustang reached over and put his palm on Elodie's cheek. She immediately leaned against him. "Except for the lying in the dirt part, I worried about the same things with you. I don't know how it happened, but you're so far under my skin, El. And I like you there."

"Same," she said with a smile.

Mustang ran his thumb over her lips briefly, then forced himself to pull back and concentrate on driving. He could sit there with her all day, but he'd rather get her home.

"So...you didn't answer my question," he said. "Anything else interesting happen while I was gone?"

"No," Elodie said with a shrug. "I worked; some tourists were a pain in the ass, but most were cool. I cooked; I already told you that your freezer is stuffed full. And I may or may not have bought a new chair for your bedroom."

Mustang frowned. "Babe, I don't want you spending money on me."

"I didn't," she insisted. "I did it for *me*. Kai took me to the huge swap meet thing at the stadium one afternoon, when I was going stir crazy. I was really careful though, and we didn't stay long. I saw the chair and couldn't resist. It's got the most comfortable cushions and you just sink into them. It's ugly as hell, I'll warn you right now. I need to get it reupholstered to cover up the orange and brown flowers that are all over it, but I figured I could do that later. I put it right in front of the window in your bedroom, and it's amazing to sit there with the window open and listen to the waves. And...it's big enough for two."

Mustang could picture her sitting there in his mind, and he couldn't wait to share that chair with her. "How much was it? I'll pay you back."

"You will not," she said forcefully.

"Whoa," he said in surprise. "I didn't mean to offend you."

She sighed. "No, I'm sorry. I didn't mean to jump down your throat. It's just that you've done so much for me, Scott. You've made me feel wanted and cherished, which I needed... you have no idea how much. A chef is usually in the background, and only thought of when something's wrong with the food. And in New York, I was just the hired help. Then I was on the run, trying to stay under the radar.

"But you saw me. *Me*. You've asked for nothing in return for all your kindnesses, and I hate feeling as if I'm mooching off you. When I saw this chair, I knew it would be perfect for that spot in your room, next to your bed. I don't want you to feel as if you have to pay for every little thing. I've been on my own for a very long time; I don't want or need to be a kept woman. Okay?"

"Okay," Mustang said immediately. "But you need to understand that it's not in my nature to let you pay for shit when I know how little you have. I don't mean that in a bad way, it's just not escaped my attention that you have very little in that room you rented. I want to give you the world, El, and I don't want you spending your hard-earned money on me. If you want to buy something, by all means, go for it, but be forewarned, I'm never going to be comfortable with you spending a ton of money on me."

"I understand. This chair was as much for me as it was you, though. Same goes with food. I don't want you getting weird when I come back from the grocery store with ten bags full of food."

Mustang pressed his lips together. He didn't want her

spending her own money on food they'd both eat, but he understood where she was coming from. "How about this, when we shop together, I pay. When you're on your own, I won't complain when you pay."

"Are you going to let me go to the store by myself when you're not on a mission?" she asked.

It was a very insightful question, and it told Mustang that she knew him pretty well already. "Yes?"

She laughed. "Right. We don't have to hash everything out right this second, but as long as you realize that I'm in my thirties and not twelve, and expect to contribute to our relationship and not mooch off you, we're good."

Mustang couldn't believe that he wanted to continue arguing his point. He should be glad she didn't want him to pay for everything. If she was any other woman, he'd be grateful she wasn't trying to milk him for all he had, but with Elodie, he wanted to pamper her. Wanted to make sure she wasn't denying herself anything. She'd had a rough time of it lately, and all he wanted to do was make her happy.

As if she could read his mind, she said, "Just being with you makes me happy, Scott. I don't need anything fancy. You know I'm happy shopping at the ABC Stores. I love that they're on almost every corner here. If we ever move, I don't know what I'm gonna do without my Maui Onion potato chips, and being able to bop down to the ABC to get sunglasses, fresh pineapple, sunscreen, and a swimsuit cover-up...all in the same shop."

"It's called Walmart," Mustang teased.

Elodie wrinkled her nose. "It's not the same thing. Believe me."

"It kinda is. You know all the crap in there is mostly made in China, right?"

"Shut up. You're ruining my Hawaiian experience."

Mustang laughed.

She beamed. "God, it's good to have you back. I'd gotten way too used to talking to myself. Even more than usual."

"Is that chair big enough to have sex in?" he blurted.

Elodie stared at him for a second, then her smile widened. "Oh, yeah," she breathed.

"Good. Because that's what we're doing first," he informed her.

"Fine by me. You gonna strip me in the foyer again, or are we gonna try to make it to the bedroom this time before we get naked?"

"You keep talking about being naked, and we might not even make it up to my apartment."

"You've showered, right?" she asked nonchalantly.

"What?"

"Showered. I'm not making love with you if you've still got crud on you from whatever country you were in."

Mustang did his best not to run them off the road as he burst out laughing. God, Elodie was the only woman who could make him this happy. "I showered, babe. You definitely would've known if I hadn't when you first saw me. It wasn't pretty."

"Okay. Chair sex, then I'll give you a tour of the freezer and you can decide what you want to eat, then I want to be on top in our bed. I've been sleeping there by myself and fantasizing about fucking you for way too long. Then maybe we can shower and sit in the chair and watch the ocean together while you tell me what you can about your mission."

Mustang almost choked. "Damn, woman."

She beamed. "Hey, women can get horny too, you know."

Luckily the entrance to his apartment complex was just ahead. Mustang didn't know if he could wait any longer to be inside her once more.

"Oh, and I should probably let you know that I *did* do something else while you were gone."

"What's that?" he asked.

"I called Kalani two days after you left and asked if she'd go with me to the women's clinic. She picked me up...and I'm now the proud owner of a birth control implant. It's in my arm and will last up to four years. If I want to get pregnant before then—which, if I'm being honest, I probably will because I'm not getting any younger—it can be removed."

Mustang parked his truck and stared at her for a long moment. She was smiling shyly over at him. He could barely wrap his mind around what she was saying. What *was* she saying?

"I also got tested while I was there, just in case," she added. "I didn't think anything was wrong, but I wanted to let you know that it was okay to have sex with me without a condom."

"I...you..." Mustang cleared his throat. Shit, he had to get himself together, but his cock was pulsing so hard, he wasn't sure he could walk. "I'm clean too," he managed.

"I figured. So...I'm thinking we can ditch the condoms...if you want. It's okay if you're not comfortable with that yet though. I know it's still early in our relationship and I—"

Her words cut off as Mustang stepped out of the truck and stalked around to her side. He didn't give her time to ask what he was doing. He simply opened her truck door and yanked her out. This time, he threw her over his shoulder.

He heard her laughing as he strode toward the apartment entrance.

"So, maybe we'll start with foyer sex, then move to the chair and the other stuff," she told him.

Yeah, that sounded more like it. Mustang knew he wouldn't be able to hold off long enough to get her to his room. Just like that first night, he had to be inside this woman. And he could take her bare. It would be a first for him, and he couldn't fucking wait.

The second he was inside his apartment and she was on her feet once more, their hands were all over each other. It took way longer than he wanted to get her naked because she still had on her bathing suit under her clothes, but he was on his knees at her feet with his mouth on her pussy before she could catch her breath.

"Scott!" she exclaimed.

The tangy taste of her excitement exploded on his tongue, and Mustang gripped her hips hard, hoping he wasn't going to leave bruises as he feasted on the woman he loved. She was as primed as he was, and within two minutes, she was writhing in his arms, begging for more.

Before her orgasm had finished, he shoved his pants and underwear over his ass, not bothering to take them off, and picked up Elodie.

Leaning back against the door, she wrapped her legs around his waist and looked into his eyes with so much love, Mustang thought he was going to explode before he even got inside her. Holding her ass with one hand, he reached for his cock with the other and lined himself up to her weeping slit.

He held his breath as he slowly slid inside her. He was thick, and she was tight, but as usual, she felt absolutely amazing. Even more so without the barrier of the condom between them. He held her gaze as he began to fuck her hard, fast, feeling closer to her than he ever had before. It was as if ditching the condom had metaphorically removed all barriers between them.

"I love you," he blurted…then stilled.

He hadn't meant to tell her yet. He wanted to give her more time to get to know him. To do what he could to make her love him back. He prayed he hadn't just ruined everything.

Her eyes got wide and filled with tears. Mustang panicked for a split second.

"I love you too," she whispered.

Mustang thrust inside her hard one more time and came. Right then and there with no more effort whatsoever. He filled her pussy with the largest load of come he'd ever let go. It felt as if he'd never stop.

Knowing she loved him back was the biggest turn-on— and the largest relief he'd ever known.

Without pulling out of her, Mustang held Elodie to him and turned around and headed for his bedroom. He had to shuffle in an undignified way since his pants had fallen around his ankles, but he wasn't going to stop, not if it meant letting go of Elodie. She leaned into him and he felt her soft puffs of air against his neck as she tried to catch her breath.

Upon entering his bedroom, he leaned over and grabbed the blanket from the bed and threw it over the ugliest chair he'd ever seen. Elodie had warned him that it needed to be reupholstered, and she hadn't been lying. But if they were going to be spending a lot of time hanging out in this chair, he didn't want to get it all gross by having sex in it.

He sat—and groaned. She was right. The chair was fucking fantastic.

Elodie braced her knees on either side of his hips and sat up, smiling at him.

"Are you laughing at me, woman?" he mock growled.

"Me? No, would I do that?" she asked not so innocently.

Mustang sobered. "Say it again," he ordered.

She took his head in her hands and stroked his beard. "I love you." She didn't even hesitate.

Mustang's cock twitched inside her, and she groaned as she shifted on his lap. Amazingly, Mustang was ready to go again. He only hoped he'd last longer this time. He would've been embarrassed at how he'd prematurely ejaculated already, but he supposed he could be forgiven. It had been two weeks since he'd come, he was fucking bare inside her for the first time ever, and the woman he loved more than life itself had just admitted she felt the same way.

"Hang on," he warned, waiting for her to grab hold of his shoulders before he began to fuck his woman once more.

Later, much later, after they'd eaten, and showered, and made love again, Mustang was lying in bed with his arm around Elodie, listening to her snore slightly against his bare chest. He was beyond tired, but more satisfied than he could ever remember being.

Mustang kissed her temple then shut his eyes, glad that she was safe. And he vowed to keep her that way.

* * *

Andrew scowled at the apartment complex in front of him. He was tired, hungry, and in need of a shower. Hawaii was supposed to be paradise, but so far it had been nothing but a pain in his ass. The traffic sucked, it was way too hot and fucking humid, and it had taken him longer than both he and Paul wanted to find Elodie fucking Winters.

But he'd done it. *Finally*.

It had been easy to figure out that the Navy SEALs who'd rescued the *Asaka Express* were stationed in Honolulu. The area code of the guy's number led him straight to the Joint Base Pearl Harbor-Hickam. Paul had paid off a contractor who had access to personnel records and had received the names of the SEALs who'd been on the cargo ship with Elodie. It hadn't been difficult to pay someone else to trace the phone numbers of those men. There was only one who had the right digits Valentino had remembered.

Scott Webber.

Andrew had hightailed it to Honolulu after getting the man's description, address, and vehicle information. It wasn't until he was already in the Aloha State that he'd been informed by his insider that the SEALs were away on a mission. It should've been the perfect time to grab the bitch and take care of her once and for all...but while he'd been able to see her with his own eyes, he hadn't been able to get near her. Since Andrew's arrival, Elodie had only left the SEAL's apartment to go to the harbor. A guy had picked her up and dropped her off every day of the last week, and the security in the apartment complex was too intense for him to slip inside unseen. There were cameras everywhere.

Andrew had managed to find the only spot in the parking lot where he'd likely be out of range of the security cameras. All the way in the back corner by the street. His nondescript, four-door black rental blended in just fine, but with the lack of access to Elodie, he'd been forced to bide his time and try to come up with another plan.

He'd hoped to have everything taken care of before Mr. Navy SEAL arrived back from his mission, but he wasn't so lucky. He'd watched from the harbor parking lot as his target and the SEAL had almost fucked right on the dock. And he'd recognized the look of lust on the man's face before he'd carried Elodie into the building a short while ago. She'd be even harder to get to now.

But not impossible. Earlier that morning, Andrew had finally come up with the perfect plan, but he had to wait until Sunday to execute it. It was costing Paul a fortune but would be worth it in the end. And Andrew couldn't fucking wait. All he wanted to do was get back to New York. He was so sick of this bitch.

Andrew started his car and pulled out of the lot. There was no need to watch the apartment complex all night, not when his plan was in motion. He'd been very careful in his surveillance so far, not wanting Elodie to have any inclination she was living her last few days on this Earth. The element of surprise was one of his favorite things, and he knew without a doubt the bitch was going to be surprised. Even dating a Navy SEAL wouldn't save her from Paul's wrath. She might think she was home free, hiding out here in paradise, fucking a damn SEAL...but she was wrong.

The mob always won in the end. Always.

CHAPTER NINETEEN

Elodie stood at the end of the dock and hugged Scott, hard. It was Sunday, normally her day off, but she'd had no problem doing Perry and Kahoni the favor of taking a client out on a fishing trip. They'd taken a chance and hired her even though she'd had no experience, which meant a roof over her head and food to eat. And the job had allowed her to stay in Hawaii and eventually run into Scott. She'd do anything for the owners of the *Fish Tales*.

"You're really going into work?" she asked Scott. He'd had a couple days off after his mission, and as much as he enjoyed her company when she wasn't working, she knew he was itching to get back to work himself.

"Yeah, just for a bit. We did our after-action review the day after we got back, but I want to read it through and make sure we didn't leave anything out."

Elodie was impressed by Scott's thoroughness. He took his job as team leader very seriously, and she loved him all the more for it. "Okay."

"I'll be here around noon to pick you up though. Maybe we'll head up over to Makapuu today. What do you think?"

Elodie nodded. Makapuu was one of the best body-surfing beaches on the island, but she wasn't getting in the water. No way.

Scott chuckled. "I know you're just humoring me, but I appreciate it. You can read a book while I body surf for a while, then I'll take you to Waimanalo and we'll eat at Smokey Ranch Barbeque. Guarantee it'll be the best barbeque you've eaten."

"Guarantee? You seem to forget that I'm a chef who's eaten at some of the best restaurants in the country," Elodie told him.

"I haven't forgotten. But I promise you'll love this place."

"All right, but I want lunch first. You'll get carried away at Makapuu and by the time you're done, I'll be starving."

"Deal," Scott said with a smile. "For the record, I was gonna bring you a snack to tide you over, but we can still eat first."

"You're so good to me," Elodie told him.

"I love you, it's my job to be good to you."

She'd never get tired of hearing him say he loved her. Elodie no longer worried about what was "right" and "normal" in a relationship. When it came to Scott and her, normal didn't apply. She was content with how things were going and had the utmost confidence that they would make it as a couple. "I love you, and I'll see you later."

"Have fun and be safe," Scott said.

"I will. I'm looking forward to being a little more relaxed today. With it being just me and Kai and only one guest, we don't have to be as formal with things. Hopefully the guy'll be cool."

"I hope so too, for your sake." Then Scott leaned down and kissed her. They'd started out the morning with lots of easy cuddles and caresses in bed. They were both tired from making love the night before and hadn't felt the urge to do more than talk quietly before getting up and starting their day.

Elodie gave Scott another hug, then picked up her backpack and started down the dock. She turned and gave one last wave before turning her attention to the *Fish Tales*. Kai was already onboard and he greeted her with a hearty "aloha!" when she came aboard.

She spent about twenty minutes getting the boat ready while Kai did paperwork and checked everything over to make sure it was seaworthy. The last thing they wanted was to get stranded in the middle of the ocean.

Their guest for the day showed up right on time.

"Hello?" a deep male voice called out.

Elodie went out on the back deck and waved at the man standing at the end of the small gangplank.

"Aloha! Are you Steven Miller?" she asked.

"That's me!" the man said jovially. He was wearing a pair of jeans and a polo shirt, not exactly fishing gear, but Elodie had seen guests show up in just about everything, so nothing surprised her anymore. Steven had dark hair that looked like it had been greased back with some sort of oil. His nose was a bit long and kind of hooked at the end, and his teeth were rather yellow. He was clean shaven and his brown eyes were bright, and he looked eager to start the day.

He was also holding a takeout container. "I brought doughnuts and coffee," he said as he came onboard.

"That was nice of you," Elodie told him. "But you didn't have to. We have snacks and coffee onboard."

"Well, I wasn't sure. I've never done this before," Steven said. "I'm super excited though."

"That's great. I'm Melody, and Kai will be our pilot and the other guide helping us today."

Elodie got Steven seated and gave him the liability paperwork to fill out. She also handed him the rules and regulations for the trip. No smoking, an explanation of what would happen if he caught a fish, as well as his one-day fishing license to sign. The cost was included in the charter.

He laughed and joked with both her and Kai as he finished filling out the paperwork and they got the boat ready to go.

"So your family wasn't too keen on fishing?" Kai asked after Elodie had given Steven the safety briefing and then showed him where the life jackets were stored and how to put one on in the case of an emergency.

"Nah, Margaret and the girls are still sleeping. They aren't morning people and would rather spend their time shopping in Waikiki and hanging out on the beach. They were more than happy to let me do this on my own. I can't wait to catch a marlin. The guys back home in Massachusetts will be so jealous!"

The small talk continued as they began to head out toward the Pinnacle, the fishing spot Kahoni had suggested they try first. Kai was up in the small wheelhouse and Melody was entertaining Steven, passing the time until they could put out the lines.

He was actually very interesting. He'd said that he was an insurance salesman, and she could totally see that. He was outgoing and gregarious and frequently made her laugh. He told her stories about his wife and daughters, and explained they'd come to Hawaii on a business trip slash vacation. He'd gone to a few meetings and made some contacts while his family shopped.

The only thing that seemed off about the man was the fact he wasn't wearing a wedding ring. Elodie didn't think too much about it, as there were lots of reasons a man didn't wear a ring. Steven wasn't hitting on her, so she didn't think it was because he was trying to pick up women.

When they reached the spot where they'd had good luck fishing in the past, Kai came down, and he and Steven baited and set the lines.

Fishing wasn't exactly Elodie's favorite thing to do. It was actually quite boring, waiting to see if a fish took the bait. Then the boredom turned to excitement as the guests tried to reel it in. She sat in the shade and did her best not to look too unenthusiastic. Usually on these trips, she'd be occupied with talking to and entertaining children or the other guests who weren't actively fishing. But since it was just Steven on this trip, and Kai was discussing the different kinds of Hawaiian fish in the area, she was left to her own thoughts. And of course they turned to Scott.

She'd much rather be spending the morning with him, but she couldn't really complain when she was in Hawaii, earning overtime, and it was such a beautiful day.

When Kai came inside a short while later and headed for the stairs to go up to the wheelhouse, she frowned in confusion. "We're leaving?"

"I talked about heading out to the Penguin Bank and he was all for it. He seems eager to go out to deeper water, and when I mentioned the possibility of seeing sharks, his eyes lit up." Kai chuckled. "I don't know why you tourists get turned on by sharks so much."

Elodie shuddered. "I'm not a tourist, and besides, I could go my entire life without seeing a real-live shark and be perfectly happy."

"He doesn't seem too interested in fishing anyway," Kai went on. "All he's talked about is how different things are here compared to Massachusetts. He's also curious as to how *you* came to be working on a charter fishing boat in Hawaii." Kai grinned. "You have to admit, it's kinda funny, you aren't exactly the typical employee."

"You mean I'm too white and too old and not into surfing," Elodie said with a chuckle.

"Exactly. Your turn to entertain while I get us farther out into the deeper waters," Kai said.

"Thanks," Elodie muttered. She wasn't concerned that

Steven had talked about her to Kai, she knew she wasn't what people expected when they signed up for the charter. For some reason, people always seemed surprised to find a woman on the boat when they arrived, as if women couldn't be fishermen or employed by a fishing vessel. As long as she was under the Columbus family's radar, she didn't care if the tourists wondered what her story was.

Thirty minutes later, the *Fish Tales* was bobbing in the deeper waters far off the coast of Waikiki. Elodie didn't particularly like it when they came out this far, but it was all a part of the job. At least this trip would be done soon. They only had two more hours before they'd need to head back in.

She was somewhat lost in her head, thinking about going to Makapuu with Scott later and making a mental note to reapply her sunscreen. Her skin had definitely gotten darker since she'd been in Hawaii, but she still burnt way too easily, and she wanted to protect herself as much as possible.

A weird noise from the back deck where the poles were in the water made her turn around.

Steven was standing on the back deck with his arms at his sides, staring at her with an expression she couldn't decipher.

A shiver went through her, and for the first time, she felt uneasy. Elodie took a step toward the doors separating the inner seating area from the back deck—then froze when she saw what Steven was holding.

A gun. It had a longer barrel than she'd expected.

Then she noticed Kai. He was lying face down on the deck behind Steven, not moving.

Her instincts kicked in, and she spun and bolted for the stairs that led up to the wheelhouse.

She knew the door wouldn't stop Steven for long, and she was literally in the middle of nowhere. There was no place to hide on the small boat, not like when she was on the *Asaka Express* and had endless places to hide from the pirates.

"Elodie!" Steven called out, and she shivered again...

Then realized he'd used her real name. He hadn't called her Melody.

Her heart sank.

Fuck. Paul Columbus had found her. Steven wasn't him, of course, but he was obviously a trusted member of the family.

Adrenaline coursed through her body as she looked around the wheelhouse. There was no way she could get back to shore before Steven, or whatever his name was, burst into the small space. He was going to kill her. She knew that as easily as she knew her name.

He confirmed it with his next taunting words.

"You can't get away, Elodie. This is it. You've had a good run, but your time is up. You knew you'd never get away from us."

Elodie looked at the small side window in the wheelhouse and reached for the latch. She wasn't going down without a fight. She had too much to live for. She had Scott. And friends. A life. A few months ago, she might've given in, but not now.

She wiggled her upper body out the window and managed to get her feet out and under her without falling off the side of the boat. There was a narrow ledge around the upper part of the boat, and she shimmied around it, frantically trying to come up with a plan. It was only then that she remembered the emergency location beacon Kahoni and Perry had installed on the boat, just in case. It would automatically be triggered to transmit their location if the ship sank, but it could also be manually activated from the wheelhouse.

But it was too late to go back. She saw Steven's head pop through the window she'd just climbed out of. He laughed at her.

"Where are you gonna go, Elodie? There's nowhere *to* go. Look around you, you're not gonna survive this. Come back inside and I'll make your death quick and painless."

Elodie inched farther away from him until she was overlooking the back deck. Looking down, she once again saw Kai lying on the deck, blood pooling under him. She wanted to cry. This was exactly what she didn't want to happen. Someone else getting hurt or dying because of her.

Panic began to set in. What was she going to do? She had very few options here. She had no weapon, and Steven could easily overpower her. She didn't believe for a second that he'd kill her quickly. The nasty gleam in his eyes belied his words.

"Hey, girl."

She jerked in surprise and saw Steven looking up at her from the lower deck. He'd moved fast, getting from the wheelhouse to the deck seemingly in seconds.

She scooted around the ledge once again, so Steven wouldn't have a direct line of fire if he decided to shoot her while she was up here.

She looked out across the water and could barely make out Diamond Head. Kai had played right into his hands, bringing them out even farther on the water. And since it was Sunday, there weren't nearly the amount of fishing boats running today. Quickly glancing around, Elodie realized she couldn't see even one. They were literally the only boat out this far, this early.

"You're making this so much harder than it needs to be," Steven mocked. "Come down before I'm forced to shoot you while you're up there. You know your body will just fall into the sea and sink to the bottom where you'll be eaten by fish and sharks."

And just like that, she knew that was his plan all along. He was going to dump her body into the ocean and no one would ever know what happened to her. Scott would forever wonder if she'd ran off on him or if something had happened.

No, he'd *know* she would never up and leave without a word. But even knowing that, her disappearance would devastate him.

Her mind was racing, trying to come up with a solution to her predicament. A way to come out of this alive.

And then, just like that, Elodie knew what she had to do.

Everything within her rebelled, but she knew it was the only way. The one chance she had of making it out of this alive. It was a slim chance, and so many things could go wrong, but she literally had no other choice.

She turned her head and saw Steven leaning against the back railing of the boat, staring at her. He could've shot her at any time, but instead he was enjoying her panic. The evilness in his eyes was as clear as day now, and Elodie knew without a doubt if he got his hands on her, she was in for a world of hurt.

"I'm sorry, Kai," she whispered.

Then inched as far forward on the boat as she could, took a deep breath, and jumped.

"No!" she heard Steven shout as she fell through the air, then all she could hear was the whoosh of the water closing over her head.

Afraid Steven would shoot at her in the water, she stayed under and held her breath as long as she could as she frantically did her best to get as far away from the boat as possible.

When she finally had to come up for air, she turned to look at the boat. Unbelievably, she'd managed to get at least twenty-five meters away. Steven was still standing on the back deck. He hadn't run up to the wheelhouse to try to steer the boat closer.

As she tread water, Elodie did her best to try to calm herself. Her heart was beating close to two hundred beats a minute, and she knew she'd pass out if she didn't slow her breathing.

"What now?" Steven called out to her. "You do know how stupid that was, right? Look around, Elodie. You gonna swim back to shore?" He laughed. "Not hardly. You'll never make it. Come back to the boat, and I'll make a deal with you."

Elodie didn't bother to ask what kind of deal. He was lying, and she knew it. She wasn't stupid; if she got back on that boat, he'd kill her. Slowly. Her only chance of getting out of this was for Scott to realize something was wrong when he came to pick her up, and she and the boat weren't there.

"Bitch! I said get back here! Now!" Steven called out when she didn't start moving toward him.

In response, Elodie kicked her legs and moved farther away.

She saw Steven pacing back and forth on the deck before he turned and went into the seating area. When he appeared in the wheelhouse, she tensed. He could easily run her over or get closer and shoot into the water.

She heard the engine start up and watched as the boat sputtered and spun in a few circles.

She would've laughed if the situation wasn't so dire. It was obvious the man had never driven a boat before. She'd been given lessons by Kahoni when she'd first been hired, and he'd also explained the oddities of his boat. For some reason, when the steering had been installed, the mechanic had put it in backward. So if you wanted to go right, you had to turn the wheel to the left. It was confusing, but the owners had laughed and said it was a fun quirk. She'd gotten used to the awkward steering, but was glad she didn't have to be in charge of driving very often.

She watched as the boat shot forward and Steven's head disappeared from view above the helm.

Kahoni and Perry had also put in a very powerful engine. If you didn't baby the throttle, it would jerk forward, as it had just done.

Steven managed to get the boat a little closer to where she was, despite his ineptitude, and despite her trying to swim away from the boat. He came back down to the back deck and raised the pistol, and even though she didn't hear shots being fired, Elodie saw the water splash up in front of where she was treading water. The reason the barrel of the gun was so long was clear now...he had a silencer on the weapon.

Ducking underwater once more, Elodie did her best to swim what she hoped was out of range of the bullets.

When she came up for air again, Steven was leaning over the railing of the boat.

"You know what? This is better!" he shouted. "I was gonna make this quick and easy, but I like this. Paul will too. You can stay out there. You'll eventually get tired...it'll be harder and harder to stay afloat. You'll get dehydrated, and with the sun beating down on you all day, you'll fry like a bug on a hot sidewalk. Not to mention there's a storm coming in this evening...if you make it that long. I've heard the riptides in Hawaii are pretty brutal too. And then there're the sharks. And I've got a parting present for you...all the bait you planned to use to help me catch a fucking fish? I'm gonna chum the water. Maybe a shark will think those big toes of yours are fish and he'll take a bite. Munch-munch!"

Elodie was crying now; she couldn't help it. She was terrified. When she'd jumped into the water, she didn't really have much of a plan, she just knew she needed to get away from Steven. But now reality was sinking in. She was in the middle of the ocean, way too far out to be able to swim to shore, and she was most likely going to die a long, slow death. Just like Steven and Paul wanted.

"I didn't *do* anything!" she cried out.

"You said no to the most powerful mob boss in New York!" Steven screamed back. "No one says no to Paul Columbus!"

And with that, Steven turned and headed back inside. Seconds later, he was back and pouring buckets of bait into the water. He dumped some over each side and even off the back. She knew from experience how bloody and stinky those bait buckets were. Many a guest had complained about them, but she'd always patiently explained that the stinkier the bait, the more appealing it was to the creatures in the sea.

Looking around frantically as she tried to swim away from the boat—and the crazy man trying to kill her—Elodie didn't see any fins, but she knew it was only a matter of time.

Steven lifted his weapon and shot off a few more rounds, but she was getting farther and farther away. Then there was silence for a moment before the engines of the *Fish Tales* fired up again and the boat lurched once more. It wobbled side to side as Steven did his best to control the powerful engine, then headed toward the island of Oahu, barely visible in the distance.

For a second, Elodie simply stared at the back end of the boat with a mixture of relief and horror. Then she panicked again. Steven had left her in the middle of the ocean; she was way too far out to swim all the way back to shore.

But then again, she was alive. He hadn't managed to shoot her. So there was that.

"What now?" she mumbled as she continued to tread water.

But that was the thing—she had no idea what to do. Stay put? Swim toward Diamond Head, which she could just see on the horizon? Would Steven come back? For some reason, she didn't think that was his plan. He'd been pissed he didn't get to shoot her, but he'd also been pretty gleeful when he'd laid out all the ways she could die out here. The man was certifiably insane, but he hid it extremely well. She hadn't thought he was anything but a married father of two, glad to get away for a little rest and relaxation while on vacation.

The tears came again, and this time they wouldn't stop. Elodie thought about Scott. About how much she loved him and how lucky she'd been to find that kind of love, even if it was only for a short time.

Then she got mad. Then she cried again.

Her emotions were all over the place, and as time went

on, and she bobbed up and down in the waves, she got more and more tired. And dehydrated. The Hawaiian sun was brutal, burning the top of her head, shoulders, and face. She had no idea how much time had gone by, but somehow she knew this suffering was only the beginning of the hell she was going to go through.

But Elodie wasn't going to give up. She hadn't lived through a hijacking and being pursued by a mob boss to die now. She was going to fight to live. If she made it out alive, she'd still have to worry about Paul coming after her again, or sending someone else. He knew where she was now, and there wouldn't be any way to keep her survival out of the papers. People ate this kind of shit up.

Woman survives out in the ocean for days. Click here for story.

She could see the posts on the Internet now. Her story would be fucking click bait, and she'd have to run again. Find somewhere else to hide.

What was the point of trying to live when she'd just be hunted down again?

But then Scott's face sprang into her mind. How he looked when he smiled down at her. How his beard felt against her skin as he kissed and caressed her. How proud he'd looked when the soufflé he'd made had come out perfectly.

A renewed energy swept over her.

Elodie would fight to live for Scott.

She loved him so damn much and would do anything to spare him the pain of not knowing what happened to her. She wouldn't wish that on her worst enemy...well, all right, maybe she would on Steven or Paul.

Elodie knew she was a bit delirious, and she took a deep, calming breath. Then she fixed her gaze on Diamond Head in the distance...and began to swim toward it.

Maybe she'd run into another fishing boat on her way, and she wouldn't have to swim the entire distance. Maybe a dolphin would come up beside her and let her grab ahold of its dorsal fin, then tow her in. Or one of Hawaii's famous green turtles, a hona, would have pity on her and let her take a ride on its back.

She didn't care how it happened, but she was going to get back to Scott no matter what it took.

CHAPTER TWENTY

Mustang looked at his watch for what seemed like the tenth time. The *Fish Tales* was late. He shouldn't be as worried as he was...but for some reason, he couldn't help but feel as if something was very wrong. Their charters ran like clockwork. In the past, on the rare occasion Elodie was going to be late, she called him. She had the disposable phone he'd given her and always carried it with her. The signal was sometimes shitty out on the ocean, but she'd always managed to get through.

His sixth sense had never failed him before, and Mustang didn't feel at all bad about pulling out his phone and disturbing Kahoni on his day off. The man had given him his number before he'd been deployed and told him to call anytime. Maybe Kai had contacted his boss and let him know they were having engine trouble or something. If anything was wrong with the boat, Kahoni would know.

"Hello?"

"Hi, Kahoni, this is Scott Webber, Melody's boyfriend."

"Aloha, Scott. What's up?"

"I'm at the dock to pick up Melody, but the boat's not back yet. I was wondering if you'd heard from Kai about any engine trouble or anything they might be having? Or maybe their guest wanted to stay out longer?" Mustang asked, looking for any reasonable answer as to why the boat hadn't been back at the time it was supposed to be.

"Really? That's strange. Hang on...I'm gonna patch Perry into the call."

Mustang waited impatiently for the second boat owner to be added to their discussion.

"Perry?"

"I'm here," the other man said.

"Scott, you still there?" Kahoni asked.

"Yes."

"Okay, so Scott says the *Fish Tales* isn't back yet. Have you heard from Kai?" Kahoni asked Perry.

"No. Not today. Give me a second and I'll check the GPS tracker."

Mustang sighed in relief as he paced in front of his truck. He hadn't realized the owners had a GPS onboard, one that could be tracked, but he shouldn't have been surprised.

He waited impatiently as Perry worked on pulling up the location of the boat on his computer.

"That's weird," he said.

Mustang stopped walking. "What's weird?" he asked.

"It's showing the *Fish Tales* is at Ko Olina Marina."

Impatient, Mustang asked, "Where is that?"

"Well, it's out by Barbers Point. You're at Ala Wai Harbor down by Waikiki, right?" Perry asked.

"Of course I am, that's where the boat left from and where it's always returned."

"Shit, what the hell is our boat doing out at Barbers Point?" Kahoni asked.

That was what Mustang wanted to know as well. He hadn't received any calls from Elodie saying there had been an emergency or a change of plans regarding where they were going to dock.

Something was terribly wrong—and he needed to find out what. "I'm headed there now," he told the men.

"I will too," Kahoni said. "Although, I'm on the other side of the island at my daughter's birthday party, so it might take me a while."

"I can't leave my kids home alone," Perry said. "I need to go over to the neighbors' and see if anyone's home and if they can watch them. But I'll be there as soon as I can."

"Stay in touch," Kahoni told Mustang.

"I will," he promised, then hung up. He climbed into his truck and immediately dialed Aleck's number.

"Yo, what's up?"

"I need you and the rest of the team to meet me at Ko Olina Marina."

"Why? What's wrong?" Aleck asked, immediately going into SEAL mode.

"I don't know exactly. Elodie's boat wasn't at their normal harbor when I got here and when Perry tracked it, it's all the way across the island at a harbor they've never docked in before."

"Shit, okay, I'll call the others. You been able to get ahold of Elodie?"

"No." Mustang's response was short and to the point.

"Fuck. Don't panic," Aleck said, and Mustang figured he was speaking to himself, as much as he was his team leader.

"It's Columbus," Mustang said as he drove way too fast toward the interstate.

"We don't know that."

"Yeah, we do," Mustang countered. "Get Pid on this. See what he can find out. We haven't had any pings on Columbus or his capos. Elodie didn't sense anything out of the ordinary, and neither have I. If this is him, or more likely someone from his family, they're better than we assumed."

"I'm on it. Don't do anything crazy when you get to that marina," Aleck warned.

"No promises," Mustang told his teammate. "If Elodie's been hurt, someone's gonna fucking pay."

"Yeah, they are," Aleck said. "No one fucks with one of our own. We'll see you soon."

Mustang clicked off the Bluetooth and gripped the steering wheel tightly with both hands. This was bad. He knew it. Call it instinct or intuition. But he knew whatever he was going to find on that boat wasn't going to be good. He just prayed he wouldn't find Elodie's body.

It took longer than he wanted, even going fifteen miles an hour over the speed limit. But when Mustang pulled into the parking lot of the Ko Olina Marina, it was chaos. An ambulance was parked haphazardly in a handicap spot near the front of the docks, and there were six police cars there as well.

Mustang ran up to where the cops were blocking access to the dock.

He could see the *Fish Tales* at the very end of the dock—with a rope tying it to a lamppost. Definitely not normal docking procedure.

"That's the boat my girlfriend was working on," Mustang told one of the police officers. "What's going on?"

The man looked remorseful, and Mustang's heart just about stopped beating. A stretcher was being pushed down the dock toward them, and he couldn't tear his eyes from it. The officer lifted the yellow police tape and the paramedics pushed the gurney under the barrier.

Mustang looked down and saw a man lying on the stretcher. Kai. He was both relieved and freaked the fuck out at the same time. "Kai!" he called, but the police officers held him back from getting too close.

Kai's head turned, and he said something.

The paramedics immediately stopped pushing the stretcher toward the ambulance and motioned for the officers to let Mustang move closer.

"Where's Elodie?" he asked, not remembering to use her fake name.

"Jumped," Kai said weakly. "Steven shot me in the back. I pretended to be dead...heard him taunting her. Said he was gonna kill her. She jumped overboard. I passed out before I found out what happened though. I'm so sorry..."

Mustang put his hand on Kai's shoulder. "I'm gonna find her," he told the man. It was a miracle Kai had survived a point-blank gunshot to the back, and he prayed they'd get another miracle and find Elodie was still alive as well.

The paramedics decided he'd had enough time to talk to their patient and wheeled him away.

"Sir? We're gonna need some information on your girl-friend," one of the officers said, but Mustang was done with them. His blood ran cold thinking about Elodie jumping overboard to try to escape the man sent to kill her. Had he succeeded? The likelihood of her being able to get away from a man with a gun, in a boat like the *Fish Tales*, while she was swimming in the ocean was unlikely. But he wasn't going to rest until he knew the truth.

Elodie hated the ocean. She'd joked about it often enough. How she was scared of sharks and killer whales, and the most she'd do was walk in the water on the beach. Hell, she wouldn't even go in past her knees, no matter how much Mustang cajoled.

But he couldn't think about that now. He had to concen-trate on finding her. Then he'd deal with the man or men who'd dared try to take what was his. And there was no doubt in his mind, Elodie was fucking *his*.

The police officers were calling after him, trying to get him to stay and answer their questions, but Mustang had spotted Midas and the rest of the team arriving.

He didn't waste any time in letting them know what he'd learned. "Kai was shot in the back, ambushed. But he's alive.

He told me Elodie jumped overboard to try to get away from the guy. That's all I know."

Jag looked up and nodded. "Surveillance cameras. I'll work with the staff to access them and see who got off the boat."

"I'll call my friend who took us fishing and see if his boat's available for us to use," Aleck said.

"I'm calling Tex," Slate said in a low, hard voice.

"What's he gonna do?" Midas asked.

"He's gonna find a way to end this Paul Columbus guy once and for all," Slate said. "We all know he knows people who will be able to make sure that once we find Elodie, this shit doesn't happen again. Should've done it before now and this wouldn't have happened."

Mustang agreed with his friend. He'd been lax with Elodie's safety. It wasn't that he hadn't believed she was in danger, he'd just thought that after so much time had passed and when nothing seemed amiss, that maybe the mob had given up on her.

He should've known better. It wasn't a mistake he'd make twice.

But then, he might not have a chance to make a mistake like that again. If Columbus's goon had managed to kill her, he'd have lost the best thing that had ever happened to him.

Mustang's phone rang, and he looked down and saw it was Perry calling. He didn't want to talk to him right now. He needed to be doing something other than standing in a parking lot with his thumb up his ass. He needed to be looking for Elodie, but he also knew the other man was worried about his boat, Kai, and Elodie as well, and had a right to know what was happening.

"Did you find them?" Perry asked as soon as Mustang answered.

He summed up the situation as best he could, and ended with, "But from what I can see, the boat is fine."

"Fuck the boat," Perry spat. "I can't believe that asshole shot Kai—and that Melody jumped overboard! What do you need from me?"

"What do you mean?"

"Kahoni and I aren't idiots. We know you're in the Navy, and Kai let it slip that you're SEALs. I know you're on this. What can we do to help?"

Mustang couldn't help but be impressed with the man.

"Ask him about the GPS," Pid said.

Mustang put the phone on speaker and held it out as the team gathered around. "Go ahead," he told Pid.

"Does the *Fish Tales* have a GPS system onboard?" Pid asked.

"Of course. There's one system that tracks the boat itself, that's how I knew where it was, and another that's used when we're on the water to keep us oriented. We mark the points where we find fish and where other boats have said they've had success."

"Does it run nonstop? Will there be a record of where the boat's been?"

"Definitely," Perry said. "I can look it up and send you the track."

"Perfect. The sooner the better," Mustang told him.

"I'm also gonna make some calls to other boat owners and see if they'll go out and help look for Melody. You need anything, and I mean anything, you call me or Kahoni. We know a lot of people on this island. She may not have been here long, but she's like family to us."

"Thanks," Mustang said. He was trying to keep his composure, but it was getting more and more difficult.

He hung up and turned to his team. He was at a loss as to what they should do next.

"I'm gonna call the commander and see if we can get a chopper up. He'll also contact the Coast Guard and get them on this too. We're gonna find her, Mustang. I swear to fucking God, we'll find her," Jag swore.

Mustang nodded and turned to stare out at the ocean. Before, he'd always been calmed by looking at the waves, but now they seemed to mock him. Elodie was out there. Somewhere. He knew it. He had no idea if she was alive or dead, but she was out there—and he needed to find her.

* * *

Elodie was used to being by herself. It had been hard to make friends with her intense schedule as a chef, and after she'd fled New York, she hadn't dared reach out to many people. She didn't mind her own company and had no problem entertaining herself with a book or mindless TV.

But the feeling of being alone while bobbing in the waves in the middle of the ocean was something completely different. It was as if she was the only person left in the world, and it was terrifying.

She'd been in the water all day and the sun had finally begun to fall from the sky, giving her a bit of reprieve from its scorching rays, but she didn't like the look of the storm clouds gathering behind her. She'd been able to keep Diamond Head in view all day, which was somewhat comforting, although it didn't seem to be getting any nearer, no matter how hard or long she swam toward it.

For the first time in hours, negative thoughts crept into her brain. No one was going to find her out here. She was literally a needle in a haystack. Even if Scott figured out what happened and came to look for her, Kai had headed off their planned route to deeper waters.

She didn't like the ocean, but that didn't mean she wasn't a good swimmer. It was what had kept her alive all day. She swam toward shore when she could, but mostly she conserved her energy and floated on her back. She was hungry, exhausted, and terrified, but she refused to give up.

Elodie had never been as thirsty as she was right this moment. She'd thrown up a bit from swallowing the salty seawater, but now there was nothing left in her belly to come up. The salt was sucking the life from her body as fast as the sun had. She knew better than to drink the water all around her, but with each passing minute, she was afraid she'd give in to the temptation.

Earlier, she'd could've sworn she saw a boat in the distance, and she had raised her arm, waving it around hysterically while screaming for help, only to realize she was hallucinating. There was no boat. No one was there to rescue her.

At this point, if Steven returned, she'd gladly get back on the boat. Even when she knew he'd shoot her the second she climbed onboard. Anything would be better than dying out here in the middle of the ocean.

She felt something brush against her leg—and screamed in terror, lurching backward as best she could. Heart beating frantically, Elodie tried to see under the water, to get a glimpse at what was about to eat her.

When she saw a fin break the surface five meters from where she was treading, she whimpered.

Then another fin appeared. And another.

She was surrounded and was about to be shark food. Scott wouldn't ever know what had happened to her. There would be nothing left for him to find.

Suddenly, she heard a weird sound. A high-pitched whining, almost, and she whipped her head around.

A dolphin was staring at her from less than ten feet away.

As if it saw her gaping at it, the mammal bobbed its head up and down, then dove beneath the surface.

Elodie licked her dry and cracked lips uneasily. Another dolphin lifted its head from the water and made some clicking noises before disappearing. The dolphins began to play all around her, gliding through the water with ease, coming close but never touching her.

As scary as this situation was, and as terrified as she was that she was going to die, Elodie couldn't help but be awed by the somewhat magical display going on all around her. She had no idea why the dolphins were there or what they were doing, but somehow, she suddenly didn't feel so alone.

Until she saw it.

A bigger fin about fifty yards away.

She blinked, and for a moment wasn't sure if she was hallucinating again. But then it resurfaced—and she knew without a doubt that it wasn't a dolphin. She panicked again, and began to swim as fast as she could in the other direction. The dolphins kept pace with her, swimming next to and around her as she flailed and tried to get away from the shark.

It was ridiculous, that shark could reach her in seconds. She was no match for it. She was in its world now. She was the prey and it was definitely the predator. In her head, she imagined it wanting revenge for all the fish the *Fish Tales* had stolen from the ocean. It was ridiculous, but she wasn't exactly thinking straight.

Eventually, she got so tired she had to stop and rest. Her head was on a swivel, trying to find where the shark went, but she couldn't see any sign of it. It had either gone below her, ready to swallow her up from underneath, or had deemed her not worthy of a proper meal.

But all through her panicked retreat from the shark, the dolphins had stayed nearby. When she finally got her bearings and realized she'd been swimming in the wrong direction, *away* from Oahu instead of toward it, she wanted to cry once more.

With the waning light and approaching storm, it was getting harder and harder to see Diamond Head. In the dark, she'd have no idea which way to go, she'd be completely lost. Not only that, but she'd begun to shiver. The water off the coast of Hawaii was warm, but it was far below her normal body temperature. Swimming had helped keep her warm, but the chill was seeping into her bones more and more.

One of the dolphins swam close enough that Elodie could reach out and barely touch its rubbery-smooth skin. Her earlier thought that maybe a dolphin would let her latch onto it and take her into shore sprang to mind once more. She envisioned herself making friends with the things, like the boy in the movie *Free Willy* did with the killer whale.

"Find Scott," she found herself telling the mammal. "Go tell him where I am. But you're gonna have to be fast. I'm not sure how much longer I can hold out. I'm trying, but I hate the ocean. No offense."

The dolphin didn't reply, but it did nudge her hand before sinking below the surface once more.

Elodie turned over onto her back and stared up at the sky. She couldn't see any stars, partly because it wasn't quite dark enough yet but also because clouds were quickly moving in.

Closing her eyes, Elodie bobbed up and down in the waves and let her mind wander. She tried to remember every moment she'd spent with Scott. The good times and the bad. If she was going to die, she was going to do it with the man she loved on her mind.

CHAPTER TWENTY-ONE

Mustang stood at the bow of the boat and strained his eyes to see something. Anything. It had taken way too long to not only get the information they needed to get a starting point for their search, but also to get Aleck's friend's boat.

The Coast Guard had been called, and they had boats out looking, but so far hadn't had luck in finding Elodie. Mustang knew, after hearing Kai's story about being shot and how the man after her was firing at Elodie from the boat, that the Coasties thought there wasn't much chance of finding her. But he'd never give up. She was out there, counting on him to find her.

The police had immediately tried to check the GPS system on the *Fish Tales*, but had found it shot all to hell. Whoever had shot Kai and been sent to kill Elodie wasn't as dumb as Mustang had hoped.

But Perry had quickly come to their rescue when they'd called to give him the news. He'd retrieved the day's data from his computer and passed the information to the SEALs...but when Mustang had seen where the *Fish Tales* had been that morning, he realized the search for Elodie wasn't going to be quick and easy. There was a lot of ground to cover, too much. Knowing she was out there somewhere, and needed his help, was almost too much for Mustang to take.

It was Slate who had calmed him down, which was ironic, considering the man was the most impatient out of everyone on the team.

"We're gonna find her," Slate had said.

Desperate for reassurance, Mustang had asked, "Do you really think she's alive?"

"Yes," Slate had said without hesitation. "Because I've never seen anyone have such an instant connection like the two of you. At first I was skeptical, but now I understand it's because you two were meant to be together. There's no fucking way you found something so special, so rare, only to lose her now."

His words had comforted Mustang then, but now he was completely and wholly focused on the ocean in front of him. The Coast Guard had recommended they not go out because of the approaching storm, but his team had ignored the warnings. They were fucking Navy SEALs, there was no way they were scared of the ocean. Besides, if Elodie *was* out there, and had been all day, they all knew it was unlikely she'd last through the night.

Mustang held a high-powered spotlight used mostly by law enforcement. Jag was holding another as he stood next to him, searching as well. They scanned the waves in front of them as Pid and Aleck searched the water on either side of the boat. Slate was in the back doing the same. Midas was driving, plowing through the waves as if they weren't even there.

The rain fell almost sideways, pelting the boat and its occupants, but Mustang didn't even feel it. He was soaked to the bone, but merely blinked the water out of his eyes when it interfered with his sight.

They'd studied the coordinates Perry had retrieved from the GPS data and charted a distance about five miles from the Pinnacle, where they'd said they'd be fishing. Then they'd gone to Penguin Bank and the boat had been idle there for about forty-five minutes before making a beeline for the shore...more than an hour before the boat should have docked at noon.

The surveillance cameras at the Ko Olina Marina had shown a single man leaving the *Fish Tales* after haphazardly parking the boat. He hadn't even pulled into a slip, had just pulled up to the end of the dock and wrapped the rope around the light pole. Officers were working on tracking where the man had gone from there, but Mustang knew where he was headed. Back to New York.

Pid had identified him as Andrew Ferry, one of Paul's capos. There had been no record of him leaving New York, but he was obviously using a false name to travel under. Kai had called him "Steven."

Slate hadn't said much about his phone call with the infamous Tex, except to relay the man was "on it."

At the moment, Mustang couldn't think about anything past finding Elodie. They'd deal with the Columbus family once he had her back safe and sound. The alternative, that he wouldn't be able to find her, was unthinkable and unacceptable.

But the longer they went back and forth in a grid pattern in the area where the last coordinates had shown the *Fish Tales* to be, and where it was likely Kai had been shot and Elodie had jumped overboard, the more stressed Mustang got.

"Come on, where are you?" he muttered, knowing he wouldn't be heard over the sound of the engine, the wind, and rain. His eyes strained to pick out even the smallest thing that was out of place.

Then something moved off to his left.

Mustang swung the light around and watched as a dolphin leaped out of one wave, into another. It did it again...or maybe it was a second dolphin, Mustang wasn't sure. It wasn't unusual to see dolphins in the ocean, but these weren't playing at the bow of the boat or in their wake. They seemed to be traveling the same speed as the boat.

Mustang couldn't take his eyes off the animals. He'd always enjoyed watching the dolphins play, but there seemed to be more to their actions than jumping through the boat's waves. But then again, he could be imagining things.

For a split second, the boat rose to the top of a wave before crashing down—but that was all it took for Mustang to see something *else*. Something that made his heart almost stop in his chest.

He banged on the plexiglass protecting Midas as he stood at the helm and pointed to the left. He'd seen something on the other side of where the dolphins had been jumping in and out of the waves.

The boat immediately turned in that direction. The waves now crashed against the boat sideways, which was dangerous as it could swamp the fishing vessel, but Mustang didn't care. Obviously, Midas didn't either as he headed in the direction Mustang had indicated.

At first he thought he'd been seeing things that weren't there. All around them were nothing but white caps. And they were headed *away* from Oahu now, not toward it, the direction they assumed Elodie would try to go if she was conscious.

But then, as another wave crashed against the boat, Mustang saw what he was looking for. What they were *all* looking for.

A person was floating face up in the storm. Lying still as if taking a nap.

Mustang held up his fist, the universal sign for "stop," but Midas had already seen what he had and cut the engine.

Mustang's teammates crowded around him, and he shoved his light at Aleck. He ripped off his boots and shoved his pants down his legs. Not bothering to strip off his T-shirt, Mustang dove off the front of the boat without hesitation.

Not one of his teammates tried to stop him. They were well aware he could hold his own in the angry ocean. They'd trained for this shit, and no one would get between him and his woman.

Mustang knew his team would be steering the boat as close as they could get, and readying the first-aid kit and whatever else was needed to take care of Elodie until they could get her to shore, but his attention was on the woman floating just in front of him. His arms moved through the water faster than he'd ever moved before—and suddenly he was next to her.

For a fraction of a second, he wasn't sure how to proceed. If he should just grab her or if he should let her know he was there, to avoid scaring her.

And of course, the thought that she was dead wouldn't leave his mind. If he touched her, and she was stiff and cold, he'd never recover.

But in typical Elodie fashion, she took the decision out of his hands. As if she sensed him next to her, her eyes popped open and she stared up at him.

"Took you long enough," she said, almost too softly for him to hear.

Mustang wanted to laugh and cry. God, he fucking loved this woman.

He slipped an arm around her chest and pulled her against him, resting her body partially on top of his as they floated in the waves. She felt cold, too fucking cold. She was also very lethargic and didn't move at all. Mustang felt her body completely relax against his.

"Sorry it took so long, babe. But I'm here now."

"Hate the ocean," she mumbled.

"I know you do, but I'm so fucking proud of you," he told her.

"Kai..." Her voice trailed off.

Mustang eyed the boat with his teammates, coming closer. "He's okay. He's alive."

"He is? Thank God! I jumped," she informed him.

"I know, Kai told us."

"Did you find Steven?"

Luckily, Slate was reaching for them at that moment, so he didn't have to break the news that the man who'd done his best to kill her and her friend had escaped...still lived to try to kill her again.

Slate held on to Mustang's shoulders as Pid reached for Elodie.

"Don't fight them, El, we'll have you out of the water in two seconds."

"Don't like the ocean..." she repeated.

And just as he'd promised, thirty seconds later, both he and Elodie were out of the waves and she was lying on the deck of the fishing vessel they'd borrowed. As Midas floored it and headed back toward shore, Aleck wrapped a mylar warming blanket around her. Mustang curled up against her side as Jag kneeled on her other side to start an IV.

It wasn't the ideal conditions for attempting to stick a needle into her vein, but the SEALs had operated under much worse conditions, and within seconds, Jag had a saline line hooked up in her arm.

Mustang kept his eyes on Elodie's. She looked horrible. Even in the meager light from the cabin of the boat he could tell her face was sunburnt beyond anything he'd seen before. Her lips were dry and cracked as well.

"Temp's ninety-four point three," Pid warned.

Shit. That was way too low and they all knew it. Hypothermia usually occurred when the body temperature fell below ninety-five.

"Did you see them?" Elodie asked.

"Who?" Mustang asked, as the guys did their best to find blankets and anything else that would warm her up, or at least make sure she didn't get any colder as they made their way to shore. Midas would be contacting EMS to ensure they were waiting for them. He'd also probably get in touch with Perry, Kahoni, and the Coast Guard as well.

"My dolphins. They chased the shark away and stayed with me when I got tired."

"Fuck...confusion's setting in," Slate muttered from above him.

Mustang was well aware that when someone got too cold, they usually got confused before their body shut down completely, but this wasn't that. He knew it.

"I saw them," he told Elodie. He leaned down so his face was right above hers. His beard brushed against her chin as he spoke. "They led me to you. They were dancing in the waves trying to get my attention, and when I looked over at them, I saw you."

She smiled weakly, then closed her eyes and frowned. "I'm never gonna be free."

Mustang knew exactly what she was referring to. "The hell you aren't," he said forcefully. "Look at me."

When she didn't open her eyes, Mustang hardened his voice. "Open your eyes and look at me, Elodie."

He waited until she did as ordered.

"I didn't take this as seriously as I should've. And for that, I'm sorry. I put you in this position—but it will *never* happen again. The wheels are already turning to end this once and for all."

"I'll have to change my name again," she whispered, her voice slurring.

"You're right, you will," Mustang agreed.

"Wait, what?" Aleck said, but Mustang ignored him.

He got up on one elbow and palmed Elodie's cheek so she

had no choice but to look at him. "You'll change it to Elodie Webber. You're gonna marry me, and we're gonna live happily ever after."

She shook her head. "I won't do that to you."

"You *will*," Mustang insisted.

"Love you too much..."

"No such thing," he told her. Mustang had no idea how much of this conversation she would remember when she was better, but he didn't care. She *was* going to marry him. He couldn't live without her. No fucking way.

"Did you just order her to marry you?" Pid asked. "Smooth, Mustang. Real fucking smooth."

Mustang felt Elodie go limp beneath him and knew she'd lost her battle with consciousness. The others saw it too, and redoubled their efforts to keep her warm until they could get her medical attention.

Mustang turned to Slate. "You sure Tex can take care of this?"

"Positive," Slate said. "Said he knew of at least two teams who would jump at the chance to take care of this shit. One out of Colorado Springs and another in Indianapolis. He also told me he'd be talking to Rawlins."

"Rawlins?" Jag asked in surprise. "Dammit, I should've thought of him from the second this shit went down."

Knowing Tex was on this, and that he would probably bring in Baker Rawlins—a mysterious and dangerous-as-fuck retired Navy SEAL who lived on the island—made Mustang relax a fraction. But he'd beat himself up for the rest of his life for not letting Tex do his thing in the first place. He'd been so sure he and his team would know if Columbus made a move. He'd been wrong, and he'd put Elodie's life in jeopardy. Never again.

Paul Columbus needed to die—along with anyone else who thought his woman was expendable.

* * *

When Elodie woke up, she immediately knew she was in a hospital. She still felt as if she was bobbing up and down, but the smell of disinfectant and bleach let her know she was on terra firma.

She only remembered bits and pieces from being rescued, but knew Scott had been there, as had the rest of his team. It had taken them longer than she'd hoped, and for a while there she'd thought they wouldn't make it, especially when the rain started and she was being buffeted up and down by the waves, but she'd taken an odd comfort in the attention from the dolphins. They'd seemed to know she was on the edge of death and wouldn't let her give up. Nudging her every now and then and making sure she stayed awake.

The lights from the boat Scott had been on had seemed like another hallucination at first, but then Scott was there. In the water next to her, holding her, keeping her safe.

Turning her head, she knew he'd be next to her still. And he was. His arms were crossed over his chest and his head was resting on the back of the chair he was sitting in. His mouth was open and he looked absolutely exhausted...she'd never seen a more beautiful sight in her life.

She drank him in for a long few minutes. She had no idea what woke him up, but out of the blue, his brown eyes popped open and he saw her staring at him.

He was up and out of the chair faster than she'd ever seen him move. He hovered and seemed to be afraid to touch her.

"El?"

She tried to speak, and nothing came out but a croak. Scott immediately reached for something next to her, then had his hand behind her neck and was lifting her head to help her take a sip from the cup he held to her lips. The water was lukewarm, and it tasted so damn good. She tried to gulp it down but Scott wouldn't let her. He lowered the cup and put it back on the table next to the bed. Then he continued to hover over her.

Elodie licked her lips, wincing when she realized they were both split from dryness and the salty ocean.

Finally, she said, "Yes, I'll marry you."

He grinned, and it lit up his face. "I know you will. I wasn't giving you a choice."

"He's gonna come back."

The smile disappeared from Scott's face as if it had never been there. "No. He's not. You're gonna have to trust me on this. The Columbus family will not be a problem for you anymore. I swear on my job as a Navy SEAL, you're going to be safe from them."

Elodie had no idea how he was going to make that happen. He couldn't exactly take on the mob, but she trusted him. How could she not after everything that had happened? "Okay."

"Okay?"

She nodded.

"I love you, Elodie Winters, soon to be Webber. So damn much."

"Love you too," she whispered. Her eyes felt extremely heavy and she was suddenly exhausted.

"There are a ton of people who are waiting to see you, but they can wait," Scott told her. "Perry, Kahoni, Kalani, all the guys. Kai is bitching about wanting to be wheeled in here from his room a few floors up. The lady from the grocery store, the family who lives a couple doors down from us...hell, even the family that chartered your boat on Saturday heard you were hurt, and they want to see you before they fly back to Australia. You're very loved, Elodie, and we're all so damn glad you were so strong out there."

She wanted to tell him that the only reason she'd held on was because of him, but she was too tired.

"Sleep, babe. We've got the rest of our lives to look

forward to together," Scott told her, and she felt him kiss her forehead gently.

She fell back into a deep, healing sleep, content in the knowledge that the man she loved was there. And that he'd somehow make sure they could be together, forever.

EPILOGUE

It had been two weeks since Elodie had been fished out of the ocean. She'd spent three days in the hospital and had been recuperating in Scott's apartment since, spending a lot of time in their comfy chair in his bedroom. Scott had been going to work, but when he wasn't at her side, one of his teammates was. Kai's mother had also brought him by the day after he'd gotten out of the hospital so they could visit.

Elodie knew she'd been very lucky, and she was having a hard time even thinking about leaving Scott's apartment. She was scared. Terrified, actually. She knew Paul Columbus wouldn't give up until she was well and truly dead.

But today, Scott had cajoled, begged, and finally just picked her up and carried her to his truck. He told her it was time to get back out into the world.

She didn't agree. But she didn't want to argue with him. She was still feeling off-kilter, and she desperately wanted to believe him when he said she was safe. That she'd always be safe from here on out.

He'd brought her to Aleck's condo, and now that Elodie was there, she was glad Scott had forced the issue. She loved these men like brothers, and after she'd heard the story about how they'd all banded together the second they knew she was missing, her heart had melted for them even more.

They were rough around the edges. Many times they said the wrong thing, they swore too much, and it was obvious what they did for a living had affected them all in some way. But she loved them exactly how they were.

She was sitting on Aleck's couch, and they were all laughing and joking about nothing in particular when a knock sounded on the door. Elodie was surprised. She had no idea who it could be. Maybe someone ordered takeout?

Slate headed for the door and opened it. Elodie couldn't see the door from where she was sitting, but she heard a deep voice she didn't recognize. When Slate reentered the room, there was a man walking next to him.

Elodie had never seen the man before, but she couldn't help but take a second glance.

He was gorgeous.

He looked older, possibly in his mid-forties to mid-fifties. But men always seemed to age more gracefully than women, so she could be way off. He had black hair that was liberally peppered with silver. It was longer on top and, even as she stared, he ran a hand through it, making it stick up even wilder. His neatly trimmed short beard was more gray than black, and she definitely approved. He had on a pair of black jeans with a black T-shirt. His skin was darkly tanned and she could see the edges of a tattoo peeking out of the right sleeve.

But it was his eyes that pinned her in place. They were a dark green, almost jade, and seemed to see way too much. She knew without having to be told, this man had dark secrets.

She shivered and broke eye contact with the newcomer as Scott covered her shoulders with a throw blanket.

That was another thing, ever since her time in the ocean, she had difficulty staying warm. Her body temperature had gotten so low, her organs had been on the verge of shutting down. It seemed as if her fingers and toes were always cold now. The doctors told her that would disappear with time.

The stranger greeted each member of Scott's team with a handshake or a chin lift and then stood a respectable distance from her.

"Elodie, this is Baker Rawlins. He's a retired Navy SEAL who lives on the island," Scott told her.

"It's nice to meet you," Elodie said. "Thank you for your service." She wasn't sure why she was meeting this man, but she had no problem being polite and welcoming to anyone who Scott and his team seemed to like.

And they definitely liked and respected this man. It was easy to see in the way they interacted with him. Their behavior was almost deferential.

Baker pulled Aleck's fancy coffee table over in front of the couch, then sat on it and studied her.

Elodie shifted uncomfortably at his proximity, but he didn't make her wait to let her know what he was doing there —and why he was so focused on her.

"I heard you've been having some problems with the Columbus family out of New York."

She blinked at the way he didn't beat around the bush. She glanced at the others, and they all nodded at her with encouragement. Scott squeezed her hand. Mentally shrugging —if the guys trusted this man, she supposed she had absolutely no reason not to either—she told him, "Yeah, you could say that."

"Well, you don't anymore."

"Um...what?"

"You don't have to worry about Paul Columbus or any of his capos coming after you anymore."

"I'm not sure it's that easy," she protested. She wanted to believe him, but she knew firsthand how ruthless the man was.

"It is when he's dead," Baker replied.

Elodie frowned. "He's dead?"

"Yeah. Happened a week ago. New York's a dangerous place. Carjacking. He and the man he was with were both shot in the head, their bodies dumped, and his Mercedes was stolen."

Elodie wanted to believe this man. Needed to. But she was afraid to hope. "I'm sure whoever took his place will take up where he left off," she whispered.

Baker shook his head. "Nope. Here's the thing...Paul was an asshole. Most mob bosses are, but he'd gotten so bad, his own family hated him. His second-in-command, his son Jerry, is now in charge, and he didn't know anything about Paul's vendetta against you."

Elodie couldn't take her gaze from Baker's green one. "How do you know all this?"

"I asked him."

"You did?"

"Yeah. I know people who know people, and I took a trip to the mainland when my friend Tex asked me to step in."

"Tex?"

Baker looked over at Scott. "She doesn't know who Tex is?"

Scott shook his head. "No."

Baker met her gaze once more. "Tex is a legend. He was a Navy SEAL who lost his leg and was medically retired. He's a computer genius who knows *everyone*. And I mean that literally. He has connections upon connections. Slate gave him a call, and he promised to take care of this. It should've been done before you got hurt."

Elodie saw him give Scott a look, and she bristled.

"Don't blame him," she said adamantly. "This isn't his fault."

"It's okay," Scott said, squeezing her hand once more. "He's right. I should've taken the entire situation more seri-

320

ously. Called Tex from the start. Just because neither of us sensed any danger didn't mean it wasn't there. Obviously."

"Anyway, I met up with a team from Indiana and got the details about Paul's unfortunate accident. Then I met with Jerry Columbus. We had lunch."

Elodie was having a hard time wrapping her mind around what Baker was telling her. He met up with a team? Had lunch with a mob boss? Who *was* this guy? But she didn't get to ask any of her questions as Baker continued.

"I raised the subject of Paul's obsession with you, and Jerry said he had no idea what I was talking about. That as far as he knew, you were a chef who'd quit abruptly. He's very happy with the new guy they hired to take your place."

"What about the guy who came out here and tried to kill Elodie?" Midas asked.

"Andrew Ferry. He was killed along with Paul," Baker said. "Turns out the man's been wanted for homicides all over the US. His DNA ties him to murders in New York, LA, Miami, Chicago, and some backwater little town in Virginia called Fallport. A team of experienced search-and-rescue guys were training in the foothills of the Appalachian Mountains, and they stumbled across the bodies of two men who'd been tortured and dumped. Was the talk of Fallport for quite a while.

"Anyway, as well as the DNA found here in the States, he's also been linked to murders in London, Paris, and Berlin, as well. The man was literally a serial killer, and Jerry Columbus isn't sorry he's dead."

"What's going to prevent Jerry from coming after Elodie?" Slate asked.

Elodie was grateful for the question. She wanted to know that as well.

"Because he gave me his word," Baker said without hesitation.

The other men all nodded—but that wasn't enough for Elodie. "And that's it? You trust him?"

"I don't trust him as far as I can throw him," Baker retorted. "I trust no one. But he knows you're off limits, and that you aren't going to be a problem for him."

"I'm off limits?" she asked.

"Yes. You're under Tex's protection. And mine. And Silverstone's. And Rex's. That was enough for him to know if he did something so stupid as to try to take up where his asshole predecessor left off, his entire family would suffer. But he's *not* stupid, he's willing to let bygones be bygones. As long as you don't go to the cops with what happened while you were in the Columbus family's employ, you'll be fine. You go your way, he'll go his. All's well and good."

Elodie's head spun. She didn't know Tex. Or who or what Silverstone was. And had never heard of any Rex. And why was Baker willing to take her under his protection?

Nothing made sense...but when she looked up into Scott's eyes, all her questions disappeared. He trusted Baker, that was obvious. All the men around her did.

All she'd wanted was for this nightmare to end. And now that it apparently had, thanks to this Tex guy and Baker, and she was grateful. She was definitely not going to go to the cops about something a dead man had supposedly done. She just wanted to forget it happened at all.

"Thank you. I'm gonna make you the biggest, most delicious apple crumble you've ever eaten in your life. And anytime you want a home-cooked meal, all you need to do is ask and it's yours."

"Done," Baker said with a completely straight face. "I've got your number, so I'll be in touch." Then he stood up and nodded at the rest of the men and headed for the door.

"Wait!" Elodie exclaimed, standing up and waiting for the mysterious Baker to turn around.

"Yeah?" he asked.

Elodie moved without thought. She walked toward Baker and put her arms around him before she chickened out.

He hesitated for a split second, as if surprised anyone would dare touch him. Then she felt his arms wrap around her.

"Thank you. I'm thinking since I'm a chef, and your first name is Baker, this was meant to be. Anything you want, anytime, I'm in your debt," she told him.

She felt his arms tighten briefly, then he cleared his throat and stepped back. She had no choice but to let go. He raised a hand and ran the backs of his fingers over her cheek before turning to Scott. "She's sweet. Don't find too many like that anymore. Don't do anything to fuck it up."

"Not planning on it," Scott said as he came up behind her and wrapped his arm around her waist.

Baker nodded at them once more, then he spun and headed for the front door.

The second it closed behind him, Elodie turned to face the guys. "And thank all of *you* for helping to find me. For calling this Tex guy. For getting the Coast Guard involved. For all of it. I owe you."

"You owe us nothing," Scott said.

"Wait a minute," Midas said. "I could use a good apple crumble."

"I don't even know what that is, and I think I could too," Aleck threw in.

"I want her to make us some more burgers," Pid added.

"I'm thinking you can probably make some kick-ass Thai food," Jag suggested.

"Chocolate cake," Slate told her.

Elodie chuckled. "Done. Maybe not all at the same time though. We'll have lots of get-togethers so I can make everyone what they want."

As the rest of the team started discussing what they wanted her to make for them first, Scott turned her toward him so they were face-to-face. "Now you've done it," he warned.

Elodie chuckled. "I'm happy to cook for them. I owe them everything. Where did this Baker guy come from? What's his story? He's kind of scary."

"He is," Scott agreed. "But he's a good man. He's seen a lot of shit in his life and is kind of a hermit. He lives up on the North Shore and spends his days surfing, trying to outrun his demons, I guess. But the admiral of the base seems to have him on speed dial. He's used as a consultant for a lot of intense missions and, as you found out, he's got some pretty powerful connections as well. If he says he's got your back, he's got your back."

"Is it really over?"

"Yeah, babe. It is."

Elodie closed her eyes and leaned into Scott's chest. "It seems hard to believe."

"Believe it. So when are you going to marry me?"

Her eyes popped open. "Seriously?"

"Yeah. I'm thinking a beach wedding. Low-key. Nothing fancy. I don't do fancy."

"We'll talk about it," she told him, her mind already racing, thinking of ideas for their wedding.

"I love you, Elodie. I promise not to let you down as badly as I did with the Columbus situation ever again."

"You didn't let me down," she protested.

"I did, but it won't happen again."

She decided to drop the subject. She'd known deep in her bones that Paul Columbus was going to catch up to her at some point. *She'd* been the one who'd gotten complacent. Thank God no one had been killed. They'd all been very lucky.

"Do I get to invite Baker to our wedding?" she asked.

"You can invite whoever you want, but don't get your hopes up that he'll come. He really is a hermit. I'm surprised he agreed to come here to talk to you today. I think he wanted to make sure you understood that he really does have your back, and that you're safe."

"I like him. He's broody and intense and kinda terrifies me...but I still like him."

Scott kissed her forehead. "Me too, babe. Me too."

* * *

Elodie didn't know how it happened, but two weeks later, she was standing on the bow of a yacht Scott had rented, having just said her vows to love and cherish her husband for the rest of her life.

He'd talked her into getting married on the ocean, even though she'd been terrified of getting on a boat again. The memories had threatened to overwhelm her when she'd stepped onboard, but she'd been so busy with getting dressed, with Kalani fussing over her, and making sure everyone was having a good time, she'd soon forgotten to be scared.

She and Scott said their vows on the top deck as a beautiful sunset bloomed behind them. Everyone was there—well, everyone except Baker. He'd declined but said he was happy for both her and Scott.

Kai and his mother, Perry and Kahoni and their families, Scott's team, of course, and Scott had even found Manuel and flown him out as well. She hadn't seen him since she'd left the *Asaka Express*. She wore a replica of the first dress she had on when she'd gone out to dinner with Scott, after they'd accidentally run into each other again.

Scott had gone crazy and bought as many duplicates of the dress as he could find. Not only that, but he'd bought them in different sizes, saying he wanted her to be able to wear the dress no matter if she gained or lost weight in the future. It was a beautiful gesture, and she loved him all the more for it.

The dark purple dress with white and hot pink petals was as far from a wedding gown as she could get, but she wouldn't have wanted to wear anything else. Scott had on a pair of black board shorts and a Hawaiian shirt that matched her dress almost perfectly. They both had leis around their necks, as did all the guests. The mood onboard was jovial and relaxed, and Elodie loved that she was sharing her special day with her new friends.

"Happy?" Scott asked as he hugged her body from behind. Elodie never felt safer than when she was in his arms. Being in the ocean would never be her thing, not anymore, but since she was now married to a man who practically had gills, she'd need to get comfortable being around and on the water.

"Very," she told him.

They stood there, listening to the party going on behind them and enjoying the view as the sun began to dip below the horizon.

Then Elodie gasped as she saw two dolphins frolicking in the bow waves. "Look!" she told Scott.

"I see them. Did you know dolphins swimming by a boat are a sign of good luck?" he asked.

"When I was out there, a shark started swimming around. I was so scared, but then a pod of dolphins surrounded me, keeping me safe. And toward the end, right before you found me? There were two that stayed right by my side. I could even touch them, they came so close. Do you think they're the same ones?" Elodie knew the chance of that was slim to none, but she could dream.

"I don't know, but dolphins are smart. Many people think they're even smarter than humans. It wouldn't surprise me if they'd known exactly what they were doing when they helped you. And that they know you're here now."

Elodie sighed in contentment and watched the pair of dolphins playing in the water. Then she turned and looked up at her husband. "I love you."

"And I love you," he replied. He leaned down and kissed her long, slow, and deep. It had taken a while for Elodie's libido to return after her ordeal, but lately she'd been even hornier than she'd been before everything had happened.

"The only bad thing about a reception on a boat is that we can't sneak out early," she said between kisses.

Scott smiled against her lips. "Who thought of this idea anyway?" he complained.

"Um...you did."

And he had. Scott had practically planned their entire wedding himself. She'd been in charge of the menu, but otherwise, he'd done everything else.

"I'll make up for it when we get to the hotel."

He'd even rented the honeymoon suite at the Halekulani Resort, complete with a home theater and plunge pool in the bathroom of their suite. It was over the top and totally unnecessary, but Elodie couldn't wait to experience it.

"I'm gonna hold you to that," she said with a smile.

"Hey, you guys gonna come and shove cake in each other's faces so we can eat it yet or what?" Aleck called out from nearby.

Elodie smiled.

"We're comin', jeez, keep your pants on," Scott grumbled.

"That was gonna be my line," Aleck joked before disappearing.

"Suck a fucking smart aleck," Scott griped, but he smiled as he said it.

She laughed. "I like your team. All of them. I'm glad you guys have each other's backs."

"We do," Scott agreed. "Come on, let's get this cake thing done, then the first dance, then I'll bribe the captain to take us back early."

Elodie knew she should argue, tell her husband that she wanted their guests to be able to stay and party late into the night, but she wanted to be alone with Scott. She couldn't wait to start the rest of their life together.

* * *

"Shit," Mustang swore again as they waited for their commander to arrive to the emergency meeting he'd called.

"Sorry, man," Midas told him. "Sucks that you're still officially on your honeymoon and we get called up for a mission."

Mustang shrugged. "Par for the course, I suppose. And Elodie and I weren't doing anything other than hanging out at my place anyway. It's not like we had a trip planned or anything."

"Riiiight. Hanging out at your place," Aleck joked.

"Shut up," Mustang told him, throwing a pencil at him from across the table.

They were all waiting for their commander to arrive to tell them more about the mission they'd be leaving on the next day. Sometimes they had weeks to plan, other times, in the case of emergencies, they were sent out almost immediately.

Midas leaned back and listened to the team give Mustang crap. The truth of the matter was, they were all thrilled for their team leader. Elodie was amazing. Down-to-earth and funny. She didn't seem to resent the time her new husband spent with them, and she was a hell of a chef to boot.

"Thanks for coming on such short notice," the commander said the second he entered the room. He was passing out folders before he'd sat down. "This mission is very time sensitive. As you all know, there was an American and a Danish aid worker kidnapped from Somalia about three months ago. The kidnappers have been demanding ten million dollars to release them. The Danish man's brother has raised half that, but says there's no way he can get any more. The State Department has been trying to negotiate with the kidnappers, without luck. We've had several proof-of-life videos, but intel's come in that the Danish man is very sick, and time is running out for them both."

"We're going in?" Pid asked, the excitement easy to hear in his voice.

"Yes. You'll go in under the cover of darkness to retrieve the hostages and kill the kidnappers. The information we have on the hostages is in the folders I just handed out."

Midas flipped open his folder and saw a still shot from one of the proof-of-life videos that had been sent. The woman had brown hair that looked as if it hadn't been brushed or washed in ages. Her face was sunburnt and her hazel eyes were filled with fear. The man had blond hair and blue eyes, and he looked pissed and defiant, even in the photograph.

He'd heard their names were Dagmar and Elizabeth, but that was about all Midas knew. He perused the file—and froze when he read the information listed for the woman.

Elizabeth Lexie Greene. Age thirty-three. Graduated from Grant High School in Portland, Oregon.

Fuck. He *knew* her.

Lexie had been in his graduating class. She'd moved to Portland their senior year. They were in different circles— Midas had been on the swim team and was very popular, and being a newcomer, Lexie had mostly hung out on the fringes of their class. Midas had been in the top ten academically, and the information in front of him said that Lexie had been in the bottom twenty percent.

His mind went back to senior English class. They'd been assigned to work together, and while at first he'd been disappointed he hadn't gotten to work with the girl he'd been crushing on at the time, he'd found that Lexie had great ideas about their project and was a pleasure to work with. Usually he put off group projects until right before they were due, but she did a lot of the legwork, and they'd finished well ahead of the deadline. He had no idea why her grades weren't good, because he'd found her to be smart, funny, and engaging.

He hadn't thought of her since graduation, but now he couldn't help but compare the woman in the picture in front of him to the teenager he'd known in his youth.

Why was she in Somalia? How had she gotten kidnapped? Was she all right? Was she scared?

Of *course* she was scared.

Midas clenched his teeth together. This was one mission they wouldn't fail. It was rare their missions became personal, but there was no way he was going to leave Africa without her. She might not remember him, but he remembered her. And Midas was going to do whatever it took to get her home safe and sound.

* * *

Elizabeth Lexie Greene lay on the pallet her captors had given her months ago and did her best to try to blank her mind. She stared up at the stars winking in the night sky overhead, trying to remember which one was the North Star. It was hopeless; she had no clue which star was which.

She'd never been a good student, much to her dad's chagrin. She'd tried, she really had, but when she tried to read, the letters got all jumbled up. She knew now that she was dyslexic, but growing up, she'd just thought she was stupid. Even her dad had lost patience with her so many times and told her she was a "retard." She hated that word to this day. It was so repulsive and discriminatory.

Her mind buried unpleasant thoughts of her past, and she gazed at her desolate surroundings. How had she even ended up here?

Oh, yeah, she'd been volunteering at a food bank back in Portland, Oregon. Years ago. Had overheard two of her coworkers talking about an aid organization Food For All, that did what it could to get help those less fortunate. So after researching the company, and liking the mission statement and all that they were doing to try to help others, she'd signed up.

Fast forward a decade, and she was still doing it. She'd been in Somalia when she and one of the head honchos of the organization, a Danish man named Dagmar, had been grabbed off the street right outside the organization's building. They'd been driven into the desert...and had been here ever since. They'd been beaten and practically starved. And living in the desert wasn't exactly fun, but at least she and Dagmar were mostly ignored now, as long as they didn't step out of line.

The fact that the kidnappers were asking for ten million dollars was a joke. They'd at first asked for five million, and when Dagmar's twin brother had come up with the money, they'd upped the ransom to ten million instead. Five for each of them.

Lexie wished they'd accepted the five million for Dagmar and let him go while trying to get more money for her. He wasn't doing well. At all.

She suspected he might've had a mild stroke last month, and he hadn't been the same since. His speech was slurred, and he kept forgetting where they were and what was going on. The captors were getting impatient with him, and she'd overheard them talking about handing them both over to another guy in the area, someone who hated foreigners.

If that happened, she was as good as dead.

She didn't want to die. Life hadn't exactly gone the way she'd hoped, but she still had visions of settling down, starting a family, and living the American dream.

Hopping from one country to another wasn't conducive to finding someone to spend the rest of her life with. But she'd finally gotten to a place where she wasn't ashamed of her disability, or herself. She wasn't the smartest person in the world, but she was kind and loyal.

Sighing, she closed her eyes once more. Of course, then she'd been kidnapped. She might not get to enjoy her newfound self-acceptance for long.

The hardest thing about being a captive, other than not eating and constantly praying someone wouldn't decide it would be more fun to beat and rape her than ignore her, was the boredom. There was absolutely nothing to do day after day, hour after hour, beyond watching the sand blow by.

She prayed their aid organization was doing all they could to free them. She didn't think she and Dagmar were important enough for the military to get involved, but a girl could dream.

Lexie fell asleep thinking about the day when commandos would storm their little camp, kill all their captors, and free them. It wasn't likely, but then again, being kidnapped in the first place wasn't very likely either, and it had happened.

Lexie needed her very own hero. And she needed him now.

* * *

Will Lexie get out of that hole? Of course she will! But what comes after remains to be seen! Find out what happens between Lexie and Midas in the second book in the SEAL Team Hawaii— *Finding Lexie.*

Want to talk to other Susan Stoker fans? Join my reader group, Susan Stoker's Stalkers, on Facebook!

Also by Susan Stoker

SEAL Team Hawaii Series

Finding Elodie
Finding Lexie (Aug 2021)
Finding Kenna (Oct 2021)
Finding Monica (TBA)
Finding Carly (TBA)
Finding Ashlyn (TBA)
Finding Jodelle (TBA)

SEAL of Protection Series

Protecting Caroline
Protecting Alabama
Protecting Fiona
Marrying Caroline (novella)
Protecting Summer
Protecting Cheyenne
Protecting Jessyka
Protecting Julie (novella)
Protecting Melody
Protecting the Future
Protecting Kiera (novella)
Protecting Alabama's Kids (novella)
Protecting Dakota

SEAL of Protection: Legacy Series

Securing Caite
Securing Brenae (novella)
Securing Sidney
Securing Piper
Securing Zoey
Securing Avery
Securing Kalee

ALSO BY SUSAN STOKER

Securing Jane

Delta Force Heroes Series
Rescuing Rayne
Rescuing Aimee (novella)
Rescuing Emily
Rescuing Harley
Marrying Emily (novella)
Rescuing Kassie
Rescuing Bryn
Rescuing Casey
Rescuing Sadie (novella)
Rescuing Wendy
Rescuing Mary
Rescuing Macie (novella)

Delta Team Two Series
Shielding Gillian
Shielding Kinley
Shielding Aspen
Shielding Jayme (novella)
Shielding Riley
Shielding Devyn (May 2021)
Shielding Ember (Sep 2021)
Shielding Sierra (TBA)

Badge of Honor: Texas Heroes Series
Justice for Mackenzie
Justice for Mickie
Justice for Corrie
Justice for Laine (novella)
Shelter for Elizabeth
Justice for Boone
Shelter for Adeline
Shelter for Sophie

Justice for Erin
Justice for Milena
Shelter for Blythe
Justice for Hope
Shelter for Quinn
Shelter for Koren
Shelter for Penelope

Ace Security Series
Claiming Grace
Claiming Alexis
Claiming Bailey
Claiming Felicity
Claiming Sarah

Mountain Mercenaries Series
Defending Allye
Defending Chloe
Defending Morgan
Defending Harlow
Defending Everly
Defending Zara
Defending Raven

Silverstone Series
Trusting Skylar
Trusting Taylor
Trusting Molly (July 2021)
Trusting Cassidy (Dec 2021)

Stand Alone
The Guardian Mist
Nature's Rift
A Princess for Cale
A Moment in Time- A Collection of Short Stories

Lambert's Lady

Special Operations Fan Fiction
http://www.AcesPress.com

Beyond Reality Series
Outback Hearts
Flaming Hearts
Frozen Hearts

Writing as Annie George:
Stepbrother Virgin (erotic novella)

ABOUT THE AUTHOR

New York Times, *USA Today* and *Wall Street Journal* Bestselling Author Susan Stoker has a heart as big as the state of Tennessee where she lives, but this all American girl has also spent the last fourteen years living in Missouri, California, Colorado, Indiana, and Texas. She's married to a retired Army man who now gets to follow *her* around the country.

She debuted her first series in 2014 and quickly followed that up with the SEAL of Protection Series, which solidified her love of writing and creating stories readers can get lost in.

If you enjoyed this book, or any book, please consider leaving a review. It's appreciated by authors more than you'll know.

www.stokeraces.com
www.AcesPress.com
susan@stokeraces.com

facebook.com/authorsusanstoker

twitter.com/Susan_Stoker

instagram.com/authorsusanstoker

goodreads.com/SusanStoker

bookbub.com/authors/susan-stoker

amazon.com/author/susanstoker

.

CPSIA information can be obtained
at www.ICGtesting.com
Printed in the USA
LVHW050845290321
682812LV00006B/26

9 781644 990681